'**Haunting and atmospheric,** *The Hiding Place* lingers in the dark spaces of a home as Amanda Mason deftly crafts a steady, creeping tension. As the Elder House's secrets are revealed, Mason shines a brilliant light on the unsettling extents of desire'

A.J. Gnuse, author of *The Girl in the Walls*

'**An unsettling, supernatural tour de force** ... with a back story steeped in local history and plot teeming with everyday anxieties, **Amanda Mason has created a new gothic myth** ... personal histories and past horrors entwine to trap the reader in a **claustrophobic, terrifying** embrace'

Daily Mail

'**Satisfyingly unsettling,** this is a hugely atmospheric novel that **oozes with uncanny menace**'

Lucie McKnight Hardy

There's nothing like a haunted house to get the heart racing and this **deliciously dark contemporary gothic tale** set in Whitby will do just that ... **Hugely atmospheric** the writer builds the tension gradually – **unsettling and creepy,** it's a perfect supernatural read'

My Weekly

'*The Hiding Place* has everything; **chills that build, an immersive setting and a wonderful clash between the present and the past,** the living and the dead. At the heart of this **haunting** novel are characters so real and compelling their stories continue to resonate long after reading'

Jess Kidd

'A masterful, unnerving thriller'

Woman's Own

The
Hiding
Place

Amanda Mason was born and brought up in Whitby, North Yorkshire. She studied Theatre at Dartington College of Arts, where she began writing by devising and directing plays. After a few years earning a very irregular living in lots of odd jobs, and performing in a comedy street magic act, she became a teacher, and has worked in the UK, Italy, Spain and Germany. She now lives in North Yorkshire and has given up teaching for writing.

Her short stories have been published in several anthologies, including collections from *Parthian Books*, *Unthank Books*, and *The Fiction Desk* and her debut novel, *The Wayward Girls* was published in 2019. *The Hiding Place* is her second novel.

The Hiding Place

Amanda Mason

ZAFFRE

First published in the UK in 2021
This paperback edition published in 2022 by
ZAFFRE
An imprint of Bonnier Books UK
4th Floor, Victoria House, Bloomsbury Square,
London, England, WC1B 4DA
Owned by Bonnier Books
Sveavägen 56, Stockholm, Sweden

A CIP catalogue record for this book is
available from the British Library.

ISBN: 978–1–83877–194–2

Also available as an ebook and an audiobook

1 3 5 7 9 10 8 6 4 2

Typeset by Palimpsest Book Production Ltd, Falkirk, Stirlingshire
Printed and bound in Great Britain by Clays Ltd, Elcograf S.p.A.

MIX
Paper from
responsible sources
FSC   FSC® C018072

Zaffre is an imprint of Bonnier Books UK
www.bonnierbooks.co.uk

For my mum, Sylvia, with love.

There was no signal. Of course there wasn't; there never was here. The house was too close to the cliff, overshadowed by it. But still she gripped the phone tightly, staring at the screen, willing the little bars at the top to fill up, trying to think.

The kitchen was a mess, and she was sitting on the floor, backed up against the cupboard under the sink, her legs splayed out – not very elegant, not very ladylike – and she could smell blood.

No. That was just her stupid imagination.

Get a grip, she thought, her fingers aching as she clutched the phone in both hands. *Get a grip, get up and* – she paused, lifted her head, listened.

It was faint, too faint to be sure, but wasn't that . . . ? She strained to hear. Couldn't she hear someone upstairs, moving slowly, deliberately along the first-floor landing?

Now, she thought, her heart hammering. *Get up now.*

She'd put it back, hadn't she? She found herself wishing that alone would be enough. She could still feel it, her talisman, her little piece of luck, warm in the palm of her hand, soft and yielding. The way it seemed to – fit. That had been the hardest part, giving it up, even after everything went wrong. Even though she knew it was the right thing to do, the only thing to do; even when she'd wanted to keep it close.

She grabbed the edge of the sink, slowly pulling herself to

1

her feet, then straightened up, trying to ignore the dull ache deep in her belly. She'd given up so much already.

Don't lose your nerve.

She shifted the phone from one hand to the other, flexed her fingers, listened. She could definitely hear footsteps. They were not so much moving across the landing as resonating deep inside the fabric of the building, inside her. The sound was comforting, in its way.

At least she wasn't alone.

The front door scraped open and – there was no mistaking it this time – someone stood hesitating on the threshold. Upstairs the footsteps stopped.

'Hello?'

It was him.

She'd made it clear he needed to keep this to himself, their arrangement. And later when they asked, she would say that she had come back to the house to retrieve her phone.

Her heart pounding, she moved silently to the corner of the room, to the fuse box.

Maybe he'll go away.

She could hear the door rattling softly on its hinges as he pushed it further back. It was dark in the hall, she knew, gloomy.

There was a shuffling as he tried to make up his mind. It wouldn't be long, a few seconds at most before he stepped inside.

She would say she had come back to the house to retrieve her phone and – and . . .

She had found him there, and no, she'd had no idea – there was no reason for him to be in the house, no reason at all.

And there had been nothing she could do.

An accident, she thought as she reached up, opening the cupboard door.

2

She had been too late.

'Hello?' His voice soft, uncertain.

The floorboards shifting as he stepped inside. The noise upstairs started again, bolder now, insistent.

She placed her hand on the switch, closed her eyes, and pushed.

1

Nell looked up at the gate; its slender fleurs-de-lys curves at odds with the worn sandstone buildings either side of it. It was new, wrought iron, unpainted, unfinished, the pale pewter grey standing in stark contrast with the rest of the long cobbled street and its mismatched Georgian shop fronts, the low doors and the sagging bow windows.

'Unbelievable.' She shook her head.

'What now?' said Chris.

'These yards aren't private. They've no right to block it.'

'Well, it's not blocked, is it?' said Maude. She reached past Nell and pushed; the bolt was hanging loose, and the gate opened easily enough, clattering against the enamelled sign that had been set into the wall, BISHOPS YARD. 'See?'

'It's out of place,' said Nell. 'And it's ugly.'

'Yes, well, grab a bag, would you?' Chris opened the car boot. 'Best not hang around.'

The journey had taken longer than they'd expected, a combination of motorway delays and too many stops to accommodate Maude's alleged travel sickness. Then they'd been late collecting the keys from the letting agency up on the West Cliff.

'I'll go over with you,' the woman had said, 'get you settled in,' but there'd been no mistaking the relief in her eyes when Chris had declined her offer. The shop was empty, the sign flipped to CLOSED and Nell had the impression that the rest of the staff had left for the day.

'We'll manage,' Chris said. 'My wife's a local girl.'

'Really?'

'We've kept you waiting long enough, and I'm sure you need to get home.'

The woman picked up a folder and two sets of keys, glancing at Nell, most likely trying, and failing, to place her. 'Well, if you're sure.'

'We'll be fine,' Chris said. 'Thanks.'

But Nell had forgotten about the one-way system, or maybe it was new, and once they'd left the agency, they'd had to follow the road up onto the cliff, and down onto the seafront, before driving up the harbour to cross the little swing bridge into the east side of town. Over the river, they'd turned onto the cobbled street, slowing the car as they checked the names of the yards. Chris had parked as close as he could, up on the pavement, more or less.

'It's a gate, it doesn't have to be pretty,' said Maude, picking up her rucksack and leading the way.

'Well, thank you for your insight, sweetheart,' said Chris, 'I'll be sure to—'

Nell nudged him and shook her head.

Maude counted off the numbers on the houses as they walked up the yard. There was a narrow gutter running the length of it, not quite central, not quite straight, carving its way through the worn cobbles. 'One, two, three,' to their right, 'five, six, four,' to the left. She came to a halt at the bottom of a flight of stone steps, steeply pitched, shallow and uneven. 'That doesn't make sense.' She looked up at Nell, frowning. 'Why is it like that?'

'Oh, I don't know.' Nell considered the question; most of

6

the houses were low sandstone cottages with neat pantile roofs; one or two had well-tended planters by their doors. Numbers five and six were no less orderly, but were built of red brick, and were set further back. All the houses were silent, their windows blank and grey, and it was impossible to tell if they were occupied or not. Nell wondered if the three of them might be the only inhabitants of the whole yard.

'I think,' she said, 'it depends how you look at it.'

Maude followed her gaze, 'Yeah?' she said.

'Do we have to do this now?' asked Chris, squeezing past, 'Can't the history lesson wait?'

Maude chose not to take her father's side, for a change. 'Those look new,' she said, 'so, the houses are numbered in the order they were built?'

'Not our place and maybe not the cottages, but yes – anything that came after them.'

Maude absorbed this. 'Right,' she said, then she pointed to the next house, which was about halfway up the steps. 'Is that us, then?'

'No.' SPINNAKER COTTAGE was engraved on a brass plate fixed to the bright blue door. 'We're right up at the top.' Nell couldn't be sure, but there seemed to be movement at one of the windows, someone watching them perhaps as they gawped at the yard like a bunch of tourists. They had shown Maude the pictures, of course, when they'd booked it, but she'd barely acknowledged them, dismissing her father's enthusiasm for the house, the town, the whole trip with a single word: *whatever.* Twelve going on twenty-one, as Chris had taken to saying.

It wasn't so easy to dismiss in real life. Elder House stood at the top of the steps, stiff, formal, imposing, looking down on the rest of the yard. It was rigidly symmetrical, solid, with stone mullioned windows and diamond shaped lead lights. The

7

roof was slate, and there was a grey-greenish tinge to the dressed stone; it was old – but unlike its neighbours – there was something untouched about it.

Dark, Nell thought, the way the house backed up against the cliff like that, she doubted it ever got much direct sunlight, even at midday. And it didn't look like a holiday let, there was nothing quirky or inviting about it. She turned and looked down the yard. The way it veered ever so slightly to one side meant it was impossible to see the street from here; the effect was oddly isolating.

Chris paused and called down to them, 'Are you two coming, then?'

Maude rolled her eyes, 'Yes. Right. Fine.' Nell took her time following her.

The steps led up to the left side of the house, and to the narrow flagged path that ran around it. There was a sheer drop of ten or twelve feet between it and their nearest neighbour, Spinnaker Cottage, and Nell had to resist the urge to warn Maude to stay away from the edge. She was a sensible kid, as a rule.

Chris was waiting for them by the front door. He found the right key, inserted it into the lock, struggling with it as it seemed to stick, shudder, then give. The door opened into a hall, a gleaming parquet floor dominated by a wide, wooden staircase. It was silent and the air was still; the house smelt faintly of beeswax polish and lavender, and underneath that, something else, something . . . Nell couldn't place it. They stood there for a moment, the three of them, waiting.

'Are we going in, then?' Maude pushed past her father and dropped her things at the foot of the stairs.

Nell followed her, flicking on the hall light, hoping to dispel the gloom. A sharp prickle of static electricity took her

8

unawares, and she caught her breath; Maude turned away, not quite masking a smirk.

There was a door to the left, and Nell opened it, revealing a long room that ran right through the house – the kitchen-diner. At the far end, on the counter, next to the Aga, there was a welcome pack, a cellophane-wrapped hamper filled with someone's idea of essential groceries and finished off with a shiny blue bow.

They had done a decent job of knocking through a wall; the shift from polished floorboards to worn flagstones was all that indicated there had once been two rooms where now there was one. The leaded windowpanes lent the room a slightly greenish cast.

Without thinking, Nell crossed the kitchen, squatted and lay her hand against the stone floor. It felt cool beneath her palm, and – this must have been imagination – slightly damp.

She stood up. There was a smell here too, although this was easier to place; it put her in mind of wet soil and rotting vegetables. It might have been the rag rug in front of the Aga, but it seemed new enough, the regular, clipped tongues of fabric springing up from the sacking base. Maybe they were the first visitors of the summer season, that would explain the damp, unused air of it all.

She didn't like it.

More than that: she didn't want to stay. The thought took her by surprise, and she tried to ignore it. It wasn't as if she had a choice.

It took a couple of trips to get everything out of the car, and by the time they were done, Chris's mood was beginning to sour. 'Next time,' he said, 'we choose somewhere with parking.'

'You were the one who wanted to stay in a yard,' said Nell.

9

'You're the one with the big old family party to go to.'

It wasn't really her fault, of course, the house, the trip. Nell had glanced at the invitation when it had come, more than a month ago, then put it to one side, intending to send a polite refusal, but never quite getting around to it.

Chris had picked it up from her desk one day, when they'd been discussing Maude, and the long summer that was suddenly stretching out in front of them. 'There's always this,' he said, opening the card before handing it to her.

There was an email address and a phone number printed inside, with the time and the date underneath the announcement: *David and Jennifer Galilee, Silver Wedding Anniversary.* There was a handwritten message too, although the writing was unfamiliar.

It would be great to see you, if you could find the time.
   Love, Jenny and Dave x

'We won't know anyone.'

Chris raised a sceptical eyebrow.

'You know what I mean,' Nell said. 'You won't know anyone. And I'll – it'll be awkward.' She couldn't remember the last time she'd spoken to her cousin, her dad's funeral, probably.

'It's up to you,' Chris said, 'but you never know, it could be fun. It might be nice to get away for a bit. Get Maude away from – everything.'

'It's a long way to go, just for one party.'

'Then we make it worth the effort. Stay on for a bit, show her the sights.'

'There are no sights.' She stood the card on her desk. The photo on the front showed a yacht sailing out of the harbour on a clear summer's day. 'Do you think she'd like it?'

10

'I don't see why not. It's the seaside, isn't it? Everyone likes the seaside.'

They hadn't been back since Maude was small, six or seven years ago, when an ice cream had been a treat, paddling in the sea an adventure. Before the arguments and the sulking, before everything had become so complicated and Maude's easy affection had been replaced by something more guarded, more unpredictable. The rush of nostalgia took Nell by surprise. 'Go on then,' she said, before she could change her mind, 'but don't blame me if she gets bored.'

She had pretty much left everything up to him after that. 'I don't mind where we stay,' she'd said, 'as long as we're together.'

She hadn't imagined he'd settle on somewhere so big, so uncompromising.

'Can I choose my room?' Maude was already halfway up the stairs.

'Sure,' said Chris. 'Go and have a look around. Don't mind me. I'll be having my heart attack in the kitchen, out of the way.'

Maude didn't look back.

Nell leant back against the banister. 'Well,' she said, 'here we are.'

'Hmm.' Chris pulled her into a gentle hug, resting his chin on her head as he looked around the hall, taking it all in.

'This is all very – showy,' Nell said. 'Very posh.'

'But . . .'

'There's a weird' – she hesitated – 'smell. Don't you think?'

'A smell?' He held her at arm's length. 'Seriously?'

'Well, yes. Haven't you noticed it?'

'No.'

'It's not so bad here, but in the kitchen it . . .' She didn't much like the way he was looking at her, as if he found her amusing, and ever so slightly foolish. 'Forget it,' she said. 'It's just . . . it's not very us, is it?'

'Isn't it?'

Chris had shown her the posting on the website, and she remembered flicking through images of a fitted kitchen with an electric Aga, cosy sofas and a log burning stove in the living room, exposed beams and leaded windows. She hadn't really taken it in. Her mind had been on other things.

She tried again. 'It feels . . .'

'What?' That same expression. Amused. Superior.

Wrong. It felt wrong.

'I like it,' said Chris. 'It's solid. Classy. There's a bit on the website about its history, former occupants and all that. You should—'

'Dad! Da-ad!' Maude's voice echoed down the stairs.

'What?'

'Come and see.'

'No.'

'You said I could choose.'

'But not this, obviously.'

'Why not?'

It was pretty impressive, Nell had to admit. The master bedroom: oak panelled, with an open fireplace, and dominated by a big brass bedstead. The ceiling was a little low perhaps, and its exposed beams seemed to dip slightly, but the room had an air of understated, if impersonal, comfort. There was a pitcher and ewer perched on a table underneath one set of windows, and a chest of drawers beneath the other. There was no wardrobe, but there were cupboards built into the wall either side of the tiled chimney breast, their tiny brass latches fitting flush against the painted wood.

Maude didn't mean it, of course – Nell could see that, she had no more intention of claiming this room than she did of letting either of them forget she was here on sufferance; the brief truce her interest in the yard had signalled was clearly over.

She fixed Nell with an accusing stare. 'He said.'

'You know perfectly well what your father meant.' Nell walked to one of the windows. Below them, to the left, the door to Spinnaker Cottage opened and a woman came out. She was blonde, wearing jeans and a waterproof jacket. As she walked down the yard, her scarf, a monochrome geometric design, fluttered in the breeze.

'Any other room,' Chris said, 'but not this one.'

'It's not fair.'

'We need the double bed,' said Chris, certain, surely, of the reaction this would provoke.

'God,' said Maude, after a horrified pause. 'You two are gross.' She turned and strode out of the room.

'What?' asked Chris, meeting Nell's gaze. 'What have I done now?'

'Nothing,' said Nell, turning her attention back to the window, 'but you can tell she's just spoiling for a fight, can't you?'

'Well, what am I supposed to do when she's being such a – brat?'

Just take a breath, Nell thought, just listen to her. 'Oh,' she said, the blonde woman had reappeared and was walking up the steps, a determined expression on her face as she headed straight for Elder House. 'I think we have a visitor.'

She could hear them, talking by the door downstairs. She'd sent Chris to deal with the woman, and now she sat on the bed, listening to the rise and fall of their voices, running her hand over the soft blue and white quilt. Her limbs were heavy, she was tempted to kick off her shoes and lie down, curl up and close her eyes, to leave the house to Chris and Maude as she slept.

Maybe it wouldn't be so bad, once they settled in.

The woman's voice was rapid and determined, Chris's responses, deeper, more considered, and gradually his voice came to dominate the exchange. After a while they said their goodbyes and Nell heard the door close.

She stood up and went to the window again, just in time to catch a final glimpse of the woman walking down the yard, upright, brisk.

'Nell!' Chris called up the stairs. 'I just need to move the car.'

'OK.'

She heard him go into the kitchen, then emerge again. As he left the house, he slammed the front door behind him.

The floorboards on the landing shifted and sighed.

'Maude?'

But there was no answer, evidently she was yet to be forgiven. She thought again about the online posting for the house. There had been no reviews, she remembered. No user comments. The owners must be new to the holiday-let business. Maybe that was why the place felt so . . .

Expectant.

Maude passed along the landing again; her footfalls muted by the carpet but still managing somehow to signal her discontent. Maybe she should have a word.

She had assumed that Maude would take the back bedroom, but when she opened the door, it was empty. 'Maude? Hello?'

14

She waited for an answer, as if Maude might be hiding some-where. It was only when she went back onto the landing that she noticed the steps, the wooden ladder that seemed to be fixed permanently in place, leading up to a hatch-door and the attic.

'I thought I'd lost you,' Nell said, climbing the last few rungs.

'I'm exploring,' Maude said, 'I mean, if that's all right.' She'd retrieved her bags from the hall and was bent over her rucksack, fiddling with the straps. Nell wasn't sure, but she thought she might have been crying.

'Of course it's all right.' Nell straightened up cautiously and looked around. Sleeps ten, the online ad had said, which had struck her as optimistic, even given the size of the place, but she had forgotten the attic. The beds here were no more than bunks, really, thin mattresses on wooden frames, two set at each side of the room, underneath the sharply pitched eaves, and separated by a narrow red rug. On the far wall, an old brick chimney snaked up to the ceiling, clinging to the white-wash. 'Do you like it?' she asked, keeping her tone carefully neutral. 'Up here, I mean?'

Maude abandoned the bag on the rug and turned to look at Nell, stepping back a little, out of reach. 'It's OK.' She looked hot and grubby, her hair coming loose from its ponytail; a little rounder in the face these days, a little taller too.

'There's a bedroom downstairs, next to the living room, you know.'

'That's for kids.'

'Or the one next to the bathroom. That's practically en-suite, if you think about it.'

'I like it up here.'

'It isn't too – gloomy?' The air was stale, still. She would be much better off downstairs, surely, closer to Nell and her father.

15

Maude didn't bother to answer, she went to one of the dormer windows, and after struggling with the catch for a moment, opened it as far as she could. 'I can see the roof,' she said, stretching up on tip-toe.

'Can you?' Nell stood behind her. Here, on this side, the back of the house, there was no view to speak of, just the dull grey slates and the looming cliff. Nell lay her hand on Maude's shoulder and squeezed reassuringly. 'Well. You don't have to decide right now, if you don't want to.'

Maude didn't answer. She turned and wriggled free, working her way around the room, opening the rest of the windows one by one, before facing Nell once again. 'It's OK,' she said, 'This will do.'

There was another pause. 'Are you—?' Nell began, but downstairs, the front door opened and closed, and distantly she could hear Chris calling out. Maude picked up her suitcase and set it on one of the beds, unzipping it. 'Go on,' she said, without looking up.

'Right,' said Nell, 'don't forget to ring your mum, once you're sorted.'

Maude pulled a book from the suitcase and set it carefully to one side. 'I won't,' she said.

Behind her, one of the windows shuddered, rattling in its frame as a breeze caught it; the room seemed to shift, to expand and settle again.

2

Maude took her time unpacking; not that she'd brought that much with her. One bag only, her dad had said, and it had taken her best efforts to bump that up to one suitcase and a rucksack, nagging him into slipping a couple of extra books into his stuff too.

He hadn't changed his mind about her laptop, though. They were all going to share his, that was the plan. No unsupervised internet for Maudie. Fine, she'd find a way around that as well; maybe if she asked him when he was on his own. It was always a lot easier to get her own way if Nell wasn't around.

She lay on the bed nearest the cliff – the bankside, that's what Nell called it – and a seagull shrieked somewhere up on the roof, sounding a little bit too close. She felt as though she was tucked up in a nest, a crow's nest, as if they were at sea.

She considered the view, the sloping, whitewashed ceiling and the bare beams that held everything in place. Oak, she supposed, but she wasn't really sure how a person could tell. It was interesting, the way the beams slotted together, the way the structure of the roof, the house, was revealed, like a skeleton. Especially up here, where it was all so bare.

Elder House was very old, her dad had made a point of telling her that when he'd booked it, because she liked History at school and generally got good grades in it, and apparently that was what they were concentrating on now: the positives.

She knew what he was doing, though. It was a sort of bribe, to make her go along with their stupid holiday, and when she'd asked exactly how old the house was, he'd gone all vague. He'd tried to show her stuff online, and that had actually been interesting, but he had spent so much time hovering over her shoulder, reading paragraphs aloud, watching her click on the links, she had begun to feel stifled. It had been easier in the end to close the laptop and pretend she wasn't that bothered.

Maybe she should ask again, maybe he'd leave her alone this time.

She followed the line of the central beam, tilting her head a little, watching the very last of the evening light from the dormer windows cut across the ceiling, splintering into shadows that shifted and settled in the corner of the room. They could make her join in, she thought, but they couldn't make her happy about it.

When she noticed the marks, she wasn't sure what they were at first. A scrawled date, perhaps. Or maybe someone's initials – the man who'd raised the beams leaving his name behind.

There was a wooden trunk in front of the chimney. Maybe if she yelled for her dad, he'd help her move it and . . .

No. She was still annoyed with him, with all of them, really, Nell and her mum, too. All of them going on as if she was to blame, as if nothing had changed. The way they kept telling her she had to be grown up now, *a proper big sister* now her mum had finally given birth, and her weekend visits with her and Callum had turned into stupid family days out with baby Leo always in the way. She had her own room at their house, but she could tell they didn't really want her there, not any more.

The trunk wasn't heavy, and there were rope handles. She could move it herself; she wanted it closer to the bed anyway. She could use it as a dressing table.

She dragged it into position and climbed on top.

The marks were faint, but quite deliberate, carved into the central beam that formed the ridge of the roof. She had a powerful urge to run her fingers over them, but of course she couldn't reach. She wondered who had made them, who had seen them last.

Craning her neck, tilting her head back for so long, trying to focus on the marks had made her feel dizzy, and she had to jump down from the trunk before she lost her balance entirely. It was quite pleasant, though, the light-headed rush, the way the room seemed momentarily to dip and swoop around her.

If she took the bunk closest to the cliff, then this was what she'd see when she opened her eyes first thing in the morning, and last thing at night too, half hidden in the dark; jagged peaks, a capital *N* or *M* – like an *M* for Maude – repeated over and over, and circles too, circles overlaying circles, like a flower, or a maze. She didn't want the big room with the brass bedstead, anyway. It was modern, fake. This was better; this, Maude decided, was hers.

Nell found Chris in the living room, his bag and jacket abandoned in the hall; he was sitting on the sofa, frowning at his laptop screen. 'Are you OK, love? Chris?'

'Yes. Sorry.' He looked up. 'I was just wondering what the Wi-Fi password is.'

'No idea. It'll be in the folder, I expect.'

'Which is . . . ?'

'I don't know. Where you left it?' Nell switched on the lights, then sat next to him, sinking into the cushions. Someone, she realised, should be thinking about dinner; lunch had been a long time and at least three counties ago. 'You could at least pretend not to be desperate to check your email, you know.'

Chris closed the laptop, then reached out to squeeze her hand. 'Sorry.'

'Hmm.'

'How is she?'

Nell glanced involuntarily at the ceiling. 'Hard to say. She's decided she wants to sleep in the attic.'

'That sounds suitably Dickensian for the poor suffering child.'

'Hmm. Did you manage to do your usual thing with that woman, the unhappy blonde?'

'Usual thing?' Chris's face was a study in mock outrage. 'I'm sure I don't know what you mean.'

'I'm sure you don't too.' Nell stretched out her legs. 'But she went away happy, yeah?'

'She was a bit pissed off about the car, because did we know we were blocking access to the whole yard. But I apologised very nicely, and told her we wouldn't make a habit of it.'

'That's my boy.'

'I think her bark is worse than her bite. She seemed friendly enough, once we'd got things settled. I had the distinct feeling she was angling to be asked in.'

'Wow. Fast work, love. Even for you.'

He shrugged. 'Well, you've either got it or you haven't.'

Nell considered her husband. He looked worried, she thought, underneath the smile and the easy charm. There was something going on, and she might have asked, if she hadn't heard Maude coming down the stairs.

She poked her head around the door. 'I'm hungry.'

'Did you ring Jess?' asked Nell.

Maude rolled her eyes. 'Yes. And I'm still hungry.'

'Right.' Chris shook himself free and put the laptop to one side and stood. 'Fish and chips all round, then?'

Nell nodded. It had been a long day, that was all, she thought, a long drive with too many delays, and nothing more than that. She should have insisted they break the journey; it wasn't as if there had been any need to rush. 'Sure,' she said. 'That would be great.'

Chris said it would be quicker if he went on his own, which meant Nell was left behind, in charge of Maude and the kitchen.

They played around with the switches, working out which one matched each range of lights, the small halogen bulbs that were embedded in the ceiling and the showier adjustable spotlights over the kitchen counters and the oven. But it didn't matter what they did, what combination they tried, they couldn't seem to make the room quite bright enough.

'Right,' she said, 'that will have to do. Plates. Cutlery. Glasses.'

There was a certain pleasure in opening the cupboards, in discovering where things were kept, in passing judgement on the owners' taste; it was as if they were trying on someone else's life for a while. Someone with expensive tastes, was Nell's verdict, even if everything did feel impersonal, cold.

'There's no salt,' she said as Maude set the table, 'and we need vinegar too.' She opened the fridge. 'There's butter, and they left us some milk, but we'll need more.'

'You should write it down,' said Maude.

'I should,' Nell said, 'or maybe you could write it for me?'

That was a request too far, though, Maude simply sighed and fussed with the knives and forks on the table.

Nell opened the welcome pack, fishing out the coffee. 'Can you find us some mugs, please?'

'I don't want coffee.'

'And you don't have to have it.'

'I want a cold drink.'

Nell took a deep breath. Maude was tired, she reminded herself; they all were. 'Coke?'

'Diet. Please.'

'I'd better ring your dad, then,' said Nell. 'Have you seen my phone?'

'Dunno. In your bag?'

'Have you seen my bag?' Nell looked around the kitchen. She must have left it in the living room.

It was almost fully dark now, but even with everything switched on, including the lamp in the window, the front room too remained on the gloomy side. She retrieved her phone, but as she swiped the screen she noticed the battery was low.

'Shit.'

She rummaged in her bag. No charger. It was, she suspected, still in the car, the car now at the other end of the street in the residents' car park.

Still holding her phone she went back into the kitchen. 'Maude, can I borrow—' Maude was standing completely still, looking up at the ceiling. 'Maudie?'

'The lights went out,' said Maude. 'Here.' She pointed to the spotlights over the dining table.

'Right.'

'It wasn't me.'

'I switched on the lights in the other room. Maybe we've tripped a fuse.'

The fuse box was in a corner cupboard above the work-top. 'See?' One switch was down and the others were all in place. Nell flicked it back up and the lights blinked on again. 'Sorted.'

She closed the cupboard door and the room seemed to dim again. The spotlights above the counter blinked out. Nell swore

22

softly, and opened the cupboard again. The next fuse in the row had tripped. 'Fine.' Nell pushed it back into place and they stood waiting, the two of them, just in case it happened again.

'OK.' Nell closed the door gently, as if that would somehow make a difference. 'Can I use your phone?'

'What for?' Maude's tone was defensive.

'To ring your dad?'

'What for?'

'To get him to pick up some more milk, and some Diet Coke, for you. Come on, Maude, please, there's no need to be so . . . Mine is pretty much dead. Please.'

After a long pause Maude pulled the phone out of her jeans pocket and handed it over. 'Here,' she said.

The phone was locked, but Nell knew the password.

Maude watched her closely as she tapped at the screen, hitting the icon to call Chris – but nothing happened. Nell frowned. 'There's not much of a signal,' she said turning to look out of the window at the bankside. 'We're too close, I suppose.' She tried the kitchen door, but it was locked. She went into the hall and opened the front door, stepping out into the chilly evening air with Maude following close behind. The call connected at last, but went through to voicemail almost immediately.

'Damn,' said Nell softly, turning away from Maude. 'Chris, can you fetch some milk back with you, and some Diet Coke for Maude and – I don't know – some salt, vinegar—'

'Chocolate,' said Maude, 'and ice cream.'

'Did you hear that? Chocolate and ice cream too, please.' Nell ended the call. She should have thought to check about the mobile signal, they used to have the same problem at her dad's house.

'Can I have it back now?' Maude was staring at her, hand extended.

Nell glanced down at the phone. There was nothing on there that shouldn't have been, no icons for email or the internet. All that had been carefully removed by Chris. Maude's phone was being used for calls and texts only; she barely even used it as a camera these days.

'Sure.' She handed it back. 'Thanks.'

One of them should check her messages, of course, but maybe she'd get Chris to do that later. They should unlock the kitchen door too, she thought, as they went back inside, another job to go on the list.

Chris returned to the house with fish and chips for three, a family-sized bottle of Diet Coke and a pocketful of Kit-Kats. No ice cream, no milk, though.

'Sorry,' he said as he helped Nell plate up the food. 'I didn't see you'd called.'

'We'll live,' said Nell, 'as long as there's something sweet for madam.'

'Well, I do know my girl.'

'Who were you talking to?' – Maude was hovering behind them – 'when Nell rang?'

'What?' Chris concentrated on transferring a piece of fish to a plate.

'She couldn't get through. So who were you talking to?'

'No one,' said Chris. 'Work. Sam. I just wanted to—' Above them the lights flickered and died.

'Not again,' said Nell.

'I told you it wasn't me,' said Maude.

'I never said it was.' Nell opened the cupboard. 'It's an old house, and underneath all the improvements, the electrics are still a bit . . .' She flipped the switch back up. 'Dodgy.'

'That's a technical term, is it?' said Chris.

24

'Funny,' said Nell.

'Yeah. Funny,' said Maude, picking up her plate and taking it to the table.

Maude didn't really mind washing-up when she got to do it with her dad, although she always made a point of complaining, just so they both knew she was doing them a favour. Sometimes it was the only part of the day they got to spend together, just the two of them.

He hadn't thought to buy washing-up liquid, but luckily there was a bottle hidden away in the cupboard under the sink. There was a supply of bin liners and a dustpan and brush, and other cleaning things too. She supposed the owners wanted their house left nice and tidy.

'You all right then, Maggot?' That was an old nickname, from before. He only ever used it when he wanted to make up for something.

'Suppose so.'

'And you're all right up in the attic?'

'Yup.' She made a point of drying the plate she was holding particularly carefully. She wondered if she should ask about the internet again.

'It's not too lonely up there?'

'Nope.' She turned the plate over, dried the back of it. She could feel him looking at her, considering his next move.

'Well, OK then.' He tipped the washing-up bowl into the sink, and they both watched the suds circle and swirl. He might be interested in the marks in the attic, Maude thought. They could go up and take a look together, just the two of them. In the living room they heard Nell switch the TV on, the familiar theme for the news wafting through the open door. The lights over the sink wavered a bit, then settled.

Her dad dried his hands. 'Shall we go and find something fun to watch?' he said.

She was supposed to say yes, obviously.

'If you like.' She added the plate to the pile. 'I'll put these away first.'

She could hear them talking as she returned the plates to the right cupboard. Talking about her, probably, and how unreasonable she was being. She folded the tea towel and hung it carefully where she'd found it, on the handle of the oven door. She didn't really want to go and join in, she'd rather be on her own; but then again, she didn't really see why they should get to spend the night together, all cosy, as if everything was all right.

She switched off the lights by the sink and the kitchen suddenly seemed smaller, closer, and the dining table, still illuminated by overhead lights, very far away. Outside, in the street beyond the yard, someone called out to a friend. Maude couldn't quite hear what they were saying, then someone laughed and their footsteps faded away.

She stretched up and opened the cupboard that held the fuse box. The fuses were all labelled, kitchen, range, dining area, living room, hall. She was tempted for a moment to flip one just to see what would happen. That was a stupid idea. She closed the cupboard door and stood for a while, gazing out of the kitchen window, into the dark.

3

Nell wasn't sure what had woken her at first. Not Chris, who lay next to her, curled up on his side, wheezing softly under his breath, and not Maude, who had retreated to her attic at bedtime, with little of the usual fuss. The house was still.

The church bells up on the cliff, she thought, striking the hour. Or the morning light, bleeding in around the edge of the curtains.

She never slept well in the summer, the light nights and early dawn left her restless and irritable. She stretched and raised her head cautiously, wondering if she dare risk picking up her phone to check the time, and beside her, Chris shifted, catching his breath before going back to sleep, the gentle wheeze now more pronounced.

She wondered if she should give him a nudge, get him to turn over before he graduated to full-on snoring, but she settled for changing position herself, rolling onto her back none too carefully, hoping he might take the hint.

She stretched out under the light summer quilt and waited for sleep to return. She tried to still her breathing; slow, deep, controlled breaths. The light from the window was bothering her, but she was reluctant to get out of bed. Once she was on her feet, that would be that, the day would have officially begun.

She closed her eyes.

Outside a seagull opened its throat, its shrill call echoing down the yard.

27

The noise didn't bother her, it was the sound of her childhood, something she barely noticed, even these days when she visited her home town less and less. It might disturb Maude, she supposed, not that there weren't seagulls at home, but they were closer here, more insistent. And it would be entirely typical of her to make a fuss, just for the sake of it, just to remind her father that their holiday was an ordeal to be got through, not a pleasure. Never mind that most kids were still in school and once they were done here, she'd be off to the South of France with her mum and stepdad.

And the new baby.

Nell hoped she wasn't going to kick off about that trip too. They were lucky they could leave the gallery for this long, but once they were back Chris would have to work, doing all the admin and sales, and Nell – well, if things worked out, if she was right this time, then she should probably plan on spending as much time as she could in the workshop, before everything changed, for good. It would be useful to get a few ideas down on paper while they were here. She had been thinking about combining sea glass and pearls, as well as doing some simpler stuff in silver.

She found she was looking at the exposed beams that ran across the ceiling. Too low, too close, and underneath the lavender scent of the fresh bedding, that smell again. She felt the first faint stirrings of nausea – too early for that, surely – and took a breath in through her nose, held it, then exhaled slowly through her mouth. For a moment she imagined nudging Chris awake, telling him she'd changed her mind, persuading him they should pack up and leave – she pushed the thought away. She lay still and tried not to think about the smell as her stomach settled. She didn't much like the house, but Chris and Maude seemed happy enough. She'd have to get used to it.

She closed her eyes, then opened them again.

She needed to pee.

She pushed open the bathroom window as far as she could and leant out. The sky was clear and according to her phone – balanced precariously on the sink – it was just a little past seven.

She wasn't going to get back to sleep now.

She still felt off-colour, and her mouth was dry; she ran the cold tap and took a couple of sips of water, but it didn't help much, the water tasted funny, almost metallic.

As she was using the loo, she thought she heard something, a slow muffled tread that came to a halt outside the door, and as she looked, the door handle seemed to tremble slightly, as if whoever was on the other side was touching it, thinking about trying it.

'Just a minute,' she said, flushing the loo, running the taps.

When she opened the door, there was no one there.

While she waited for the kettle to boil, Nell unlocked the kitchen door and went outside. The path led to the back of the house where it had been widened a little in an attempt at a patio. She wasn't really sure what the owners had been thinking, it was the very opposite of inviting; damp and gloomy, more than likely in perpetual shadow.

Beyond the flagstones – cleverly matched but not as old as the ones at the front of the house, Nell guessed – behind the wheelie bin and the narrow strip of gravel that marked a boundary, the land rose abruptly to meet the foot of the cliff. Half-hidden in the long grass were the remains of a low wooden fence, collapsed and peeling, held together by brambles and nettles, forming a rough square that swept up the incline of the bank. There was no obvious way in.

She glanced back at the house; it wouldn't hurt to take a quick look.

She followed the fence, stumbling slightly as the land rose unevenly. After two or three paces, she glanced to her left and was surprised to see another house, small, self-contained, with a red pantile roof, tucked away behind the cottages opposite; as if it had been forgotten as the yard below it had evolved.

Like Elder House, it was nestled up against the cliff, only it had the luxury of a little garden, constructed in tiers, well tended and bursting with colour.

She carried on, following the fence as it turned right, and just as she was beginning to think there was no way in at all, she more or less stumbled over the gate. It didn't make sense, she thought as she bent to lift the latch, hiding away the entrance like that.

Nell stepped inside, the long grass was cool and slick and almost immediately she slipped again, her foot catching in a narrow hole – rats, she thought, remembering the tales she and her friends used to tell each other about the bankside when they were kids, rats tunnelling away into the cliff – and only righting herself at the last moment.

From this vantage point all she could see was Elder House looming in front of her, and the little cottage to her right. As she edged forward her feet came in contact with the odd brick or bit of rubble buried in the undergrowth. Shoes might have been a good idea. She stopped and tried not to think about what else might lie broken and rotting out of sight.

She glanced up at the house again, and had the oddest feeling she wasn't alone.

Time to go back.

She turned, then lost her balance, she took a step and where there should have been solid ground, there was nothing. Her ankle gave way and she collapsed onto her hands and knees, wrenching her foot.

'Shit.' The pain was sharp enough to bring tears to her eyes. She'd managed to fall into a patch of nettles too. 'Shit, shit, shit.'

'Hello?'

There was a woman standing behind her, on the steps by the corner of the house. She was in her fifties, perhaps, her untidy dark hair streaked with grey, and she was wearing a scarf and a baggy jumper over faded jeans. She was carrying two hemp shopping bags, well-used and bulging.

'I . . .' Nell was fighting the urge – foolish, she knew – to claw her fingers into the earth, to stop herself falling any further.

She couldn't focus, she couldn't . . .

Breathe.

'Are you all right?' The woman stepped onto the patio, and placed her bags carefully on the ground, her expression fixed, determined.

Nell struggled to her feet, took a breath. 'Fine.' Her voice was little more than a croak. She coughed, cleared her throat, tried again. 'I'm fine, thanks.'

The woman watched as she made a point of pulling the gate shut before retracing her steps back onto the path. 'They've let it, then,' she said, looking up at Elder House.

Nell nodded. 'We got here yesterday.' She wiped her hands on her pyjamas, she was still a bit breathless, and felt more than a little foolish. It was a relief to be standing on solid ground.

'Nice.'

'Yes.'

'Gina Verrill,' the woman said, extending a hand. 'That's my place up there, Rowan Cottage.'

The hidden house, with its beautiful garden.

'Nell. Nell Galilee.' She tried not to wince as they shook hands, the nettle stings were starting to burn.

'Galilee. That's a local name.'

'Yes, it is. I – I haven't been back for a bit, but – yes.'

The woman looked at her appraisingly, taking in the pyjama bottoms and the faded T-shirt. 'I used to know a Rebecca Galilee; she lived up on the Ropery, fifteen, twenty years back.'

Nell wasn't really in the mood for this, she should have stayed quiet, or at least used Chris's name.

'My gran.'

'So, you'd be . . . Linda's daughter.'

'That's right.'

'And your dad . . .'

'Thomas.'

The woman smiled. 'Yes,' she said, 'Of course . . .'

Nell stepped back, folding her arms. She wished she'd bothered to get dressed before deciding to clamber around the bankside; behaving like an idiot visitor.

'She was a lovely woman, your gran, always friendly, always interested in people.'

'Yes. She was.' Nell had long since grown used to the fact of her grandmother's death, even if it still puzzled her occasionally, that she hadn't lived to see Nell leave school, graduate, marry. At least her dad had met Chris, although he hadn't approved.

'Are you here for Dave and Jenny's party, then?'

'That's right.'

'It'll be nice for you to catch up with everyone, I expect.'

'It was very good of them to invite us, I haven't really stayed in touch since – well – my dad . . .'

'That'll be Jenny, bless her. Dave's a good lad, but he's left her to sort most of it out. She got it into her head that she would invite everyone who was at the wedding in the first place.'

'Right.' A surname popped into her head out of nowhere, Marsay, Jennifer Marsay. She had a vague memory of the wedding reception, held in one of the villages up the valley. A couple of illicit pints of cider, a boy kissing her in a darkened car park as the disco lights bled out of the pub windows; everyone walking home through narrow country lanes because they couldn't get any taxis. She could walk past David Galilee in the street now and not recognise him. 'We thought we'd stay on for a bit, afterwards so we – you know . . .' She gestured towards the house.

The stinging was getting worse and as she flexed her fingers Nell suspected her pyjama knees were smeared with grass stains.

'Here.' Gina bent and tugged at a broad-leafed plant growing at the edge of the patio. 'Try this.' She crushed the leaf and pressed it into Nell's hands. A dock leaf.

'Thanks,' said Nell. 'Would you like to come in, for a cup of tea, or something?' She wasn't sure why she'd offered, other than it felt like a neighbourly thing to do. The thought of breakfast made her stomach churn.

'Oh, no,' said Gina, looking up at the house – and it was there again, very faintly, that fixed look, not disapproval, more . . . distaste. 'I'll let you start your day in peace.' She nodded towards the sandstone cottage at the top of the path. 'I'll see you around, I expect. Or you're welcome to call into the shop.'

'The shop?'

'Sheela Na Gig. You can't miss it, it's just on Church Street, two doors on from the bookshop.' She picked up her bags and smiled at Nell. 'Bye for now, then.'

*

Maude was standing by the sink when Nell limped back inside, still clutching the crumpled dock leaf. Her hair was tousled and her face flushed and creased from sleep; she was holding a glass of milk.

'Morning, sweetheart.'

'Hmm.'

It was better than nothing, Nell supposed.

'What happened to you?' asked Maude.

'I tripped . . .'

'You woke me up.'

'Really?'

'Something did.'

'Seagulls?'

'No.' Maude stopped to consider. 'It was – I don't know – something thumping. What's that?'

'A dock leaf, for nettle stings.'

'Does it work?'

'A bit.' Nell dropped the leaf into the kitchen rubbish and turned on the tap to wash her hands. The burning had subsided into a dull itch, and a constellation of small white blisters was scattered across both palms.

'What were you doing?'

'I was – exploring.' Nell nodded towards the bankside. 'And I lost my balance.'

Maude edged forward, peering through the window. 'Aren't we a bit close? To the cliff? What if there's a landslide?'

Nell wasn't sure she was joking. 'There hasn't been one since the eighteenth century,' she said, drying her hands carefully on a tea towel, 'so I think we're probably OK for the next few weeks.'

'Is that what happened to the other houses?'

'What other houses?'

'There's a book in the living room, some Victorian photographer. There used to be a lot more of them, all down the street, sort of pressed up against the cliff.'

'No.' Nell couldn't help smiling. 'No, I was . . . I think most of them were knocked down in the 1950s.'

'Why?'

'They were, like – tenements, very overcrowded.'

'Slums?'

'Not exactly.'

'Dad said there's stuff about the house on the website.'

'Did he?'

'He showed me. He said I could read it if I want. Can I?'

'Sure, but you know, later.'

It was the wrong answer, of course, and Nell felt a twinge of sympathy for her stepdaughter as her enthusiasm seemed to visibly dwindle.

'OK.'

'Do you want to help with breakfast?'

'If you like.' Maude looked up at the cliff again, frowning. 'It's very close,' she said.

'You'll get used to it,' said Nell. 'Come on. We'll get started, then you can go wake your dad up.'

4

All the other houses in the yard were most likely, in Nell's opinion, holiday lets. Which meant the blonde woman who'd come to the door last night would soon be gone. They had the party next weekend, then they'd have the rest of their stay to themselves; time to relax, to look after each other. It had been a good idea, after all, she thought; a family holiday was exactly what they needed, they'd make it work. She'd make it work.

Someone had bolted the gate, and after opening it – and shepherding Maude and Chris through first – Nell didn't bother to close it again.

'What shall we do?' said Maude. 'Where shall we go?'

If they turned left, they'd walk past Nell's childhood home, and it might be nice to climb the bankside there and take the short cut up to the headland and the abbey. They'd stop halfway up the path and Nell would show Maude where she used to live, pointing out the kitchen window, and her old bedroom above it. But the lace curtains and potted geraniums would have vanished. It wouldn't be the same; it wouldn't be home.

'We should really get some shopping done,' Nell said. 'Get organised.'

'Boring,' said Maude.

'Yeah,' said Chris, 'so boring.' The two of them ganging up on her, as usual.

'So what do you suggest?'

'Well,' said Chris, hooking his arm through hers, 'we could go for a walk instead. You choose, Maudie, shop or beach?'

'Beach, please.' Her response almost instant, as if they'd planned it behind Nell's back.

The beach hadn't changed, it was still scruffy and windswept in the dull morning light, reminding Nell of when she was a little girl, and all the times they'd struggled across it; she and her gran, with their bags and their towels and the fading windbreaker. The careful pacing of the sand to find the right spot.

It all seemed so very long ago.

Nell stopped to take in the view as Chris marched on towards the Nab, where the cliff curved down and into the sea, forming a natural harbour that was extended and reinforced by the long sandstone pier stretching towards its twin across the estuary. She was almost halfway along the strand, the broken trail of dried seaweed and sticks, with the odd seagull feather trapped and fluttering in the breeze. Maude stood next to her, looking out at the harbour mouth, facing due north.

The sky was grey and the horizon blurred with fog, a sea fret was settling in; Nell closed her eyes and let the sound of the tide, the gentle hiss as waves broke softly against the beach, wash over her.

'Oh! Sorry!'

The dog didn't so much run into Nell as bounce off her. She opened her eyes as the border collie, all salt fur and soft growls, circled her, a stick in its mouth. Maude skipped back out of the way; she wasn't used to dogs, and without thinking Nell moved in front of her, trying to distract it.

'Flossie! Floss!' The dog chased its tail for a moment or two as a girl made her way up the beach, half walking, half running. 'Sit, Floss!'

The collie finally dropped to the sand, and began to gnaw at the stick.

'Sorry,' said the girl as she drew closer, 'she's not dangerous or anything, but I think she might be a bit deaf.'

'Maybe keep her on a lead then,' Nell said, glancing at Maude, 'not everyone is comfortable around dogs.'

'Floss won't hurt you.' The girl smiled reassuringly. 'She's too lazy.'

'Even so,' said Nell as she turned away, 'it might be the sensible thing to do, don't you think?'

She concentrated for a while on following the high water mark and then crossed it, stepping over onto the wet sand, pock-marked with pebbles and shingle and broken shells.

'That was a bit – rude,' Maude said, catching up, 'telling her off like that.' She sounded impressed.

Nell glanced back down the beach, the girl was still there, the dog dancing around her.

'I wasn't telling her off. Was I?'

'A bit. Yeah.'

'Well. She should keep the stupid thing under control. Are you OK? You weren't – frightened?'

'I'm all right,' said Maude. 'Come on. Dad's waiting.'

'I win,' said Chris, leaning back against a boulder at the foot of the cliff. 'You two have been ages.'

'You never said it was a race,' Maude pointed out.

They stood there, the three of them, no one sure what to do or say next.

'Right,' said Nell eventually, 'since we're here—'

'Seriously?' Nell couldn't tell if Maude's incredulity was sincere or just part of the game. 'I'm not, like, six, you know.'

'Come on. Please,' said Nell. 'Just – I don't know – three good pieces of sea glass. Stuff I can use.'

Maude rolled her eyes. 'I should get paid for this,' she said.

Nell couldn't find anything at first, nothing but shells, mainly mussels, some hinged open but most single. There was the odd cockle, and a few limpets, but then, just as Chris was getting bored, abandoning the hunt to take photos with his phone, she seemed to get her eye in and by the time she'd circled back to the slipway that led up onto the pier she had gathered a pretty decent collection.

She sat on a rock and spread everything out, discarding the smaller pieces and the ones with any sharp edges. The largest, around the size of the tip of her thumb, pale green and rendered faintly opaque by the grinding action of the sea, was definitely worth keeping.

'I hardly got anything,' said Maude, dumping a handful of shells and pebbles, and some scraps of pottery in front of Nell.

'It's not so bad,' Nell said, sorting through the offerings. Two smaller pieces of glass, the size of a fingernail, and darker, a rich bottle green, might do as well. She took her time sorting through their finds before making her final selection, long enough for Maude to lose patience and wander back down the beach. She picked up a stick and bent down to draw something in the wet sand.

'Have you got anything useful?' Chris leant against the rock beside her.

'Oh. You know.' The breeze was ruffling his hair, the light brown that was beginning to be threaded with grey, and he hadn't bothered to shave that morning. The faded blue of his shirt – a gift from Nell, and one of her favourites – brought out the blue of his eyes. She sat back, looking at him thoughtfully.

'What?' he said. 'What's wrong?'

'Nothing.'

'Does it really bother you that much? The house? I know it's a bit over the top, but with everything so last minute – and I thought you'd like it.'

'No. Of course not, it's fine.'

'Because you have that look on your face,' he said, 'the one where I can't tell if you want to draw me or—'

'Shush.' The kiss to shut him up turned into something more purposeful, until Nell, aware of Maude and her new policy on public displays of affection, pulled away. 'You're a terrible distraction,' she said.

'I aim to please.' He settled back onto his rock, looking at Maude as she continued making marks in the sand. 'How's she doing, do you think? Really?'

'You have to stop asking me that.' Nell slipped the glass into her pockets. 'I think the best policy is to keep everything low key, normal. No fuss.'

'Hmm.' He didn't look convinced.

'She was asking about the internet this morning. She's interested in the house.'

'Is she?'

'Which is good, right? At least she's showing a bit of enthusiasm.' Nell paused. She wasn't sure he was listening. 'She has to get through this on her own, love. You can't do it for her.'

'I know.' He took her hand, tugging gently at her fingers. 'And you? How are you?'

'You have to stop asking me that too. Especially, you know . . .' Maude was turning in a wide circle, dragging the stick through the sand.

'Yeah, I know. But have you . . .'

It was funny the way he couldn't quite bring himself to ask,

41

to say it out loud. They were neither of them superstitious, but it was as if to put it into words, to even acknowledge the possibility might jinx it.

'Not yet,' said Nell. 'I mean, I could, there are tests you can do early, but I'd rather wait until – you know – I've actually missed a period.' The date was highlighted on the calendar on her phone.

'But you do think . . . ?'

'Yes. Yes, I do.'

They sat quietly for a moment, holding hands, looking at the sea, at the mist rolling in.

'It's not – it's not the best timing, is it?' said Chris, then, 'Not that I'm not happy, I am, of course – but . . . you know.' He glanced at Maude.

'No. No, it isn't. Sorry about that,' she said. 'We'll work it out, though.'

Chris sighed softly, then raised her fingers to his lips, kissed them and stood. Brushing sand off his jeans, he called out, 'Hey! Maude! Maudie!'

Maude looked up, dropping the stick and waiting, both hands on her hips, as Chris jogged towards her. Nell couldn't hear, but from the way he pulled his phone from his pocket and Maude backed off, shaking her head; he was clearly trying to persuade her to pose with him for a selfie.

Nell left the discarded glass and shells on the rock and followed him slowly. By the time she caught up with them both, Chris was duly admiring the drawings in the sand – huge, stylised flowers, nodding their heads over undulating stems – as Maude danced around him. She wasn't really sorry, despite what she'd said; she wasn't about to let anyone, or anything, make her sorry about this.

*

42

Dad and Nell took their time following Maude off the beach, they wandered slowly behind her, acting all – weird. Her dad was doing that thing of being a bit too touchy-feely, as if it made up for him being at the gallery all the time, and Nell was playing along. They kept stopping to pick up more bits of glass and pebbles, and her dad kept taking photos.

Maude made a point of walking quickly and not looking back; it wasn't as if she needed them. She wasn't a little kid anymore. She reached the steps up to the little pier and sat on one of the low wooden benches; she had kept some of the things she'd found and was busy inspecting her treasure when they caught up with her.

'What have you got there, Maudie?' her dad asked.

'Nothing.' She shoved everything in her jacket pocket as she stood. 'Can we go up onto the cliff now? Can we go and look at the abbey?'

He rolled his eyes, and puffed out his cheeks as if she was being unreasonable, but he wasn't going to say no, not when he was trying so hard to make out everything was all right.

When they finally decided to head for home, the church clock was striking the hour, and the sun had vanished. They walked slowly down the street, pausing at the entrance to the yard; the fog had reached the town and the air was thick and damp.

As they walked up the steps, Nell shivered, suddenly aware that none of them were properly dressed for this weather, for the dull unpredictable days of early summer.

Chris had insisted they buy kippers for lunch.

'You can see their faces,' Maude said, unwrapping the grease-proof paper, 'it's gross.'

'More for Nell and me, then.'

'Hmm.' She extended a grubby finger and gingerly lifted one of the fish. 'How do you cook it?'

'Technically, it's cooked already,' said Chris, 'but I'll fry them up to warm them.'

'Or grill them,' said Nell, looking up from the glass she was arranging on the dining table, 'and open the door and windows maybe, so you don't stink the whole house out.'

Chris grinned at her, then whispered something in Maude's ear which made her laugh, and Nell turned her attention back to her sea glass. She thought she might take a photo. She turned on the overhead lights, but that didn't help; they seemed to turn everything yellow, and as she was considering what to do next, they flickered gently, a warning.

'Fine,' she said softly, turning the lights back off. 'Fine. Can you guys call me when the food's ready? I'm just going to take these upstairs.'

'Sure,' said Chris, barely bothering to look up.

The light was better in the bedroom, if she balanced the glass on the window ledge. She'd left her phone charging by the bed, using the cable Maude had begrudgingly loaned her. She unplugged it, checked her messages, decided she could safely ignore most of them, and took a couple of shots of her finds.

When she was done, she took a few more pictures of the room itself; she wasn't sure why, other than she had the vague feeling that was what people did these days, and maybe Chris would want to put them online. She got a decent shot of the bed and the wooden panelling and was just considering the tiles around the fireplace when the room seemed to lurch and her vision blurred. Still clutching the phone, she sat heavily on the bed, the frame rattling against the oak panels. She

44

swallowed, licked her lips; it was there again, that odd metallic taste in her mouth.

Could it be a symptom? If she were pregnant then there were all sorts of changes going on in her body; she tried to remember what she'd read online, stuff about cravings, what she should and shouldn't eat, sudden aversions to particular tastes and smells. She couldn't remember feeling this way before, off-balance, the nausea, her mouth dry all the time. Oddly, this made her feel ever so slightly optimistic, even though a small part of her still insisted that surely this was far too early for her to feel any real difference in herself. She took a deep breath and let it out gently, then she became aware that someone – Maude, she supposed, was making their way up the stairs, presumably to tell her lunch was ready.

She stood, not wanting to be found looking and feeling out of sorts, and called, 'It's OK, I'm coming.' Then she took a couple more steadying breaths before she went back down to the kitchen.

Now that the fish was on her plate, Maude was even less keen. 'It smells,' she said.

'It smells delicious,' said Chris.

'Ha.' She picked up her knife and fork, prodded at the pinkish grey flesh. 'There are loads of bones,' she said. 'We should have gone to the chip shop instead.'

'You can't live on chips,' said Nell.

Maude picked at her food. 'You can die from that, you know, fish bones. You can choke to death.'

'And you know this how?' asked Chris.

'Everyone knows,' said Maude.

Suddenly, inexplicably, Nell was ravenous. She began to cut her food, then, dropping her knife, she used her fingers to pull the fine bones from the clump of fish on her fork, before popping it into her mouth, it tasted glorious, oily, sweet and smoky.

Maude was watching her suspiciously.

'It's fine,' said Nell, 'try some.'

'Hmm.' Maude picked at her food, spearing a few flakes of fish, staring at them resentfully before taking a bite.

'OK?'

Maude swallowed. 'I can feel them,' she said, 'the bones.'

'They won't do you any harm,' said Chris.

Maude picked up another forkful, larger this time, and took another bite.

'See?' said Nell. 'Fine.'

'It's all right, but I don't see why—' She stopped, trying and failing to clear her throat.

'Maudie?' Chris said. 'Have a drink of water.'

She shook her head, then coughed.

'It's OK,' Nell said. 'Just do as your dad said and—'

Maude leant forward and spat her food back onto her plate; half chewed flesh, grey and glistening, but with no discernible bones, not that Nell could see, anyway.

'Jeez, Maude,' said Chris.

'I could feel them,' said Maude, raising a hand to her throat, and she shot Nell a look of pure resentment, 'inside.'

'Brown bread,' said Nell, before there was yet another scene.

'What?'

'Brown bread,' Nell said again. 'My gran always said to eat brown bread with kippers, and that way if any of the little bones get stuck, the bread sort of sweeps them away.' She looked at the mess on Maude's plate, and she could feel it too, a prickling sensation at the back of her throat, as if something was caught there.

Maude took a tentative bite of bread and began to chew.

Nell looked down at her plate, concentrating on not thinking about the prickling, which seemed to be getting worse.

'Good girl,' said Chris.

Maude regarded them both suspiciously, then picked up her knife and fork and began to prod at the fish again.

Nell took a sip of water. The whole house was going to stink of smoked kipper, she thought, despite the open windows. But at least it was masking the other smell, that scent of damp, decaying earth that bothered her so. She cleared her throat softly and cut into her fish again, the bones were as fine as hair, she reminded herself; they couldn't possibly do any harm.

Maude struggled through the meal. She quite liked the taste, she supposed, but that thing with the bread didn't really work; she was sure she could feel all the tiny bones scratching her throat every time she swallowed.

'Can I go upstairs now?' she asked, pushing her plate to one side.

'I suppose so,' Nell said. 'Don't you want to go out again?'

'Not really.'

'Maude.' Her dad used his warning tone.

She took her plate to the sink. If you craned your neck you could almost see the edge of the cliff.

'It's fine,' said Nell, 'do what you want to do, sweetheart.'

'OK.' Maude made a point of rinsing her plate before leaving it in the sink, and going upstairs. She wasn't really sure what she wanted to do, but at least she could get away from them both for a bit.

She tried her phone once she was back in the attic. She was still allowed to text people, as long as either her dad or Nell checked her messages, only the signal up here was rubbish.

And anyway, everyone she knew was at school. She thought about this for a moment – double French with Ms Patterson – and blinked away the tears, she hadn't thought going on holiday would make her feel so left out, and she'd definitely never thought she'd miss French. She dropped the phone on her bunk.

She emptied her pockets, found an old tissue, and sat on the bed, wiping away the sand from the pebbles she'd collected, smooth and pale and almost the colour of amber, arranging them carefully on top of the pine trunk.

She wasn't sure what to do next.

There were books, of course, the ones she'd brought from home, and the ones she'd found in the living room; it was a family joke, the rate she went through them. The book she had found about the street was interesting, the one with the old photos, but what she really wanted was to find out more about the house. Maybe she'd go back down in a bit and see what else she could find. Or she could draw instead.

Maude was the best at drawing in her year – probably in the school – and she had packed a pad and some pencils, mostly at her dad's insistence. He thought she was going to be an artist, like him, and Nell, but Maude wasn't sure. The more he pushed, the more she felt herself pushing back. Art wasn't even her favourite subject; just because you were good at something, it didn't mean you had to like it. But she'd got into the habit of treating drawing like a diary, and there was something about the patterns on the beam, something special, satisfying.

She picked up her sketch pad and took it to the bed; she looked up at the marks, at the circles and the petals they enclosed, staring at them for the longest time, and then after a while, she opened a music file on her phone, found something she liked, and began to draw.

5

Nell made some tea and she and Chris took it into the living room. She found her book and settled herself in one of the chairs by the window. The light was dull, and the room felt a little chilly; she wondered if they shouldn't think of lighting the log burner that evening.

Chris took the sofa and opened the laptop. 'I'm just going to look at some emails,' he said, 'unless you want this?'

'No. I'm fine, thanks.' She'd check her phone again later.

Nell had finished her drink and been reading for a while before she realised that Chris was still sitting there, hunched over the laptop.

'Chris?'

'Yeah?'

'Are you OK? Only . . .' She gestured towards the computer.

'Right.' He looked down at the screen. 'It's fine. I'm just – Sam sent a few bits and pieces over.'

'Really?' They had agreed that Sam was more than capable of running the gallery while they were away.

'It won't take long.'

'Then it can't be that important.'

'Do you need the laptop?'

'No.' That wasn't the point.

'Do we have plans? Something else I should be doing?'

49

'Well. No . . .' You're not here, though, she wanted to say, you're off somewhere on your own, again.

'Then I'll get on.'

'Chris—'

'I'm sorry, am I disturbing you?' His tone was sharp and she wished she hadn't said anything. He stood, picking up the laptop. 'I'll take this out of the way, then.' And it seemed to her that as he left he made a point of closing the door a little too firmly behind him.

She wasn't going to follow him, she thought, trying to get back into her book, not when he was being so unreasonable, not when the whole trip had been his idea anyway, a way to make up for – for everything. Tears began to prick at her eyes.

This wasn't like her – she wasn't usually so easily upset. They didn't quarrel, she and Chris, they didn't snipe at each other. The day had started so well. She tried to focus on the printed page in front of her. It was fine, she told herself. They'd had a long trip, and they were still tired and it wasn't unreasonable for him to keep in touch with Sam and the gallery, and the way she felt – well, maybe it was her hormones or something. Maybe.

The words on the page dipped and swam in front of her. She put the paperback to one side and stood, inspecting the books on offer on the shelves underneath the window, before picking out an old hardback with a familiar title, *The Lore and Legends of the North Riding*. There was a series of thuds upstairs as Maude walked along the landing, then another one, more distant, in the attic perhaps, as Nell took the book back to her seat and finally the house settled into an uncomfortable silence.

*

Maude was always surprised how quickly the time passed when she was drawing. When she stopped she'd filled a dozen pages, faithfully copying the design on the rafter at first, simple circles overlapping, elegant and precise, but then allowing herself to play, creating ever more complex and elaborate variations on a theme. At some point her music had finished, and she hadn't bothered to find a new album. She'd written a few things too, bits of sentences, half-formed thoughts, scraps of things she wished she could say out loud. She put her pencil down and yawned; she was tired, hungry too. She closed the pad. She'd look at it later, decide whether or not to show the marks on the beam to her dad.

Downstairs, Nell was in the living room, staring out of the window, a book in her lap. Maude hesitated by the door, not sure if she wanted to speak to her or not. They used to get on all right – but ever since the new baby, Leo, had arrived, Nell had been all moody. Maude didn't want to think about why that might be. Her mum and Callum were quite happy without her now, they were a new family – new and improved – and she didn't want them giving her dad and Nell any ideas.

She went into the kitchen and her dad was working at the dining table, just like he always did at home. She leant up against his chair and wrapped her arms around his shoulders. 'I'm hungry,' she said.

'Good grief, Maggot. Where are you putting it?' He tapped the mouse and the gallery home page appeared onscreen: *Clarke Galilee: Fine Art & Jewellery.*

'Can I check my messages?'

'Maybe later.'

Which meant no. Suppressing a sigh, Maude took herself off to investigate the kitchen, but there wasn't much left of the welcome pack, and she'd finished the last of the Kit-Kats that morning. 'We need to go shopping,' she said.

'OK. Maybe you and Nell could go, then?' her father said absently. 'I just need to do a bit more here.'

'Do I have to?'

'Come on, Maude. Play the game.'

Maude gave her father a long stare, before sighing theatrically. 'Fine,' she said, 'I'll go and tell her.'

When Nell was a child there had been a butcher's, a grocer's, several fishmongers', a post office, and a small supermarket on the east side of town, but they had all long gone. If they wanted to eat, they'd have to do their shopping over the bridge, just like everyone else, at the supermarket built on the old dock. Trying to stifle her irritation with Chris, who could at least have offered to help, Nell led the way down the steps and out onto the street. The mist clung to them, dulling the light, blunting the edges of the buildings.

'Is it far?'

'No, not far.'

'It's cold. It's supposed to be the summer.'

'It's the fog. It'll clear soon.'

'It's creepy,' said Maude.

'Atmospheric,' said Nell, and Maude snorted softly.

If anyone had asked a year ago how well she got on with her stepdaughter, Nell wouldn't have hesitated. *Fine*, she'd have said, *she's terrific*. They'd always had a solid relationship, or so she'd thought.

But a year was a long time, and now Maude was trying to cope with a new step-father and a new half-brother, and there were times when Nell suspected that neither she nor Chris was up to the job of parenting any more, days when no matter how she tried, she simply couldn't say or do the right thing.

There were a few people about as they walked towards the bridge. Maude was right, it was cold for late May, the fog muting the town and all its inhabitants. They crossed the river in silence.

The supermarket was quieter than Nell had expected – the schools hadn't broken up yet, but she'd have thought the weekend would be busier than this – and the two of them took their time filling their trolley. Nell found she was looking more carefully than usual at the other customers, wondering when she might notice a familiar face, if anyone would recognise her.

They strolled slowly down the aisle, past the household section, towards toiletries and personal hygiene, and suddenly, not knowing for sure felt like the worst thing in the world. She stopped and forced a smile. 'Shall we get some more biscuits, or some chocolate?' she asked.

'Well, yeah,' said Maude as if the answer were obvious.

'Do you want to go and grab some, then? Only don't go mad, OK?'

'Yeah, sure, whatever.' Maude didn't look back. As soon as she was out of sight, Nell headed over to the shelves, scanning them for a testing kit. She didn't have long, and there were far too many to choose from. Her hand hovered over the one she'd used last time, when she'd been so certain, so very sure. Only that felt like tempting fate, as if she'd get the same result all over again, the same sense of crushing failure, of shame. A single vertical line. Not pregnant.

Maude would be back any second.

The writing on the cellophane wrapped packets began to waver.

'I got some cake as well.' Maude dropped her haul into the trolley, chocolate, biscuits, a lemon drizzle loaf.

'Do you think you got enough?' It was quite an effort to move away, to feign idle interest in the shelves.

'You've got to hit all the food groups, Nell.'

The girl on the till asked if they wanted the shopping delivered.

'Yes, please,' said Maude.

'We'll be fine,' Nell said, picking up her share of the carrier bags. It wasn't rational, this sudden urge to know, but she couldn't help herself. 'Will you do me a favour?' she asked Maude as they walked towards the exit.

'Depends.'

'Just hang on here, with our stuff, will you? I forgot— I'll be back in a minute.'

'Really?' Maude rolled her eyes.

'Really. I won't be long.' Nell ducked back into the shop.

She was fairly sure Maude couldn't see which section she was in, not from her place by the door, and before she could think too much about it she grabbed a testing kit, one she could use early; it was generic, cheap, but it would do, and as an afterthought, she picked up a packet of tampons.

'Sorry,' she said, making a show of putting her tampons in her bag as she walked swiftly back towards Maude.

Maude didn't bother to answer.

It was almost high water, Nell realised as the bell rang and the long gate was fixed into place, blocking the road and bringing all traffic on both sides of the bridge to a halt. A man, tall, balding and wearing a blue boiler suit, walked to the centre of the bridge to operate the opening mechanism. They were going to have to wait. Maude sighed and dumped her shopping bags at Nell's feet.

'It must be cantilevered. If we wait and watch you'll see it lift to let the boats through.' The woman behind them was explaining to her friend, and Nell moved away, ignoring the temptation to correct her.

The bridge opened using a swing mechanism which moved the two sections horizontally, and today only one half swung open to allow a handful of yachts – blurred silhouettes in the mist – to sail up the harbour to their moorings. It didn't take too long, just long enough.

'Hello?' The voice was tentative, but not so uncertain that Nell could get away with ignoring it. She turned around. It was the blonde woman from yesterday.

'Yes?'

'Hi. I think I saw you arriving at Elder House?' She was Nell's age, more or less, but her manner was younger, the way she inflected her statement to make it into a question, the tilt of her head. 'In Bishops Yard? I think I spoke to your husband?'

'Yes.'

'Oh good. I thought it was you. I saw you in the supermarket, lurking by the shampoos.' She was carrying a basket, loaded with shopping, which she shifted from one arm to the other before sticking out her hand. 'Carolyn,' she said, 'Carolyn Wilson?'

'Hello.' Nell took the hand. Surely there was nothing more for the woman to complain about?

'I don't normally thrust myself on visitors when they arrive but . . . Sorry, I'm really not being clear. I thought I recognised you, and please forgive me if I got this wrong . . . but it is you, isn't it? Nell. Nell Galilee. We were at school together.'

The bridge swung back into place with a soft thud, and after a moment or two the gates were opened and the small crowd that had gathered began to swarm past.

'I – yes.'

'I thought so. I used to see you around, now and then – but never to stop and chat. And then of course your dad passed away. Two or three years ago.'

'Five now.'

'Goodness. Has it been so long? Are you back for David's party?'

The same question. It was inevitable, of course. 'Yes, that's right.' Nell couldn't place the woman. There was nothing familiar about her. If she hadn't called her by her name, Nell might have told her she was mistaken, that they had never met at all.

'And this is your daughter?' The woman turned her smile onto Maude who was edging closer, all ears.

'My stepdaughter; Maude.'

'Hello.'

'Hi,' said Maude.

'Do you need a hand?' asked Carolyn. 'With your shopping?'

'No. No, we're fine.' Nell picked up her share of the carrier bags, which were slick and beaded with moisture. 'We'd better get on though.'

'Well, we'll go along together, shall we?'

Carolyn insisted they join her for coffee, and Nell couldn't quite make her initial refusal stick. 'We should get on,' she'd said, 'finish unpacking.' She'd looked to Maude as if she might back her up at this point, but Maude had avoided her eye, smiling politely at Carolyn instead.

'Oh, that can wait, surely.' Carolyn led the way up the steps and into Spinnaker Cottage. 'You're on holiday, after all.'

The front door opened straight into a long low kitchen, dominated by a battered pine table heaped with magazines and piles of clothes, some ironed, some still waiting to be dealt with.

'Sorry about the mess,' said Carolyn, dropping her bags in front of the fridge. She switched the kettle on and began to open cupboards, picking out mugs and a cafetière. 'Now, Maude, what would you like? We have milk, or would you prefer some apple juice?'

'Juice, please,' said Maude.

The door opened. 'Ah, there you are,' said Carolyn. A teenage girl, maybe sixteen or seventeen, with long fair hair stood in the doorway. It was, Nell realised after a moment, the girl from the beach. 'What have you been up to?'

'Revision, at the library.'

'I see. Evie, this is Nell, we were at school together, back in the dark ages. And this is Maude.'

'Oh right, hi.' A polite smile. 'We met this morning, didn't we? I'm sorry about Flossie, she gets a bit over-excited sometimes.'

'She wasn't bothering you, was she?' Carolyn looked pained.

'No,' said Nell, 'not really. It's just that Maude's a little uncertain around dogs. I might have been – overprotective.'

As if on cue, Flossie appeared, her claws skittering over the tiled floor; she shook herself vigorously, yawned, then seemed to notice the visitors in the house for the first time. As she advanced, Maude drew back.

'Oh, she won't bother you, will you?' Carolyn, bent down to stroke Flossie's head. 'She's the most dreadful pushover really.'

'I can put her in the other room if you like.' Evie said.

Maude shook her head. 'That's OK.'

'Evie, sweetheart, would you mind clearing a space on the table?'

'I really am sorry,' Nell said, again, 'I think I might have been a bit – forceful earlier.'

'Please don't worry about it. She was pushing her luck, she

57

thinks everyone on the beach is fair game.' Evie picked up a Moses basket and put it on the table, gathering up the piles of ironed clothes and dropping them inside. She smiled at Maude who was still keeping a careful eye on Flossie and lowered her voice conspiratorially, 'Mum's right, though, she's a soppy old thing really, she won't bother you.'

'Goodness,' said Nell, more to fill the growing silence than anything else, running her fingers over the basket's woven wicker handle. 'I haven't seen one of those for years.'

'It used to be mine.' Evie flicked a glance at her mother, who was busy decanting milk into a china jug. 'Apparently.'

'And mine before that,' said Carolyn, setting the jug and cafetière on the table. 'It's for a baby,' she said to Maude, as they sat.

'Yes,' Maude said. 'I know.'

The conversation stuttered on. Carolyn had clearly kept in touch with more school friends than Nell had. Stories of marriages, divorces, births and – increasingly – health scares, left her feeling mildly bewildered. Some of the names mentioned were familiar, but many were not – and Nell began to doubt that she had ever exchanged more than a few words with Carolyn Wilson during their time at school.

'I don't know how you keep up,' she said.

'Facebook.'

'She has more friends than I do,' said Evie, reaching across the table and picking up a biscuit.

'You're not on there, are you?' Carolyn said to Nell, sliding the plate away from her daughter and towards Maude, smiling approvingly as the younger girl helped herself.

'God, no.'

'Not even as a business?'

'Well. Yes.' Nell shouldn't be surprised, she supposed, that Carolyn seemed to be aware of what she did for a living – given the way she had kept up with half the sixth form – but she felt a moment's discomfort. 'But I don't – there's nothing personal on there. Chris deals with all of that.'

'What business?' asked Evie.

'I make jewellery,' said Nell.

'Really?' said Evie, her face lighting up. 'What—' But her mother spoke over her.

'It's a bit more than that,' said Carolyn.

'It really isn't.'

'Nell is Clarke Galilee, well, half of it.'

'Right. I don't . . .' Evie hesitated, puzzled.

'She's famous.'

'Hardly.'

'Successful, then.'

'I suppose so.' Nell said. 'We've been very lucky, that's all it boils down to.'

'It's nice of you to come back for David and Jenny's party, it's such a long way,' said Carolyn.

'We're on holiday,' said Maude. 'We're staying for ages.'

'We have a good team at the shop,' said Nell. 'And I'm not working on any commissions at the moment, so we thought we'd – spend some time here.'

'It's not a shop, it's a gallery,' said Maude. 'Dad doesn't like it when she calls it a shop.'

'We sell things, don't we?' said Nell.

'We're building a bigger gallery,' said Maude, 'in a barn. It's going to be epic.'

Nell couldn't tell if she was serious. 'Yes, Maude. Thank you,' she said.

'Business must be going well,' said Carolyn.

'Yes, I suppose it is.'

There was a brief silence.

'I have a magazine,' said Carolyn, 'they did a feature on you, the Style section of – the *Sunday Times*, was it?'

'That was ages ago.'

Months. Probably close to a year.

They fell silent again. Flossie sniffled, circling herself before settling down in front of the oven. Maude shifted in her seat, sipping at her apple juice.

'You have a lovely house,' said Nell, eventually, hoping they wouldn't be offered a tour. 'Have you been here long?'

'Thank you, yes. We've been here – what – two years now?'

'Three,' said Evie.

'I suppose so. Gosh, the years just start to blur after a while, don't they?'

'Is it very old?' asked Maude.

'Eighteen hundred or thereabouts. We have the deeds upstairs, well several deeds, actually. It's absolutely fascinating. The first owner was a sea captain,' said Carolyn, 'a master mariner. And it was quite the little community here once upon a time. There was a haberdashers', an inn, an apothecary – people don't realise these yards were so busy, so full of life. And now, of course, all the other houses have gone for holiday lets.'

'Isn't it odd? Being the only permanent family in the yard?' asked Nell.

'A little, but we're used to it, I suppose.'

'And there's Gina Verrill,' said Evie, 'she's been here a lot longer than we have.'

'Oh yes,' said Carolyn, 'Gina. Have you met her yet?'

'Only in passing.'

'She and Mum don't get on,' Evie said to Maude, reaching for another biscuit.

60

'That's enough for now, don't you think?' Carolyn said softly, and Evie sat back, letting her hand fall into her lap.

'Really? She didn't strike me as being – difficult.' Nell didn't really want to know, but she couldn't see any way out of the conversation.

'The trouble is,' said Carolyn, 'that she's been here for so long, she thinks it gives her some sort of – authority, over the yard, over us.'

'Mum.'

'Well, she does, sweetheart. She has quite an attitude problem, to be honest. The whole business over the gate, for one thing.'

'The gate?' Maude flicked a quick glance at Nell. 'Did you do that?'

'Eventually, yes,' Carolyn said. 'Once we'd overcome all of Gina's ridiculous objections. You'd think she *wanted* visitors to use the yard as a toilet on their way home from the pub.'

'Ew.' Maude wrinkled her nose.

'Exactly. She claimed it was out of character for the street.'

'Isn't it?' Nell asked, not catching Maude's eye.

'Goodness, no, lots of the yards used to have gates, including this one.'

'Why?' asked Maude.

'To keep visitors out,' said Carolyn.

'Or to keep locals in,' said Evie, and Maude smiled.

'Then there's the drying ground.' Carolyn turned to face Nell. 'It's next to Elder House, well, behind it, really. It's just a little patch of land.'

'Yes.'

'Gina says it's private,' said Carolyn, 'which is absolutely not the case, I mean, you'll know that. Historically speaking, drying grounds were always communal areas.'

61

The idea sounded plausible, Nell had a vague memory of looking at some old photographs with her gran, patches of laundry hanging lopsided, like flags, between the crowded galleries of houses. But even so, she found it hard to imagine that any piece of land available in a yard might go unclaimed by one household or another. 'Well, I suppose since no one needs one now—' she began.

'That's hardly the point,' said Carolyn.

'Mum,' Evie shook her head.

Nell finally gave in to the temptation to look at her watch. 'Well, I suppose we should go,' she said, standing. 'But thanks for the coffee.'

'You should come over for dinner sometime,' said Carolyn, and 'meet Ollie.'

'Oh. That's very—'

'We'll fix something up for later on in the week, shall we? Or' – Carolyn saw them to the door, blocking it for a moment – 'we could walk to the party together.'

'Oh, I'm not sure—'

'Well. If you feel like it.' She stood back, out of the way, and Nell stepped outside, avoiding any kind of direct reply. Maude followed suit, keeping her distance from the dog.

Evie caught Flossie by her collar as she made a bid for freedom. 'Bye,' she said.

'Well,' said Nell, as she unlocked the door, 'that was all very – full on.'

'She was all right,' said Maude.

'Really?'

'Yeah.'

Not like Nell at all, although they had the same sort of accent; educated, but with the soft flattening of the vowels.

And the biscuits – homemade – had been very nice. 'Evie seemed all right too, not, you know, snobby.' Maude glanced back at the cottage; a proper house, she thought, with a proper mum.

They took the shopping into the kitchen and Maude watched as Nell began to unpack it. She was looking tired, and a bit pale. Once upon a time Maude might have felt sorry for her, but now – not so much. She watched her put a bottle of Diet Coke in the fridge, then made a point of getting it out again and opening it.

'Glass,' said Nell as Maude raised the bottle to her lips. She thought about ignoring her, but settled for a barely audible sigh as she did as she was told.

'What's for dinner?' she asked.

'Can't you wait? You must be full of biscuits.'

'It's all the sea air.' She opened a cupboard, pulling out a box of crackers. She bit into one, scattering crumbs all over the flagstones. 'Were you really at school with Carolyn?' Maude asked, because Nell hadn't seemed pleased to see her at all.

'I don't know,' Nell said slowly. 'Probably, yes. But I don't remember her.' She looked embarrassed, and a little anxious. 'It's a bit – awkward, really.'

'Well,' Maude said, 'it was a very long time ago.' She looked out of the kitchen window and up at the bankside beyond. 'Can we eat out there tonight?'

'It might be uncomfortable, don't you think?' said Nell. 'There's no table, we'd have to eat off our knees.'

'We could have a picnic.'

'We could. Tomorrow, perhaps, if we plan what we want to eat.'

'Did there used to be houses there?'

'Where?'

63

Maude gestured towards the drying ground and Nell drew close to the window, pushing it open a little further. 'I don't think so,' she said. 'There might have been something, but it would have been terribly cramped.'

'I can see a wall.'

'There's a fence.'

'Inside that.'

'Can you?'

'I think so.' She frowned. 'There's something there, anyway.' She slid past Nell and opened the kitchen door.

'Maude. Maudie, what are you up to?'

'What does it look like?' Maude scrambled up the bank as quickly as she could before Nell could catch her.

'Don't,' Nell said, 'It's too steep.'

Maude snorted as she opened the little gate, then stepped into the drying ground. But Nell was right – it was steeper than she expected and the ground shifted beneath her feet; she lost her balance for a moment, wheeling her arms out before steadying and edging carefully down the incline.

Nell had come out as far as the fence; she looked pale and cross.

Maude stopped, squatted and plunged her hands into the long grass. 'Bricks,' she said, 'with a sort of a gap in them.' A hole for a post.

'Maude. I mean it.'

Maude looked at her, considering her next move. It was all very ordinary, the little patch of land, but then, somehow – not. Too high, too lonely, too cold; she felt trapped. Elder House, the whole yard, seemed very far away.

'Please, Maudie.'

She stood up slowly, and wiped the soil off her hands; she was shivering and her heart thudded uncomfortably. But she wasn't about to let Nell see there was anything wrong. 'OK,' she said, 'I'm coming.'

Nell watched as Maude closed the little wooden gate behind her and made her way carefully down the bankside. She had a vague memory of once seeing photos of laundry being dried on the beach, so a drying ground in the yard, she supposed, must have been highly prized.

It didn't feel like a communal space, though. It felt – private, isolated.

Elder House seemed to muffle any noise in the yard and the street beyond – and it was the sort of quiet that seemed to press in on you, once you noticed it. For a moment there it was again, that odd smell, damp and stale. She couldn't tell if it was outside the house or in; maybe it was on her clothes, her skin. Maybe it was in the stones.

'Are you OK?'

Maude was breathless, her cheeks were flushed. 'I'm fine. Can I go up to my room now?'

Nell was struck once more by how far apart they had drifted; she couldn't remember the last time Maude had offered to spend time alone with her, just the two of them, hanging out.

'Sure,' she said.

6

Evie worked through the rest of the afternoon and early evening until she could no longer ignore the hunger pangs. She closed her laptop and wandered out onto the landing. As she passed by her parents' room, she glanced inside.

Carolyn was sitting on the bed, her jewellery box in her lap. She was lost in thought, the top section with its neat little velvet compartments was on the duvet next to her and she was idly stirring through the contents of the base.

'Mum?'

'Hello, darling.'

'What are you doing?'

'I can't find the match to this, see?' Carolyn tilted her head, the better to show off an earring, silver and studded with turquoise stones, which Evie recognised as one of mum's good pieces, something expensive.

She sat on the bed beside her and picked up the discarded tray. 'Are you going out?' she asked, wondering if she might be allowed a takeaway if this was the case; a curry, curry and rice and naan bread. Just the thought of it made her stomach rumble.

'No. I just – I haven't worn them for a while, that's all.'

Evie tipped the contents of the tray out onto the duvet and set about refilling it, picking out all the bracelets first, concentrating on untangling the slender gold and silver chains, picking gently at the knots and shaking them free. 'What's the occasion?'

she asked. The earrings were an anniversary present, she knew, but her parents' anniversary was in February.

'Oh, there's no occasion,' said Carolyn. 'I'd almost forgotten I had them, but they're hers, you see.'

'Sorry?'

'Nell Galilee's. She designed them.'

'Oh.' Evie digested this new information. 'Right, so you want to wear them now?'

'Well, I'd like to find the second one, if I can. Then I'll worry about finding an occasion to wear them.'

Evie moved on to the earrings, a jumble of silver wire, beads, pearls and sparkles, pairing them up carefully, putting them in place, in their plush blue nests. So many birthdays and Christmases and anniversaries, so many surprises.

'Is she famous, then? She didn't seem to like the idea much.'

Her mum smiled. 'No, maybe not famous, not in the way you think. But she's certainly done better for herself than most of the girls I was at school with. She made the jewellery that was used in that TV show you liked, the one with the actress.'

'I think you're going to need to be a bit more specific.'

'Anyway, because of that, there was quite a bit of attention.'

'The *Sunday Times*?' Evie might have read the article, she followed stuff like that, fashion, design, although she didn't remember it, or recognise Nell.

'Right.'

It was quite restful, sorting everything, picking up the odd broken bits and pieces. Maybe, if she was lucky, her mum might pass on something she'd got bored with, something she no longer cared for. If she managed to find the missing earring, then that would certainly earn a couple of brownie points and these things were important.

'Could you tell?' Evie asked. 'When you were at school, could you tell she was going to be successful?'

'Ha.' Carolyn darted forward, then held up the second earring, smiling. 'Got it.' She slid it through the hole in her ear. 'What do you think?'

'Nice,' Evie said, automatically, but the earrings were more than nice; they were – stylish. There was nothing difficult or complicated about them, they were simple lengths of polished silver, with turquoise beads clustering at each end. But there was something about them, something elegant and considered, something about the way her mother, who was inspecting her reflection in the mirror, turning her head this way and that, seemed to light up because of them that made Evie want to try the earrings for herself. 'They're lovely,' she said.

'Hmm.' Carolyn was barely listening now.

Evie went back to her task, unpicking the mess of her mother's discarded finery. 'Was she, like, arty, then?'

'Helen. The teachers always called her Helen, but she preferred Nell. Does that make her arty?'

Evie picked up a knotted length of silver chain. 'I don't know. Maybe. Not if she was obnoxious about it.'

'I don't suppose she was, not really,' said her mother, 'no more obnoxious than the rest of us, anyway.'

Evie concentrated on untangling the chain, which proved to be the remains of a silver bracelet that had once held a collection of charms. She remembered it from when she was a kid; there was the bell, and a flower, an anchor, a tiny ship, and a shoe – a ballet slipper. She had the idea that the shoe represented her, although what the other objects signified, she couldn't say. She shook the chain out; there were gaps where other charms had long since been lost and the catch was missing from one end. 'This is pretty,' she said, holding it up, and the bell tinkled gently.

'That old thing,' said her mother.

Evie's dad was home later than usual, but he'd at least texted Mum, and the lasagne wasn't completely ruined by the time they all sat down together. He was an architect and had recently taken on the renovation of some flats in an old building on the West Cliff. It was his first big commission in a few months, this and the prospect of more work to follow, seemed to be worth the price of the long hours and his increasing absences from home.

'Revision going well?' he asked Evie.

'Fine. You know – fine, thanks.'

'You know you're going to ace it, don't you?'

'*If* she puts the work in,' said Carolyn.

Evie wished they could find something else to talk about.

'Well, she knows that, don't you, sweetheart? And you?' He leant across the table, topping up Carolyn's wine. 'Good day?'

'Oh, the same old same old, really.' Carolyn was wearing a pair of silver earrings that Evie hadn't seen for a while, not the Clarke Galilee ones, these were heavy silver hoops; nice enough, in Evie's opinion, but a bit too young for her mother, a bit too ostentatiously cool. 'We met the new holiday-cottage people.'

'Which ones?'

'Elder House, of course.'

'Ah. Right.'

'And it turns out that I know them,' said Carolyn. 'Well, her. She's Nell Galilee.'

'Sorry?'

'She's a jewellery designer,' said Evie, who'd spent the time waiting for her father googling her new neighbour. Her work was lovely, most of it in the style of her mum's earrings, spare

70

and simple; lots of semi-precious stones and sea glass set in silver, exactly the kind of thing that appealed to Evie, the kind of thing she might like to do herself one day, if only she could talk her mum around. It was expensive too, she'd marvelled at the prices people were willing to pay; wishing she could afford some of it.

'She's an old school friend,' said her mother.

'Really?' Oliver didn't look convinced. He had opinions about her mother's old school, Evie knew, opinions that were strong enough to have Evie sent to a private school just outside of town. Until last September, anyway.

'Really. She grew up just down the road, in one of the council houses by the harbour.'

'And had the good sense to get out?'

'Well, she's not got any family here, not anymore.' Carolyn said. 'Cousins, obviously, David Galilee; they're here for the anniversary party.'

'Just the two of them, is it, in a house that size?' Oliver asked.

'There's a daughter.'

'Stepdaughter,' said Evie.

'Right. Well, the jewellery business must be booming, that's all I can say. If they can afford to take that on for the week.'

'Longer, I think,' said Carolyn.

'If they stay,' said Evie.

'Well, why wouldn't they?'

'I don't know. The house is a bit – creepy, isn't it?'

'Some people like that sort of thing,' said her father. 'Ghosties and ghoulies and things that go bump in the night. What about whatshisname, that guy who wanted to bring his ghost walk up the yard?'

Carolyn shook her head. 'Complete and utter nonsense.' She frowned at Evie. 'I can't imagine what's brought this on.'

71

'Some people can't get enough of it,' said Oliver.

'Not Nell Galilee,' said Carolyn. 'Ghost stories are for tourists and incomers.'

There was a pause.

'Mum has some of her earrings,' said Evie. 'You bought them for her.'

'Did I?'

'Yes.' Her mother began to clear the table. 'You did.'

It was odd, Evie thought as she stood to help her mother, glancing through the kitchen window, the way Elder House seemed closer now it was occupied; when it was empty, it had been easier to ignore.

After dinner, Nell tidied the kitchen. Then, leaving Chris and Maude to entertain themselves in the living room, and thinking she might check her messages, she went upstairs in search of her phone. The charger snaked across the duvet, but the phone itself – and she was certain she'd left it on the bed – had vanished. She checked underneath, then made a detour to the bathroom. Maybe she'd left it in there.

The bathroom was surprisingly small, given the size of the house, and in the short time they'd been in residence she, Chris and Maude had managed to clutter every available surface with an astonishing array of toiletries. Discarded towels were slung over the bath, and a pair of Chris's trainers had been kicked under the sink.

There was no sign of her phone.

She tried to retrace her steps. She was sure she'd left it on the bed. The door had been open and the phone in plain sight.

Maude.

Once the solution, uncharitable as it was, presented itself, it was hard to ignore. Maude, currently banned from all unsupervised

72

internet use and from all her accounts. Chris had logged her out, deleted all the apps himself.

It's for your own good, Maudie.

Nell's phone was logged into the house's Wi-Fi, and the temptation must have been too much. She stood on the landing, looking at the little ladder that led to the attic. It couldn't hurt, she decided, to take a look, maybe even retrieve the phone quietly and have a private word with Maude afterwards.

It wasn't there. Not as far as she could see, anyway. Not on or under the bed, not in Maude's empty suitcase or rucksack. She had looked inside the chest of drawers too, but once she'd found herself concentrating on how best to search without disturbing its contents, she'd stopped.

Maybe she'd got it wrong. Maude would be furious if she found Nell searching her room, and she would have every right to be. Nell looked around the attic one last time. It was stuffy up here, she could at least open the windows, air the place out a bit.

She was just fixing the latch in place when she noticed the book, Maude's notebook, lying open on one of the bunks, half a dozen coloured pencils scattered over it, and an uncapped pen leaking ink onto the clean duvet cover. She bent down and began to tidy everything up, then it happened. Somewhere behind her in the attic, a shuffling, footsteps; the near imperceptible shift in the air that meant . . .

Maude clambered up the ladder. 'What do you want? What are you doing up here?'

'Nothing. I – opened the windows. It was – stifling.' Nell was still holding the notebook.

'What are you doing? That's mine. That's private.'

'I'm not doing anything. I was tidying up.'

Maude crossed the room in a few paces and snatched her sketchbook. 'I can do that myself if I want to, I'm not stupid.'

'I was looking for my phone—'

'Well I haven't got it.' Maude's response was near instantaneous.

'If you borrowed it, it's OK—'

'I haven't borrowed it. I haven't taken your stupid bloody phone.'

'Hey,' Nell said, 'watch it – that's not how you speak to me.'

'Really? And what are you going to do about it?' Maude clutched her book to her chest. 'Are you going to tell on me? This is my room and you can't just come up here and mess with my things.'

'I'm just—'

'What's this?' Neither of them had heard Chris approach, and as he stepped off the ladder, Nell felt the childish urge to do exactly what Maude had accused her of, to tell on her, to get her into trouble.

'She,' said Maude, 'is going through my stuff.'

'I'm sure she's not,' said Chris.

'She bloody is! She thinks I've nicked her stupid bloody phone.'

'Hey.'

'What?' Maude turned on him. 'What have I done now? She was going through my private things, she was searching my room—'

'I thought Maude might have borrowed my phone – you know . . . I just came up to check and I wasn't' – she turned to Maude – 'I wasn't going through your stuff.'

'You could have asked me.' Maude's tone was anguished, she was, Nell realised, close to tears. 'You didn't have to be such a bloody bitch about it.'

74

There was a moment when Nell could have broken the silence, could have apologised, taken Maude in her arms and hugged her and told her, that whatever it was that had gone wrong they could surely put it right, but she left it a fraction too late, and it was Chris who spoke first.

'I think that's enough, don't you?'

'It's not—'

'I said that's enough, Maude. Now, do you have Nell's phone?'

'No.'

'Because we are going to look for it.'

'Fine.' Maude sat on her bed, drawing her legs up, wrapping her arms around her knees. 'Go for it.' She sat there in silence, simmering with rage as Chris and Nell quickly went through her belongings, opening and closing drawers, emptying her bag, bending down and checking underneath the beds. Nell losing all interest in actually retrieving the phone as she went.

It wasn't there.

'Right.' Chris stood in the centre of the room, he looked very tall, very severe, and Maude on her bunk, much younger, sadder. 'I think an apology is in order.'

Maude looked up at him. 'What?'

'You don't speak to Nell like that, and you don't use language like that.'

'And what about me, where's my apology?'

'Chris . . .' Nell started, but he ignored her, as he usually did at this point – Maude was, after all, his daughter, not hers. Nell wondered again how they'd got here, Chris as the voice of authority, and she little more than a spectator.

He waited for a moment or two, then shrugged, and walked towards the ladder. 'Suit yourself,' he said, 'but until Nell gets an apology, you're grounded.'

'Grounded how?' said Maude. 'Early bed and no supper? Big

deal.' But her bravado was wavering, surely her father could see that.

'You won't go to the party,' said Chris, not missing a beat. 'Not unless you say you're sorry.'

'Fine,' Maude slumped back onto the bed. 'I didn't want to go anyway.'

Nell didn't want to leave, Maude was clearly upset, and the last thing they all needed was for a stupid error of judgement on her part to continue escalating. But Chris had his don't-mess-with-me face on, and a united front, that was the rule when dealing with Maude.

She followed her husband down the ladder; she could barely look the poor kid in the eye.

Chris led the way back into the living room, the TV still paused on the film he and Maude had been watching. He sank into the sofa wearily. 'Shit,' he said, then he looked up at Nell, 'you could have asked her first,' he said. 'You could have been a bit more subtle.'

'I just meant to take a quick look. I didn't think it would be – such a big deal,' said Nell.

'You know what she's like. Any excuse to kick off these days.'

'Yes, well. It's done now.' She looked around the room, it was gloomy, even with the TV on; chilly too now the sun had gone down. They should definitely light the log burner, try to make the place a little more inviting. 'You don't think,' she said, 'we were a bit over the top with the whole grounding thing?'

'We? Me, you mean?'

'She was angry. She didn't mean it.'

'That's no excuse.'

If she'd lit the fire earlier, then they'd be settled in front of it now, cosy, a family watching the stupid film together, laughing at it.

'She can't be allowed to speak to you like that, no matter how angry she is,' said Chris.

'I suppose so.'

He looked weary, disappointed. 'But, to be honest, if you'd just thought a bit about how to handle her, then . . .' He let his voice trail away.

'So it's my fault, then?' Nell said, flatly.

Chris picked up the TV remote. 'I'm just saying if you could be a bit more careful around her, then that might help.' The film leapt back into life and Nell was left with the sensation that out of the three of them, she was most at fault, lacking some vital sort of instinct.

Not a real mum, at all.

Maude cried for a bit. Hot angry tears. It was so unfair, all of it, but especially the way her dad always took Nell's side. She curled up on her bunk and cried until her nose ran and her head ached. It wasn't as if she'd even touched Nell's bloody phone. She wished she had.

She rolled onto her back and looked up at the ceiling, at the beams and the marks there. She couldn't see them properly, because it was getting dark, but that didn't matter, she'd looked at them enough to know them by heart. She'd been planning to tell her dad and Nell about them; at least, she'd been thinking about it. It was the sort of thing her dad would get all interested in for a bit, and that might have been nice, to have something they could share. But then Nell had come up and searched her room, *searched* it – the sobs threatened to break through again – and they'd ganged up on her.

She wiped her face, it was gross, all snotty and wet. She sat up gingerly; she needed to blow her nose. She went to the ladder and listened carefully before making her way down to the bathroom.

She made sure to bolt the door before she cleaned herself up, scowling at her reflection in the mirror; she looked all red and blotchy.

Grounded, she thought. Big bloody deal.

Back on the landing all was silent. It was a funny house, a bit too big for them, a bit too cold, even though it was supposed to be the summer; a bit too quiet. The door to the big bedroom was ajar, and Maude thought she could hear someone moving around in there – her dad, maybe. If he saw her, if he saw she'd been crying, then maybe he'd give her a hug. The thought was almost enough to make her tearful again.

She pushed the door open, but the room was empty. She hesitated, then stepped quickly inside.

She didn't bother to switch on the light. It was tidy, like a hotel room. That would be Nell, not her dad – such a control freak. A floorboard underneath the carpet groaned softly as she crossed the room and looked out of the window, down the darkened yard, although some of the cottages had their lights on, casting a dull yellow glow across the cobblestones. She sat on the bed, trying to work up the nerve to open a drawer – she'd go through Nell's things, and see how she liked that. If she found the phone maybe she wouldn't give it back, maybe she'd keep it, use it.

She didn't think she could quite dare to do it though. It would be just her luck for Nell to walk in at the wrong moment. She strained her ears to try to work out what was going on downstairs. She couldn't hear voices, so they weren't arguing, but she could hear something – the TV. They had gone back to watching the film, as if everything was all right.

The beams in this room didn't have any marks, not as far as Maude could tell, but the wooden panels on the walls gave her the strange sensation of being trapped inside a box. She stretched out a hand, ran a finger down one of them, the brass bedstead groaning as she shifted her weight. The panels were original to the house her dad said, which meant they were old, very old.

Not as old as the drying ground, she thought. And it was like she was back there again, all alone in the cold, waiting. She didn't want to think about that.

She caught her breath as something tugged against the pad of her forefinger, catching the skin. There was a fine line running down the wood, parallel to where it had been slotted into its frame; a hairline crack. She leant closer, even if you knew it was there, it was hard to make out; she wondered if it too had been there since the house was built.

She raised her finger and inspected it, a fine sliver of wood had caught in the skin, *a spell*, Nell called them; she pulled it free and a bright droplet of blood bloomed in its place. She popped her finger in her mouth and sucked, all the while considering the panel and the crack that ran down it – how it fitted into place, and what might lie behind it. She leant forward again, digging her fingernails in, trying to pull the panel free, but it didn't move.

Downstairs, a door opened, then closed – someone had gone into the kitchen.

Maude stood and took one last look around the room, her finger stinging, then on impulse she knocked on the panel sharply, rapidly, three times.

Nell didn't really like the house that much, she could tell. Fine, then Maude would definitely like it; they could ground her all they wanted, she would make this house her own.

7

Nell woke up suddenly, as if someone was standing over her, calling her name, and for a few moments she wasn't sure where she was, until the unfamiliar shadows in the room gradually resolved, revealing a chest of drawers, windows, the door left slightly ajar, and Chris beside her, dead to the world. Pushing back the duvet, she got heavily to her feet and stumbled to the bathroom to use the loo. It was cold. The window was open. She closed it, resisting the temptation to look out at the drying ground below. When she was done, she switched off the bathroom light and, stepping onto the landing, she paused and listened. She had the oddest feeling that she wasn't alone, that quite apart from Chris and Maude there was someone, something else in the house, that the house was – waiting.

Chris stirred as she slipped back under the covers, reaching out for her, pulling her close.

She didn't wake again until morning. She rolled over in bed and looked at the window, the blue curtains wafted in the breeze. It was a bright day, as far as she could tell, no fog, at least.

She fell asleep again, briefly, deeply, but not for long, not long enough to dream. Distantly, she heard Chris's phone sound, its ringtone an old-fashioned bell, no one answered it, though.

Someone was knocking at the door.

She didn't move at first; if there was no answer, they would, she reasoned, give up and leave. Which struck her as a wonderful idea.

Only they didn't.

'Nell! Nell, are you up yet?' Chris's voice drifting up from the bottom of the stairs.

She opened her eyes; she'd overslept.

She threw back the duvet. 'Yes. Just a minute.' Grabbing yesterday's jeans and T-shirt, struggling to pull them on. She ran her fingers through her hair.

She could at least leave the room tidy, she thought, pulling the duvet roughly into place, and then she noticed it; a long scratch on the wall behind the bed. They must have knocked the bed post against it. The thought was followed by a flush of embarrassment, then guilt. How would they explain that to the woman in the letting office?

She bent over the bed and looked more closely. It wasn't a scratch, it was a crack, running vertically down one panel. She traced it with the tip of her finger, maybe they had overlooked it and it had been there all along; maybe the old house wasn't quite so picture perfect after all.

'Nell!'

'Yes! I'm here!'

She left the bedroom door open, and ran downstairs.

'We thought you'd like some brownies, well, blondies, really. I always make too many,' said Carolyn. 'Raspberry and white chocolate.'

'That's very kind of you.'

Nell tugged at her T-shirt, still trying to catch her breath. Her phone lay on the kitchen counter, and she couldn't help glancing at Maude who was hovering beside it, not bothering to disguise her interest in the foil-covered plate Carolyn was holding. Chris was filling the kettle at the sink, evidently Carolyn and Evie, who was standing silently by the open door looking mildly embarrassed, were staying. Nell took the proffered plate and unwrapped it. 'Would you like one of these?'

'Goodness, no,' Carolyn said. 'Those are for you and Chris, Maude too, if she likes them.'

'Yes, please,' said Maude, helping herself. Nell found herself looking at Chris for some sort of cue. She was fairly certain that people who were grounded didn't get to eat blondies for breakfast, but he made sure not to catch her eye.

She wondered where the phone had come from, who had replaced it. 'It's very kind of you,' she said.

'Well, I've got to be honest, I do have an ulterior motive. I just wanted to have a quick word with the both of you, if that's OK.'

'Mum,' said Evie softly, but Carolyn ignored her.

'I've been thinking about the drying ground, you know?' she went on. 'And the thing is she can be so unreasonable. Gina.'

'Can she?'

'Everyone knows they were communal. The way people just annex them these days, claiming they were gardens, digging them over, fencing them off.'

'So you're saying everyone should have access to it?' Nell said.

'Well. Not visitors. Obviously. But residents. Locals.'

'I'm sorry. I don't quite follow,' said Chris.

'I mentioned it, didn't I?' said Nell. 'About the drying ground.'

'Oh. Yes.' He looked vaguely out of the window. 'Maude said something.'

'If you were able to – well, if you wouldn't mind us using it?' Carolyn said. 'Not every day, of course . . .'

'I'm sorry, I don't quite understand,' Nell said. 'You need to be speaking to Gina, surely. If she says the land is hers—'

83

'Oh. Oh no.' Carolyn looked at Evie, smiling apologetically. 'No. The thing is, Gina says the drying ground belongs to Elder House.'

'Oh,' Chris said. 'So, it's ours? Part of our agreement?'

'Well, that's her opinion – but she's wrong, do you see?' Carolyn went on, 'Historically, they were always shared spaces.'

'Look. I'm sorry,' said Nell, 'but – I don't really see what you'd use it for. We're certainly not going to . . .' People didn't need to dry their washing outside anymore, did they? And the prospect of simply sitting out there, sunning yourself, struck her as slightly ridiculous, it was too dark, she thought, too cold. 'And it's not ours, we can't give you permission.'

Silence seeped into the room. Nell wondered if she'd caused offence. She looked at Carolyn, trying to temper her words with a smile. Surely she could see how absurd her request was, how inappropriate. Nell had the feeling there was something wrapped up in Carolyn's request that she was missing, something she – an outsider after all those years away – couldn't see. She had the sense she had wandered into a dispute she only half understood.

'No, I'm sorry,' Carolyn said finally, 'you are absolutely right. It's because you're local, you see – I sort of forgot that you're not staying. And of course you don't want us trooping up here every evening—'

'It's not that . . .' Although, of course, it was.

'Which we wouldn't. It's just – it's the principle of the thing.'

'I really don't think that it's something we can help you with.'

There was another silence, then Carolyn gave a sad, self-deprecating smile. 'Oh, good lord, you must think I'm dreadful. But you do understand – I wouldn't ask if we weren't old friends.'

'The thing is,' Nell said, her heart thudding, *just do it, say it, get it out in the open*, 'and I know this is going to sound a bit odd, but I've been thinking about – about school, about – us – and – I'm not that sure, really, that I actually remember . . .'

Carolyn didn't seem to be listening. 'Do you mind,' she asked, heading towards the hallway, 'if I just nip up and use your loo?'

The silence that followed was punctuated by the kettle whistling shrilly, then switching itself off. 'Sorry,' Evie said, 'I know she's a bit – determined.'

'That's OK,' Nell said, casting about for something that would spare Evie having to further excuse her mother. 'It's just – well, it's not up to us, is it? And the next set of people who rent this place might not want anyone . . .' Her voice trailed off.

'Picnicking behind the bins?'

'Well. Yes.'

'It's not that she wants to, not really. Dad thinks she's—' Evie came to a halt. 'He's not that bothered about it. She just gets – focused on things, you know? She's very hot on local history, and tradition, rights of way and all that.'

'It's fine,' said Nell, 'absolutely fine. Sit down, have a cake before Maude eats the lot.' She caught Chris's eye as they set about making some coffee, setting aside a mug of instant decaf for herself. The poor kid, having to apologise for her own mother.

Evie sat at the dining table and looked around the room. 'I've never been in here before,' she said, 'It's very – nice.'

'It's all right,' said Maude, helping herself to another blondie.

'It's the oldest house in the yard,' said Evie.

'How do you know?' Maude asked.

Evie smiled. 'Like I said, Mum's very into the whole local

history thing.' She fell silent and began to fiddle with the bracelet she wore, a tiny silver slipper suspended from a fine red ribbon.

'That's pretty,' said Maude, sounding uncharacteristically shy.

Evie extended her wrist, the charm was knotted in place and on either side of it there were two fragments of shell, pale pink, curving like little cups. 'I made it,' said Evie. 'It's just junk, really. The hardest bit was finding shells with natural holes, 'cause I don't have a proper drill, but then I worked out I could use bits of periwinkle. It still took me ages to find the right-sized pieces, though.'

Nell placed a mug of coffee on the table, it was nice of Evie to bother with Maude, she thought, to make an effort to be so kind. 'Maudie's right, that's very clever.'

'Thank you. I've only just started thinking about it, seriously. Making stuff.'

Upstairs, distantly, the toilet flushed and a door opened.

'I was wondering,' Evie went on, 'about – well, studying design—'

'Really?' said Chris, his interest piqued. 'Have you got anywhere in mind?'

'Not really, not yet,' said Evie, 'Mum thinks—'

Wiping her hands down the front of her T-shirt, Maude sighed and stood up.

'Where are you off to?' Nell asked.

'The loo. God, Nell, relax.'

'Hey,' Chris said.

'It's fine,' said Nell. 'Sorry, Maudie. I didn't mean anything.'

Maude didn't answer, she settled for rolling her eyes at Evie as she left the room and bounded up the stairs; her bare feet slapping against the wooden treads.

Evie took a sip of her too-hot coffee. 'I was wondering,' she said, 'if you, if either of you—' She was interrupted by a thud on the landing.

'Dad!' Maude's voice echoing through the hall. 'Dad! Nell!'

'I am so sorry,' Carolyn said when they were all in the bedroom. 'I really don't make a habit of wandering into people's bedrooms uninvited.'

Evie was the last one in, reluctant, edging towards the window.

'It's fine, really,' said Nell.

'I just glanced in as I was passing and – it shouldn't look like that, should it?'

It was definitely bigger, Nell thought. A distinct line running perhaps twelve inches down one of the oak panels, parallel with the bedpost, with another crack, vertical, jagged, running horizontally across the top. There was the beginnings of a gap, as if someone had tried to tug it open.

'And when I came up, Carolyn was in here and showed me,' said Maude. 'Is it a cupboard?'

'It's not a cupboard, there's no hinge,' Nell said. 'It's just – come loose.'

'We must have knocked it somehow,' said Chris.

'So it's your fault?' A disapproving tone crept into Maude's voice.

'Good God, when did you become the holiday police, Maggot?' said Chris.

'It's no one's fault,' said Nell. It seemed to her that there were too many of them in the bedroom, all too eager to offer an opinion. Chris bent down and shoved the bed to one side.

He pulled gently at the edge of the wood and it gave a little. 'I think it's a void,' he said, peering in.

'Sorry?'

'A little gap, in the wall.'

'A hidey hole,' said Maude, sounding pleased.

'We need a torch,' Chris said.

Evie pulled her phone out of her pocket. 'Will this do?'

'Thanks.' He let the beam of the torch app, which was surprisingly powerful, play up and down the panel. 'I wonder if the bed has been holding it in place.' He ran his fingers over the pale edge of the wood; the damage ran the length of the grain, and there was another crack, threading its way along the bottom of the panel. He edged it open a little more.

'Well, it should be easy enough to repair,' said Carolyn, 'there'll be some sort of insurance cover, I suppose.'

There was a pause.

'There's something here,' Chris said.

'Can you see?' Nell stood back and held up the phone. Chris bent close and looked inside, the blue-white beam trembling slightly.

'No. Not really,' he said, pulling at the wood and trying to slip his hand in. The gap was too narrow, too narrow for Chris at any rate.

'Can I try?' Maude asked.

'No,' said Nell.

'Rats can get ever so hungry all alone in the dark,' said Chris, standing now, pulling a face at Maude, who for once didn't seem to get the joke. She moved closer to Evie, who slipped an arm around her shoulder and gave her a gentle, reassuring hug.

'For goodness' sake,' said Nell, frowning at him. 'There's nothing to be afraid of, Maudie.'

'Fine,' said Chris. 'You give it a go.'

There was no way of avoiding it. Nell gave the phone to

88

Chris and knelt, and – trying not to think about rats, or spiders, cobwebs or . . . dead things . . . she slid her hand into the gap.

There was a sort of shelf. She ran her fingers gently across the surface – lightly ridged in places, dusty and cold – making sure to press into the corners; her fingernails scrabbling against the stone.

It was maybe twelve inches long and went back three or four inches into the wall. She could feel herringbone marks cross hatched into the stone, like little crosses.

'There's nothing there,' she said.

'Are you sure?' said Carolyn, who had been watching intently.

'Yes.' As she drew her hand back her fingers brushed over the cool stone and caught against something. 'Shit.'

'What is it?' asked Maude.

She had them now, both Chris and Carolyn were leaning in closer and Nell found she was tempted to give them a fright, to start screaming as if there was a rat after all, something with teeth.

'I'm not sure.' She felt around carefully, trying not to think about what she might be catching under her nails. 'Oh.'

'What?'

It wasn't stone. Whatever it was gave slightly under the pressure of Nell's fingers. It was soft, collapsed – something dead.

'I think it's . . .'

Skin.

She wrapped her hand around it and carefully, she pulled it out into the light.

It was a shoe.

'Well,' said Carolyn, lifting it up, tilting it this way and that.

'Is there another one?' asked Maude.

'No.' Even if there was, Nell wasn't about to shove her hand back into the wall.

It was made of leather, stained and worn; thick with dust. A child's shoe.

'How old is it, do you think?' asked Evie.

'I don't know, as old as the house?' Nell rubbed her fingers against the leg of her jeans. She wanted to wash her hands; she wanted to get into the bath and scrub everything away.

Carolyn handed the shoe to her daughter, who turned it over, examining the sole.

'Shouldn't we show it to someone?' said Maude.

'Who?'

'I don't know.'

'Gina, perhaps?' said Evie, looking up. 'Or, you know, someone else at the museum.'

'They're hardly professionals,' said Carolyn.

'I suppose not.' Evie handed the shoe back to Chris. She looked glad to be rid of it.

'But what will you do?' Carolyn asked as Nell saw her to the door.

'We'll ring the letting agent and they can worry about it. It's not our problem.'

'Of course,' said Carolyn, pausing on the step, 'but if you do find anything else, you will let me know – I mean, it's an incredible thing, isn't it? For it to have been hidden away all this time. It does make you wonder.'

'There wasn't anything else,' said Nell, flexing her fingers.

'Oh. Well, we'll see you at the party?'

'Of course.' Nell's smile was fixed firmly in place.

'Right, Good. I'll see you then.'

Nell closed the door and leant her head against it.

'Can we keep it?' They had put the shoe on the dining table and Maude was leaning over it, prodding gently at the worn leather.

No shoes on the table, Nell's gran would say, *it's bad luck*. And Nell found it was quite an effort not to pick it up and set it down on a chair instead. 'No,' she said, running the hot tap and squirting washing-up liquid into her hands as Chris and Maude continued to fuss over the shoe, him taking photos from every angle.

Nell dried her hands on a tea towel and watched as Maude ran her thumb across the top of the grimy leather, tracing out the shape of someone's foot – *this little piggy went to market, this little piggy stayed at home*. It had been worn for as long as possible, until the leather at the very front had begun to lift from the sole, and the heel had begun to stretch and buckle. It was plain and simple, with four eyelets for a lace of some sort punched unevenly into the top.

It was small enough to fit in the palm of her hand, stained and battered, inexplicable.

'Maude has something to say to you,' said Chris, looking up from the shoe. 'Maudie?'

'Sorry.' Maude stood up straighter, tugging at her T-shirt, giving the impression of looking at Nell, without actually making eye contact. 'For saying – what I said.'

'Oh.' Nell glanced at Chris.

'We had a talk,' he said. 'Earlier. While you were asleep.'

'Well, that's OK,' said Nell, 'I mean, it's not OK that you said it, but . . .' The old Maude would have given her a hug by now, a bit teary that she'd upset Nell, perhaps; they'd be making a joke and moving on.

The old Maude wouldn't have called her a bitch in the first place.

'There's no harm done,' said Nell, glancing at her phone; she'd check it later, the call log, the search history, just in case.

'So, what do you fancy doing today?' Chris said. He looked annoyingly well rested.

'Nothing,' said Maude, turning her attention back to the shoe. 'There's nothing to do here.'

'Well, that's just not true,' said Chris. 'We could go on the beach.'

And that was it, Nell realised. Apparently they were going to carry on as if nothing had happened. 'It might be a bit too cold for that today,' she said. 'You guys could take a drive out somewhere, perhaps?'

'Where?' Maude ran her finger across the leather again, and Nell felt the oddest urge to slap her hand away. The smell in the kitchen had got worse and she shouldn't have had that coffee, decaf or no, her stomach was acid, churning,

'I don't know, down the coast to Bay, perhaps, or inland, up onto the moors.'

'Don't you want to come?'

This was a trick question, of course.

'I'm not feeling too clever today, to be honest,' Nell said. 'I didn't sleep very well. Anyway, you two don't need me to have a good time.'

Maude said, looking at her father, 'Can we go? Just you and me?'

'I don't know,' said Chris, looking thoughtfully at Nell.

'There's a little museum at Bay, or rather, there was,' said Nell. 'Natural history, and a bit about the lifeboat there, you might like it.'

Maude tilted her head to one side, waiting, daring her father to say no. 'What about this?' she said, gently patting the shoe.

'It'll keep,' said Nell.

Chris nodded. 'Go and get your jacket,' he said, 'and don't take all morning about it.'

'OK.'

Nell waited until Maude was out of the room before sitting at the table, her head ached and her eyes were sore.

'Are you sure you don't want to come?' he said.

'I'm sure. It's fine. I'm fine; she's obviously dying to have you to herself for a bit. Just try not to completely ruin her with treats and sugar.'

'As if.'

'Did she say?' Nell asked. 'That she took it?'

'No.' He leant against the counter, picking the phone up, inspecting it, then carefully putting it back in place. 'It was just here when I came down this morning.'

'And you didn't ask?'

'Is there any point? She's apologised.'

'But don't you want to know why she took it?'

'I think we can work that out ourselves, love. It won't happen again.'

Nell considered the shoe, small and ugly on the table in front of her. 'One of us should ring the letting agency,' she said, 'I'll do it later.'

'OK,' said Chris. 'Thanks.' He pulled his own phone out of his pocket, frowning at the screen. 'I'll just give Sam a quick call – can you go and sort Maude out?'

Nell knocked gently on the ladder to Maude's room, before climbing up it. 'Hey,' she said, 'are we good to go?'

Maude didn't look up, she was on her knees in front of her bag. 'I can't find my orange flip-flops.'

'Are you sure you packed them?'

'Of course I am.'

Nell decided to ignore her tone. 'Do you really need them?'

'Well, yeah. It's a holiday?'

Nell knelt down, checking under the bed. 'It's still early in the season, you know. It might be a bit too cold for flip-flops.'

'Cold?' Maude looked unimpressed. 'Honestly, this place. I don't know why we bothered.'

'Oh, you know. To catch up with family.'

'Your family.'

'Yours too, Maudie.'

There was no reply and Nell concentrated on the discarded clothes and half-read books Maude seemed to be stockpiling under her bed. 'We have the time now, don't we? And this way you get to go to France too. Two holidays instead of one. You lucky thing.' Something rattled along the floorboard, and Nell picked it up; a tiny toy soldier, encrusted with mud, long forgotten by a former occupant.

'They're not there,' said Maude, 'I looked.' She closed the bag and gazed around the bedroom, dissatisfied. 'Do I have to go?'

'Sorry, what?'

'To the party. Dad says I'm not grounded any more' – an expression something like defiance crossed her face – 'but actually, I don't think I *want* to go.'

'Why not?'

'I don't know. It'll be all adults, boring.' Maude could get like this sometimes, anxious about strangers, new places, new things.

'You don't know that.' Nell put the soldier on top of the wooden trunk, wiped the dust off her hands.

'Is Evie going?'

'I'm not sure.' And if she was, she might be old enough to drink, she'd hardly want to hang out with Maude all evening. 'But there'll be other kids. Probably.'

'I'm not a kid. I could stay here, on my own.'

'I don't know, sweetheart. We'd have to have a chat with your dad.'

'Yeah. Whatever.' Maude sat on the bed, defeated.

'Why don't you make a move?' Nell stood up, brushing her knees. 'We can always buy a new pair, if they don't turn up.'

Maude didn't reply, but began shoving her feet into her red trainers.

'What else do you need?'

'Nothing.' Her hair tumbled over her face, obscuring her expression as she tied the grubby laces.

'Maude . . .'

'What?'

She should ask about the phone. If Maude had taken it they needed to clear the air; they should try to work things out, just the two of them. Maude was very still, her shoulders unnaturally tense.

'Nothing. Come on, let's not keep your dad waiting.'

8

It was astonishing, Nell thought, surveying the remains of breakfast, the amount of mess both Chris and Maude could generate. She did her best to tidy up, vaguely aware she should eat something. She covered up Carolyn's plate of blondies – too rich, too sickly – maybe some toast, maybe later.

The shoe had been abandoned on the table. She picked it up and after a moment or two's unease – the leather was creased and dirty, the stitching was rotting in places, and even with the dust wiped inexpertly away by Maude, there was something faintly unclean about it – she settled for putting it in the cupboard under the sink. She would ring the letting agency before Chris and Maude got back, but not right now. There was something else she needed to do first.

She retrieved the pregnancy testing kit from her bag and, running her dates through her head just one more time, she made her way upstairs.

She was sitting on the side of the bath, reading through the instruction leaflet when she heard it.

A door slamming shut, rattling on its hinges, startling her.

They were back. She refolded the leaflet clumsily and shoved it into its box, pushing the whole thing to the back of the bathroom cabinet. She'd have to find a better hiding place for it later.

She went out onto the landing. 'Hello? Chris?'

They must have forgotten something, or perhaps Maude had changed her mind. 'Hello?'

There was no reply.

But there was someone there. She could feel it, a shift in the atmosphere; she wasn't alone.

She walked slowly downstairs, expecting someone – Chris, Maude, maybe even Carolyn again – to come into view, smiling, apologising for startling her. But no one did and the silence was alive, as if there was someone just out of sight, waiting.

'Maude?'

She hesitated.

'Carolyn?'

She couldn't think why Carolyn might need to call back, delivering more baked goods, perhaps, in another attempt to lay claim to the drying ground. The more she thought about it, the more Nell was convinced that Carolyn knew perfectly well she had only the haziest recollection of their schooldays, and what was more, she suspected she was enjoying the mild discomfort this uncertainty provoked.

But if it wasn't her . . .

Someone chancing their luck then, hoping to find the cottage empty, hoping to get in and out before anyone noticed.

Her phone was in the kitchen, on the counter. So was her bag, her wallet, her money, credit cards. It would be inconvenient to lose them, but ultimately they were all replaceable. But she'd called out; hiding wasn't an option.

She took the stairs carefully, listening for a clue, any indication of which way she should turn. In the hall she paused again. They'd fallen into the habit of using the kitchen door to come and go, but they'd locked the front door, hadn't they?

She couldn't remember.

It was cold in the hallway, damp – and the light was dim.

To her left, the living room door was shut. To her right, the door to the kitchen was open, and beyond it was the back door – which she had very definitely not locked when Chris and Maude left.

It might have been the wind, but she thought she could hear the front door shudder a little, as if someone was testing it.

She didn't stop to think, if she did that she'd never move, and then . . . She took a breath and turned right – it was just half a dozen paces to her phone. She moved swiftly, purposefully, through the open door, then skidded suddenly as she lost first her footing, then her balance, her momentum causing her to fall heavily against the dining table, leaving her breathless as she slammed her hands against the top of it, bracing herself.

Everything stopped; then she stood, slowly, tenderly, taking stock, her arms shaking. Lying on the floorboard was a scrap of rubber and foam, bright orange, missing a few of its sequins now, but familiar enough; she had slipped on one of Maude's flip-flops. Where had it come from? How had any of them missed it?

She picked it up, and behind her, in the hall, the front door shuddered again. She hurried across the kitchen, snatching up her phone, turning and scanning the room.

Empty. Empty. Empty.

But still it didn't feel empty.

'Hello?' she called out, still convinced there was someone in the house with her, someone just out of sight. 'Maude? Is that you?' She glanced down at her screen. There was no signal; there never was a bloody signal here. She grabbed the door handle and pulled, but it was stuck – locked – using both hands now, locked after all, locked *in* – and as she struggled with it she lost her grip on the phone and it smashed face down onto the flagstone floor.

Leave it, Nell thought, just leave it.

She tried the door again – turning the key back and forth, she felt the mechanism click into place, so surely it couldn't be, couldn't be – and after pulling frantically at the handle for another few seconds, she managed to unstick it, tug it free, staggering back a little as she did so.

She righted herself and all but walked straight into Gina Verrill.

The thought occurred to Nell that Gina had been pulling at the door too, that the pair of them had been engaged in some ridiculous tug of war, and she had the terrible urge to laugh.

'Are you all right?' Gina was peering past her.

'I . . .' Nell stood back, looking around the kitchen, which was empty, perfectly ordinary. Back in focus now. 'Of course I am. I – I'm fine.'

'Am I interrupting?'

'No. Not really. I was just . . .' She could feel her cheeks reddening. She was still clutching the stupid flip-flop, she bent down and picked up the phone. The screen was broken, of course, covered in a dense network of fine cracks.

'Ouch,' said Gina.

'Yes,' said Nell, tears pricking at her eyes. 'That was – stupid of me.'

'What happened?'

Nell rubbed her arm, she had scraped it from wrist to elbow, right along the bone; it took a moment or two for her to remember. 'I slipped,' she said, 'smacked right into the dining table.'

'Slipped?'

100

'I was in a rush, not looking where I was going, it was just . . .' She glanced behind her again at the empty kitchen. 'My own stupid fault. And then I dropped my phone.'

Gina was looking more closely at her now.

'It's fine, honestly. Why don't you come in?'

'Oh.' Gina stepped back. 'No. No, I don't think so. I just wanted to drop these off.' She held out a small paper envelope, the kind used to hold photographs and negatives.

'Oh, thank you.' Nell tried to swallow, her mouth was dry. 'Are you sure?' Suddenly the idea of company was very appealing. It might have been her imagination, but the smell was back, stronger, despite the open door; damp and sour, sickening.

'Tell you what,' Gina said, 'why don't we go up to mine instead?'

Nell followed Gina up the path to the little house. A ceramic tile by the door bore an image of a leafy branch and a name, ROWAN COTTAGE. The sandstone seemed blunted, by time and the weather, the sash windows were in need of sanding and repainting, but it was very still, self-contained, peaceful.

'Come in, come in.' Gina led the way into the kitchen, opening the back door into a tiny garden, the terraces clambering up the cliff, thick with greenery of every shade and dotted with patches of colour; pale pink valerian, buttery gold toadflax, foxgloves and geraniums. Closer to the house there were herbs in weathered terracotta planters, and a small but neatly organised vegetable patch.

'This is lovely,' said Nell.

'Thank you,' said Gina. 'Now, something soothing perhaps, chamomile? Or ginger?'

'Oh, whatever you're having, thanks.'

They sat at the kitchen table. It was a pleasant room, slightly old fashioned, a little untidy, family snapshots, a small boy grinning up at an unseen photographer; more recent selfies of a teenage girl were dotted along the shelves and stuck with magnets to the fridge. With the garden occupying what space there was between the house and the cliff, the whole room was filled with a cool green light.

'They're a bit tatty,' Gina said, pushing the paper wallet towards her. Nell opened it, and tried to focus. There were two photographs inside. One was in colour and had been taken outside someone's house, an older woman was standing by the front door. Her hair was pulled back from her face, she wore glasses, and a floral apron covered her clothes; she rarely wore make-up, Nell remembered, but liked a nice perfume – Elizabeth Arden, Lily of the Valley. It was her grandmother, Rebecca. The second was in black and white, the same woman, but younger, her arms linked with another woman Nell didn't recognise, both caught striding down the pier, smiling brightly at the unseen photographer.

'Where did you get these?' Nell placed them carefully on the table, side by side; almost afraid to touch them.

'I've no idea, pet. Not really. My gran knew Ida, Ida Green – that's her with your gran – and I inherited all her old photos. I was actually looking for a few pictures of Dave and Jenny, you know, for their anniversary.'

'I remember this.' Nell pointed towards the colour shot. 'The house, I mean.'

'Your gran and Ida were neighbours up on St Mary's Crescent.'

'Really?' Nell picked up the black and white photo again, frowning, 'I can't quite . . .' The name was familiar, though the memory shimmered, just out of sight. A shadowy figure leaning over her, pressing something small into her hand.

102

'I thought you might like them,' said Gina.

'That's so kind of you, thank you,' said Nell, oddly touched by the gesture.

'You're welcome. She was such a nice lady, kind.'

'Yes. She was.' The photo began to blur. Nell cleared her throat, and tried to smile.

'And if you don't mind – are you quite all right, pet?' asked Gina. 'In yourself? Only you seemed a bit – worried, back at the house.'

It seemed easier to start with Carolyn. Nell took a sip of chamomile tea, breathing in the sweet floral scent. 'The thing is,' she said, 'I don't remember her at all.'

'But you went to school together?'

'Evidently.'

'Don't you have any old photos?'

'Not really. Well, at home, packed up in boxes.' Nell picked up the pictures of her gran again, she'd show them to Chris and Maude, maybe get her old albums out once they got back home.

'And she'd be the right age?'

'I guess. I don't think I've got the nerve to ask.'

'The trouble with Carolyn is that once she's got an idea in her head, she won't let it go.'

'Yes, I'd sort of gathered that.' Nell leant back in her seat, looking around the room. Elder House was all very well, stylish, comfortable, but it was – cold. Unloved, perhaps. Not like Rowan Cottage, which for all its clutter was relaxed and inviting; a proper home. 'She does seem very determined about the drying ground.'

'Of course she does.'

'She seemed to think it's sort of – communal?'

103

'It probably was, once. But the deeds I've seen for the house are quite clear. As of 1882, the drying ground at the back of Elder House belonged to Elder House.'

'You've seen the deeds?'

Gina smiled. 'I volunteer at the museum, for the Lit and Phil. It's amazing the things we have on file, and in 1882 the house was bought by a Dr Bishop – hence Bishops Yard, it was actually Elder Yard before that. He was a very successful man, quite the local worthy, and he donated all of his collections and paperwork to the Society. She's wrong, and we've got the proof in black and white.' She sighed softly. 'We've had this argument before, and I daresay we'll have it again.'

'But why? I mean, if it's as clear cut as you say, why does she keep pressing her point?'

'Oh, I don't know.' Gina smiled sadly. 'She's just one of those people who likes her own way, I suppose, and she cannot stand to lose an argument. Believe me, I should know.'

Nell thought of the gate, so new, so out of place.

'How long have you lived here?' she asked, carefully tucking the photos back into their wallet.

'Getting on for thirty years, now. We did this place up ourselves. That is, my husband did. Jack.' Gina pointed to a framed photo on the wall, a snapshot of a man in a checked shirt and jeans, a pair of glasses pushed up onto the top of his head. 'It was his business, you see – doing up older buildings. But – you know, sympathetically.' A boy, Maude's age, perhaps, stood next to him, his expression a little sheepish. Gina smiled sadly. 'It's just me now.'

'Oh. I'm sorry.'

'Thank you, it's been a few years now, and you get used to it after a while.'

'Does your son live close by?' Nell asked, it wasn't unusual for people to move away in search of bigger, better opportunities, a more exciting life; she'd done it herself.

'Oh, no.' Gina looked almost apologetic. 'Robin – he died too. Not at the same time, that would have been – no. It was . . .' she hesitated, 'a long time ago.'

'I'm so sorry. I had no idea.' Nell looked around the room, struggling to find the right thing to say, and to her horror she felt her throat tighten and tears threaten to rise; to lose a child – it must have been unbearable.

'My Jack worked on quite a few places in the yard actually,' said Gina, pouring more tea. 'He used to do a fair bit for Oliver Wilson, back when he was just starting out, before he and Carolyn – well, when she was a bit easier to get along with. He did your place, the first time round.'

'Really? It feels very new, still,' said Nell, grateful for the distraction Gina was so obviously providing.

'There was a lot more work done on it a year or so ago, a new roof – everything. They took their time, too. We had workmen traipsing up and down the yard for months, their lorries blocking the street. There was a good deal of money spent, by all accounts.' Gina fell silent.

'Who owns it now?'

'Oh, I did know the name – Crow? Crowne? Something like that – no one local. I've never laid eyes on them.' She hesitated. 'There's nothing wrong with it, is there?'

'No. They did a lovely job,' said Nell. 'But it just feels – it's not very . . . welcoming.'

'That's the thing with these holiday places, isn't it?' said Gina. 'They're pretty enough, but it takes a family to make a home.'

'But it's a funny spot, don't you think?' Nell said. She was tempted to mention the noises she'd heard, and the sense she'd had that there had been someone in the house, to tell Gina about the shoe, and the void in the bedroom wall. 'I mean, it's not just me, is it?'

Gina looked at her steadily, then she seemed to come to a decision. 'The thing is, pet, I'm probably not—'

The light dimmed as a figure appeared in the doorway, blocking it briefly before stepping inside; a girl in school uniform, dark-haired and wearing lots of eye make-up.

'Hello, Gran,' she said, dropping her rucksack in front of the fridge.

'Hello, love, I wasn't expecting to see you today.' Gina stood, kissing the girl on her cheek. 'Nell,' she said, 'this is my grand-daughter, Kym. Kym, love, this is Nell.'

'Hello.'

'Hi.' The girl smiled politely, briefly.

'Nell's staying at Elder House, with her husband and daughter.'

'Stepdaughter, actually,' said Nell.

'Oh. I didn't know they'd let it out.' The girl's gaze was direct as she leant back against the kitchen counter, assessing Nell and her grubby T-shirt, her baggy jeans. 'What's it like?'

'Kym,' said Gina softly.

'I just wondered.' Her eyes wide, a picture of innocence. 'I've never been inside,' she said to Nell.

'It's – fine.' Nell, glanced at Gina. 'Probably a bit big for us really.'

'I can't remember the last time anyone lived there.'

'Well, this is only temporary, I'm afraid.'

'Pity, Gran could do with some new neighbours.'

'That's enough,' said Gina, and Kym grinned at her.

'Nell is Dave Galilee's cousin. She's here for the party.'

'Lucky you,' said Kym, then. 'Sorry, I've been hearing a lot about this party.'

106

'Don't be,' said Nell. 'My stepdaughter's not too keen on the idea either.'

'I saw Louise this morning,' Gina said. 'She's still looking for someone reliable.'

'Cleaning holiday cottages?' Kym pulled a face. 'Really?'

'It's good money. It would do until you found something else.'

'Can't I come and work in the shop with you? Or I could help out at the Lit and Phil.'

'Kym did some work experience with us,' Gina told Nell, 'and now we can't get rid of her.'

'It was interesting,' said Kym.

'I'm sure it was,' said Nell. She'd spent many rainy afternoons wandering around the museum when she was a kid.

'And we would have you back like a shot, pet. Only there's no money to pay you.'

'The shop then.'

'I can only offer you the odd shift.'

'Well that's that,' said Kym, kicking her bag out of the way and opening the fridge, 'skivvying it is.'

Nell stood up. 'I should go.'

'There's no need,' said Gina. 'You're welcome to stay for lunch.'

'Oh, that's tempting – but I should get back. Another day, though? Or you could come down to the house, take a look around, see how it's changed?'

'We'll see. I wouldn't like to intrude.'

Kym glanced at her grandmother, but didn't comment.

'Go through the garden, pet,' said Gina. 'Just follow the path round.' She walked Nell to the door. 'Call in any time, if she gets a bit too much for you, Carolyn. And I daresay I'll see you at Dave and Jenny's do.'

'I could babysit.' Kym was still standing by the open fridge. 'I mean – if you want? If your little girl doesn't want to go to the party?'

'Kym,' said Gina, 'don't.'

'What? I'm being friendly, helpful.' She grinned at Nell. 'And only a bit pushy.'

'Oh,' Nell said, 'I'm not sure. She's not actually that little, she's twelve.'

'Or not, you know – only if you need someone just to keep her company—'

'I'm sure Nell can make her own arrangements,' said Gina.

'Can I think about it?' Nell asked. 'Have a word with my husband and let you know?'

'Sure. Gran's got my number.'

'Right. I'll be in touch, then.' Nell opened the door, then hesitated, looking around the kitchen one last time. 'Thanks,' she said, 'for the photos, and for the tea and sympathy.'

'Any time.'

Nell smiled and Kym thought she might say more, but instead she stepped out into the garden and vanished from sight.

'Sympathy?' Kym said. 'Did I interrupt something?'

'Not really.' Gina sat back down at the table. 'Just Carolyn Wilson being – well, you know. And I don't think she likes the . . .' She hesitated, frowning. 'Well, you know what visitors can be like, if something doesn't suit them.'

Kym closed the fridge and took the seat opposite her. 'Are you cross?' she asked. 'Am I in trouble now? About the baby-sitting?'

'Your mother won't be pleased.'

'I can manage her. It's you I'm worried about.'

Gina looked at her. 'Well, I'd rather you didn't,' she said, 'but I don't suppose that counts for much.'

'Don't be like that.'

'What good will it do? Poking around that old place.'

'I don't know,' said Kym. 'Think of it as . . . scratching an itch. Getting it all out of my system.' She helped herself to the last of the ginger biscuits.

'You'll spoil your dinner.'

'You have to stop fussing.'

'So I've been told.'

Kym smiled at her. 'It'll be fine,' she said. 'Trust me.'

Nell didn't feel like eating, and she didn't much want to go back up to the bathroom and deal with the pregnancy test either, suddenly it felt like tempting fate; if she didn't know, she couldn't be wrong. She passed her hand absently over her belly, no harm done, she reminded herself, blinking away an image of her crashing into the table, of falling – worse than that. She wished she'd gone with Chris and Maude after all. She wasn't looking forward to spending the rest of the day alone in the house.

She thought she might ring the letting agents, but a brief inspection of her phone confirmed that conversation would have to wait. The damn thing was useless, its screen cracked and blank, and there was nowhere in town to get it fixed, of that she was certain.

The best thing to do was to work.

She started off at the little table in the living room, laying out the glass she'd collected so far, playing with it, grading it by size, colour, translucence. Resolutely not thinking about earlier, and absolutely not listening out for any other odd noises. But after a while she'd decided the light wasn't good enough, the windows were too small, the ceiling too low, and switching on the overhead lights didn't help. There was, it seemed to her, a low-level buzzing that filled the room and never seemed to go away, not even when she switched the lights off again. She felt – hemmed in.

She gathered up her pencils, and as she crossed the hall, the sea glass balanced precariously on her sketch pad, the front door rattled again, like a warning. Nell stopped, waited, but all she could hear was the thudding of her heart, the glass on the paper in front of her trembling. She took a breath and carried on into the kitchen, and as she was organising her pieces all over again on the dining table, she heard a dull thump far above her in the house. A window left open, she told herself. Nothing to worry about.

She took a seat, picked up a pencil, tried to concentrate, but the kitchen wasn't any better, the smell seemed to have faded, but it hadn't entirely vanished, and she found herself wondering about the house, and if anyone else felt so – unsettled here.

In the end she took everything outside onto the patio, spreading out their old picnic blanket and contriving a seat out of a pile of fresh towels – she didn't care to risk any of the cushions from the sofa. She had her pad with her, and a few pencils; she fetched the washing-up bowl out too – it held a couple of tepid inches of water – and she took a few moments to drop each piece of glass back into it, ignoring the suspicion that she'd allowed the house to force her out.

She told herself she was cleaning the glass, but really, she liked the way the water added depth and shine, the way the droplets created the illusion of facets as she picked out single pieces and held them up to the light. She sat cross-legged, arranging and rearranging the glass on sheets of damp paper, letting her mind run free. She shifted her position, until she had her back to Elder House, and after a while she picked up a pencil and began to work.

110

Kym took her usual route home, out of the yard, past Nell Galilee – who didn't look up from whatever it was she was doing near the drying ground – down the street then up the bankside, following the paved footpath the council had finally created after generations of locals had worn the route into the side of the cliff. The path was steep, but there were benches placed along it at intervals, and Kym sat on the last one, right at the top. She liked the view from here, you could see how the town had developed. The oldest houses were crammed into the streets nearest the river, and tucked close under the cliff. Then as the years had passed, and the railway brought visitors to the town, bigger houses had appeared, inland and up on the West Cliff, grander houses, organised and ambitious, set in wide streets. And finally there were the newer builds, modern housing estates, springing up on the outskirts of town; it always reminded her of the rings in a tree trunk.

She was in no hurry to get home, her mum wasn't exactly a worrier, and Kym had the feeling that she might welcome some time on her own. Recently she'd started to talk about the future, not just this year's exams, but A levels and uni and Kym moving out. She didn't seem too unhappy about this prospect; they were talking about it to get used to the idea, Kym thought, the both of them.

You couldn't quite see her gran's cottage from here, but Kym could more or less place it among the jumble of red roofs to her right. Bishops Yard. She used to think the name connected it to the abbey, until her gran had pointed out it was more likely to be named for the family that had once lived there, despite the lack of an apostrophe. Greens Yard, Lengs Yard, Blackburns Yard, even – to the amusement of tourists – Arguments Yard had all been named for the families that once had occupied them; the streets here told all sorts of stories, if only people thought to look.

Nell Galilee had seemed nice enough; maybe she'd let Kym have a look around one day, if the babysitting thing didn't come off. She'd have to find a way to ask.

Her phone buzzed, and she pulled it out of her bag, her heart sinking when she saw who was calling.

Tyler. She'd managed to avoid him at school, where he was making a show of ignoring her, and where no one knew about the calls and the texts, because it was not cool to be seen to be wanting her back. But apparently he wasn't taking the hint.

She didn't answer. She was in no mood to talk to him, and when the buzzing stopped only to be replaced moments later by the soft chime that indicated she had a message, she didn't open that either.

They were done, and it was about time he got used to the idea.

About time the both of them did.

'Kym? Is that you?'

'No. It's Taylor Swift.'

Kym dropped her bag by the stairs and went into the kitchen. Her mum, Kate, was sitting at the kitchen table, a cigarette in one hand, a book in front of her. She was wearing one of Kym's T-shirts, Debbie Harry scowling in front of black and white parallel lines.

'Be a pet then, Taylor love, and stick the kettle on.'

'Have you been going through my stuff again?'

'I didn't think you'd mind. What's wrong? Too young?' Kate looked down at herself, squinting. 'Doesn't it suit me?'

'That's not the problem, Mum.'

'Oh. Sorry.'

Kym didn't really mind, she supposed, even though there were times when she wished her mum didn't look so – appealing. She had fallen pregnant when she was sixteen and on a good day she still looked as though she was barely in her twenties.

Kym pulled out a chair and sat down. 'What are you reading?'

Kate held the paperback up, *The Valley of the Dolls*. 'I found it in a charity shop,' she said. 'Bargain.'

'I'm shocked, Mother. Shocked, I tell you.'

'You can borrow it when I'm done, if you like. School all right?'

'Yeah, fine.'

'And your gran?' Her mum didn't much approve of Gina, and she was always making a big deal about not bothering her, as if she was some old lady, frail and easily confused.

'She's OK. Sends her love'

Kate snorted softly. 'If you say so.'

'Mum?'

'Yes?'

'You wouldn't mind if I did a bit of baby-sitting, would you?'

'Who for?'

'Some visitors – in the yard.' She didn't need to say which yard.

Kate put her book down. 'Is this Gina's idea?'

'No, I met this woman, and I just offered. She didn't seem too sure, really, she said she'd have to check with her husband.

113

It might not come to anything, but you know – if it did.' She tried to sound as if she didn't much care, one way or the other.

'As long as it doesn't interfere with your exams, then.'

'As if.' It was weird, the way everyone was going on about the exams, AS levels, because she knew – they all knew at school – there was always next year, and they were going to get rid of them anyway.

'Right. Well. If you really want to.' She picked up her book again. It wasn't that she wasn't interested, Kym knew, it was that she wasn't willing to push. Her own mother had pushed and look where that had led. And there was no need for Kate to know which particular house the visitors were renting.

'Tea?' Kym said. She'd make them both a drink and then take herself off to her room, maybe get out her notes on the yard, on the house; just in case.

'Yes, please.' Her mum was already lost in her reading, and what she didn't know wouldn't hurt her.

10

Nell worked outside until the sun began to sink below the rooftops, and the afternoon air began to chill. She had a few ideas she was pleased with, collars and cuffs of beaten silver, inset with sea glass, and she felt calmer now, more herself.

It was simply a case of finding the right piece of glass for each design. She picked one up, ran her thumb over its slightly pitted surface, then held it to her eye; it was almost too opaque to see through, and rendered the world a watery green.

She had no idea of the time, she rarely wore a watch and never when working, and she'd become so absorbed in her collection, she'd managed to ignore the chimes of the church clock on the cliff.

She stood up slowly, her limbs had stiffened – sitting cross-legged on damp stone all afternoon had maybe not been such a good idea. The drying ground was right in front of her, in full shadow. She couldn't imagine anyone choosing to spend time there, if the house was unsettling, then the little patch of land was downright – wrong. Dark and damp, unloved and overgrown – her skin rose in goosebumps just looking at it.

She gathered up her drawing things and took them inside, stacking them on the dining table. On her way back to fetch the glass, she picked up her phone and swiped at the broken screen, hoping for a miracle.

Nothing.

She tried to remember if she'd bothered to insure this phone and where the nearest store might be if she had. They'd have to make a day out of it, she supposed, which might not be a bad thing.

The microwave clock told her it was past five. Chris and Maude would be back soon, she should be thinking about dinner.

She went out and gathered up the glass, scooping it into the washing-up bowl, then deposited the bowl on the draining board. She thought for a moment, then opened the cupboard door and considered the shoe.

There was no way to date it, at least, not to her inexpert eye. It was simple and plain, a product of an age where function was more important than fashion. She picked it up; it must have belonged to a small child, three or four years old, just past the toddling stage. She could imagine sliding the shoe onto a foot, tying the leather lace tight. If she closed her eyes, she could almost imagine the gentle pressure of the child's foot against her hand.

It felt – familiar.

It was cold in the kitchen, and Nell shivered.

She heard them coming up the steps, Chris and Maude, and had managed to slip the shoe back into place and close the cupboard door by the time they rounded the corner.

'Hi.'

'Hi.' Maude headed straight for the biscuit tin. 'What's for dinner? I'm starving.'

'I hadn't thought.'

'Hi, love.' Chris looked tousled, tired. A whole day with Maude seemed to have taken its toll. He kissed her, absently placing a carrier bag on the counter.

'Good day?' Nell asked.

'It was all right.' Maude opened the fridge. 'Can I have some Coke?'

'Sure,' said Chris.

'What's this?' Nell opened the bag, 'A present? For me?'

'No,' said Maude, 'for me.'

There was a box inside the bag.

'Replacement flip-flops,' said Chris. 'Apparently she can't live without them.'

'Hey.' Maude put down her glass. 'They're mine.'

'Sorry.' Nell stepped back, looking at Chris as Maude opened the box.

'They're cheap enough,' he said.

'Look.' Maude slid the flip-flops onto her hands; they were a bright aqua blue and decorated with red and purple foam shells, she danced them in the air.

'Very tasteful,' said Nell, 'and completely unnecessary. I found your old ones, well, one of them.'

'Oh.' Maude blinked at her. 'Well, these are nicer anyway.'

'I tripped on it,' Nell went on. 'Look.' She held out her arm; the graze was beginning to fade. 'I fell. I nearly cracked my head open.'

'Sorry.' Maude looked at her dad. 'I didn't mean to – where was it?'

'By the table,' said Nell, 'if you looked after your things a little more carefully—'

'I said I was sorry.' Maude's eyes filled with tears.

'It's all right, Maggot,' said Chris, reaching out to ruffle her hair, and for once she didn't shy away. 'There's no harm done, is there?'

'No. I . . .' Nell found she couldn't face yet another row, not when they'd barely got over the last one. 'I broke my phone, though.'

'We'll sort something out.'

'And you do need to take more care of your stuff, Maude.'

'Yes. Sorry.' Maude sat down and kicked off her sneakers. 'Where's the shoe?' she asked putting on the new flips-flops. 'What have you done with it?'

'I put it away,' said Nell. 'It's under the sink.'

'Nell. That's not very . . .' Maude struggled to find the right word. 'Respectful.'

'We can't just leave it lying about, certainly not in the mess you two make of this place.'

'Here we go.' Chris picked up the shoebox before Maude could answer. 'Perfect.'

'It's too big,' said Maude.

'Fine.' Chris grabbed that day's paper and pulled a couple of sheets free. 'How about this?'

Nell moved to one side and watched as Maude retrieved the shoe from under the sink, and Chris wadded up the paper, the both of them positioning the shoe carefully, as if it were something delicate, precious. They were very alike, the same colouring, the same sense of humour, and a shared tendency for sudden wild enthusiasms.

'You've caught the sun,' she said, 'both of you.'

'Dad forgot the suncream,' said Maude.

'You fuss too much,' said Chris. Nell wasn't quite sure where that comment was directed.

When the shoe was finally arranged to Maude's satisfaction, she asked her dad, 'Can I keep it up in my room?'

'I don't think so, Maudie.'

'Well, that's not fair.' She gazed sadly into the box.

'You'll get over it.'

'We need to ring the agents, let them know about the panel,' said Nell, 'and – everything.'

'It's a bit late now,' said Chris, 'I'll do it tomorrow. Now, who wants to help with dinner?'

'Do I have to?' Maude looked up at her father. 'I'm so tired.'

'No,' said Chris, 'not if you don't want to.'

'Cool,' said Maude. She slid the lid carefully onto the shoebox before turning her attention to the biscuit tin by the kettle.

She left them to it, her dad and Nell in the kitchen. She took her handful of biscuits up to the attic, got out her sketch pad and her books and settled herself on her bunk. She'd brought the books up from the living room. Nell and her dad wouldn't mind, they loved to see her doing something normal like reading, something safe.

The books were quite old, leather bound with their titles stamped in gold letters down their spines. Maude suspected that half the reason they were kept in the house was because they looked good all bundled up together, but they were interesting too. There were lots of myths and legends mixed in with the historic stuff, even if it was hard to tell things apart sometimes, and she wondered if she might find out about the drying ground and why it felt so funny there, or maybe something about the shoe.

She wished she could bring it up to her room, and was briefly resentful that she wasn't allowed to keep it close by, as if she couldn't be trusted, as if she was a little kid.

She'd had a nice day with her dad, though. They'd gone to a pub for lunch and that had only been spoilt a bit by him being on his phone half the time. It was funny really, as if she was the grown-up and he was the irritating kid who couldn't leave his mobile alone.

There had been one quite long call he'd wandered off to take, leaving her all on her own at their table – she wasn't sure

119

who that had been, but her dad had looked guilty when he had finally come back.

'Don't tell Nell,' he'd said, and she'd liked that feeling, the sense that it was just the two of them against the world, against her.

She'd tried asking him about the house as they were on their way back. The sea dipping in and out of view as they drove home along the coast road. 'Is it very old, then?'

'Yeah.'

'How old?'

'I'm not sure, to be honest.'

'Can we look? Online?'

'Maybe.'

The closer they'd got to the house, the quieter he'd got, as if his mind was drifting back to boring stuff, back to Nell. But it had been good until then, just the two of them. They liked the same things, they laughed at the same jokes; they didn't need anyone else.

She'd been reading for a half hour or so before she came across a description of Elder House – the book made it sound as though the house had been important once, that the people who lived in it had been important too, rich enough to have had servants.

The house acquired an odd reputation early in its history. There are accounts from the 1600s which refer to a mysterious spirit who would knock on the doors once the household was in bed, waking family and servants alike from their rest.

'Strange knockings and noises did plague the household, and several times did the mistress of the house discover all the plate in disarray.'

She had the idea that plate meant metal stuff, cups and plates and candlesticks.

She wondered if the patterns in the beams above her had been there when that happened, if they'd been there right from the very beginning, hidden away when the spirit – whatever it was – was roaming the house.

She put the book to one side and grabbed her sketch pad. She had thought she might write about their day trip, stick in the postcards her dad insisted she buy, but as she turned the pages, looking at the designs she'd copied from the beam, that idea seemed a bit childish. There was still enough light to draw by, even if the shadows were thickening in the corner of the room. She thought about the noises, the disturbances in the house, and shivered. She didn't much like the shadows up here, but there was no way she was going to give in and move into one of the kids' rooms. She didn't much like the drying ground either – the idea popped into her head, and she found she didn't want to think about that. She switched on her lamp, and ran her fingers over the most elaborate of the designs, flowers interlocking and spiralling across the page, so beautiful, so *safe*. It was almost as if her hand needed to copy the marks, as if the action might soothe her, save her.

She picked up her pencil and began to draw some more.

As she worked she could hear Nell walking across the landing towards the big bedroom – no, the bathroom; and she smiled as she worked, thinking about the smashed-up phone, because after everything Nell had said and done, didn't that really serve her right.

Nell slipped inside the bathroom and opened the cabinet; she should definitely move the testing kit just in case Maude stumbled across it, because the last thing they needed was another confrontation, not before they were sure. Everything was stacked neatly inside, just as she'd left it; cotton buds and painkillers and dental floss and deodorant, but she was too late. The tall white box was gone.

11

'Nell? Nell, sweetheart?' Chris was sitting on the edge of the bed, holding a cup of tea. He was fully dressed, showered, shaved; he looked solemn.

'What's this?' She sat up, pushing back the covers, reaching for her phone to check the time, but of course it was downstairs somewhere, broken. 'What's happened? What's wrong?'

'I've got it all worked out,' Chris said, 'I'll be gone two days, three at the most.'

The laptop was on the dining table. Before she sat down, Nell opened the kitchen window as far as she could. The day was just starting to brighten; she hadn't overslept, Chris had simply been up and about very, very early. The air was still, she could smell fresh green outdoor scents, but as she turned back to the kitchen it was still there, underneath, something damp, something rotten. She felt sick.

The emails from Sam seemed innocuous enough at first; one ceramicist was going to be delayed in meeting an order because she was having problems with her supplier; another was complaining she hadn't been paid, which was most unlike Chris – he never let that sort of thing slide. There were other bills yet to be dealt with, attached to the emails that seemed to have been arriving on an hourly basis ever since they'd left home.

They had agreed that while they were away Sam would run

things by herself, but as far as Nell could see she and Chris had been in almost continuous contact since they'd set out on the drive north. That was something they'd need to discuss another time.

The most recent email was headed *Barn Project* and as she clicked on it, Nell thought she could hear Maude moving around upstairs. She paused for a moment, listening. Nothing.

They had always intended to redevelop the building that housed their gallery; as the business had taken off their exhibition space had grown too small, too cramped, and they had in recent months been inching towards getting permission to adapt an old barn adjacent to their current place. It was, they'd been assured by their architect, just a matter of removing all the modern improvements, and opening up the space, filling it with natural light. It had seemed to be the ideal solution. Over the years, they had fallen into their roles at the gallery with little discussion or friction – Nell was the creative one, while Chris managed the business. And as far as Nell knew, everything had been going to plan.

She opened the email and began to read.

Her tea stood untouched on the table. 'You should have told me.'

Chris sat next to her. 'I didn't want to worry you.'

'So you thought it best to worry about it all on your own?'

'Can we talk about this later?'

'You said Sam could manage.'

'And she can.'

'Then why is she sending daily updates?' She shook her head. 'Did you know? Did you know this guy . . .'

'Simeon Lee.'

Simeon Lee, chair of a local history group working to preserve Devon's architectural heritage.

124

'Did you know he was going to kick off?'

'I'd heard a rumour, but I didn't think it would come to anything. Then Sam messaged me.'

'When?' Last night? Dawn?

'Late. It's not her fault, Nell. I asked her to keep on top of things.'

'What kind of a manager can't cope on her own?'

'Oh, come on – this is something we have to deal with.'

She scrolled through the email again. 'She says that we're not going to get planning permission.'

'She thinks there might – *might* – be a problem.'

'And why am I only hearing about this now?'

'Because . . .' He hesitated, choosing his words carefully. 'When it first came up, we'd been having a tough time. You'd had – well, you know, you weren't well.'

'It was depression, Chris. You can say the word.' It had been inevitable, or so she told herself now; the natural result of an endless cycle of hope, followed by crushing, soul-destroying disappointment as Jess's pregnancy – accidental, but such a *joy* – had progressed without a hitch to a home birth and a healthy baby boy, while she, Nell, continued to – fail. There had been days when she thought she might actually go mad with longing, days when she could not bear to hear about Maude's mum and how well baby Leo was doing. Even now she found it hard to take any real interest in him, and on the rare occasions they were all in the same room together she made sure to keep her distance. It had all been so – unfair.

He glanced up at the ceiling guiltily, as if Maude might overhear. 'It was difficult, for both of us. Then he seemed to go off the boil for a bit; then there was the stuff with Maude.'

Days when all Chris seemed to see or hear was his daughter, not his wife.

'Even so.' She stood and took her cup to the sink, tipping the cold tea away.

'I didn't think it was all going to kick off so quickly.'

'We should never have come away. I told you—'

'We needed this.' He stood up, scraping his chair across the floorboards. 'We agreed we needed to get away. Anyway, it's not like you couldn't check the gallery emails whenever you wanted; you didn't, I did.'

'What the hell is that supposed to mean?' He always did this, shifting the argument, making it sound as though it was her fault. She didn't understand where it had come from, this sudden emergency that absolutely had to be dealt with by Chris, in person.

'Nothing – it's not supposed to mean anything.'

'Will you be able to get back for the party?'

There was a pause.

'Great,' said Nell. 'Brilliant.'

'Oh, come on, it's not like you don't know anyone, and you'll have Maude for company.'

'Well, we need to talk about Maude.'

'Not now, surely.'

'Yes, now, Chris. She's been going through my stuff again—'

'Can you actually hear yourself?'

'Presumably because she's worked out there are no real consequences for her misbehaviour—'

'She's a kid.'

'You can't just dump her on me and go swanning off back to work.'

'I don't see,' said Maude, 'why I can't come too.'

She had thought someone was calling her name at first, and when she had woken up properly, struggling upright in bed, she had thought there was someone in her room. Only it had turned out the raised voice had been Nell. Maude had got all the way to the kitchen door before anyone noticed her and the row stopped abruptly.

Her dad was standing by the counter, dressed for work and looking like he'd been up for hours. Nell was leaning against the Aga, barefoot and bleary eyed, still wearing her pyjamas. 'You'd be bored,' he said. 'Besides, you'll be much better off here, having fun. Going to the party.'

'I told you. I don't want to go to the stupid party.'

'Then' – Chris glanced helplessly at Nell – 'you don't have to. We'll sort something out.'

'It isn't fair.'

'The sooner I go, the sooner I'll be done.'

'It's still not fair.'

'I'll be back before you know it.' His bag was by the door, and he picked it up. 'Do I at least get a hug?' he asked, and after a moment Maude obliged. She thought Nell might refuse, she was still so furious with him. But eventually she crossed the room, reaching up to give him a quick peck on the cheek.

'Drive safely,' she said, 'ring us when you get there.'

'I will.'

'I mean it.' She glanced at Maude as if she was in trouble again, 'there are some things we still need to sort out.'

'Promise.' But he was halfway out of the door.

Maude was in her pyjamas too, she couldn't even walk him to the car. He gave her a quick, guilty grin, and then he was gone. She crossed her arms and looked up at Nell. 'Well this sucks,' she said.

'It won't be for long.' But Nell didn't look any happier than Maude felt.

*

127

She had to rely on texting to talk to Imogen. The whole conversation had been difficult, stuttering along because the mobile signal in the house was so rubbish, and once she was done explaining that her dad had totally abandoned them, it had been time to stop because Imogen had school.

Maude picked up a book and lay back on her bed. She'd finally found one that promised to be about magic and stuff, and there was even a little bit about patterns like the ones on the beam – 'witch marks', they called them: *the act of carving the protective design may in itself hold power, the intention being just as potent as the image itself.* It seemed to Maude though that whoever had written the book hadn't been too sure about their facts. She found herself reading the same short paragraph over and over again, tying to make sense of it.

She looked up, from time to time, staring so hard at the flowers and repeated initials on the beam above that she thought if she closed her eyes, they would still be there, printed onto her retinas. It was Nell's fault that her dad had gone, you could tell from the look on his face when he'd said goodbye; he'd looked relieved, like he'd wanted to get away.

She ruined everything.

She read for a little while, skipping from chapter to chapter, there were lots of odd stories mixed up with scientific-sounding explanations – but there was nothing connecting Elder House and these marks in particular. Nobody else seemed to know about them.

Maude dropped the book on the floor and stood up, opening the nearest dormer window as far as she could. The diamond-shaped panes of glass looked a little smoky, as if the lead was bleeding into them. She leant forward and breathed onto one, and then traced her initial into the mist. Her jagged capital *M* echoed the ones up on the beam. Maude. Maude. Maude.

In the corner of her eye, the shadows under the roof seemed to shift. But when she turned to look, there was no one there.

She found Nell sitting at the dining table with a mug of coffee, shoving her bits of glass around like they were counters in a game. She hadn't said much more once Dad had left, just given Maude a not-quite-there smile, and gone upstairs to get dressed as if everything was totally fine.

Maude wandered over, Nell was playing with the darker colours, the emerald greens, and bright leafy shades. She had arranged them like a chart, by size and depth of colour; and had picked out a couple for closer examination.

'Maude?' Nell had a funny expression on her face, she looked worried, worried and a bit cross. 'Have you been – tidying up the bathroom?'

'No.'

'Moving things around?'

'No.' She pointed to the table. 'Is that all you've got?'

Nell looked at her closely, as if she was trying to catch her out. 'Nope. There's some in the bowl, on the draining board.'

'Can I sort them?'

There was a pause and Maude wondered what it was she was supposed to have done now. Nell's phone lay abandoned on the kitchen counter, still broken.

'If you like. But keep them at the sink, yeah? Just pick out the pieces you like and put them on a tea towel.'

Nell had left all the pale pieces in the bowl. Maude ran the cold tap for a little while, for no other reason than to watch the light bounce off the glassy pebbles.

She could sort of see why Nell liked this bit so much, why – once she was done – she'd look at the order she'd created, then sweep them altogether and start again. She glanced over towards the table; Nell was drawing, her head bent over her sketch pad. The stuff she made was quite nice, she supposed, if you liked that sort of thing. And Nell had used to be all right, too, when Maude was little. She'd always been kind, friendly, without trying to get all mumsy with her, and they'd got on OK really. Then Maude had found out, about Nell, about her dad; the big secret they had all kept from her.

She didn't want to think about that right now.

She wished she could think of a way to get back at them, at her.

Maude ran her fingers through the water. There were a few quartz pebbles she had slipped in with the sea glass. She was forever trying to get Nell to use them in her pieces. She never did though. Maude picked one out, a tiny perfect egg, a pale blue-ish white, veined in grey. She put it on the window ledge and watched the lustre fade as it dried. She found a second, then a third. She picked them up and slipped them into her pocket. Nell wouldn't miss them.

She wiped her hands on her jeans and opened the kitchen door, it was cool in the shadow of the house, and the stone was damp and gritty under her bare feet. You could hear the street from here, but it was a dull far-away sound, the yard was very quiet and still. The drying ground didn't look like anyone had touched it for years and Maude edged a little closer, the skin on the back of her neck rising into goosebumps. It felt like—

'What are you up to, Maudie?' Nell was in the doorway, her arms folded, still cross.

'Nothing.' Maude edged past her stepmother back into the house.

It felt like when you played hide and seek, and you knew someone was there but you couldn't see them, you could only

130

feel them. She slid her hand into her pocket and gave one of the quartz pebbles a quick squeeze, it felt solid, real, comforting.

Nell closed the kitchen door. 'We agreed, didn't we,' she began, but Maude cut her off.

'No more climbing around on the cliff, Nell. Yes. I remember. I wasn't going to do anything.' She looked around the kitchen, she wished her dad hadn't gone off like that; he would have had a plan for the day, they'd be out somewhere by now, *doing* something.

Someone had shoved the shoebox to one side of the kettle and Maude picked it up.

She took it to the table and opened it. 'What are we going to do with this?'

'You're not supposed to be messing around with that.'

'I'm not.' Maude picked the shoe up and noticed how Nell flinched a little when she placed it in front of her. It was creased and slightly greasy looking, but the funny smell, as if it had been locked away somewhere damp for a very long time, was starting to feel familiar, comforting. 'I'm interested.'

'It's not a toy.'

'I know.' Maude pulled out a chair and sat down with a thump. 'But what are we going to do with it?'

'Nothing. It's not ours.'

'We could find out about it.'

'How?'

'The internet.'

'It's too nice a day to be staring at a screen.'

That was such a rubbish excuse. Maude thought for a moment. 'The museum, then? Evie said the museum might want it.'

'Did she?'

'When everyone was talking. She said about Ginny.'

131

'Gina.'

'We could go and see.'

'It's . . .' But Nell seemed to think again, she pushed her workbook to one side. 'OK. We could take it up and – I don't know – we could see if Gina is around, have a chat with someone.'

'Excellent.' Maude pushed her chair back, ready to go.

'But we are not keeping it, Maude. You do understand that, don't you?'

'Yes, Nell,' she said, placing the shoe back in its box, and trying to sound as though she meant it.

Nell hadn't been to the museum for years. She and Chris had never bothered to take Maude on their previous visits, reasoning that she was too young, and it would have been too much effort, tucked out of the way as it was, in the park, far from the more obvious attractions of the seafront and the harbour.

'Is this it?' Maude looked up at the building: Victorian, red brick, solid and respectable. Double wooden doors, matching brass doorknobs shiny with use.

'It is.'

Nell led the way in.

It hadn't changed a bit.

There were dinosaur skeletons fixed into the walls and surrounded by glass-topped cabinets of smaller fossils, all carefully classified. Other cases contained Iron Age flints and pottery shards, Roman glass, and medieval tiles. More held domestic objects from every conceivable era of history, or exotic items from distant lands brought back by long-forgotten sea captains.

There was a whole room dedicated to ships in bottles, and to larger, extraordinarily elaborate models, fully rigged and

132

ready to sail, while another was dedicated to the history of bathing costumes. The walls were lined with thickly varnished portraits of serious, solid men; and beneath them, more displays; jet jewellery; scientific instruments; spectacles and pocket watches; hats and gloves and bonnets.

Even the huge glass cases filled with the taxidermied birds Nell had hated so when she was a child were still in place. The whole museum was a gentleman's cabinet of curiosities.

'Do we have to pay?' Maude's voice echoed through the silence as they approached the reception desk, piled high with postcards and guidebooks, key rings and leaflets advertising summer season attractions.

'Yes,' said Nell, noting that the stuffed crocodile she remembered was still there too, raised up on its back legs, a donation box slung around its neck. 'Only residents get in for free.'

'We're residents, aren't we? And anyway, we've brought something to show them.'

'Nice try, but no,' said Nell, rummaging in her bag for her wallet, smiling apologetically at the woman behind the counter. 'We'll buy our tickets and have a look around and worry about finding Gina later.'

'Is it Gina Verrill you're after?' the woman asked as she took Nell's money.

'Well, if she's available.'

'Oh, yes.' The woman handed over their tickets and a folded leaflet. 'I'll let her know she's got visitors.'

'Thank you,' said Maude, taking possession of the leaflet, which proved to be a printed map. 'Follow me, Nell.'

They took their time; inspecting the cabinets of embroidered samplers, before moving on to examine the fading school books filled with rows of exquisite copperplate writing. Maude wandered off to look at a display of toys and Nell gravitated towards the jewellery exhibits, keeping half an eye on her stepdaughter as she darted from one glass cabinet to the next. Nell smiled; she should have thought of this before; now she was older, this was exactly the sort of thing that would keep Maude entertained for hours.

'Hello. You found us then.' Gina was standing by the desk, holding a clipboard and file, a lanyard with an ID pass strung around her neck.

'Yes,' said Nell, 'we did.'

'Hello?' Maude looked up from the dolls' house she was examining, an exact copy, Nell remembered, of the big house opposite the park. She looked from one woman to the other, expectant.

'Maude, this is Mrs Verrill, she lives in Rowan Cottage in the yard. Gina, this is Maude, my stepdaughter.'

Maude smiled. 'You'll never guess,' she said, 'what we found.'

'We shouldn't really be in here,' said Gina, 'what with you not being members, but I'm sure Mrs Agar won't tell, if you won't.'

The elderly lady sitting at a desk, working her way through an old-fashioned card index, looked up and smiled.

Maude turned to Nell. 'Did you use to come in here too?'

'No,' said Nell as she looked around the room, which was lined with bookcases, most of them locked. 'You have to be a member of the Lit and Phil to be allowed in.'

'The Literary and Philosophical Society,' said Gina, 'though who exactly is literary and who is philosophical is never very clear.'

'Like a private club?' Maude asked.

'Sort of,' said Gina, leading them to a polished oval table

placed in the centre of the room. 'Right, let's have a look at your treasure.'

Maude had insisted on carrying the shoebox inside her rucksack. Now she slid it out, handing it to Gina. Gently, Gina opened the lid and peered in.

It seemed to Nell that she hesitated a little before reaching inside and lifting out the shoe. 'We found it in the house,' she said.

'In the bedroom. In the wall,' said Maude.

'And we were just – wondering about it.'

'Well,' said Gina, softly, 'would you look at that.' She placed it on the table. 'Sheila, have you got a minute?'

'Goodness.' The old lady, Mrs Agar, made her way across the room. 'In a wall, you said?'

'Yes. On a little stone shelf.'

'So, it wasn't – lost?' Gina asked.

'No.' This hadn't occurred to Nell before, but someone must have placed the shoe on the shelf quite deliberately. 'No. I don't suppose it was.'

'What do you think?' Maude asked.

The two older women exchanged looks. 'I think I'd need to check,' said Gina.

'You could try Dr Nathan,' said Mrs Agar.

'Who's Dr Nathan?'

'Sally Nathan. She's an archaeologist; officially she's working on a project up at the abbey, but she comes in here sometimes, to use our archive.' Gina looked down at the shoe again. 'I could ask.'

'Or you could keep it,' said Nell. 'I mean, isn't it better off in a museum?'

'Easier said than done, I'm afraid,' said Gina. 'Donating something is quite a complicated process, and it's not really yours to offer, is it?'

'No. I suppose not.'

'You could leave it with me, though,' said Gina, 'and I'll see what Dr Nathan thinks.'

'No,' said Maude.

Nell turned to her. 'Hey,' she said, 'think about your tone, please.'

'Are you sure?' said Gina. 'I'd take very good care of it.'

'No.'

'Maude.'

'Sorry.' Maude leant over the table and pushed gently at the shoe, edging it further towards the centre. 'But it belongs in the house.'

'She has a point, you know,' said Gina, 'I could take some photos, then? Would that be all right, pet?'

Maude nodded but it was gone, Nell realised, the sunny relaxed mood they'd been enjoying; they were back to where they had started.

Gina seemed to sense it too. 'Good. Right. Would you like to hold it for me?' she asked Maude. 'And when we're done, I'll show you some other finds from the yard.'

Leaving Mrs Agar to her card index, they followed Gina back out to the public part of the museum, into the section dealing with the abbey.

'So,' Gina said, leading the way to a cabinet set against the wall, 'are you ready for the boring history bit?'

Maude nodded.

'Right. Well. Short version. The abbey we see today is medi-eval—'

'Gothic,' said Maude, surprising Nell. 'We went round it the other day, didn't we?'

'We did,' said Nell, 'but I didn't think you were paying attention.'

136

Maude rolled her eyes. 'More attention than you and Dad,' she said.

Gina smiled. 'Well, you are correct, Maude. But the site itself is much older than that, and once housed an earlier community, and – probably – an earlier abbey.'

'When?' asked Maude.

'Seventh century, or thereabouts, making it an Anglian community. And what we have here,' Gina continued, gesturing towards the cabinet, 'is a plan of that community. It's a bit hard to understand because we've superimposed a plan of the medieval abbey, but if you think of it being like a little village, with a church, and accommodations for the nuns and monks, and a farm, and a graveyard – they were probably quite self-sufficient.'

Nell leant in, but the map made little sense to her, blotches of grey squashed up against each other, the outline of the abbey dominating.

'And there was a wall, or a fence,' said Gina, 'or some kind of a boundary, at least. And the bit that concerns us ran parallel with the cliff edge, along here' – she pointed – 'above the yards on our street.'

'Above Bishops Yard?' Maude asked uncertainly.

'That's right,' said Gina. 'We're here. See?' She pointed to the map. 'And inside the boundary, we have the abbey, the community, and outside the boundary there's a midden. A rubbish dump. And over the years, as the rubbish piles up and the cliff erodes . . .'

'It falls down into the yards?' Nell said.

'Our yard?' said Maude.

'That's the theory, more or less.' Gina moved along to the next cabinet. 'Anyway, this is what they found, we think.'

'You think?' Nell asked.

137

'They weren't brilliant at recording how and where finds were made back then. These pieces all come from the same collector and were certainly discovered at more or less the same time, probably in the drying ground behind Elder House.'

There were a few jet beads, and some metal strap ends, one – delightfully – shaped like an owl. There were two tiny keys, and several fragments of richly coloured glass, amethyst purple and peacock blue, a few stones used to weigh spindles, a handful of pins, and part of a comb. The comb was quite a complicated thing, constructed from several pieces neatly joined and plugged together. It might have once been white but was now a grubby yellowish grey, with a pattern of faint vertical scratches running along it.

'Is that ivory?' Nell asked.

'Animal bone.'

'Gross,' said Maude.

'Clever, though.' Nell looked closer. 'They've had to make little bone pegs to hold it all in place. They've even decorated it.' The scratches weren't random, they were closely bundled together, purposeful.

'Those are runes,' said Gina. 'There's a translation next to it. And it's probably the oldest piece in the whole display.'

From the private collection of Dr F. E. Bishop.
Uncovered in Bishops Yard circa 1885

The typewritten label was held in place by yellowing Sellotape.

'Why would people chuck this stuff out?' asked Maude.

'Why do people chuck stuff out now?' said Gina. 'Because it's broken, or they don't need it anymore; or it's lost, maybe, swept up by accident when someone was cleaning out the kitchen.'

138

'Hidden?'

'Could be. Though I wouldn't like to hide anything I treasured in a rubbish bin, would you? Getting it back again would be – messy.'

'Yuck.' Maude walked around the cabinet, leaning forward to read the typed labels. 'Why did they want to go digging around in a rubbish dump?'

'Good question. I think they thought it might tell them about life in the abbey. They weren't proper archaeologists, but they were educated, interested.'

'Dr Bishop,' said Maude, 'of Bishops Yard.'

'Careful,' said Nell as Maude leant forward onto a cabinet, pressing her fingertips against the glass.

'Oh, she's fine, aren't you?' said Gina.

Maude smiled briefly in response, shifting her rucksack onto her shoulder. Inside the bag was the box, and inside the box was the shoe. Nell was obscurely disappointed that no one was willing to take it off their hands; she had half expected they might leave it in the care of the museum. She didn't really want to take it back to the house.

'I'm hungry,' said Maude, once they were back outside in the watery sunshine.

'You're always hungry,' said Nell.

'Doesn't mean it's not true.'

'We could get a snack, I suppose,' said Nell. She pointed to the street beyond the boundary of the park. 'There used to be a bakery up there. We could take a look, if you like?'

'OK.'

'We could call in at the letting agents too, show them what they've got on their hands.' Trying to make it sound normal, just another errand.

139

'Do we have to?' Maude hitched her bag up on her shoulder.

'It won't take long,' Nell said.

Maude looked at the door, which was locked, the office beyond it, dark. CLOSED. She made a point of reading the sign out loud, then smiling sweetly at Nell.

'That's odd.' Nell tried the door, but it was bolted shut. 'It's a bit early for lunch. Everyone must be – I don't know – out? Showing houses?' Business hours were painted on the glass panel of the door: *10.00 a.m. until 5.00 p.m.*

'You'll have to come back,' said Maude, 'another time.' She smiled again. 'Come on, I'm hungry.'

'Can I borrow your phone?'

'Starving, in fact.'

'Please.'

Nell keyed in the number and left a brief message, asking someone to call back, and after checking the screen for notifications – out of habit now, more than anything else, she returned the phone to Maude who dropped it into her bag.

'You'll let me know when they ring?'

'If I'm not actually dead of hunger by then.'

'Fine. Come on.'

'Was it nice,' asked Maude, as they walked up the final few steps, following the path round to the kitchen door, 'growing up by the sea?'

'I suppose so,' said Nell, 'but it felt – I don't know – a bit cut off?' She slid the key into the lock, glancing up at the drying ground. A midden, she thought, a rubbish dump; Carolyn was welcome to it.

'Is that why we don't come here much?' Maude followed her into the kitchen.

'Not exactly.'

'Then why?'

'It's a long way, and we never seem to have enough time.' Lots of reasons, Nell thought, none of them quite good enough. It was too hard, sometimes, walking through the same streets, where it seemed like nothing had changed, but of course, everything had. There were so many memories and even the happy ones were hard to bear. 'It's different now,' said Nell, 'I don't have any family to visit, and all my friends moved away.' She put their shopping on the counter, a loaf of wholemeal bread, some biscuits and a treat each. The cake Nell had chosen suddenly seemed less appealing, the familiar blue and white paper bag spotted with grease.

'You have cousins, lots of cousins.' Maude, until recently the only child of two only children, did not.

'Yes. Well, we're not close.'

Maude frowned, picking up the little envelope Nell had left on the counter. She pulled out the photos. 'Which one's your gran again?'

'This one.' Nell pointed her out. 'You've seen her before.'

Maude nodded. 'Do you remember Gina?' she asked, 'From before?'

'Everyone knows everybody here, it's that sort of town.'

'But do you?'

'No. Not really. She's a bit older than me.'

'What about her?' Maude pointed at the other woman in the photo.

'Ida? Sort of. From when I was very little. She was old-fashioned,' said Nell. 'I think she used to give me sweets when she saw me. Or money, sometimes. But I don't remember talking to her.' It was a feeling, more than a memory. She'd been a little girl, no more than four or five. A shiny ten pence piece tucked into her hand. 'When I was a kid, grown-ups – older people, like my gran's generation – were very separate from children, you know?'

Maude peered closely at the pictures. 'You look like your gran.'

'Do I?' Nell said. 'A bit, I suppose.' The same dark hair, something about the chin and mouth.

'Did she know your mum, too? Gina?'

'I think so. Maybe. My mum died when I was little. I was six.' Maude knew this story already, there were photos of Nell's mum back at home. Her mum and her dad and her grandmother, all of them gone now.

'What was she like?'

'I don't know. Pretty. Kind.' Nell had only the vaguest memory of her mother, a house at the top of a steep cobblestone path, a crowded kitchen, the windows steamed over and the smell of vegetables cooking. A young woman with long dark hair taking her by the hand and smiling down at her.

She felt it again, that familiar burst of love, punctuated by the tug of grief, missing the woman she barely remembered, wondering what she'd make of the person Nell had become.

Maude was still staring at the photos. 'And this is her mum?'

'You're very full of questions today.'

Maude pushed the photos back into the envelope. 'You never talk about her,' she said, 'you never talk about here, either.'

'Yes, well,' Nell said, 'it wouldn't mean much to you, would it? You'd only be bored.'

'If you say so.' Maude stood, dropping the photos on the table, heedless of her chair scraping the polished floorboard, 'I'm going upstairs to read.'

Nell thought about checking in with Chris, maybe even

asking if he'd moved the pregnancy test, and what he thought about getting Gina's granddaughter to babysit at the weekend. Then she realised Maude had taken her bag, her phone, the box, and the shoe upstairs with her too.

12

Her first exam was in the dining hall, and everyone gathered at their lockers putting their bags away; the rules about what they could and couldn't take in with them were displayed on pretty much every door and notice board in the building. There was a lot of murmured panic as friends compared nerves, competing – or so it seemed to Kym – to be the most unprepared for the ordeal ahead. She could see Evie Wilson shoving her bag up onto a shelf, picking up a pencil case, then slamming her locker door shut. As she did, something fine and vivid slithered to the floor, briefly catching the light as Evie turned and headed down the corridor. No one else seemed to notice.

Kym caught up with her just as the dining hall doors were opened.

'Hey,' she said, tapping Evie gently on the elbow, 'you dropped this.'

'Oh.'

It was a silver shoe, a ballet slipper, on a thin red ribbon. Kym held it up and it danced in the air.

Evie held out her hand. 'Thanks,' she said, and Kym released the makeshift bracelet, letting it pool into Evie's palm.

They all had them, of course. Lucky charms, dangling from bags and pencil cases, or hanging from a necklace, hidden beneath a school shirt and tie.

'Not that you need it,' said Kym.

'Well.' Evie tucked the slipper into her pocket. 'It can't hurt, right?'

'I suppose.'

'You mean you've not brought anything with you?'

Kym lifted her pencil case – transparent as per the rules, as if they were all going through airport security or something – and shook it, rattling around in the bottom there was a piece of flint. It was flat and grey, shaped liked an arrowhead and worn smooth by the sea, with a natural hole running through it, about the size of the tip of her little finger. 'My gran,' she said, as if that explained everything. 'I've had it for years.'

It had been that last summer between primary and big school. They'd been for a walk on the Long Sands and Gina had found the stone, wiping it clean and insisting Kym keep it with her for luck. She'd dropped it into her school bag when she'd got home, and every time since, when she'd transferred all her stuff to a new bag, she had picked it up and thought about chucking it away. She never had, though, always dropping it in at the last moment with all her usual bits and pieces. This morning she'd made a point of hiding it away inside the pencil case.

'A rock,' said Evie. 'Nice.'

'It's a hagstone,' said Kym. 'If you look through them you can see into the other world.'

Evie looked sceptical. 'And can you?'

Kym smiled. 'If I can, it looks disturbingly like this one.'

People were moving past them, taking their places. Among them, Kym couldn't help noticing, was Tyler, swaggering the length of the room with his mates, laughing loudly, and very obviously not looking in her direction.

She watched for a moment, waiting for him to turn and catch her eye, to yell something funny or irritating. But he held his nerve, and she felt foolish for expecting anything else; it was what she wanted, after all.

'I suppose we'd better get on, then,' said Evie, following Kym's gaze as Ty pulled out his chair and took his place. 'Good luck.'

Kym went to her own seat, took a deep breath, and tried to concentrate.

'Right. Time's up, stop writing, please.' Ms Roberts, the invigilator stood, smiling slightly at the collective sigh as everyone sat back and began to exchange sheepish grins.

Kym had to suppress the urge to yawn, she felt odd, a bit light headed. She'd glanced up once or twice, just to check how Ty was doing, but he was too far forward for her to see properly, and after a while, absorbed in her own work, she had forgotten to look.

She hung back at her desk, unpacking and repacking her pencil case until he was well out of the way, as people drifted past, getting ready to compare horror stories, no doubt.

By the time she got out of the room, the corridor was full, and Kym let herself be carried along with the crowd, to the lockers first, then when she'd picked up her bag, back down the corridor, through the double doors and out into the pale sunshine.

She felt lighter, freer, now she was outside, and not even catching another brief glimpse of Tyler at the centre of a group of lads, all loudly whooping and shoving each other around, could spoil her mood. He caught her eye, grinned, and it took a ridiculous effort on her part to pretend she hadn't seen him. The sudden lurch she felt when she caught sight of him was habit, nothing more, she told herself as she walked away. They were done.

As she turned the corner, she was surprised to see Evie Wilson head down, fiddling with the earbuds for her phone, her usual gang of friends nowhere in sight.

On impulse, Kym made an effort to catch up, 'Hey, how did it go?'

'Oh. Hi.' Evie pulled a face, halfway between a grimace and a grin. 'OK, I suppose. You?'

'Same.' Kym fell into step with her as if they walked home from school together all the time. 'Nothing that sitting the real thing next year won't put right.'

'God, don't. I can't even imagine . . .' Evie's voice trailed away. 'My mum, you know?' she said.

'Yeah, well, I can guess,' said Kym. 'Mine's just as bad.'

'Really?'

'Yeah.' They walked towards the traffic lights at the bottom of the hill; ahead of them, on the other side of the road, strolling past the park, were Marnie, Lauren, Sophie and Grace – Evie's usual crowd. The lights changed and Kym glanced at Evie who seemed to be very determined not to notice her friends. 'I've told her the exams don't matter,' she went on, 'that it's next year that really counts, but she won't have it.' It was an exaggeration, of course, Kate wasn't that bad.

'No. Nor will mine. Dad's OK, he's a bit more laid-back, you know. But she—'

Deep in her bag, Kym's phone buzzed. 'Sorry,' she said, rummaging inside, and as she stopped, Evie stopped too, seemingly unbothered that she had no chance now of catching up with her mates. Kym wondered what might be going on there. 'Missed call,' she said, when she finally laid hands on her mobile. 'Ty.' Not so cool, after all.

148

'Oh, right. Do you want to call him back?'

'God, no.' Kym frowned at the screen, then dropped the phone back inside her backpack. 'He really needs to get over himself.' She looked up at Evie. 'We split up,' she said.

'Oh.' Evie looked embarrassed. 'I didn't realise.'

'No reason why you should,' said Kym, 'it's no big deal.'

'Isn't it? Haven't you been going out, like, forever?'

'No.' Kym tried to look offended. 'Only a year, well, two years. We were just mates before that.' There were photos at home, picnics and birthday parties, stretching back as far as nursery school. She and Ty had known each other their whole lives, had been best friends for as long as she could remember.

'It must be – weird – not being around him anymore.'

'Yeah,' said Kym. 'But it's not like . . .' She slowed her pace, trying to work out how much she wanted to say. 'I want to go to uni, you know? Get on. Get out. Tyler doesn't. He's staying on to keep his dad happy, but honestly, he's just marking time until he can go and work with his uncle. He reckons he'll set him up with some sort of apprenticeship.'

'That doesn't mean you have to split though, does it? There's holidays, and once you get your degree you can live where you want.'

'You sound like him.'

'Sorry.'

Kym smiled. 'Anyway. Who the hell marries their first boyfriend?'

'Or their cousin.' Evie's expression was deadpan.

'Unfounded rumour, Evie. I'm shocked.' They crossed the road. 'Anyway, find me a lad I'm not related to in this town. If you go far enough back, we're all bloody cousins. My mum's pleased, though. She likes Tyler well enough, but she was starting to get this look on her face whenever I was late getting

149

in, like she was worried I was going to get pregnant and fuck everything up. Which is a bit rich, if you ask me, but there you go.' She took a breath, grinned. 'So, what about you?'

'Sorry?'

'Are you seeing anyone? Dating?' She managed to put inverted commas around the question.

'Oh, God, no.' Evie was actually blushing.

They turned the corner and the bridge came into view. In the distance the girls, Marnie and Sophie and the others were indulging in a round of goodbye hugs before going their separate ways. 'There was someone, but I kind of got it wrong and things didn't really work out.'

'Yeah? Who?'

'Someone at my last school.'

'Right,' said Kym. '*That* sort of boyfriend.'

Evie rolled her eyes. 'So it's definitely off, then?' she said. 'You and Tyler?'

'Definitely,' said Kym. Almost definitely.

The town was beginning to fill up, even though the schools weren't out yet. You could always spot the tourists, they seemed to take up too much space, to walk too slowly. The milder weather had brought them out, clotting the streets.

'What are you going to do,' Kym asked as they crossed the bridge, 'in the summer?'

'Do?'

'Yeah. A job? I've been let off a bit, because of revision, but once term ends . . .'

'Oh,' said Evie. 'Yes.' Except of course things were different for her, it was written all over her face. They'd go off somewhere on holiday, the Wilsons, somewhere warm, somewhere beautiful. Of course they would.

'My gran keeps going on about a friend of hers who runs a

150

cleaning business, you know, holiday lets and all that. She's looking for someone. Five pounds an hour.' Evie clearly couldn't tell if this was a bad or a good thing. Kym didn't bother to enlighten her.

In another life, they might have been friends, she thought. If Evie's mum and dad hadn't sent her off to her posh school, if Kym's gran had been more . . . forgiving. It was odd that they had the yard in common, but knew so little about each other. The only thing she knew for certain about Evie was that she felt sorry for her. Her mum was a pain in the arse, and clearly now there was something going on between her and her mates. 'Right then,' she said. 'I'll see you, I suppose.'

'Actually,' said Evie, rummaging in her bag. 'If I give you my number, then, if you hear of anything, any jobs, you could let me know?'

'OK,' said Kym, a little surprised. 'Sure.'

Evie rattled off her number and Kym keyed it into her phone, sending a text, just the single word: *Hi.*

Evie's phone buzzed softly. 'And if you get fed up of revising, we can always hang out?' she went on. 'You know, if you feel like it.'

And the thing was, she seemed OK, despite her parents, and the private school. There was something sweet and slightly awkward about the offer, as if they were both back in primary school, as if they might have a chance to be friends after all. The summer stretched out threateningly beyond exams. There'd be a job of some description, but no one to talk to – not with Ty out of the picture – no one to listen. 'Sure,' Kym said.

It might be useful too, getting to know Evie Wilson a bit better.

'OK. So. I'll see you around.'

'Yeah, see you.'

Kym watched Evie walk up the street and turn into the yard. Apart from anything else, Carolyn Wilson would definitely be pissed off.

13

'I don't see,' said Maude, 'why I have to have a babysitter when I'm not actually a baby.'

'I know,' said Nell, 'but I couldn't leave you here on your own.' She was trying to do her make-up, only there wasn't enough light in the bathroom; her face in the mirror had an alarming greenish cast to it, and Maude was blocking the doorway. 'Think of it as having a friend over.'

Maude brightened at this. 'Could I ask Evie, then?'

'Is Evie your friend?'

'She says hello when we see her in the yard.' They'd bumped into her a few times over the past week. When she was on her way to the beach, more often than not, tugging Flossie along on her lead.

'Does that really count?' Nell fumbled with her eyeliner, frowning. When had everything become an obstacle race; overcoming Maude's objections, rationalising decisions, suggesting compromises.

'People usually get to choose their friends for themselves.'

'Another time,' Nell said. 'You can invite Evie over another time.' She might even say yes, she seemed like a nice girl, thoughtful. 'Did you check your phone?' she asked. 'Were there any messages for me?'

'No.'

She should check, for herself, she knew, but she wasn't about

153

to get involved in another argument about rules and boundaries and privacy, another time, maybe, when Maude was in a better mood.

'What's she like?' Maude asked.

'Who?'

'Kym?'

'I don't know. Nice.'

'Oh,' said Maude. 'Good. Glad to see you checked her out properly.'

Maude went upstairs. Her phone lay on the bed, but a quick tap on the screen revealed that, as usual, there was barely a signal. Her growing collection of shells and pebbles, the quartz ones she liked so much, was crowding the window ledges. She went round the room, checking they were all in place, arranged just the way she liked, before retrieving the shoebox from its hiding place under the bed.

She knew she wasn't supposed to mess around with the shoe; that was one of the conditions about keeping it up in the attic. She wasn't supposed to touch it, because it was old, fragile, important, but she couldn't help it. And after all, she wasn't doing any harm. She opened the box and lay down on her bunk, balancing the shoe on her belly.

She lay still for a moment or two, trying to imagine how it might have looked when it was new, when it still had its twin and had been used, worn by someone's child.

Maude closed her eyes and tried to imagine the child – a little boy, she decided, for no real reason at all – running through the house. The soft leather shoes padding over the flagstones in the kitchen, the toes scuffing as he stumbled up the wooden stairs. She began to wonder again if Nell would notice if she sneaked the shoe into her bag when they left; if there was any

154

way she could hide it from both Nell and her dad. There had been two messages so far from the woman in the letting agency. Maude had listened to them both before quietly deleting them. It wasn't her fault, she decided, that her phone signal was so rubbish here.

Nell's voice on the landing below startled her, and when she opened her eyes, there was someone in the corner of the room, watching her. She sat up abruptly, and the shadows resolved themselves into one of the unused bunks, its pillows piled up and crumpled. No one there after all. Looking down, she found that she was clutching the shoe in one hand. The leather was warm and she was glad she had hold of it. It was like the marks on the beam; it made her feel safe.

'Hi. Maude?'

Maude put the shoe back in its box, gave it a minute, then peered down from the attic.

The babysitter didn't really look like a babysitter; she was wearing lots of make-up and she had thick black hair, too black to be natural. She was wearing skinny jeans and a sweat shirt, and inky blue nail polish.

'This is Kym, sweetheart, she's going to . . . keep you company this evening.'

Nell was wearing lots of make-up too, for her, and a dress, something a bit clingy and the colour of violets. The dress was expensive, but she'd had it a while, and it looked to Maude to be getting a bit tight. She'd piled her hair up on top of her head; she was looking pretty, but anxious. And she wore shoes with spiked heels – they didn't look comfortable at all.

'Hi.'

'Do you want to come down?'

'If I must.'

Nell led the way into the living room and Maude could see Kym taking it all in, but trying to look casual about it, her gaze travelling around the room, across the bookshelves and along the beams. 'I'm hungry,' Maude said, 'are we going to eat soon?'

'There's pizza on the way,' Nell said, 'if you want to come and help set the table.'

They all trooped into the kitchen, with Nell pointing out the obvious, back door, kettle, fridge, and Kym nodding along.

'This is very good of you,' she said, as if Kym was doing her a favour instead of being paid for the evening. 'I'll have Maude's phone with me if you need—'

'You can't,' said Maude, 'the battery's flat.'

'Honestly, Maude—'

'I can ring my gran if I need to,' said Kym. 'Or the Yacht Club? Would that be OK?' As if now Nell was the one doing Kym a favour.

'Sure,' Nell said. 'Yes. OK.'

The party was large enough, informal enough for her late arrival to go unremarked upon, and Nell was grateful for that, at least. She hadn't wanted to leave the house until she was sure Maude was settled, and there was even a bit of her, she suspected, that didn't really want to go to the party at all.

It wasn't that she wanted to avoid anyone, but now Chris had abandoned her she couldn't imagine finding anyone she'd be happy to spend the whole evening with. There was a reason she'd lost touch with people; she'd grown up, moved on, and so had they. You didn't have to stay in the same town your whole life, for God's sake, especially not one like this – small, insular, quaint. She could barely remember why they'd accepted the invitation in the first place.

She stood at the doorway of the Yacht Club's first-floor function room, clutching a bulky gift bag, feeling very alone, and slightly foolish.

There was a bar running the length of the room and, at the far end, French windows that opened out onto a shallow balcony. Opposite the bar a buffet had been laid out and in one corner, a young man stood behind some record decks. It was all unnervingly reminiscent of school discos, and as if on cue an old Robbie Williams track kicked in.

Bloody Chris, she thought.

Maude clearly wasn't happy about the whole babysitting thing, and Kym could hardly blame her. They were sharing a huge pizza, with Maude ignoring the bowl of salad Nell had placed on the table to accompany it, and answering Kym's well-meant questions with single words and the occasional eye roll. It was going to be a long night. Nell had told Kym to help herself to anything she might fancy in the fridge, but she wasn't sure if that meant the wine in the door. Probably not – not with her being all responsible.

Her phone buzzed and she pulled it out of her pocket. It was Ty again. She lay the phone on the table and watched as it shuddered its way towards voicemail and silence.

'Who's that?' Maude asked, craning her neck to get a better look at the caller ID. 'He's fit. Is he your boyfriend?'

'Ex-boyfriend.'

'Really? Did he dump you? You must be gutted. Is that why you didn't want to go to the party?'

'Excuse me,' said Kym, playing up the outrage. 'I dumped him.'

Maude snorted. 'Yeah, right,' she said, then, 'Really? Why, though?'

'None of your business.' Stifling a smile, Kym picked up another slice of pizza.

Maude sighed theatrically. 'People never want to talk about interesting stuff,' she said.

'Private,' said Kym, 'it's private, OK?'

'Did you go out with him for a long time?'

'Long enough.'

Maude was staring at her thoughtfully. 'I'm not allowed to pierce my ears yet,' she said. 'It's so not fair.'

'Oh.' Kym raised her free hand to her ear, slightly thrown by this sudden change of subject. 'Well, what can you do?' she said. 'They always expect you to be so reasonable about the things they say you can't have.' She looked around the kitchen, trying to be casual. 'I mean, you can argue about it, but that only makes things worse – like it's proof you're immature or something.' They had taken the old house and tried to open it up by knocking a wall through. You saw it all the time, of course, people making improvements bit by bit, priding themselves on retaining period features, the character of a place, barely aware that with every inconvenience they removed, every decision they made, they were obliterating history.

But here, it was as if underneath the renovations the house was still – itself, solid and unchanging. The bare floors were cold with a suggestion of damp, the leaded windows lent the whole interior a grey-green light that wasn't entirely healthy. And there was a weird smell.

She almost laughed. Ty would completely take the piss if he could hear her. She wondered how she might get the kid to show her around.

'Yeah.' Maude looked pleased. 'I mean, like tonight, I could have kicked off about Nell going off and leaving me behind.

158

Or about you – I would have been fine on my own, and anyway, I was going to ask Evie over.'

'Evie Wilson?'

'Do you know her?'

'Yeah.'

'Only she wouldn't let me.'

'Nell?'

'I could have made a fuss though, if I'd wanted.'

'But then you just come off as immature. Again.'

'Exactly.' Maude turned her attention to the last of her pizza.

'It won't be any fun, you know,' said Kym, 'the party; just a bunch of people talking, and old blokes dad dancing all over the place.' She almost felt sorry for the kid.

'Hmm.' Maude crammed the last bit of crust into her mouth, then pushed her empty plate away. 'Do you want dessert?'

Kym's stomach groaned. 'In a bit,' she said. 'We could watch a DVD, if you like?' There was a shelf in the living room, Kym had noticed, filled with the usual holiday-let stuff, friendly-family fare, and the odd rom-com.

'I've seen them all.'

'Oh. Right.' Kym started clearing the table, gathering up their plates and taking them to the sink. It was weird, seeing the bankside from this perspective, its shadows lengthening in the evening light; the house was much closer to the cliff than her gran's cottage, too close, claustrophobic.

Kym picked up the untouched salad and placed it inside the fridge 'So, what do you want to do?' she asked, conscious of the little jolt she felt – anticipation, perhaps. Or fear.

Nell was clutching a glass of sparkling water and standing by the bar as she chatted to David and his wife, Jenny. They had covered work, and then kids, and Chris's apologies, before they were joined by new arrivals and David moved the conversation on to sailing. Nell took a sip of her drink, her back was aching and her shoes pinched and she wondered if she might slip away and find a seat.

She was looking around the room when a middle-aged woman approached, smiling anxiously; Nell straightened up and fixed her own smile in place. 'Cheryl.' The right name came to her at the last moment. 'It is Cheryl, isn't it?' Her cousin.

'Nell. I thought it was you.' Cheryl pulled her into a hug. 'We've got a table, come and sit with us.'

It was surprisingly easy to fall into conversation, and easier still when first Cheryl's husband, Ben, then her daughter, Nancy, joined the table. Nancy took it upon herself to point out several of the half-familiar faces around the room, offering an inventive running commentary on them, and Nell could feel the knot in her stomach, the anxiety she'd been trying to ignore all day, gradually unravelling. This was fine, she'd stay for a couple of hours then make her excuses and leave.

Cheryl leant forward. 'I heard you're staying in Bishops Yard.' Nell knew better than to be surprised, that everyone in town knew everyone's business was a given. 'That's right,' she said. 'Elder House, right at the top.'

'Really?' Cheryl widened her eyes. 'Rather you than me.'

Ben smiled, 'Don't you start,' he said.

'Am I missing something?' Nell looked around the table.

'Nothing,' said Ben, 'nothing at all. Just some daft ghost story made up for tourists.'

'Tourists and incomers,' said Nancy, taking a sip of her drink. 'Do you remember that bloke who did the ghost walk? He'd take people up the yard and onto the steps and with no thought that it might upset Gina.'

'Gina?' said Nell.

'Standing there in his top hat and tails, going on about how Elder House has never been at peace. Like he'd know anything about the place at all.' Nancy glared at her mother. 'And which everyone knows is a load of nonsense. Anyway, they put a stop to it, said it was an invasion of privacy.'

'Who did?' said Nell.

But before Nancy could reply, Nell became aware of a familiar figure cutting through the crowd: Carolyn, closely followed by a man Nell didn't recognise – her husband, no doubt. She caught Nell's eye and waved. Nancy picked up her empty glass and grinned apologetically at Nell. 'Who do you think?' she said. 'He can't have known, but even so, you'd think he'd bother to check.' She stood up. 'Drink?'

Nell shook her head. 'No. I'm fine with this, thanks.'

'OK, well, good luck.' Nancy turned and headed towards the bar, saying hello to the Wilsons as she went, but not breaking her stride.

Carolyn bent down to hug Nell as the man claimed one of the empty seats at the table. 'Well, this is . . .' Carolyn looked around the room, then sat in the chair Nancy had left vacant, pulling it closer. 'This is all very nice.'

Nell decided to take the comment at face value. 'It is, isn't it?'

'Ollie, this is Nell, Nell, this is my husband, Oliver.'

'Nice to meet you.' Oliver extended a hand. He looked pleasant enough, solid, stocky, with red hair and freckles.

Carolyn scanned the room. 'Where's Chris?'

'He couldn't make it,' said Nell.

'Oh?'

'He had to go back to the gallery to deal with some work stuff.'

'That sounds serious,' said Carolyn.

'It's not. It's really not,' said Nell. 'He'll be back in a couple of days.'

'You should come to us for dinner,' said Carolyn.

'There's really no need—'

'Supper, then. I insist. Maude too. We can't have the two of you rattling around that old house all on your own and we'd love to have you, wouldn't we, Oliver?'

'Of course.'

'I need to . . . check.'

'Tomorrow? Please. I hate it when people are vague and never make proper plans.'

'Well. Yes. Great. Thank you.'

Cheryl picked up her drink and Nell found she couldn't quite meet her cousin's eye. 'That's very kind of you,' she said to Carolyn. 'Thanks.'

'It'll be fun.' Satisfied, Carolyn took a deep breath and continued to look around the room.

'We were just talking,' said Cheryl, 'about that bloke who used to do the ghost walk.'

'Oh.' Carolyn wrinkled her nose in distaste. 'Him.'

'Funny way to make a living,' said Oliver, 'I can't imagine there's much money in it.'

'It was all very – theatrical,' Carolyn said to Nell. 'He dressed up as a Victorian gentleman, top hat and cane and – but honestly, it was ridiculous, superstitious nonsense, with people traipsing up and down the yard at all hours.'

'Hardly that,' said Oliver, 'I don't think he meant any harm. Gina Verrill said—'

'Gina,' said Carolyn, 'is just as bad.'

'Really?' Nell couldn't help herself, 'in what way?'

Carolyn looked around the table. 'Oh, it's nothing,' she said, 'only, she does like to play the wise woman, doesn't she? With her garden and her herbs, and her remedies—'

'I suppose she is a bit of a kitchen witch,' said Oliver, 'but then—'

'It's just so irritating,' said Carolyn, 'the way she tries to tell people what's good for them all the time, as if she knows best.'

An awkward silence spread around the table.

'Oh, look,' Carolyn said, tapping Oliver gently on the wrist, and nodding towards a tall middle-aged man at the centre of a family group. 'Is that Peter Chappell over there? I didn't know he was coming up for this, and there's Laura, too; we should go and say hello.'

'Good God, woman, we only just sat down,' said Oliver.

'Well, how often do we see him these days?' said Carolyn, standing. 'Come on, five minutes, just to be polite.'

Nell sipped her water and watched as the two of them crossed the dance floor, Oliver following his wife, the whole room ebbing and shifting around them.

'She doesn't change, does she?' said Cheryl.

'I wouldn't know,' said Nell, 'to be honest, I don't really remember her. From school, I mean.'

Cheryl looked at her thoughtfully. 'Do you not? Mind you – she was in my year, and I was the year behind you, so maybe you wouldn't.'

'What was she like?'

'Oh, like I said, she doesn't change.' Cheryl picked up her drink. 'She was always a little bit full of herself, maybe. Always keen to hang out with the cool kids.'

Nell watched as Carolyn and Oliver negotiated a complicated round of greetings and introductions. 'Right.'

'Don't listen to me,' said Cheryl, 'there's no harm in her, and

163

he seems all right too. It's just that she was always one of those girls who wanted to be – let in, I suppose. And she never could take no for an answer.'

Kym didn't like Maude's room; she couldn't have said why, exactly, but everything felt odd, off.

It started with the climb up the little ladder, perhaps. There was something about the angle of it, the way the treads were set a bit too close, a bit too steep; or maybe it was the way you just sort of emerged into the room, head first, with that funny gap between the last step and the attic floorboards.

The ceiling seemed to pitch too sharply, and at the far end of the room the red brick chimney stack clung precariously to the wall. It was almost as if no improvement could reach here; the idea struck her again, more forcefully this time, it was as if the house still possessed its stubborn, untouched essence.

'This is – nice.' Kym sat down on one of the bunks, the one opposite Maude's.

'Are you all right?'

'Fine.' It was just a room, a plain, whitewashed attic.

'You're not going to throw up, are you?'

Kym smiled. 'I'm supposed to be the one looking after you.'

Maude rolled her eyes, 'Oh, please,' she said.

Nell made her way to the buffet and picked up a plate. She wasn't hungry, but she didn't feel like sitting down, making polite conversation. As she slowly worked her way along the table, not finding herself tempted by anything on display, she was relieved to see someone else, a man she didn't recognise, join her cousin. Introductions were made and he took Nell's empty seat, leaning across to say something to Cheryl that made her smile.

164

'You've escaped, then?' Gina was standing at the end of the buffet, a platter of fresh sandwiches in one hand.

'For a bit.'

Gina considered the spread in front of her, then rearranged a couple of plates, making space for the one she held. 'There,' she said. 'It's not pretty, but it'll do.'

'Did you do all this?' It was impressive, the sheer amount of food, carefully arranged and portioned, but the thought of eating made Nell feel dizzy, sick.

'Goodness, no. We all did a bit – I just told Jenny I'd help keep an eye on things. Tidy away empty plates, bring out fresh stuff when it's needed. There's the same amount again, stacked up in the kitchen.'

'I didn't realise I was supposed to bring something. No one said.'

'Oh, don't you worry about that, love. There's more than enough.' Gina nodded towards the empty plate Nell was holding. 'Are you not going to use that?'

'Actually,' said Nell, 'I don't think I am.' She put the plate down; she shouldn't have come. 'I don't have a phone at the moment,' she went on, 'but Kym knows to ring you if – if she gets worried or anything. I hope that's all right.'

'Of course it is.'

'Sorry. I'm not usually so – anxious.' She looked at the table, and suddenly she didn't know why she'd come out, what she'd been thinking of. She shouldn't have left them alone in the house.

'This is so strange,' she said, looking around the room, 'everyone looks so familiar, but then – not. I'm not really sure who's who. I'm not really sure why I'm here.'

'Did you see the photos in the foyer?' Gina asked.

'I don't think I did.'

Gina smiled. 'Come on, then,' she said.

There were two large easels set up at the far end of the corridor, between the stairs and the ladies' loos; they were covered in family photographs.

There was the wedding that Nell half-remembered, a formal portrait of David and Jenny, she looking remarkably glamorous, he young, handsome and happy, surrounded by all their guests. It only took a few seconds for her to find herself, and Gran and her dad.

'Jenny asked people to dig out their own pictures for them.'

'Really? I didn't . . .' The truth, when it occurred to her, left her a little deflated. 'They didn't think I'd come, did they? They just sent the invitation to be polite.'

'I expect they thought you'd be too busy.'

'I expect so.' It was foolish, she thought, to feel so left out, when it was entirely her own fault for staying away for so long.

Nell leant forward, looking more closely at the group photograph. She'd kept her gran and her father waiting while she was trying to get her hair right, her dad by the front door, yelling at her to get a move on. The expression on his face when she'd finally gone downstairs, though, in the new Top Shop dress her gran had insisted on buying her, and her strappy sandals. 'Look at you,' he'd said, smiling, extending an arm in an exaggerated gesture of chivalry.

He'd not lived to see her marry Chris.

There were other photos too, some of the faces were familiar, many more were not. Her gran would have been able to name everyone, of course.

'Are you here?' Nell asked.

'There.' Gina was standing next to a tall bespectacled man,

166

he in a dark blue suit, she in a pale green floral dress, a large hat half obscuring her face. 'We'd only been married a few months ourselves.'

'I don't remember meeting you,' said Nell.

'I'm not surprised, pet. We must have seemed very old and settled to a teenage girl.'

'Is Carolyn here?'

'I'm not sure.'

Nell stood back for a moment. The rest of the display was taken up with more informal pictures, and the same faces kept reappearing, holding babies; holiday snaps, Christmases, anniversaries. The faces grew older, and, gradually, some faces vanished.

'When did you last visit?' Gina asked.

'Oh, about a year after Dad's funeral, probably.' Six, seven years ago.

'That's a while.'

'Yes. Well.' Nell cleared her throat, moved on to the next easel. 'We were in Exeter by then, and there was work to worry about.' She smiled sadly. 'There's always work. The last time – it wasn't the same, without my gran, without my dad. I kept expecting to . . . And then of course, there's nowhere to stay. It's not . . . home . . .' Her voice trailed away.

She had seen them everywhere, that was the trouble, in the pubs, walking along the beach or down the street. Then there had been the well-wishers, people stopping to chat, to ask how she was, curious glances flickering over Chris and little Maude; they were married by the time they made that last visit. Her father was gone, and that was unbearable.

'After a while, it didn't seem like we had a reason to come back,' Nell said, 'and then – time passed, you know?'

'I do, pet.'

167

Nell turned her attention back to the photographs. 'Is that her?'

'Carolyn, you mean?' Gina squinted at the image, 'it could be, I suppose.' The picture appeared to have been taken at some sort of party, there were children – teenagers, really, sitting around a table, and behind them, a handful of adults.

'That's your gran, there.' Gina pointed to an older woman, caught in profile, saying something to the woman next to her. 'And that's Ida.'

She was wearing a floral blouse tucked into a dark skirt, her grey hair pinned up away from her face, the smiling young woman in Nell's photograph seemed to have vanished. 'Maude was asking about her, but I couldn't – what was she like?'

Gina thought for a moment. 'She was the sort of person everybody knew. People would go to her, for – help, advice and – things. Even remedies, you know, instead of going to the doctor for a prescription.' Gina hesitated. 'I heard a rumour once that when she was young – that girls would go to her if they got into trouble – back when they would have had no choice.'

Nell's eyes widened, 'Really?'

Gina nodded. 'It was a different world,' she said. 'Hard.'

'I sort of remember her from being little, but I don't really remember her being a particular friend of my gran. Certainly not in later life.'

'Well, people move on, don't they? They change jobs, or get married, they outgrow each other. And she could be difficult, if you crossed her. I always thought there was something – inflexible about her.'

Nell looked closer. In front of Ida was Carolyn Wilson – Nell was certain it was her – grinning confidently at the camera. 'Were they related, then? Carolyn and Ida?'

'I don't think so. But once Carolyn's mother left . . .' Gina glanced at her. 'You'll not remember that, then? The poor lass's mum just upped and left when she was, what, twelve years old?'

'No. I didn't – I didn't know that.'

'Well, Ida helped out for a while, I know that much. She meant well, I suppose, even if she was a bit set in her ways.'

Nell looked at the photos again, trying to remember, but any solid recollection of Ida, or of the girl Carolyn Wilson had been, remained frustratingly out of reach.

'Are you glad you came home?' Gina asked.

The question took Nell by surprise. 'It's not been – what I expected,' she said, 'and it's not ideal, Chris being called away. Parties are much more his sort of thing.'

'When's he due back?'

'I'm not sure. It seems to depend on some meeting. But a couple of days, I hope.'

They'd spoken that afternoon; the conversation had been short and self-consciously upbeat. The longer he stayed away, the less they seemed to have to say to each other.

'I should have gone back with him, really. Only it took such an effort to get here, and there's Maude . . .' Other people had brought their kids, Nell had noticed, although she hadn't recognised any of them, or any of their parents, come to that. But even so, she should have made more of an effort to persuade Maude to change her mind.

Nell might have said more, but the door to the function room opened suddenly as two young women exploded into the corridor, one of them brandishing a packet of cigarettes as they giggled their way downstairs. The music seemed to swell in their wake and suddenly Nell felt foolish; she barely knew Gina, after all.

'No,' she said, 'ignore me. I'm just being – I miss Chris a bit more than I thought I would, that's all.'

'Well, if you're sure,' said Gina. 'I should go. I said I'd sort out the cake.'

'I'll come and help,' said Nell.

'You will do no such thing,' said Gina. 'Get yourself back into that party. Go and catch up with a few people.'

Maude had made herself at home. Her clothes were strewn over the beds and the little chair in the corner. She was using a pine trunk as a dressing table and it was covered in all sorts of random bits and pieces – hair clips and junk jewellery and shells off the beach, lip balm and a scented body spray. There was even a tiny toy soldier, slumped on his side, his painted redcoat peeling. Her phone lay abandoned on the bed, its screen dark and smeary.

They had opened the windows, Maude taking particular care not to dislodge her collection of pebbles, but the room was still stuffy and there was something else too. It took Kym a moment to place it, it was as if they had just snuffed out a candle and the wick was still smouldering.

'Don't you mind it?' she asked, 'being a bit – cut off from the rest of the house?'

'That's sort of the point,' said Maude.

'Do they not get on, your dad and Nell?'

'I suppose so.' Maude sat on the bed. 'But sometimes – I just want to be left alone.'

'Fair enough.'

'You could stay over, if you like,' said Maude.

'What? Here?' Kym looked around the room. 'Wouldn't they mind? Your mum and dad?'

'Nell's not my mum.'

'Yeah, sorry.'

'Here.' On the floor, propped up against the trunk, there was a small mirror, with a couple of snapshots pushed into the frame. Maude pulled one of them free. 'That's her, my real mum.'

The woman in the picture was smiling, and she had her arms around a little girl, five or six years old, but still definitely Maude; all chubby arms and frizzy hair.

'She looks nice,' said Kym. 'What happened?'

Maude took the picture and concentrated on sliding it back in place. 'They split up.'

'And you stayed with your dad?'

'Mostly. I mean – I go and stay with her too.'

The other photo was the two of them, her dad and the mum, smiling like neither of them knew what was coming.

'My dad's dead,' said Kym.

Maude turned to look at her, her eyes wide. 'Oh.'

'Yeah.' She didn't talk about it as a rule, and she never just blurted it out like that – she wasn't really sure why she'd mentioned it now. Maybe to get Maude on side a bit, maybe so she'd know it wasn't so unusual not to have both parents around. Maybe because he was on her mind these days, because he felt so – close.

She could see Maude struggling with what to say next, her curiosity battling with her good manners.

'He died before I was born,' said Kym. 'It's just been my mum and me ever since I can remember.' Probably best, she decided, to leave it at that for now.

'I'm sorry,' said Maude.

'Yeah. Me too.'

'They took me out of school early,' said Maude, abruptly. 'We're supposed to say it's because we're on holiday. But actually, it's the other way around, we're on holiday because I'm not in school.'

171

'Oh.' This was unexpected. 'Why's that, then?'

'I'm not supposed to say.' Maude looked anxious, suddenly. 'There was a big meeting at school and – we're supposed to be moving on.' The phrase didn't sound natural, and Kym had the impression that it was something Maude had heard, probably more than once. 'I'm going back, though, in September.'

She didn't sound too happy about that and Kym could imagine why; she felt an unexpected rush of sympathy. 'You're lucky, to have all this to yourself,' she said, looking around the attic. 'It's – cool.'

'It's not ours, though,' said Maude.

'It is for now.'

Maude thought for a moment. And Kym had the sense that the kid was trying to come to some sort of decision. 'Do you want to see something *really* cool?' she said.

14

'It's good, isn't it?'

The problem was there was no overhead lighting, so they'd had to clear the trunk, pull it into position underneath the beam and then Kym had climbed onto it. Standing on her toes, she'd even attempted to take a few pictures.

'Kym?'

'What?'

'No one else knows about them.' Maude frowned. 'I mean, I don't *think* anyone else knows about them.'

'You haven't told your – Nell or your dad?'

'No.'

'Why not?'

'Dunno. It's my room, not theirs. And they're all weird with me now. Like they can't leave me alone, and – I just want something for myself. That's all right, isn't it?'

Kym sat next to Maude on the bed, scrolling through the pictures. She'd thought there was only one mark on the beam at first, some workman carving his initials *MM*, bold and crude, and not much to get excited over. But he'd repeated it over and over again, then, further along, she'd noticed another design, more abstract this time.

'That one looks like a flower,' said Maude.

'Yes.' It was simple enough, a circle, and inside the circle six narrow ellipses, petals. Kym looked up at the ceiling again. It

173

was dark outside now, properly dark, and the lamps up here weren't really strong enough, but there were definitely more.

'You have to promise not to tell.'

Kym looked down at her, almost amused. 'Do I?'

'Please.'

'Why?'

'I told you,' said Maude, 'they'll get all weird and there's no need, I was reading about—' She stopped mid-sentence. 'Did you hear that?' she said.

Someone was knocking at the door.

The sound was muffled at first, but once they'd climbed back down the ladder it was clearer, more distinct. Someone thumping on the front door with the side of their fist, over and over again.

'Is something wrong?' Maude asked as she followed Kym along the landing.

'I don't know.'

Because it wasn't regular knocking, a quick one-two-three and then a pause, someone waiting patiently on the doorstep for an answer; it was swift, steady, relentless. The door vibrating so violently that Kym half expected it to burst open.

Maude edged closer. 'Could it be, like, the wind?'

'Could be,' said Kym.

The door shuddered one last time, then fell still.

'Should we check?' Maude, didn't move. 'I mean, there might be someone there?'

God, I hope not, Kym thought. 'Sure,' she said. 'You go back up to your room though, OK?'

She waited until she was sure Maude had scrambled back up the ladder, then she walked down the stairs, nice and steady, purposeful.

Someone had knocked while they were in the attic, that was

174

all, and when they hadn't got a reply, they'd become impatient, rattling the locked door. Worst case scenario, it was some visitor from the yard, pissed off because they couldn't raise anyone to lend them a cup of sugar or something.

Kym placed her hand on the Yale lock, shiny and new, and took a deep breath; now she thought about it, the silence was worse than the noise.

Just a neighbour, she told herself, if she was really unlucky it would be Carolyn Wilson, come to complain about something or other; worse, expecting to be invited in. She ran her fingers over the latch.

Behind her, through the kitchen, at the back of the house, there was another sudden explosion of sound, as someone started pounding at the kitchen door.

And suddenly it all made sense.

Tyler.

'Kym!' Maude was clattering down the ladder.

'It's all right,' Kym called out, 'It's just someone messing about.' Ty, she thought as she moved through the dining area, Ty hanging about outside, knocking on the doors, winding her up because he didn't like to be told no. Because he knew what would get her attention and how she felt about this house.

She reached the back door in a few strides, not even bothering to switch on the lights, unlocked it and flung it open.

There was no one there.

'Kym?' Maude was a few paces behind her.

'Stay here, OK?' Kym hesitated for a moment, then plunged into the darkness.

She could hear him, a few steps ahead, just out of sight, and as she rounded the corner, she wondered if she might catch him in the act, hammering on the front door. Tosser.

There was no one there. He'd obviously had enough, but she could probably catch him before he made it to the end of the yard. She set off down the steps, wishing she had the nerve to run, but fearful of stumbling in the dark.

'Ty! Tyler!'

She'd just reached Spinnaker Cottage when the yard was flooded with a pale orange light. 'Shit!'

She'd forgotten about the security lights.

Kym stood still, feeling foolish, vulnerable; the yard was obviously empty. She turned, scanning the shadows. To her left, the door to Spinnaker Cottage slowly opened. 'Hello?'

'Hi. Evie. Sorry.'

She was wearing leggings and a T-shirt, she looked as if she was ready for bed. Behind her, half hidden in shadow, a dog growled softly, and Evie nudged it back out of the way with her leg. 'Is everything all right?'

'Yes. Of course it is. I'm just – babysitting for Nell Galilee.'

'Right.' Evie looked up towards Elder House where Maude stood, barefoot, peering anxiously down at them. She held something in her hands, a toy perhaps, a teddy bear. 'And how's that going, then?'

Maude took a couple of hesitant steps towards them, pale under the security light, a thin line, a fine thread of scarlet unspooling from wrist to elbow. Blood. The dog growled again, then gave a single harsh bark.

'Shit.' Kym ran back up to Maude, vaguely aware that Evie was close behind her, matching her stride, taking the steps two at a time. 'Shit, shit, shit.'

It turned out that Evie was remarkably calm in a crisis. It was she who managed to get Maude to give up the shoe she'd been holding. She'd discarded it as quickly as she could, her

176

expression more than simple mild distaste, and got Maude over to the sink where she was examining her wound.

'Did you see anyone?' Maude asked.

'No. He's – there's no one there.'

'Should we call the police?'

'I'd rather we didn't,' said Kym, glancing at Evie. 'I'm pretty sure it was Tyler – messing about.'

'The good-looking guy on your phone.'

'Yes.' Kym picked up the shoe and examined it carefully, moving across the room until she was under a spotlight.

'So, is he your boyfriend or isn't he?' Maude asked as Evie held her hand under the cold tap, cleaning the deep puncture in the pad of Maude's thumb.

'No,' said Kym, 'not anymore. I told you.'

'But it was just a joke, yeah?'

The kid was getting a bit of colour back in her cheeks. A pin, very old, blackened with age, had been forced into the seam of the shoe, so tightly Kym couldn't pull it free – and as Maude had tightened her grip, it had pierced her skin; how she hadn't felt it and dropped the damn thing was a mystery. As it was, the wound was deep enough to have produced an impressive amount of blood. Kym didn't like to think what might have happened if she'd caught herself just an inch or so lower, if she'd managed to puncture one of the blue veins in her wrist.

'There.' Evie switched off the tap. 'It's stopped bleeding, I think.' She grabbed a length of kitchen roll, wadded it up and pressed it against the younger girl's hand. 'You won't need stitches or anything. I mean – I don't think you will.'

Maude looked up at her with anxious eyes. 'Thank you.'

'I'm sorry,' said Kym, 'if he frightened you. Tyler. I'll have a word with him. Several words. He shouldn't have done that. You stay here with Evie. OK?'

'OK.'

She slipped outside into the cool evening air, but there was no reply when she rang him, only his stupid voicemail, and she didn't leave a message. When she went back into the house, Evie and Maude were sitting at the dining table, talking quietly. 'How are you feeling?' she asked.

'Fine.' Maude raised her hand and peeled back the kitchen roll. 'It's stopped bleeding.'

'Good.' Kym joined them at the table, feeling inexplicably weary; one evening – just a few hours, really – of being responsible for someone's kid and she was exhausted. 'If you want to tell Nell, then, that's OK.' Bloody Ty, pushing her into a corner like this. 'I mean, if you do, then she probably won't ask me to – you know, stay with you again. But if you want to – you should.' She would bloody kill him. Kill him, then dump him all over again. 'And he won't bother us again, I can promise you that much.'

The shoe lay on the table between them and for a moment Kym almost wanted to pick it up and look at it some more, to feel the warm leather give way under her hand, maybe even feel the bite of the pin against her fingers. She frowned. 'What is this about, then?' she asked.

'We found it,' said Maude.

'In the bedroom wall,' said Evie. 'Mum says it's very old.'

'I was going to show you,' said Maude. 'Only I'm not supposed to touch it. You won't tell, will you?'

'I dunno, Maude. Rules are rules.' It was old, the shoe, and there was something about it that was – damaged.

'Please.' The kid looked frantic.

'She's teasing you, Maude,' said Evie, 'she won't tell.'

Kym caught her eye and grinned.

Maude nodded, relieved. 'I only wanted to make sure it was safe,' she said.

'Maude was telling me about the marks,' said Evie, 'up in the roof.'

'Oh, yes,' said Kym, as she stood, 'those.'

Evie was standing right under the beam, her head tilted back. 'Do you know what they are?' she asked.

'We were just discussing that when Ty decided to kick off,' said Kym.

'Are they, like, a secret?'

'I don't know.'

'Can we check?'

'How?'

'The website,' said Maude, and the two older girls looked at her. 'My dad said there was stuff about the history of the house on the website. He was going to show me, only...' she stopped, hugged herself.

'Should we tell someone?' asked Evie.

'No,' said Maude, but neither of the older girls seemed to hear her.

'Maybe see what we find out first?' said Kym. 'Maybe it's no big deal. Maybe they've got a picture of them plastered over their website.'

'I don't think so,' said Maude, doubtfully, 'my dad didn't say anything.'

'And – they don't bother you?' Evie asked.

'I like them,' said Maude, standing up. 'And I think we should keep quiet about them. We won't tell anyone about Tyler, either, or me having the shoe – that way, none of us gets into trouble.' She looked from Evie to Kym, straightening up, lifting her chin.

'The kid has a point,' said Kym.

*

179

Evie didn't stay long after that. She seemed anxious, and said she ought to get on with some revision. They went back downstairs and Kym saw her to the door.

'You're sure,' she said quietly, once Maude had said her goodbyes and gone back into the living room, 'that you didn't see Tyler come up the yard?'

'I didn't see anything until you set the light off. But I'd been upstairs before that.' Evie had the sense to keep her voice lowered too. 'But it couldn't have been anything else, could it?'

'No. I suppose not.' It was foolish, to have let Ty spook her so, and she was certain it had been him. Almost certain.

'Should we tell?'

Kym glanced towards the living room. 'We promised not to.'

'She's just a kid who doesn't want to get into trouble.'

'Me and her both.' Kym smiled. She was tempted to ask Evie to stay, to hang out for a bit – she might even be persuaded to share her babysitting fee.

'Are you sure you're OK?' Evie asked.

'I'm fine.' It was the house, that was all, finally being inside the house after all this time. There was a lot to take in.

'If you say so,' Evie smiled. 'Text me if, you know, anything else happens.'

'What? So you can come charging up the steps and rescue us?'

'Oh, shut up.'

It was nice that she'd offered, though, kind. 'Yeah. Sure.' She hesitated. 'I'll text you anyway, first thing? I'll check out those marks and we can talk properly.'

'OK.'

Kym closed the door and locked it. She stood for a moment in the gloom, listening, just to make sure that Tyler hadn't

180

come back; pissed off that he'd managed to knock her off balance so easily.

Just as she was returning to the living room, just as Maude hit the volume button on the TV remote, Kym could have sworn she heard a door thudding shut; someone walking lightly along the landing. She paused at the foot of the stairs, looking up. He couldn't have got inside, could he?

Maybe she should go and check.

The light in the hall seemed to waver. For a moment she thought she could smell burning wire. Something felt – wrong. She couldn't move, didn't want to move. Tears pricked at her eyes and she grabbed hold of the banister, trying to steady herself.

'Kym?' Maude was beginning to sound anxious again. Ty and his stupid game had obviously bothered her more than she was willing to let on.

And it had been him. Almost definitely it had been him.

She shouldn't have left Maude like that, running off into the dark. And for the first time, she began to wonder how he'd managed to get up to the house, to hammer on the door and get away again, without being seen.

'I'm here,' said Kym, squashing the little flicker of fear before it could take hold, 'don't worry.'

The night was dark and still, the street empty as she picked her way carefully over the cobbles; this, Nell recalled, had always been the trouble with high heels in this town.

She had stayed for the cutting of the cake and the surprisingly heartfelt speeches. Then as the music started up again, distinctly louder, and as more people had taken to the dance floor, she had found David and Jenny and said her goodbyes. Nell had been surprised how quickly time had passed and how pleasant it had been in the end. It had been worth making the effort after all, and she was only sorry that Chris couldn't have been there too.

When she got to the yard entrance, the new gate was hanging defiantly open. She walked slowly up the steps, feeling around in her bag for the key. The light shining out from the living room should have been comforting, but the nearer she got, the more the warmth, the goodwill generated by the party, began to fade.

Rather you than me.

She took a deep breath, unlocked the door and let herself in.

Nell made sure to lock the door behind Kym, before kicking off her shoes and going through the ground floor, checking the windows and switching off the lights. In the living room, she thought she could detect an unfamiliar scent, and it occurred to her that maybe Kym had been smoking in the house and if she had, then she'd need to have a word with her.

The smell was worse in the hall. Stale. As if the whole house needed airing.

The front door rattled gently on its hinges and something – the wind, surely – nudged against it.

She placed a hand against the door, listening as the house seemed to shift and settle around her, then switched off the hall light, gasping softly again at the static shock.

She was halfway up the stairs, her shoes dangling from one hand, when the front door rattled again. A little louder this time, a little more insistent.

She paused and looked back into the darkened hall, just to make sure. The house was empty; they were quite alone.

She didn't sleep well. After a restless few hours she woke around seven, went downstairs, made a cup of tea and took it into the living room. She sat in the big chair by the window, gazing out at Spinnaker Cottage, cradling her cup, thinking.

Chris wasn't bothered by the house, and as far as she could tell, neither was Maude. But she didn't think it was her imagination – or her hormones – making her oversensitive to smells, to the atmosphere of the place. Cheryl had thought there was something odd about Elder House; she had the feeling Gina didn't much like the place either.

Her pregnancy testing kit was still missing, although she supposed that there was a chance it might – like her mobile phone – be returned.

Because that was Maude, surely.

Oh, God. Maude. The test was one thing, but if she was pregnant, what then? She felt the tears rise – how on earth would she cope if Maude carried on like this, sullen, unreliable, untrustworthy. What would they do if she continued to push them away, if the petty acts of spite began to escalate?

She pulled up her sleeve and inspected her arm, the scratch had faded, but she could still feel the sudden shock of falling, of slamming into the table.

How would she keep her baby safe?

Her head ached from lack of sleep, her limbs felt heavy, and all she had to look forward to was a day spent pretending everything was fine.

She was just considering getting up properly, getting dressed, or at least making another cup of tea when the door to Spinnaker Cottage opened and Evie came out, Flossie circling her excitedly.

She looked worried, pinched and pale. Poor kid. She clipped on the dog's lead then looked expectantly down the yard.

A moment later, Kym appeared, and Evie ran down the steps to meet her. Nell hadn't realised the two were friends.

They made an unlikely pair, Evie so proper and correct, and Kym all attitude and eyeliner.

She would get dressed, borrow Maude's phone and maybe catch Chris before he set off for the gallery.

'Did you look it up, then? The house?' said Evie as they walked quickly down the yard in an unspoken effort to avoid Carolyn.

'Yeah,' said Kym.

'Me too.' It was very swish, the new website, elegant and modern, with lots of artistic photographs of the interiors. 'So they don't know about the shoe then? Or the marks in the attic?' They reached the street and turned up towards the beach, Flossie leading the way. 'The owners, whoever they are.'

'I don't think so. It's the sort of thing they like to feature isn't it?' said Kym. 'Something spooky to give the tourists a thrill. And they never set foot in the place once they started work on it.'

'How do you know that?'

Kym shrugged, 'I used to talk to the builders a bit, if I happened to be passing.'

'Oh.' Evie, completely at a loss as how to deal with the appreciative looks and occasional comments that had characterised most of her encounters with the workmen, had done her best to ignore them. After a while they'd got the message. 'Did they notice anything? Anything – weird?'

'I don't know.' Kym looked oddly guilty. 'I was just getting somewhere when my gran had a quiet word and after that, they wouldn't give me the time of day. She can be a bit – over-protective.'

The street narrowed and they were too close, Kym's wrist brushing against Evie's hip; she stepped into the road. Flossie's claws scraped over the cobbles. 'And everything settled down last night? Once I was gone?' she asked.

'Yeah. All quiet. Maude didn't say anything when Nell got back; I don't think she will.'

They headed towards the pier, it was low tide and the beach was empty.

'So no one knows about the marks except us.'

'Doesn't look like it.'

Flossie picked up her pace as they walked down the steps onto the beach. Evie bent down and let the dog off her lead; Flossie gave a sharp bark and ran across the sand.

'So, I did a bit of a search on the internet,' said Kym, pulling her phone out of her pocket. 'What do you reckon?'

The photos on the screen weren't that helpful – glossy close-ups that gave no sense of scale, no context – but there were diagrams too, hand drawn and labelled, and much easier to digest. There were some circular designs that were bold and simple, almost childlike in their execution, and others that were astonishing in their complexity.

'They look – similar,' Evie said, surrendering the phone.

'Here.' Kym flicked through the screen again. '"Marian marks",' she read out loud, '"referring to the Virgin Mary and widely assumed to offer protection".' She glanced up, 'Those are the letters.'

'*M*,' said Evie. '*M* for Mary.'

'"Daisy wheels",' Kym continued. '"Patterns of varying complexity, and frequently found where a house might be deemed to be most vulnerable, at windows or thresholds, for example. Carved into stone, or more commonly into wood, ritual in purpose, and often referred to as witch marks. Their function is unclear, yet we must assume they held value and meaning for these houses' original occupants".'

Ahead of them, Flossie barked joyfully as she ran up and down the beach. 'How old is Elder House, do we know?' Kym asked.

'Built in the late fifteen hundreds,' said Evie.

Kym nodded. 'My gran reckons that sometimes when they were building then, they used timber from older houses too, waste not want not and all that.'

The flowers were very precise, Evie thought, as if someone had used a pair of compasses to draw them, precise, faithful, important. 'Should we tell someone?' she asked.

'I'm not sure,' said Kym, 'I mean, they're not uncommon, and they're not – sinister. Only – there's that shoe.' She shoved her phone into her jeans pocket. 'What are you doing today?'

'Revision,' said Evie, 'You know how it is.'

'I don't suppose you fancy bunking off for a bit?'

'Tempting.' Evie could feel the blush beginning to rise, she turned her attention back to Flossie who was investigating the tide line. 'But no. I can't, sorry.'

'Later, then.'

'I suppose . . .' Evie looked down at Flossie's lead and began winding it slowly around her hand. It would be tricky, getting away from the house, finding an acceptable excuse. 'Yeah. I could sort something out.' She cleared her throat, looked up. 'Why? Do they bother you? The marks?'

'No, that's just - history. But that knocking – it was weird.'

'That was Tyler, wasn't it?'

Kym looked down at her boots as they walked. 'I was wondering,' she said, 'why you came out last night, when it was all kicking off.'

'I was in the kitchen, and then the yard light came on and I saw you, and . . .' Evie stopped, her eyes widening. 'Oh,' she said, 'right.'

'If it was Ty, then why didn't the light come on before I tripped it?' said Kym, smiling. 'I didn't think, everything was so – intense.'

'Maybe he didn't come down the steps, maybe he was hiding.' The dog had discovered something of interest in a heap of seaweed and driftwood and was gnawing at it. 'Sorry, I think I need to sort Floss out, and I need to get back.' Evie raised her voice. 'Flossie, come here. Here. Bad dog.'

Flossie looked up and after a moment's consideration, began to trot back towards her.

'OK,' Kym persisted, 'but if it wasn't him? What then?'

'I don't know,' Evie said.

'I'd like to be sure, you know?' Kym pushed her hair out of her eyes, serious, determined. 'I'd like to know that it's not going to happen again.'

The conversation with Chris was brief, and it didn't help that it had been Sam who answered, her muffled comments as she handed the phone over irritating Nell; she had wanted to talk properly.

'Hi love, how are things?' Chris sounded mildly distracted, she could picture him at his desk, scrolling through his emails as they talked.

'Not brilliant, to be honest.'

'Are you OK?' The note of concern was – shamefully – gratifying.

'I'm fine – I'm – I don't know, out of sorts. Like I might be coming down with something.'

'Are you taking it easy; you know, taking care of yourself?'

She smiled. 'What a quaint idea.'

'You know what I mean.'

'I know. We miss you.' *I* miss you.

'How was the party?'

188

There was some sort of interference on the line, as if he had moved somewhere.

'Fine. It was fine.'

'And this indisposition today, not party related, is it?'

'No.' She walked through the kitchen, hoping for a better signal, irritated all over again. 'How are things with you?'

'Busy.'

'I should have come back with you, I could help.'

'Someone needs to keep an eye on Maude, and there was no point in all of us missing out.'

'But you'll be back soon, yeah?'

'As soon as I can.' She could imagine him glancing up at Sam, almost, but not quite rolling his eyes. 'Is Maude OK?'

'Of course.'

Maude was standing in the doorway. 'I'm hungry,' she said. 'Can I have some toast?'

'Sure. Do you want to talk to your dad?' Nell held out the phone, Maude pressed speaker and set it on the counter as she sliced some bread.

'Hiya.'

'Hi, love. How are you?'

'Fine. Bored.' The bread came away in uneven chunks, crumbs scattering onto the flagstones.

'Hey,' Nell said, frowning.

'Kym came round last night,' said Maude, 'when Nell was out.'

'Did you have a good time?'

'It was all right,' said Maude.

'Really?' Chris said. 'Just all right?'

'We had pizza.'

'Right. And what else have you been up to?' He had all the time in the world for Maude, of course.

'We took the shoe to the museum. But they didn't want it, so we've still got it.' She forced the bread into the toaster, then swiped half-heartedly at the mess she'd made.

'I rang the letting people and left a message.' Nell reached over the sink and opened the window, propping it out as far as it would go.

'So that's sorted, then,' said Chris.

'Not exactly—'

'When will you be back?' Maude asked.

'A couple of days. I think.'

'That's a bit vague.' Maude opened the fridge and took out the butter and the last of the milk.

'Well, it's the best answer I've got. As soon as I can, Maudie, I promise.'

'Do you know what's going to happen with Simon Lee?' Maude asked.

'Simeon.'

'Right. Him.'

Maude could have waited, thought Nell, they could have had just a few more minutes talking on their own. But no, here she was again. She had a gift for it; for inserting herself between the two of them.

'Has he got a case?' Nell asked. 'Will he be able to stop us expanding the gallery?'

'I don't know. I don't think so, but it's hard to tell.' Chris sounded tired. 'I'm sorry, love. I'd much rather be there with you guys.'

'Really?' said Nell.

'Really.' He lowered his voice. Sam was hovering nearby, no doubt. 'I miss you, you know?'

'Yeah.' She glanced at Maude. 'Me too.'

They hadn't even said goodbye properly. Nell remembered

190

when they'd first met. The excuses she'd made to spend time with him; the painful lurch she'd felt in the pit of her stomach if she ever bumped into him by accident. The knowledge, the absolute certainty of it; this is him, the one.

The disbelief when she'd discovered he was married.

'Oh, please don't start all that.' Maude said.

'What are you two going to do today?' Chris asked.

'I thought we'd take a walk, maybe go and see Gina's shop,' said Nell, 'if Maude likes.'

'Can't you sort out a new phone?'

'Easier said than done, love. There's nowhere here that can replace it. I think we'll have to take a bus to—'

'No buses,' said Maude, 'I'll be sick.' She almost sounded pleased at the prospect.

'Or, you know. We could just wait until you get back,' said Nell.

'Right,' said Chris, but it sounded like he was speaking to someone else. 'Sorry, guys, I have to go. I'll ring this evening, yeah?'

When Nell was growing up, Gina's shop had been a butcher's, an old-fashioned shop front with blue and white tiles beneath the large window, and a family name painted over the door. It was unrecognisable now. She sold joss sticks and scented candles, Tarot sets, jewellery and woolly hats, and various bits and pieces that might be described as 'alternative'. Nell could practically hear her gran spitting out the word – *hippy*.

'Hello there.' Gina was sitting behind the long, low, wooden counter, knitting. 'How are you today?'

'Fine, thank you.' Maude said. She turned to Nell. 'Can I look around?'

'Of course, that's what we're here for.'

191

Maude made her way to the back of the shop, and began to inspect the little figurines, elves and faeries, wizards and dragons that were jostling on the shelves for space and attention.

'How's business?' Nell asked.

'Slow. But it's early in the season yet.' Gina wound up her knitting and put it to one side. 'It's very nice to see you two, though.'

Maude picked up a model of an elf wielding a silver sword. 'Can I have one of these?' she asked.

'No.'

'You're no fun.' Maude drifted around the shop. 'What about one of those, then?' she said, pointing at the large glass baubles Gina had suspended in the window from brightly coloured ribbons. They varied in colour, deep reds, rich blues and silvers, greens and golds, shimmering and opalescent. 'What are they?'

'They're witch balls,' said Gina. 'You hang one in your window and they ward off evil spirits.'

'How?'

'The witch is supposed to become so fascinated with her reflection in the glass that she forgets to come inside.'

'Do you believe in them – witches?' asked Maude, rubbing at her hand absent-mindedly.

'Well,' said Gina, 'I do and I don't.'

'What's that supposed to mean?'

'Maude,' said Nell. She cast a look at Gina, half amused, half apologetic.

'That's all right,' said Gina. 'What I meant was that sometimes if people were – I don't know – wise, or knowledgeable, then that might be viewed as witchcraft.'

'But you'd want to let people like that in, wouldn't you? If you needed some help.'

'Good point; knowledge like that might be useful, especially if you were ill or afraid. You might want someone like that on your side.'

'So you'd let them in, but you'd keep an eye on them?' said Maude. 'Just in case?'

'Maybe. People used to believe you could trap a witch in a bottle, if you put in a bit of iron, like a pin, inside, and salt, or hair, or – other stuff.'

'A pin?'

'Metal. Iron in particular. Very magical,' said Gina, smiling. 'Very strong protection right there.'

Maude looked up at the bottles again. 'Is that what these are?' she asked. 'Magical?'

'Not exactly,' said Gina. 'Between you and me, these are mass produced in a factory in Romania. But they are very pretty.'

Maude turned hopefully to Nell who shook her head. 'I don't think so.'

Maude began to circle the shop again. 'Did you find out about our shoe?' she asked.

'I did. A bit, anyway. I spoke to Sally Nathan earlier and she says that it sounds like the real deal, a proper concealed shoe, probably, but not necessarily, apotropaic in purpose.'

'A pot what?'

'Apotropaic. Magic,' said Gina. 'For protection.'

'Like the witch balls?'

'Exactly. But given the shoe was in the bedroom' – she glanced at Nell – 'it might be to do with . . . well, sometimes hidden shoes are connected to fertility. And I think that's what you've got here.'

'Ew,' said Maude. 'Gross.'

'Maude . . .' said Nell, softly. She could feel it still, the warm

193

leather, the grime beneath her fingernails. She shouldn't have moved it, she shouldn't have touched it.

'But what's fertile about a shoe?' asked Maude.

'Oh, I don't know, pet. Why do people tie them to newlyweds' cars? Why do we go on about the patter of tiny feet? Some objects become – significant; talismans.'

'Like, a lucky charm?'

'Yes. Exactly that.'

'Did Dr Nathan say what we should do with it?' said Nell. 'Does she want to take a closer look at it?'

'Not really. They're not uncommon, you see. You should let the owners know, obviously,' said Gina. 'If it were up to me though, I'd just put it back quietly – privately – where it belongs. It's been doing its job all these years,' she went on. 'And I'd leave it well enough alone.'

'Really?' said Nell.

'Someone put that shoe there for a reason. Think of it as making a commitment; striking a bargain – and I think we should honour that.'

'So we definitely can't keep it, then?' said Maude.

'I'm afraid not. Have you heard from your dad?' asked Gina. 'Is he on his way back?'

'Not yet,' said Nell, trying to smile.

'Work,' said Maude, continuing her inspection of the shop. 'And it's so boring here without him.' She picked up a necklace, a long silver chain with an amethyst pendant, it spun lazily, catching the light. The shop bell jingled and a young couple entered.

'We should let you get on,' said Nell.

Maude carefully draped the necklace back onto the shelf.

'Call back any time,' Gina said. 'Here or the cottage, if you feel like some company.'

*

194

The church clock was striking the quarter hour as Evie walked up the yard. Thinking about Kym and the marks inside Elder House, and glancing in the windows of Spinnaker Cottage, it occurred to her that she didn't actually have to go straight home.

And Elder House was empty, as far as she could tell.

'Come on, Floss.' She tugged on the lead and carried on up the steps, if anyone challenged her, if her mother suddenly appeared, she'd say – that she wanted to visit Nell, to ask her . . . she wasn't sure what. That she needed an excuse at all irritated her. She'd worry about that if it happened.

The kitchen door was closed, the house was dark and still; and beyond it stood the drying ground.

If Tyler hadn't gone running down the steps and out of the yard, then he could have hidden here, in the shadows, against the cliff. There wasn't that much cover in the long grass, but in the dark, with everyone looking the wrong way, maybe he had made fools of them all.

She stepped off the path, the damp seeping into her shoes, there was a smell too, sour and—

'Flossie?' She looked down.

The dog wouldn't move.

'Come on.' Evie tugged gently on the lead. 'Come on, Floss.'

The dog dropped to the ground, and looking beyond Evie, at the bankside, she began to growl softly.

Evie tried again, less gently, then as Flossie continued to resist, she dropped the lead, 'Right. Fine.'

She walked up the bank, following the fence. It was cold in the shadow of the house and her skin rose in goosebumps. She bent down and pushed the gate open and for a moment there was nothing more than the sound of her own breath, and the conviction that it – someone – was there, just out of sight, waiting for her – inside . . . Flossie's low growl turned into a series of barks which echoed through the yard and, fearful of being discovered by Nell, by her mother, by – something, Evie backed away, scrambling onto the path, scooping up Flossie's lead and heading for home.

She kicked off her shoes by the kitchen door and looped the lead over the coat hook. She glanced down at Flossie, who had settled herself in front of the Aga. She seemed fine now, the poor old thing, and there hadn't actually been anything there – nothing she could see or touch.

Her mother's voice drifted downstairs. 'Evie? Is that you?'

'Yes.' Suppressing the familiar jolt of guilt. Her mother had been ironing – the Moses basket was filled with clean bedding and there was a pile of clothes balanced precariously on the end of the table. Evie added the clothes to the basket and picked it up, bracing herself for the inevitable interrogation as she walked slowly upstairs.

'Evie?'

'I'm here.' She nudged the bedroom door open.

Carolyn seemed to be in the process of rearranging the entire room, the bed and the chest of drawers had been pulled out of their usual positions and she was standing on a chair attempting to lift the large antique mirror that was hanging against the wall.

Maybe she hadn't noticed, if she'd been busy, then there was no reason she should have seen Evie disappear up past Elder House.

Carolyn flinched and half stepped, half fell off the chair, lurching against the bed before regaining her balance.

Evie lifted up the basket. 'Where do you want these?'

'Oh, put them down anywhere, I'll deal with that later.'

Evie looked around the room, the chest of drawers that had

previously sat underneath the window had been pushed across the room to the opposite wall, and the wardrobe to the right of the door had been pulled out at an angle as if her mother had been attempting to move it single-handed, and the little bookcase she kept by her bed had been half emptied and dragged into a corner. She dropped the basket onto a clean patch of carpet, out of the way, as best she could.

'Now, if you can just take the weight of this as I unhook it,' said Carolyn, climbing up on to the chair again, 'then that would be perfect.'

It took ages to get everything the way Carolyn wanted it. They emptied the wardrobe, dumping all the clothes on the bed, and between them they were able to shift it across the room. They tried moving the bed too, placing it against the opposite wall; but Carolyn decided almost immediately that she preferred it back where it belonged, which meant rehanging the mirror. Once it was back in place, she had Evie help her take it down again. Her indecision was exhausting. 'I don't think so,' she said, propping the mirror against the chest of drawers, 'maybe I'll get rid of it entirely. Unless you'd like it?'

It was an old-fashioned piece with an ornate frame, the glass slightly foxed in a lower corner. It had suited her parents' room, but was too big for Evie's; she couldn't imagine where it would fit. 'No, thanks,' she said.

'Oh. Well, I'll deal with that later.' Carolyn looked around the room. 'I wonder sometimes how we ended up with so much stuff. Maybe we should chuck it all out and start again.'

'Wouldn't that be a bit expensive?' Excessive too, Evie thought.

'Oh. I don't know. Sometimes you just have to cut your losses.' Her mother sat on the bed, next to the pile of clothes collapsing gently over the duvet. 'I hate this bit. When you've made such a mess you don't know where to start.'

The room looked odd, Evie thought, out of balance. It had been cosy up here before, more her mother's room than her father's perhaps, but still a comfortable space, welcoming. Now it was . . .

'Why don't we take a break?' she said. 'We'll have a cup of tea and a biscuit. Then I'll give you a hand with this.' She hadn't been able to manage much breakfast that morning; she'd been in too much of a rush to get out of the house, to go and meet Kym.

'I thought we weren't going to snack in between meals anymore.'

There was no point in arguing.

'How was your walk? You were gone for ages.'

'Oh, you know. Fine.' She'd wait until Carolyn was occupied, then fix herself a quick sandwich. She should have known better than to raise the subject of food. 'Floss was making a bit of a fuss. Up by the drying ground.'

'Was she now?' Her mother looked at her for the longest time. 'And how did she end up there?'

'I dropped her lead when I was opening the door. She didn't go in, though. I don't know why. She seemed a bit – spooked.'

'The poor old thing. And how's the revision going?'

'The same as the last time you asked, Mum.' She tried to smile.

'I'm sorry, sweetheart,' said Carolyn. 'It's tough at the moment, I know. But anything worth having involves the odd sacrifice. And you can do it, you know – you just have to put the hours in.'

'I do, Mum.' Evie hesitated. 'I did.'

And the results last year hadn't been that bad, not by any

reasonable measure. Just bad enough for her mother to insist on a meeting with Evie's head of year. A meeting that had gone on and on, picking apart Evie's grades and coursework, a meeting that had ended with her mother quietly furious with the teachers, the whole school and Evie herself. Transferring to the sixth form in town had been a relief after that, even if her mother was already beginning to go on about university. She'd settled in, made new friends, until eventually, inevitably, the rumours had caught up with her. Some stupid netball tournament where Marnie and Grace had bumped into Ellie Foster. Evie had counted Ellie as a friend in her old school, but she had clearly lost no time in letting Marnie and Grace know what she, Evie, was really like.

Such a loser.

Such a freak.

They hadn't actually said anything yet, not to anyone else, but Evie suspected it was only a matter of time; eventually the odd loaded comment wouldn't be enough.

The thought of it made her sick. Maybe Kym wouldn't care.

Carolyn sighed. 'Yes. Well, A levels are different, Evie. You have to take them seriously. Honestly, it doesn't seem five minutes since we were packing you off to nursery.' For one awful moment Evie thought her mother might cry. 'And now look at you. So . . .' Her voice faded, and Evie was glad; she wasn't sure, these days, what her mum thought of her, but mostly she suspected she was a disappointment.

Carolyn glanced at her watch. 'Goodness,' she said, 'is that the time? Back to the books, I think, don't you?'

'Are you sure you don't want me to help?' The bed was still a mess, a riot of discarded sweaters and cardigans and scarves.

'Absolutely not. Go on. Revision.' Carolyn stood, gesturing to the door.

One day she would get away, Evie thought suddenly, fiercely, and when she did, she'd stay away.

It didn't take much effort to find Tyler, not at the weekend, anyway.

His uncle's boat, the *Donna Marie*, was moored on the quay, just along from the bridge. She had seen better days, her paintwork was patched and spotted with rust, but there was a large sign fixed to the cabin, advertising the rates for a day's fishing, and there was a group of guys hanging around, boxes of tackle stacked on the pavement, clearly waiting for their turn to board.

'All right?' the man on deck was smiling at her as if he knew her. Ty's Uncle Mike, greyer and thinner than the last time she'd seen him.

'Hi. Is Tyler about?'

The man nodded and vanished into the cabin. Then Ty appeared, head down as his uncle said something Kym couldn't hear, and clapped him on the back, as if he was congratulating him. He climbed the ladder onto the quayside and shepherded her away from the boat and the men.

Even in his work gear, which was worn and faded, he looked good, tanned, fit. Away from his mates he seemed less of a boy, more the man he was going to be, and it was as strong as ever, that tug she felt deep in her belly, that connection which was a combination of affection and habit, and more recently, lust. The connection that wouldn't do either of them any good, in the end.

'I'm at work,' he said.

'Don't worry, Ty. I think they can spare you for five minutes.'

Seagulls dipped and swooped over the boat as she shifted lazily on the tide.

'You know what your trouble is? You're a bloody snob.'

'Shouldn't you at least be pretending to be revising?'

'And now you sound like my dad.' He watched the men gathering up their rods and climbing down onto the boat. 'I'm busy, Kym, I don't have time to talk.'

'You should answer your phone, then.'

'Like you answer yours?'

'Last night,' said Kym, 'what the hell were you playing at?'

'Nothing. I wasn't doing anything.' He wouldn't look her in the eye, though.

'Don't give me that – I heard you, banging at the door, trying to freak us out—'

'What? What *us*?' He looked puzzled. 'Your mum? You think I've been having a go at you and your mum? What's been going on?'

'No.' She sighed, tried to slow down. 'I was at Elder House—'

'And I bet you loved that—'

'I was babysitting someone, Ty. We were all alone and then you started battering at the doors. She's just a kid and you freaked her out—'

'Oh, piss off. No.' He stepped back, and he looked – relieved. 'I don't know what this is – but no. Not me. I—' He stopped. 'I've got to get back to work.'

'No. Hang on.' She grabbed him by the arm. 'Really? I mean – not even for, like, a joke?'

'How would I know where you were last night? On any night?'

'I don't know. You could have asked my mum, or – followed me—'

'Fucksake.' He pulled away, shoving his fists into his pockets. 'You really need to get over yourself.'

This was the closest they'd been to each other in weeks, the past month the longest they'd gone without speaking for – years. Everything about him was familiar, and safe – even if she was pissed off with him – and now, he couldn't stand for her to touch him.

One of the men paused as his mates stowed their gear, watching them.

'This is important, Ty. Please.'

'Of course it's important, because it's Elder bloody House, isn't it?' He shook his head. 'It wasn't me, I wasn't there. And if you don't believe me' – his expression was a mixture of triumph and pity – 'you can ask Beth.'

Beth Harland.

It was like being punched.

'I was round at hers on Friday night.'

Kym was absolutely not going to cry in front of him.

'We were revising. Maths. You know.'

'Yeah, I don't need the details, thanks.' She shouldn't have been surprised, Beth had always had a bit of thing for Ty. A little revision, a lot of sympathy; it didn't take much imagination to see how that would play out. But even so, she had thought they were friends.

'It's not like I didn't ring. Loads of times.'

The dopey cow.

'Fuck sake, Kym. You dumped me. You were the one who wanted to—'

'Tyler! Got to go, mate.' There was a flurry of activity on the boat as the engine started up.

'Yeah well,' she looked away. 'Tell Beth from me that diet's really working.'

'Tyler!'

'What if I've changed my mind?' Kym asked.

'What about?' Tyler edged her further away from the gangplank and the boat.

202

'Us. You.'

'Have you?'

And he'd take her back, she knew it, it was written all over his face, no matter what Beth Harland might say or do. It was as if they hadn't split at all. 'I don't know. Maybe. If I can just – work out this stuff with the house.'

And Tyler sighed. 'I shouldn't have told you, should I?' he said. 'I should never have put this stupid bloody idea in your head.' He looked back towards the boat as it shuddered into life, its engines churning the dull grey water.

'Tyler! Last chance!' Ty's uncle was on deck.

'I'll ring you then, if you like?' She'd missed him, and now to see him again, so close, so like his old self; they could work everything else out. And he was tempted, she could see that.

'Don't bother,' Tyler said, backing away. 'It's not good for you, this – it's not healthy.'

'Tyler.'

'It's not worth it.' Then he turned and ran towards the boat. He climbed onto the deck and moved swiftly to the bow, and helped cast off.

Kym stood by the bridge and watched as the *Donna Marie* motored slowly under the bridge and into the lower harbour, but Ty didn't look back.

The lighthouse was Maude's idea and the climb to the top was more difficult than Nell remembered. The twist of the spiral staircase was tighter, the walls closer and the sudden emergence into daylight at the top was dizzying.

'Careful,' she said as Maude grabbed hold of the railing that ran around the narrow ledge and leant over it.

Maude didn't bother replying, but she did, Nell noticed gratefully, step back, letting go of the railing and leading the

203

way around the glassed-in lamp. On the seaward side the wind buffeted them and Nell had to guard against the instinct to take Maude by the arm, and keep her close; she wouldn't welcome it, and after all, they were perfectly safe.

They stopped and took in the view for a moment. Even though it wasn't the brightest of days, something about the light, the way it hit the sea, the dull sandstone of the lighthouse, the peeling paint, reassured her. The air was cold and damp, but the familiar scene was comforting in a way the house was not. She didn't want to go back, she realised; there was something unnerving about it, as if they were never quite alone there, never quite— Maude glanced at her then stood carefully on the bottom rung of the railing, boosting herself up and looking out to sea – the slow steady swell of it shifting against the piers.

'Was it all right, then? The party?'

'I suppose so.'

'Did you know lots of people?'

'It was fine. Maude . . .' Nell wasn't sure how to go on. 'You're not – worried about anything, are you?'

'Such as?'

'Well it's an old house we're staying in, some people might find it a bit – creepy.'

Maude glanced at her, her expression oddly self-satisfied. 'You're not scared, are you?' she asked.

'No,' said Nell. 'Of course not.' She sighed. 'And could you get down off there, please?'

'Were you really at school with Carolyn?'

'Yes. I suppose so. When I was growing up here there was only the one secondary school.'

'That's not what I meant.' Maude bounced up and down a little, testing the strength of the iron rung, which was, Nell noted, peeling and rusted in places. 'Were you, like, friends?'

'I don't remember her,' said Nell.

'So, she's lying.'

'Oh, I doubt it. I just – it was a long time ago.' The wind whipped Nell's hair into her eyes, and she tried to brush it away.

Maude seemed to think about this, still bouncing on the railing as the wind tugged at her jacket. 'Haven't you checked? If you want to know about her?'

'Checked how?'

'Online. Facebook.'

'I don't have an account. Please, Maude, get down.'

Maude jumped gently back onto the walkway. 'Yeah, but she does,' she said.

16

Several bags of clothes joined the mirror on the landing as the afternoon went on, and Evie waited until she could hear her mother hoovering before she rapped on the bedroom door and announced that she was just nipping out to the shop.

The text had been brief.

You want to come round to mine?

It wasn't that far, and Evie was a fast walker.

Kym's house was small, and to Evie's eye, reassuringly normal; a red-brick semi-detached, built in the early seventies. Her room was normal too, lots of books and a single bed, a dressing table heaving with products and make-up; the furniture was cheap and a little bit worn, but it felt comfortable, cosy.

'I saw Tyler,' said Kym, picking up a large, spiral-bound notebook and sitting on the bed. 'He says it wasn't him.'

'And you believe him?'

Kym busied herself arranging and rearranging her notes. 'No reason not to,' she said. 'He's got an alibi.'

'Oh.' Evie looked around the room, wondering where she should sit.

'He says he spent last night revising. With Beth Harland.'

'Oh,' said Evie again.

'Yeah.' Kym had given up with the papers, her head lowered, she began to pick at her nail polish.

'Are you OK?'

Kym nodded, but she didn't look up. 'Sure,' she said.

'He's an idiot,' Evie went on, 'if he thinks Beth is – well – you know . . .'

'She's not that bad,' said Kym. 'Not really. I just thought – he could have waited just a couple more weeks, couldn't he? Now it's like we – didn't matter. Like I don't matter.'

Evie sat on the bed, next to her. 'You do though.' She tried to keep her voice light. 'Of course you do. And it's just a rebound thing, isn't it? He's probably trying to make you jealous.'

Kym shook her head. 'I don't think so.'

'Or he's getting his own back,' Evie went on, 'for being dumped.'

'No.' Kym looked up. 'When me and Ty split – it wasn't exactly like I said. I mean, it's true about uni and stuff but, to be honest, we hadn't been getting on for a while. And there was something else.' Her eyes filled with tears. 'He said I was being unreasonable, he said . . .' She wiped angrily at her face, smearing the thick black mascara. 'Oh God,' she went on, 'the thing is – it's all to do with my dad.'

The mild start to the day hadn't held, and eventually another sea fret, clammy and grey, had driven them back to the house. Maude took up residence in her chair in the living room, and once she was certain she was settled, Nell took her sketchbook and the laptop into the other room to work on her designs at the dining table.

After a while, the lure of the internet proved too much. She found the letting agent's site and clicked on the link for Elder House. The photographs had been taken one evening when the house reflected the setting sun, and someone had applied a filter that gave the building a rich glow it sorely lacked in real life. She scrolled quickly through the potted history onscreen, although she wasn't quite sure what she might be looking for. The yard, she discovered, had changed its name over the years, Black Elder Yard, Elder Yard, Bishops Yard, and the house had been built in the sixteenth century.

The links the site provided simply repeated the same information over and over again, and after a while, Nell found her attention wandering. She sat back in her chair and gazed aimlessly around the kitchen, and Cheryl's words came back to her.

Rather you than me.

On impulse, she typed the words 'ghost walk' into the search engine, and then after the briefest of hesitations, 'Bishops Yard'.

It took a little while to sort through the results. In the first company Nell tried, the walks were led by a woman, another had plenty of online reviews, but there was little detail of actual content, just the prices and the booking details. The third, however, The Man in Grey, had posted a video; a surprisingly professional trailer, cutting between various locations in the town, shot at night and filled with looming shadows and artful close-ups of a young man dressed in immaculate period costume.

At one point, he led the way into Bishops Yard.

Nell paused the video, then hit the link to the website. Neither the reviews, nor the business terms had been updated for well over a year, but there was a page dedicated to tour's highlights, which had included, apparently, The Tragedy of Dr Bishop.

Nell hesitated, she might be better off not knowing, she thought. But then, despite herself, she clicked on the link.

It was another video.

'The thing is,' Kym said, 'he was working on a house, it was being done up – because that's all bloody incomers do, buy up old cottages and knock them apart and – he was an apprentice and there was some sort of accident and it was so unfair, what they said . . .' She stopped for a moment, trying to pull herself together. 'No, it's OK.' Her voice cracked a little, but she carried on. 'But the thing is, it happened one evening, after work. When everyone else had left, he went back to the house and – it happened there.'

'I'm sorry, I don't get—'

Kym's expression hardened a little, as if Evie were being deliberately stupid. 'Elder House,' she said, 'the house they – the house he was working in was Elder House.'

'Oh, shit. I mean . . .' Evie didn't know what to say. 'Oh God, I'm sorry.'

'He shouldn't have been there,' said Kym, bluntly. 'It was empty, and they were done for the day, and he had no reason to be there.'

'Oh. Didn't anyone ask the owners? I mean – there would have been, like, an inquest?'

Again, that look. It was as if she kept giving the wrong answer.

'There was; death by misadventure,' said Kym, 'and that was that, pretty much. My gran hasn't been inside the place since, as far as I can tell – but still lives right next to it, and my mum never goes anywhere near it either. And they don't talk, not to each other, not really – they don't get on, they – they don't talk to me either. But the one thing they have in common is the way they feel about that house.' The last few words came in a rush. 'And I can't work out why he was there, no one will tell me, and I need to know.'

'Right.' Evie didn't know what to say, she'd never seen Kym looking less fierce, less sure of herself. It must be awful, to miss someone you'd never known. She took her hand, squeezed it.

210

'So. Anyway,' Kym went on, 'Ty knew all this because – well, of course he did. And a few weeks back he told me this story.' She held onto Evie's hand, gripping fiercely. 'He does a bit for his uncle, you know, taking out fishing parties, and they'd had this bloke on a charter and he lives away now, but he was born here, grew up here, and he comes back sometimes.'

'And?'

'There wasn't much fishing, according to Ty. And this bloke is a bit – he started talking about odd things that had happened in his job. He's an architect and a couple of years ago he'd come back to work on Elder House. And – he was telling them all about it and how bloody weird it was.'

'Weird how?'

'He was doing some sort of preliminary visit, a meeting with the builder on site, and he said it took him ages, he kept losing things, pens and the relevant documents and even a mobile phone. They tried ringing it, and they could hear it in the house, they even took up some floorboards, but they couldn't find it.'

'It must have been – I don't know, wedged behind something?'

'He said the house wasn't empty, that they both heard someone walking about; someone who shouldn't have been there. He said it was – freaky.'

There was a long pause.

'He was winding them up,' said Evie uncertainly.

'Maybe. That's why I thought – that's why I thought it was Ty last night. He didn't like me talking about it.' She smiled sadly. 'It's not healthy, apparently.'

'And that's why you two split up?'

'Not the point of the story, Evie. But – yeah, mostly.' She released Evie's hand, opened her notebook, smoothed down the page.

211

'You think this guy losing his phone is connected to your dad dying?'

'You sound like Ty.'

'Sorry.'

'I just wonder,' said Kym, 'what they heard and if it's . . . I wanted to talk to this guy – Pete – myself but Ty clammed up, wouldn't ask his uncle to pass on my number. So I started researching the house, because there's something about it, something – odd.'

'It's just a house.'

'Evie, you have to look at it every day. Come on.'

And the thing was, she was right, it *was* an odd house. More than that, it was – Evie thought about the drying ground and Flossie's whining refusal to go inside – wrong. 'Tell me what you got, then,' she said.

The video had been much less professional, hand-held, and presumably filmed by someone taking the tour; the segment filmed in Bishops Yard had been frustratingly brief, and Nell played it through several times.

A crowd gathered at the foot of the steps, looking up at the Man in Grey, the house filling the screen behind him.

'In the summer of 1889, Elder House was occupied by one Dr Frederick Bishop and his family.' The young man had a pleasant voice, calm, authoritative, and his audience were listening intently. 'One afternoon, he was called from his practice to his house, where it transpired his youngest child – a much longed for son, after the birth of four daughters – had gone missing. As you can imagine, the house was in disarray, the doctor's wife was distraught – it was a scene of confusion, and fear.

'The child had been left to his own devices by one of the maids, playing with his toy soldiers in the nursery, and after

212

searching the yard and nearby streets – for it was assumed the boy had left the house and wandered off – it was decided to search the house one more time from top to bottom.' He paused. 'The child was found in the attic, unconscious, his mouth bloody. He was dead.'

There was an appreciative gasp off-camera.

'He was assumed,' the tour guide went on, 'to have suffered some sort of fit, but the truth was far stranger—'

'What are you doing?' Nell had been so absorbed she hadn't heard Maude come in, swiftly, she exited the site, sat back in her seat.

'Nothing. Do you want some juice? Some lemonade?'

'Are you stalking Carolyn?'

The poor child was found to have choked on a pin.

Nell could feel it, a scrape, a prickle in her throat. She dragged her attention back to her stepdaughter.

'I'm not stalking anyone.'

'Yeah, right. You should friend her, on Facebook.'

'We've been through this, I don't have an account.'

'I know. But the gallery does,' Maude said, sitting at the table. 'I could do it for you, if you like.'

'You know the rules.'

'God, Nell.' Maude rolled her eyes. 'I won't be unsupervised, will I? You'll be right next to me.'

Nell could still hear the tour guide, the way he lowered his voice, the way he spoke about the doctor and his poor lost child as if he knew them. 'Fine,' she said, 'OK.'

They were already logged into Facebook on the laptop, which was just as well, as Nell had no clue what their password might be. She suspected that Maude knew it, which she wasn't entirely happy about, but today was not the day to bring that up. It took a few minutes, but she had found Carolyn easily enough.

'She might not respond,' Nell said. She clicked on the mouse pad, sending the friend request before she could change her mind. 'There.'

'I could google her, if you like,' said Maude.

'No. I think me stalking our neighbours is quite bad enough.'

Maude looked down at her hands, trying not to smile. 'I was thinking, I might buy Imogen something from Gina's shop, like, a souvenir?'

'I thought you didn't have any pocket money?'

'Mum gave me some.'

Maude hadn't bothered to mention this before, although Nell supposed Jess might have said something to Chris.

'I'm not sure I want to go out again.'

'You don't have to come.'

Nell hesitated.

Maude sat up straight, smoothing down her T-shirt. 'It's just up the street, Nell.'

She was about to answer when the laptop on the table pinged gently.

Carolyn had accepted her request.

There was a tap at the door, then it opened. 'You girls all right up here?' Kate asked.

Kym closed her book and started gathering up the papers they had spread across the bed. 'Fine.'

'Only I was thinking about starting tea. You're welcome to stay if you like, Evie.'

'Oh, thanks. I'd love to, but I should probably get back home, we've got guests this evening.'

'Right you are.' Kate leant against the doorframe, surveying the mess. 'Don't work too hard.'

'We won't,' said Kym.

Kate made a show of closing the door quietly.

'It's horrible,' said Evie, 'what happened to your dad. I'm so sorry.' She gathered up some of the scattered papers, neatening them, then placing them carefully on the desk. Kym's pencil case had slumped open, spilling out a collection of biros and markers. More out of habit than anything else, Evie began to tidy them away. Something prickled at the back of her throat. She wanted it all to be a coincidence, the knocking, the house, the way she had felt in the drying ground; bad luck and nothing more than that.

'But you'll help?' Kym asked. 'If I can find out – something, anything about the house?'

'Sure,' said Evie. 'If you want me to.'

Kym seemed to be waiting for more, 'Yeah,' she said. 'Yes. Please.'

At first, scrolling through Carolyn's posts, it seemed to Nell that there was no connection between the two of them at all. Most of the people she interacted with were strangers, many of them had nothing to do with the town, and Nell found herself wondering how many of Carolyn's many, many Facebook friends were people she'd actually met in real life.

'This is boring.' Maude had dragged her seat next to Nell's. 'Look through her photos.'

'We can't do that. They're – private.'

'Jeez, Nell.' Maude said. 'If she wanted to keep them private she wouldn't post them, would she?'

There were far too many to scroll through, but Carolyn had at least created albums. Several were dedicated to Evie, from babyhood, right through school, and others were clearly dedicated to holidays and trips abroad.

'There.' Maude pointed at the screen; the folder was marked 'Reunion'.

215

It was a couple of years old, but it seemed there had been a twenty-year reunion of the sixth form. This was news to Nell, and she couldn't say she was disappointed to have been left out. The faces in the photos were familiar, at least, even if most of the names weren't.

Carolyn featured in several of them, smiling broadly, she looked confident, glossy, successful.

Then with a comment – *A blast from the past!* – someone had posted an old school photo. The whole of the sixth form ranged in rows.

'Oh,' said Nell, 'right.'

'What? Do you recognise her?' Maude swivelled the computer around to get a better look.

'I recognise the photo,' said Nell; and she did, somewhere back at the house up in the loft where they kept all their junk, she had a copy of her own.

It didn't take Maude long to find her.

'There you are,' she said. 'Second row back, fourth one in.'

'Yes.'

'Nice hair.'

'Oh, shut up.'

It took them longer to find Carolyn.

'There,' said Nell, eventually. 'Is that her, do you think?'

The girl had dirty blonde hair and wore glasses, she stood at the end of the back row, and it may have been Nell's imagination, but she seemed to be standing slightly apart from everyone else.

'Could be,' said Maude. She clicked on the screen, someone had tagged a few people and a name popped out: Carrie Hudson.

'The thing is,' said Nell, 'this is two years, upper and lower

216

sixth form. I can recognise pretty much everyone in my year, even if I can't remember their names. But the people in the year below me, not so much.'

'Including Carolyn?'

'If it is her, then yes.'

'So, she was at school with you.'

'Well, yes.'

'And you don't remember her because she was in the year below you.'

'No. No, I don't.'

'And you didn't – have anything to do with her, ever?' Maude looked worried, younger momentarily.

'No. Nothing,' said Nell.

'You're sure? You never, like, fell out with her or anything?'

'Of course not.'

That solved the mystery, such as it was. Didn't it? Nell wished she could recall their encounter at the bridge, when she'd introduced herself, had she given her maiden name? She wasn't sure. Anyway, if a person was the year behind, was it still reasonable and normal to claim you had been to school together? Did the distinctions that seemed so important then carry on through later life? Carolyn had seen Nell in an article about the gallery, and seemed to have built up an acquaintance on little more than wishful thinking. There was something though, Nell realised – something prompted by Maude's question, something to do with a school trip.

'Well, there you go.' Maude was looking at the screen intently. 'Can I check my account? Just to see if there are any messages? Nell? Please?'

Nell sighed. 'Five minutes.'

'Fifteen?'

'Ten. And don't push your luck.'

217

'And then can I go out? To Gina's?'

'Straight there and straight back,' said Nell.

There was no sneaking past her mother when she got in; Carolyn was in the kitchen, making a start on dinner. 'Where on earth have you been?' she said.

'I've . . .' Evie couldn't think. 'I was at a friend's.'

'Sophie? Grace? What happened to the shop? You were supposed to come straight home. You could at least have texted. Well?'

There was no point lying, her mother was perfectly capable of ringing to check, and there was a chance that Grace and Sophie would say no, they hadn't seen Evie, not for ages now. They might even say why. It was hard to tell just how much Carolyn already knew, and best perhaps to come clean. As her father was fond of saying, it was better to ask for forgiveness than permission. 'Sorry. I was at Kym's.'

'At Gina's house?' Carolyn didn't sound very forgiving.

'No. Kym's up on Green Lane.'

'And when did all this happen? This – friendship?'

'I don't know.' Evie wished her mum would let her go up to her room. She was hot and sweaty from the walk back. She felt foolish, and obscurely guilty. 'School, you know?'

'And what were you doing?'

'Revision.' Carolyn eyed the bag on Evie's shoulder and for a moment Evie thought she was going to demand she hand it over, so she could search it. The thought made her breathless. 'We're in the same English group.' This part was not a lie.

'Don't you think,' said Carolyn, 'that you'd get more done working on your own? It's kind of you to offer to help a class-mate, but it's hardly the best timing.'

218

'I'm not . . . She's perfectly capable, Mum. We were just – going over some notes.'

'Well. I'd prefer you didn't go there again, not while you've exams to worry about.' Carolyn moved out of the way at last and Evie darted past her. 'Are we clear on that?' she added as Evie went up the stairs.

'Yes,' Evie said. 'Perfectly clear.'

Kym found her mum in the kitchen, chopping vegetables for a stew. She picked up a knife and began to help; the radio on in the background, both of them half listening to the news, making plans for the rest of the week. Kate was off on a training course on Monday, and Kym had already decided she was going to stay over at her gran's.

'You don't have to, you know. I trust you to look after yourself here.'

'I know. But – I like it there.'

Kate gave her a look, then changed the subject. 'And how are things with you and Ty? I saw him in the street today; he didn't stop.'

'It's OK, you know?'

'You're not having second thoughts?'

'No. Not really.'

'Right.' Kate looked at her. 'You'd tell me, wouldn't you? If there was anything bothering you?'

'Course I would.' The lie felt wrong, but there were some things Kym reckoned her mother was better off not knowing.

'Hmm. I don't have to go to Lincoln tomorrow, you know?'

'Don't be daft.'

'Fine. Forget it,' said Kate, turning her attention back to the chopping board. 'Forget I mentioned it.'

*

The landing was clogged with bin liners swollen with clothes, her mum's and – Evie noticed – her dad's too. Carolyn got like this sometimes; it was as if she was trying to shed the past, starting a great purge that led to renovation and redecoration. The mirror had gone, and Evie supposed other things would soon go missing too; ornaments, paintings, even things they were attached to, family photos, souvenirs, gifts. Carolyn could be remarkably unsentimental at times. She enjoyed moving house and when that was denied her, she loved to make a house over, as if they could all start again. New and improved. The only things she clung onto through thick and thin were the stupid Moses basket that now lay empty by the bedroom door – Evie had the uneasy feeling Carolyn was keeping that for her first grandchild – and the books she had transported from her childhood home to university and back again. Old, cheap and second-hand, most of them, hidden away in the bedroom, as if she were ashamed of the girl she had once been.

Evie went into her room and closed the door behind her, grateful to see everything was just as she'd left it. She dropped her bag on her bed, and went to the chest of drawers. She made a point of not looking up at Elder House. Kym was right, she had never really liked it, and now there were people there, a family; that just made it worse, although she couldn't have said why.

She opened the drawer. It was uncharacteristically untidy; underwear and tights and odd socks lay in a great tangle, exactly as they had the last time she looked. She pushed everything to one side, revealing an old chocolate box, its lid slightly buckled in one corner. It was shallow and more or less fitted the dimensions of the drawer, and, as far as she knew, her mum had never noticed it; it was her hiding place. Evie opened it.

It looked like junk, mostly; single earrings and scraps of

chain and ribbon. There was the remains of the old charm bracelet she had retrieved from her mother's jewellery box, a tie pin someone had given her dad one Christmas, which he never wore. Broken bits of costume jewellery, with clasps missing or lacking a hook. There were new pieces too, modern necklaces and bracelets from high street shops, most still bearing their prices, one or two weighed down by their security tags. Evie opened her bag, it took her a minute to find what she was looking for; she'd had to drop it inside quickly, without looking, and it had fallen right to the bottom.

But her fingers closed on it eventually, and she pulled it out, running her thumb over the surface as she dropped it into the box: Kym's hagstone, dark grey and with a single hole, natural and smooth, drilled through at one corner. It was shaped like an arrowhead, or a teardrop – or a heart.

17

The bathroom was at the back of the house, and as it was overlooked by nothing but the steep slope of the cliff, there was no frosted glass in the windows. It was almost pleasant, Nell decided, soaking underneath a layer of scented bubbles, the way the dull green light sort of slid into the room, peaceful, at least. She had opened one of the windows, just a little, and the air was still, the silence punctuated by the odd seagull cry.

She closed her eyes, tried not to think about the story she'd watched on the video, and gradually she felt the muscles in her back begin to soften, relax. After a week of restless nights, she began to drift away.

She was barely aware of it at first.

One-*two*.

One-*two*.

She listened. Someone was making their way down Maude's little stepladder the way a small child might, one step at a time, one-*two* – left foot, right foot, left foot, right foot; descending slowly.

Maude.

But – Maude clattered up and down the ladder at full speed, it seemed to be a point of pride with her. And anyway, wasn't there something familiar about this noise? Someone moving about the house; hadn't she heard this before?

One-*two*.

One-*two*.

Nell sat up, the bubbles sliding over her wet skin. She hugged her knees and listened.

One-*two*.

One-*two*.

Getting closer.

Silence.

She placed her hand on her chest and counted the ragged thudding of her heartbeat, one-*two*, one-*two*.

Her skin puckered into goosebumps. 'Maude? Is that you?'

The water was cooling, and slowly, carefully, she got out of the bath, grabbing a towel and wrapping it around herself, her hair dripping down her neck and shoulders.

She opened the bathroom door. There was no one there.

No internet was such a stupid idea. She had been incredibly good about it for ages now, conspicuously obliging; but every time she mentioned to Nell that maybe they could relax, and she could have a bit more access, Nell fobbed her off with vague promises, or worse, she logged on and sat down next to her, watching all the time, reading her private stuff. Maude lay on her bunk, gripping her phone, but that was useless too, the signal had almost entirely faded away up here.

Ten minutes, like she was a baby or something.

It wasn't fair.

She watched the shadows cast by the window frames as they shuddered gently against the ceiling and the witch marks carved into the beam.

Down in the house she heard a door close, and the soft footfall of someone coming upstairs. Nell seemed to move around the house much more slowly these days. It was as if she was ill.

Good.

Maude had two families, which was rubbish, no matter what people said. Two separate families. She had a vague suspicion that they had tried, at first, to get along, to do things together, for her sake. But the trouble was, although she tried to hide it most of the time, her mother really didn't like Nell. And Maude had got used to it after a while, two Christmases, two birthdays; and it was OK – had been OK – until *he* was born. The baby. Her brother. Two families, and no room for her in Mum's anymore.

Then she'd found out about Nell and Dad.

She felt the blood rushing in her ears, and it was as if the roof was pressing down on her, the darkened corners closing in. She sat up and swung her legs onto the floor, fighting the urge to cry; she wasn't going to be caught blubbing when Nell finally hauled herself up the ladder. Maybe she was hurt, because there was an odd rhythm to her footsteps, uneven; as if she was limping.

The shoe lay on the trunk where she had left it and Maude picked it up – she hadn't decided what she would wish for yet. She wasn't sure how you were supposed to go about *striking a bargain*, but she was going to, she was definitely going to. She held it close, clutching the shoe against her chest and shutting her eyes, and maybe it was because she'd been staring so hard at the marks on the beam, but it seemed to her for a moment that she could still see them, tiny daisy wheels floating behind her eyelids.

'Maude?' Nell stood on the landing and waited, but there was no reply. Sulking, no doubt. Or maybe that wasn't fair; perhaps she simply hadn't heard.

Nell considered climbing the ladder. But then, if she did,

there was every chance Maude would send her away, scornful of her attention.

God, Nell. I'm fine. Her moods were exhausting.

She gave her a moment or two to reconsider, to stick her head through the hatch.

But there was no reply.

The bubbles had subsided into a pale green scum, and the water was cold. Nell emptied the bath and rinsed it out. Then she went into the bedroom to get dry, get dressed.

'Hello.' Evie answered the door, stepping back and calling over her shoulder, 'Mum, Mrs Galilee and Maude are here.'

Carolyn's reply was muffled and masked by a single deep bark as the dog, Flossie, appeared from the back of the house.

'It's OK,' Evie said to Maude, 'she's not going to make a fuss or anything.' She opened the door wider. 'Come in.'

Maude smiled, but she didn't look convinced, standing back to let Nell go first.

'Thanks,' Nell said. 'And I'm not Mrs Galilee; Nell is fine.'

'Hello.' Carolyn appeared in the doorway, looking a little flushed and out of breath. She had changed out of her usual jeans into a linen frock and was wearing a pair of silver and turquoise earrings that Nell recognised as her own design. She should, she supposed, be flattered.

'Hi.' She held out the bottle of wine she'd been debating over for a good half hour, wondering if it might be too much for a simple supper.

'Oh, you didn't need to do that, thank you. Come in, come in.' Carolyn put the wine on the kitchen table, then led the way into the living room. 'Ollie, Nell and Maude are here.'

'Oh, hi.' Ollie struggled out of the sofa, as the cricket played on the TV in the background. 'Is it that time already? And this is Maude, is it? Hello, nice to meet you.'

'Hi.'

The room was cluttered, with tall bookshelves covering one wall, photos and pictures ranging across the others.

'Have a seat,' said Oliver, reaching for the TV remote.

'There's no need to turn that off on our account,' Nell said.

'Actually, I have something for Maude,' said Evie. 'If that's OK?' She looked at Nell.

'Yes. Of course.' She was a nice girl, Nell thought, kind. 'Is there anything I can do to help?' she asked Carolyn.

'Not a thing. Sit down. Five minutes, girls.' Carolyn vanished into the kitchen. As Maude followed Evie upstairs, Nell took a seat on the sofa, and asked Oliver something innocuous about batting order. Oliver answered readily enough and Nell began to relax as they watched the game unfold. After a few minutes, she let her attention wander, quietly inspecting the rest of the room.

The Wilsons had retained the sash windows and the exposed beams that were, she presumed original to the house. There was an open fire, unlit, and a variety of plants were crammed onto the windowsills. Most of the larger books on display were, Nell noticed, on boats and architecture. The room was a little worn, but it was comfortable, cosy, if a little cramped, as if the furniture belonged to a bigger house.

'This is very kind of you both,' Nell said. 'I hope Carolyn hasn't gone to too much trouble.'

'Oh, she loves to cook,' Oliver said. 'I barely get a look in.'

The sofa was too soft, Nell could feel herself sinking into it, the conversation fading as she did so. She had the impression it was going to be a long evening.

*

227

Evie's room was surprisingly small. Her desk was piled high with books. She cleared a space in the centre and opened a drawer, she pulled out a tangle of bright ribbon and began to sort through it.

'I wanted to make sure, like – you're OK?' said Evie, 'There's been no more – knocking?'

Maude shook her head, 'No,' she said. 'But it won't happen again, right?'

'Right.'

'You don't sound very sure.' Maude looked through the window at Elder House.

'Tyler says it wasn't him.'

'Oh.' It seemed very different from this perspective, taller and more forbidding. Better to be inside it than out, she thought. 'What was it then?'

'I don't know.' Evie hesitated. 'You weren't – too frightened?'

'A bit,' said Maude, 'maybe. But the marks in the attic will help, won't they?'

'How do you know that?' Evie asked, surprised.

'I was reading about them,' said Maude. 'We have lots of books in the house. They're witch marks but that means they're good luck.' Her fingers practically ached to draw the flowers again.

'I suppose so.' Evie looked at her intently. 'Do you believe in all that then? Witches and stuff?'

'Maybe,' said Maude. She did, she thought, but not quite enough to say so out loud. She liked Evie, but she didn't know her very well, and there was still some small part of her that feared she'd appear stupid, not cool at all.

'Gina does. She's got all sorts of things in her shop.'

'And how's your hand?'

'Fine.' Maude raised her palm. There was the tiny red dot on the fleshy base of her thumb, no bigger than a freckle.

'Evie! Maude!' Carolyn's voice drifted up the stairs. 'Supper's ready.'

Evie sat at the dressing table. 'OK,' she called.

'Evie!'

'Just a minute.' Evie pulled one of the ribbons free. 'I made this,' she said to Maude, 'and then I thought of you.' The bracelet held another one of her mother's silver charms, a tiny silver daisy, knotted onto pale blue ribbon. Evie wound it around her wrist, three times. 'You should keep it on, all the time.' She smiled. 'For luck.'

They ate in the kitchen, at the large pine table. The girls, Evie and Maude, sat on a bench with their backs against the wall, facing Nell. Oliver and Carolyn took a seat at either end of the table.

There were bowls of olives, and shallow dishes filled with roasted peppers, as well as large plates filled with a variety of bruschetta. Just a bit of supper, Nell thought, trying to catch Maude's eye.

'Mashed cannelloni and garlic,' said Carolyn, pointing to one. 'Tomato and anchovies there. Shrimp there. Just help yourself. Ollie, could you do the wine?'

As they filled their plates, Nell found she had to explain Chris's absence all over again. 'We've run into a bit of a problem with the new shop. He had to go back to deal with a planning issue.'

'Really?' Oliver looked interested in this development, and Nell hoped he wasn't going to offer any professional advice.

'The earrings look good,' she said to Carolyn, more to change the subject than anything else.

Carolyn pushed back her hair and tilted her head; the earrings shuddered in the candlelight. 'Anniversary present,' she said, smiling fondly at her husband.

'I can't really take any credit,' said Oliver. 'She'd been going on about them for ages, kept showing me this very fancy website – I had to be very canny about the delivery address, got you to send it to my office.'

'I didn't think he'd been paying attention,' said Carolyn, 'it was the most lovely surprise.'

It was strange to think Nell had parcelled them up and sent them off, all unawares. 'Well, you have excellent taste,' said Nell. 'So well done.'

'Is it odd?' Evie asked. 'When you meet someone and they're wearing something you designed?'

'I don't know. It doesn't happen very often. Usually, if someone's wearing something I've made, it's because I gave it to them, and that's different, I suppose.'

'You don't mix with your clients, then?' Oliver asked.

'Evidently not. Do you?'

'Hard not to, around these parts.'

Carolyn kept getting up to deal with the main course, an elaborate seafood risotto, as Nell, Evie and Oliver did their best to keep the conversation moving along.

They covered Oliver's birthplace, Brighton, and how he'd met Carolyn, university, and were just moving on to why they'd decided to move back to the coast when Carolyn – still busy at the oven – spoke again.

'Evie? Could you clear some space on the table for me? And load up the dishwasher.'

'How did you and Chris meet?' Oliver asked as Evie began to clear their plates.

'The gallery,' said Nell. 'I took some of my early stuff in, hoping he'd buy it and . . .' She hesitated. 'We sort of went on from there.'

230

'Evie gave me a present,' said Maude, extending her wrist. 'It's for luck.'

'Do you need luck?' Oliver asked.

'Every little helps,' said Evie. She glanced behind Nell, at her mother, then leant over the table, reaching for the empty dishes. 'I wanted to study Design Technology at school,' said Evie, 'But – I couldn't, you know, fit it in with everything else.'

'Oh,' said Nell.

'I'm doing Geography instead.'

'Far more sensible,' said Carolyn as Evie took the dishes to the sink.

'Did you hear about our shoe?' Maude asked. 'It was hidden in the wall.'

'I did indeed,' said Oliver, 'it all sounds highly intriguing. What will you do with it?'

'I wanted to keep it, but we're not allowed.'

'It isn't ours,' Nell said.

'I knew a bloke who once found a dead cat in his house.'

'Dad. No,' said Evie, sliding back into her seat. 'He tells such tall tales.'

'Up on Henrietta Street; it was under the floorboards, all grey and stiff, with a big grin on its face. Mummified,' said Oliver.

'Cool,' said Maude. 'What did he do with it?'

'Oliver, please. We're eating,' said Carolyn.

'But really, what?' said Maude.

'He put it back,' said Oliver.

Maude grinned. 'Which house is it in?'

'Oliver.'

Oliver raised his glass to Maude and winked.

Carolyn began to heap spoonfuls of risotto onto dinner plates. 'They've done a lovely job with Elder House, from what

231

I've seen.' She set the plates in front of Nell and Maude. 'Very stylish.'

'Who did?' Nell asked as she inspected her meal, trying to remember which types of seafood she should be wary of. 'I mean, who owns it?'

'Actually, I'm not sure. It was a holiday place when we bought here, a second home, and that was – two years ago?'

'Three,' said Oliver.

'Not that anyone seemed to use it very much. And then last year it changed hands – that was when they did it out again. It never seemed to actually be let out to anyone.' She served Evie and Oliver, then sat at the table, her own portion of food noticeably smaller than everyone else's.

'It's a shame,' said Oliver. 'I sometimes think we should never have—'

'They're not local, are they?' Carolyn went on. 'The new owners.'

'I don't think so,' said Oliver. 'Mind you, I can barely keep up with people moving in and out of the yard.'

'Visitors,' said Evie.

'Sorry,' said Nell.

'Oh, not you,' said Carolyn.

'How are you finding it? Elder House?' Oliver asked.

'It's – fine,' said Nell, carefully picking her way through her food. 'It's probably too big for us, but things were a bit – last minute.'

'We don't visit very often,' said Maude. 'Nell doesn't like it here.'

'That's not true.' Nell put down her knife and fork. 'You don't really think that, do you?' She looked around the table. 'We just don't have much reason to visit anymore,' she said.

'You didn't hang on to your family's house, then?' asked Oliver, topping up Carolyn's wine.

232

'They don't let you do that with council houses,' said Nell. 'Not if you're not actually living there.'

'Your parents should have bought when they had the chance.'

'That was never really an option.'

'That's how we were able to buy back here in the yard.' Ollie looked across the table at his wife. 'We were on the West Cliff, then we sold the house Caro's dad left her – up on Green Lane – and that gave us the boost we needed for this place. When we were first married we—'

'Are you all right, sweetheart?' Carolyn interrupted, looking at Maude. Her tone was solicitous.

Maude looked up from her plate, surprised. 'Yes, thank you.'

'If you don't like it, don't be afraid to say so.'

'I . . .' Maude looked to Nell for some support.

'Maude likes Italian food as a rule, don't you?'

'Yes. This is – lovely. Thank you.' Maude speared a large pink prawn and shoved it into her mouth.

'What was Mum like at school?' Evie asked.

'Very, very well-behaved and studious,' said Carolyn.

'Well, she wasn't called Carolyn,' said Nell. 'Carrie. Carrie Hudson.'

Just saying the name gave Nell a better sense of the girl in the photo, a bit shy, not really part of any gang or group.

'You got there in the end,' said Carolyn, raising her glass. 'It's OK. I do understand there's no real reason you'd remember me, not the way I remember you, anyway.'

'Yes. Sorry. But – you've changed.'

'I should hope so. No one has called me Carrie for years. You were one year above me, and one of the cool girls, too.'

'Oh, I was so not.'

'But that's what all the really cool people think, isn't it? Really cool people don't care about that sort of thing.' Carolyn's

233

expression faltered a little, and she looked older, suddenly, sadder. 'I remember once sitting next to you in the library in a free period. I was struggling to finish an essay for English Lit, and you were reading a copy of *Vogue*. I think you might have been the first person I ever met who read it.'

'Oh, God – that makes me sound kind of awful.'

'You and Laura McCallister were big friends, weren't you? And you went out for a bit with Mark Atkinson.'

'But he dumped me for – for—'

'Marianne Bentley,' said Carolyn.

'Oh yes, Good Lord.' Nell hadn't thought about Mark in years.

'Anyway, you were all so – the rest of us were just trying to keep up.'

'Like how?' asked Maude, leaning forward.

'Oh I don't know,' Carolyn faltered, then brightened. 'The Edinburgh trip. Do you remember that?'

'Not really.'

'It was – what, two nights – a whole bunch of sixth formers being let loose on galleries and the theatre and what have you.'

'Rock and roll, Nell,' Maude said.

'Hey, mind your manners, you.'

'Only someone suggested we didn't have to stick with everyone else. And a few of us sneaked away from this dreadful guided tour, I think it was in the Scottish National Gallery? Anyway, we all bunked off.'

'Where did you go?' asked Evie.

'I'm not . . .' Nell smiled apologetically. 'I can't really remember. I think Laura got it into her head . . .' Something about buying some dope, probably, she glanced at Maude.

'What?' Maude's tone was gleeful.

'We were going through a goth phase, me and Laura – well, quite a lot of us, actually.'

234

Some of the details came back to her: the dark gallery and the blazing hot sunshine in the street, the directions they'd got hold of. It hadn't been Nell's idea, though; she was sure of that.

'Yes?' Oliver said. 'Is this something I should know about?'

'What was it called?' Nell asked.

'Oh God, I don't know,' said Carolyn.

'The – something, something – Magick Emporium?'

'Magick with a k.'

'Sorry?' said Evie.

'It sold occult stuff,' said Carolyn. 'You know, bundles of herbs, joss sticks, crystals, black candles and chalices.'

'Like Gina's shop,' said Maude.

'Not exactly,' said Carolyn. 'These people – they took it seriously, I'm sure they did.'

Maude looked impressed. 'Did you buy anything?'

'No. We all lost our collective nerve pretty quickly,' said Carolyn. 'We tried to play it cool, then staggered back out into the daylight, more or less straight into one of the teachers.'

'Mrs Parker,' said Nell.

'She was livid,' said Carolyn.

'Yeah.' She remembered this part.

There had been a long and tedious telling off back at school. Nell had a sudden piercingly clear memory of everyone waiting in the corridor outside the headteacher's office, forbidden to speak to each other, Carrie Hudson all alone at the end of the line.

'Did you believe in all that?' asked Maude. 'Magic and stuff. Do you believe in it now?'

'I'm not sure.' Carolyn smiled across the table, indulgently. 'But when I was a girl, about your age, I knew a witch.'

'What, for real?' Maude sounded suspicious.

'Definitely. My auntie Ida, only she wasn't my real aunt, people just called her that.'

Maude looked around the table, waiting for something, confirmation, reassurance.

'Ida Green?' said Nell, and then to Maude. 'She's in those photos I showed you.'

'No way. What did she do then? If she was a witch?'

'Maude. Slow down a bit,' said Nell.

'Maybe that's a story for another time,' said Carolyn.

'The wine not to your taste?' Oliver asked, gesturing towards Nell's untouched glass. 'I can open a bottle of red, if you prefer.'

'I'm sure it's fine,' said Nell. 'I'm just not a very big drinker, these days.' Carolyn cast her a shrewd, assessing glance.

Maude picked up her fork. 'I was only asking,' she said.

'Actually,' said Nell, standing. 'If I could just use your bathroom?'

'Up the stairs and turn right,' said Carolyn. 'You can't miss it.'

The stairwell was lined with photographs, and on the first floor the door to Carolyn and Oliver's room stood ajar and Nell hesitated by the door.

A couple of discarded dresses lay across the bed, but otherwise the room was tidy, the walls painted a solid peacock blue and lights soft and discreet. There was a bookcase to one side of the bed, crammed with faded paperbacks, and it was tempting to slip inside, as some sort of obscure payback for the discovery of the shoe in the wall, to examine the shelves, to pull one free, to see what it was that Carolyn read at night, what it was that fed her imagination.

Ridiculous.

'Coffee?'

'Do you have decaf?'

'Actually, I think we might be out. Sorry.'

'Oh. Well, yes, regular is fine.' She knew it wasn't a good idea, and she rarely drank caffeine so late in the evening, but the house seemed a long way away, the yard steps ridiculously steep. 'Thanks.' She'd been sensible for weeks, half a cup wouldn't hurt.

'Ollie?'

'Please.'

'Let me help.' Nell stood up, anything to get away from the table, move around a little. She gathered up their empty glasses, putting them next to the sink. Carolyn's kitchen windows offered a view of Elder House; it seemed to overshadow the little cottage.

'How are you feeling?' asked Carolyn. 'Only I noticed – you didn't seem to eat very much . . .'

'I'm not used to such huge portions,' said Nell, 'but it was all delicious, thank you.' It had all been far too rich, though, and filled with the kind of ingredients she was certain she was supposed to be avoiding. She'd taken two guilty bites of the tiramisu, and let Maude finish the rest.

Carolyn didn't believe her, obviously. Nell had the feeling she'd like to be confided in. 'This has been lovely,' she said, 'you have such a – lovely house.'

Carolyn smiled. 'We've been very lucky. There was a time when I – we – thought we might like more kids, but mostly we've been . . .' She glanced at Evie, who was showing Maude something on her phone. 'You've never thought of having one of your own?' she asked.

'Maude's enough for now,' said Nell, turning back to the sink. 'Anyway, if we did, we'd have to move, find somewhere bigger.' That was something else to think about, another conversation she had been avoiding.

237

Carolyn looked out of the window, considering. 'Some people don't like old places,' she said, 'too much – history. But not me, I like them. I couldn't imagine living in a modern house.'

'Have you ever . . .' Nell hesitated. She wasn't sure what she intended to ask, something about Elder House and the death of the child; that was Carolyn's thing after all, wasn't it? History.

'Ever what?'

'Nothing,' said Nell, 'nothing important.' She would definitely do something about the shoe tomorrow, she thought. She'd ring the letting agents, first thing, find out why they hadn't returned her call.

Oliver looked up. 'How's that coffee coming along?'

'Nearly there,' said Carolyn.

There was no avoiding the goodbye hug. 'Thanks,' said Nell.

'We should do it again,' said Carolyn, 'before you go.'

It was a clear night, the sky a rich velvet blue and full of stars. Flossie slipped past Nell, circled around, sniffing at the damp stone. She seemed to consider heading up the steps to Elder House, staring at it for a moment, her ears pricking, before thinking better of it.

'You should come to us, next time,' said Nell, avoiding Maude's eye.

'Stupid old thing,' said Oliver, bending down and fussing over the dog.

'Well, goodnight then.'

Nell led the way up slowly, feeling strangely weary, conscious that Carolyn was at the bottom of the steps, watching.

It was dark inside the cottage and she couldn't find the light switch.

Nell dropped the key as Maude switched on the hall light

238

and moved past her, and bending to retrieve it made Nell dizzy. Her back ached and she felt faintly sick. 'Are you . . .' She straightened, steadying herself against the wall. 'Are you OK, Maudie? Did you have a nice time?'

'I'm fine,' said Maude as she headed upstairs. 'It was fine. And don't call me that, I'm not a little kid.'

Nell took the laptop into the living room and curled up on the sofa. She spent a few minutes going through her emails – junk, mostly, and newsletters from the few galleries and designers she followed. She deleted most of them without even reading them. The updates from the gallery – the ones Sam always copied her into – had stopped the day Chris had gone back. Maybe there was no need to update her. Maybe everything was going to be fine.

She thought for a moment, then opening a new email, she began to type:

Hi love,

Just a quick note to say we're fine here, apart from missing you, of course. I'd ring, or text, but Maude's taken herself off to the attic. If you ring her later, do me a favour and make her bring the phone down to me. Mine's still bust – obviously.

Dare I ask about Simeon Lee? The barn? I've not got any new emails from Sam, so is it OK to assume we're going to get through this? We could come back, you know, even if it was just to offer moral support. The seaside isn't much fun without you.

She stopped. There was no point in nagging. She hit the delete button and watched the cursor eat up her words.

Hi love,

Just a quick note to say we're fine here, apart from missing you, of course. I'd ring, or text, but Maude's taken herself off to the attic. If you ring her later, do me a favour and make her bring the phone down to me. Mine's still bust – obviously.

Speak soon, love you,

Nell xxx

She hit send, then stood and went into the kitchen. It was foolish, she told herself, to expect a response straight away.

Back in the attic, Maude sat on her bed and examined the bracelet Evie had given her, running her finger gently over the moulding of the petals.

It had been OK, really, supper at Carolyn's house. Lots of food, and all of it homemade, even dessert, because Carolyn was a proper cook, a proper mum. When she asked questions, she listened to the answers, and she was interested in people, even if she was a bit bossy.

It was funny to think of her and Nell at school, getting into trouble like that, even if Nell went on about not really remembering properly. But she did that, didn't she? She'd got all vague when she was telling everyone how she'd met Maude's dad; she had left bits out of that story too. She was good at that.

Thinking about her dad made her feel angry all over again; it wasn't fair that he'd gone off and left her behind.

She picked up her diary and flicked through it, thinking she might write in it for a while, but then her stomach began to churn, and she thought she might have a snack instead.

*

Nell was in the kitchen, standing by the sink, staring into the dark. She should lock up, get to bed, if there was no answer to her email in the morning she'd ring Chris.

Maude padded into the kitchen and opened the fridge. 'Can I have a biscuit?'

'You can't possibly be hungry. Not after that meal.'

'Is that a yes or a no?'

'It's a no. You're probably thirsty.' Nell picked up a glass from the draining board and filled it from the tap. 'Here.'

'If I drink it and I'm still hungry after, then can I have a biscuit as well?'

Nell didn't answer and, sighing elaborately, Maude reached out to take the glass.

'What's that?' Nell caught hold of her hand and turned it, inspecting her palm – there was a livid red spot on the fleshy part of Maude's thumb.

Maude wriggled free. 'Nothing. A nettle sting.'

'Sorry, I—'

Maude frowned. 'Can you hear that?' she said, looking up at the ceiling.

'What?'

'There's someone upstairs.'

'Don't be daft.'

'There is, listen.'

Nell couldn't be sure, it might just have been the thudding of the blood in her veins, but she thought she could hear someone walking unsteadily across the room above.

Someone limping. One-*two*.

It was impossible, ridiculous, because of course there was no one there. Both doors were locked, she was certain of that, and while most of the windows were open, they were far too small for anyone to get through, and anyway, nothing had tripped

241

the security lights. Apart from Nell and Maude, the house was empty.

Then why didn't it feel empty?

'They're upstairs,' said Maude.

It was a relief, in a way, that she could hear it too.

One-*two*.

Like a child.

Nell walked quietly into the hall, Maude sticking close behind. It was gloomy and silent and still, and the smell she had noticed last night, the damp, smouldering smell, was back. 'I'll go and look,' she said. 'You wait here.'

The noise, if there had been a noise, and Nell was no longer sure that she'd heard anything, had appeared to come from the front of the house – her and Chris's room. She walked slowly up the stairs.

The door was ajar, but that didn't mean anything, she often left it like that. Since Chris had left, she hadn't even bothered to close it when she went to sleep, judging it best to keep half an ear out for Maude.

There's no one here, she reminded herself, before taking a breath and pushing the door open.

It was all exactly as she'd left it, neat, tidy. The smell was worse here, and she crossed the room and opened the window, extending the latch as far as it would go. The poor little boy, she thought suddenly, dying all alone.

Then something, someone, walked slowly along the landing.

The skin on the back of her neck prickled.

'Maude?' She took a single reluctant step towards the door, and the slow, stuttering rhythm was replaced by a swifter double beat as if someone, something was skipping along the landing.

One-*two*, one-*two*, one-*two*.

242

It was better to stay hidden, surely, better not to look; but there was Maude to think of. She forced herself to move, she stepped back onto the landing and listened. Suddenly, inexplicably, above her, there it was again, footsteps pattering across wood; one-*two*, one-*two*, one-*two*. Scrabbling, like rats in the dark.

It was in Maude's room.

The air in the attic was stale and underneath that there was something else – something human, unwashed, sour.

Nell looked up at the windows, all of them open, but to little effect; she didn't know how Maude stood it. Her gaze travelled along the central beam in the ceiling. And then, finally, she saw them.

The oddest thing was, perhaps, that the marks were so – familiar. Craning her head back she tried to take them in, she'd seen something like this before, she was certain. Automatically, her hand went to her hip pocket, for her phone, her camera, but the pocket was empty.

She had seen it before, or something very like it, anyway. The letters were crude, slightly uneven, like a child's drawing; the flower image – for that's what it looked like, stylised petals – was clearer, cleaner, more practised. The memory was just out of reach – she closed her eyes, and immediately the smell in the attic grew worse.

On the beach, that first morning, Maude drawing flowers in the sand. Flowers, daisies, nodding their heads in a row. She opened her eyes. How on earth had she managed to carve them into the beam?

Maude's notebook lay on the bed, and Nell recalled their quarrel, Maude snatching the book away, furious and maybe even – frightened. She opened it at random.

They were the same designs swirling and looping across the paper, drawn in a bold, confident hand. Nell turned the page, there were more flowers, with sentences, or fragments of sentences weaving in and out of the petals.

Her own name leapt out at her.

Very faintly, on the landing below, someone was walking again, slowly, hesitantly, one-*two*, one-*two*.

Maude.

She was where Nell had left her, standing obediently by the front door. 'Nell? What is it? Who's there?'

'Was that you? Making that noise?'

'No.'

'It's not funny—'

'It's not me – I was right there next to you in the kitchen, how could it be me?'

'Because I've really had enough of this—'

'It's not fair, you always blame—'

'What's going on with those marks, in your room? What have you been doing?'

'What marks?'

'Don't give me that, Maude. I've had enough of this.' Nell began to walk down the stairs, still holding Maude's diary 'This isn't our house and even if it was you can't just – vandalise it—'

'I'm not doing anything!' Maude backed away, on the verge of tears, her rage and frustration a near physical thing, and Nell felt her own temper rising in response. 'You always blame me and it's not fair—'

'You need to tell me what you've been up to—'

'That's mine.' Maude's voice grew shrill. 'You're not supposed to touch my stuff—'

'Well, what else am I supposed to do' – Nell's voice rose in response – 'when you won't talk to me?' She took another step, heedless, at first, of the footsteps behind her. Then the hall lights wavered and Maude looked up past her and gasped. Nell turned to look up at the first floor landing, but the lights flickered once more and died. In the sudden darkness, the footsteps stopped. Nell took a breath, and behind her on the stair someone took hold of her T-shirt, bunching the fabric together tightly between her shoulder blades, and pulled.

As she fell, she heard Maude scream.

18

She couldn't breathe.

Her wrist ached and there was a vicious pain dancing around her ribs. She couldn't – breathe. Panic flooded in.

'Nell?' Maude sounded unbearably young, and very, very afraid. 'Nell?'

She forced herself onto her hands and knees, gasping, trying to calm down. She was winded, that was all, and – and – she took in a long shuddering breath, then another.

'Are you OK?'

'Yes.' Her voice was hoarse. She cleared her throat and tried once more. 'I'm fine, Maudie.' Gradually, her eyes became accustomed to the dark, and she could just make her out, a shadowy figure in front of the door. But hadn't she been closer? Behind her on the stairs? Nell wasn't sure.

'Who's there?'

Nell lifted her head, listened. 'No one,' she said, getting slowly to her feet, 'there's no one there.' She could smell something, hot metal, burning wire. 'We've blown a fuse, that's all.' She was dizzy, her lips were wet.

'It hurts,' said Maude, brushing past her in the dark, and Nell followed her into the kitchen. But when she spoke again she was somehow behind her once more, back in the hall, by the door. 'It really hurts, Nell.'

'Yes. OK. Give me a minute.'

*

Nell fumbled with the fuse box, her fingers stiff and clumsy. After a stuttering hesitation, the lights came on.

'Nell?'

'I said, a minute, all right? I'm coming.' No one there, she reminded herself, glancing around the empty kitchen. She'd checked upstairs and they were quite alone. She walked back into the hall.

Maude was leaning against the front door, pale and wide-eyed. 'God. Nell. Your face.'

Nell raised her hand to her mouth, her fingers, when they came away were daubed with red. 'It's OK.' She walked towards Maude, something cracking and splintering underneath her feet, pebbles, she thought, gravel or . . . Maude slid slowly down to the ground, hugging her knee, lifting, cradling her foot . . . Glass, Nell realised. Broken glass. The last of the water pooling on the parquet blocks, thin and reddish. Nell lifted her fingers to her face again, her lip was sore, swollen, and she could taste metal, but it wasn't her blood on the floor. It was Maude's.

Everything seemed too slow – to take too much time, running back into the kitchen and grabbing something, a tea towel to press against the wound, getting back to Maude and kneeling down next to her.

The cut extended the length of the arch of her foot. As far as Nell could see, it was clean. It was also deep. 'Can you wiggle your toes for me, sweetie?'

'It hurts.'

'I know.'

Maude moved her toes, and tears, heavy, sad, self-pitying, rolled down her face. Nell pressed the tea towel back into place, more firmly now she was confident there was no glass in the wound, but still concerned that the bleeding didn't seem to be easing.

'Right,' she said, 'I think we need to get this looked at properly, OK?'

Evie sat in the armchair by her window and took a good long look at Elder House.

It didn't much resemble the other holiday cottages in the yard. There were no flowers in front of it; there had been no attempt to soften or prettify the stone facade of the building with its dark leaded windows. Maybe the owners thought the house itself, which looked solid, serious, old, was enough. She wondered if they'd even seen it since spending all that money on it, what Kym felt every time she walked past it, what Gina felt too – knowing what she did about Kym's dad, Robin, and what had happened to him there.

It was hard to remember, sometimes, that Nell Galilee and her family weren't the owners, and that they weren't going to stay.

Her mother certainly seemed to have a problem hanging on to that idea. Ever since the house had been occupied, she'd been going on again about the drying ground – which wouldn't do anybody any good; there was something off about it, something – not right. She couldn't imagine why anyone would want to claim it.

She looked at her bed where she'd already set out her uniform for tomorrow, her school bag propped up against it. Notebook, pencil case, headphones, water bottle, apple – all packed up ready, just like she did every school night.

Nearly there, she told herself, just a few more days.

Downstairs, someone answered the door and then her mother was calling up to her, and to her father.

'What?' Evie went out onto the landing, but there was no reply, just a hurried conference of adult voices at the kitchen door.

*

There had been no choice in the end. Nell could have gone to Gina, but when she'd stepped outside, trying to sound reassuring as she promised Maude she wouldn't be long, Rowan Cottage was dark, and the lights in Spinnaker Cottage were still glowing gently.

And Carolyn hadn't hesitated.

Between them, they had helped Maude down the yard. Carolyn insisting she drive them herself, leaving Ollie and Evie at home.

At least the A & E department was still functioning. They didn't have to wait very long, and by the time they were seen by a doctor, a tall man with a reassuring manner, Maude had calmed down a little. She was, if anything, unnaturally withdrawn.

She sat on a bed in a cubicle, her legs extended, her foot raised on a folded towel. Wrapped in a blanket, shivering. Shock, Nell thought.

'Well, it's a nice clean cut, I'll give you that much.' The doctor moved to the sink in the corner and began to wash his hands. 'And I don't think you've done any serious damage there.'

'There was a lot of blood,' said Maude quietly.

'I'm sure there was. But there's nothing to worry about. We'll clean the wound, then put a couple of stitches in.'

'Will it hurt?' said Maude.

'Will there be a scar?' Nell asked.

'Nothing that won't fade over time,' said the doctor.

It had been incredibly kind of Carolyn to wait.

'You should go,' Nell had said. 'We might be a while, and we can get a taxi back if we need to.'

But Carolyn had insisted, and once they were done, and

they had made their way carefully out of the cubicle and back into the waiting area, she was still there.

'I said I'd text Ollie when we knew what was going on.'

'Thank you,' said Nell, 'but you really didn't have to stay.'

'I absolutely did,' said Carolyn. 'Maude, how are you feeling, sweetheart?'

'I'm all right.' Maude said softly, not really making eye contact.

'Yes. Well. Let's get you two home,' said Carolyn.

Nell got Maude up the steps, into the house and onto the sofa in the living room. 'Are you OK here for a minute?' she asked, her mind already running ahead to how they were going to manage showers and getting out of the house, how they were going to manage the stupid bloody ladder into the attic, what she was going to say to Chris.

'Yes.' Maude sank back into the cushions. From the kitchen there was a brisk double knock at the door. When Nell went through, she discovered Carolyn, hovering on the step. 'I'm all parked up,' she said. 'I just wanted to make sure – there's nothing else I can do?'

'You've already done more than enough.'

'Hardly.'

'Really, Carolyn. I'm so grateful.'

'Is she all right, the poor thing?' Carolyn strode through the kitchen, across the hall and into the living room, and Nell could hear her addressing Maude in cheery tones. She closed the door and looked at the clock on the microwave; it was past one in the morning. She pulled Maude's phone out of her bag and slipped outside, she tried three times, but each time the call just went straight to voicemail.

He was probably asleep.

251

He'd call back when he could.

And there was nothing to worry about. There was no real damage, and even Nell's suggestion that Maude stay off her feet for a while had been dismissed by the doctor. 'She'll judge for herself what feels right,' he'd said, 'there's no need to take any excessive precautions.'

Nell thought again of Maude stepping back in the dark, the shard of glass – slicing deep into the pale arch of her foot. She felt sick when she thought of the damage that might have been caused.

Standing at the sink, filling the glass, holding it out, and Maude trying to bargain with her.

Had she taken it? Had she?

Maude standing at the foot of the stairs, holding the glass, not holding the glass.

Nell couldn't remember.

It didn't really take two of them to get Maude back up into her room, and Nell wondered if Maude might kick up a fuss, but she seemed to welcome the attention, letting Carolyn climb up the ladder first, then she'd followed – clutching the sketch-book she had retrieved from the hall – taking the hand Carolyn offered, leaning on her as she limped across the room.

'All right?' Carolyn hovered over her as Maude lowered herself gently onto her bunk.

'Yes, thank you.'

Carolyn straightened and looked around the room. 'I can see why you like it up here,' she said. 'Very private.'

'It's a mess.' Nell picked up a shirt Maude had discarded on the floor and folded it, placing it on a spare bed, before picking up another one. Clearly, leaving Maude to her own devices up here wasn't working. She glanced up at the ceiling, at the strange

252

marks scored into the beams, soft, blurring into shadow. Well out of her reach, let alone a child's. She didn't know what she had been thinking, making such ridiculous accusations.

Maude slid her notebook under her pillow, making a point of not looking at Nell.

Carolyn smiled conspiratorially at Maude. 'It's not a mess if you know where everything is,' she said.

'No,' said Maude, 'it isn't.'

The shoe had fallen onto the floor and Nell picked it up.

Maude frowned. 'You said I could look after it.'

'I didn't mean you could dump it in with all your rubbish. Where's the box?'

'My stuff isn't rubbish,' said Maude, tugging at the bracelet Evie had given her, tightening the knot.

'May I have another look?' said Carolyn, leaving Nell with no choice than to hand it over. 'I can see why you like it too.' She sat on the edge of Maude's bunk. 'But Nell's right, you should probably keep it safe.'

'She shouldn't be keeping it at all,' said Nell. 'Not if she can't look after it responsibly.'

'But you won't take it,' Maude said, 'will you? Please?' She almost seemed to be on the verge of tears. 'I'll be careful.'

Carolyn handed the shoe over to Maude and smiled up at Nell expectantly and suddenly it was two against one, and it was Nell who was being unreasonable, and poor Maude who needed to be indulged.

'Of course not,' she said, 'but you have to remember it's not ours. You have to take very good care of it. You have to be – responsible.'

Something in Maude's expression soured. 'Yeah, right,' she said.

'Time for me to go, I think,' said Carolyn, standing. 'It's ever

253

so late; but I'll come and visit again, if you like? Check up on you.'

'Yes, please,' said Maude, before Nell could answer.

They walked down to the kitchen. 'Thanks again. You've no idea how grateful I am,' said Nell.

'Oh, you're welcome.' Carolyn gathered up her bag. 'You didn't say – what happened exactly.'

Nell hesitated. 'Power cut,' she said. 'The lights went out – and in the confusion Maude stood on a broken glass.'

Holding it out, distracted by the mark on Maude's hand, then the noise upstairs.

The glass she had left in the kitchen.

'I see.'

'It's happened before. The lights fusing, I mean.'

'Well,' said Carolyn, 'these things happen, especially in these old places, and kids are a total nightmare – if they can find something to break or trip over, they will.'

'Yeah.'

'She'll bounce back before you know it. And – if you don't mind – are you OK?' Carolyn lowered her voice. 'You must have taken a nasty tumble too.'

'I'm fine.' Nell folded her arms and stepped back, trying to smile, trying not think about the footsteps, which seemed now to have been muffled yet purposeful, or that bloody shoe and the way Maude clung onto it, and the flowers and the letters above her bed fading into the shadows: *MMM*. 'Honestly.'

'Yes, well, let me know if you need anything else.' Carolyn opened the door. 'Goodnight, again.'

19

Maude waited until she was sure they had both gone back downstairs, then – moving slowly and carefully – she arranged everything she needed on the bed; the shoe, her pad and pencils, the books she'd been reading, the salt cellar she'd pinched from the kitchen. Iron had been a bit trickier, until Nell had let her out to go and buy Issie her present. Instead of going to Gina's, she'd whizzed across the bridge to the haberdasher's – so weird, so old-fashioned – opposite the bus station. She'd bought a packet of pins, steel, not iron, but they would have to do. Nell was busy pretending to Carolyn that there was nothing wrong, but she wasn't fooling Maude.

She picked up one of the books, the one that had the description of the witch marks. There wasn't much detail in it, really, just fragments of ideas, bits of superstition, but if you thought about it – if you thought about the shoe – they sort of made sense.

Apotropaic magic, which meant you could protect yourself.

Sympathetic magic, which meant you could make things happen.

It had been a nice evening at Carolyn's house until they'd got back here and the noises started.

The noises had frightened Nell.

Good.

Maude found the page she wanted and started to read.
Serve her right.

Nell lay awake, staring into the dark, listening for – she wasn't
quite sure what. Her back ached, her mouth was dry, and sleep
– the very idea of it – was impossible. She kept replaying the
night's events in her head; sometimes Maude was holding a
glass of water as they quarrelled, sometimes she was not. She
rolled onto her side and began to rehearse the phone call with
Chris. Distantly the clock in the churchyard above chimed the
half hour.

Downstairs, a door slammed.

On the landing all was still. Nell walked down the hall and
paused at the top of the stairs, 'Maude?' She couldn't be sure,
but she thought she could hear someone moving around in
the kitchen. Muffled footsteps, the rush of water in the sink.

She should be resting her foot, not – not . . .

The kitchen was dark, it was empty, and she had the sensation that it had only recently been vacated, that whoever had
been walking there had simply stepped outside, and might be
waiting for her to follow. She switched on the lights, crossed
the room quickly and tried the door; it was locked. The cold
tap was dripping and she tightened it. Standing in front of the
windows, she couldn't see the bankside, and she was grateful
for that at least. It was an ugly little patch of land, no good to
anyone.

There was just her own reflection, pale and lonely where the
drying ground should be.

Somewhere in the dining area, and slightly muted as if it
was half hidden, a mobile phone sounded, and Nell turned.
The ringtone was an old-fashioned bell, Chris's phone. It wasn't

256

possible, of course, but her heart lifted for a moment, he was back, he was here.

The ringing was further away now, the hall, perhaps; the tone sounded once, twice more, then stopped.

But there was no one there. Behind her, out in the dark, the wind gusted briefly and the windows rattled.

The dull ache in her back had spread, and she ran her hand across her belly, as the first sliver of pain sliced into her.

Too much food, she thought, too much, too late in the evening; she should have been more careful.

Then she felt it, another spasm, deeper, and followed by a warm, sticky release, and as she doubled over, gasping, she knew that she was wrong.

It took ages to clean herself up, shaking and clumsy, rubbing at her thighs with dampened toilet roll, washing her hands and watching the rust-tinted lather swirl into the sink, then washing them again, fearful of staining the pristine towels, leaving evidence of yet another dreadful humiliating failure.

She opened the bathroom cabinet. At least she'd bought some tampons, at least she'd brought some paracetamol. The cramps were getting worse now, now she knew what they were, knifing through her, taking her breath away. She was done now; she wanted to go home, she wanted Chris. She wanted nothing more than to lay down and cry.

Front and centre, wedged between a box of plasters and a bottle of mouthwash, stood the familiar white and blue box, the pregnancy test she had bought and misplaced.

Early Detection.

Unmissable.

The sheer spite of it took her breath away.

Nell grabbed the box, and, looking for somewhere to dispose

257

of it, finally settled for wedging it in the bottom of the bin, underneath used tissues and bits of cotton wool. The tears threatening to rise again, this was unbearable.

How would she tell Chris?

What would he say?

She looked in the mirror, pushed her hair back from her face, then she heard it again.

The soft hesitant footsteps.

One-*two*.

One-*two*.

Then silence.

She opened the door and stepped out onto the empty landing, then walked to her room without looking back.

20

Nell's headache was worse than any hangover. She rolled onto her side, squinting against the morning light that edged in around the drawn curtains, and raised a hand to the back of her head. There was a good-sized lump there and a few rusty smears on the pillow case. Then she remembered the rest of it, the frantic scramble to the bathroom and all that followed, as the suffocating sense of loss rolled through her, settling over her heart; what would she tell Chris?

She sat up carefully, the muscles in her back and left shoulder were stiff and sore. Gathering her courage, she stood, swaying a little as a sharp pain cut through her hip and down her left leg. She walked unsteadily to the door, fighting the urge to cry, to get back into bed, pull the covers over her head and give in. A shower would help, and something for the pain too, then she'd set about the day.

The room seemed to blur, to tilt to one side, before righting itself.

Maude. She should check on Maude.

One thing at a time, she decided.

The shower over the bath wasn't the strongest in the world, but it washed away the dried blood from her scalp and hair; the hot water easing her muscles and the cramps in her back.

There was a graze running along her leg and the beginnings of some spectacular bruising around her ribs.

She'd been lucky really. No broken limbs.

'Shit.' The tears welled up again, and she made sure to be careful when clambering out of the shower, clinging onto the edge of the bath, moving slowly, with exaggerated care.

She began to comb out her damp hair, trying to avoid the lump on her head. Her reflection in the mirror was grey-ish, pale and tired, and she wondered if she shouldn't attempt some make-up.

Then she noticed the pins.

They were jammed into the wood at the bottom of the sash window, seven of them, with a couple more laying loose on the ledge, as if someone had dislodged them. The pins were new, the marks in the paint fresh, and there was a heap of white grains in the corner of the window, in both corners. After a moment, she licked her finger and dipped it in the coarse powder, bringing it up to her mouth to taste.

Salt.

The nausea that gripped her was sudden and vicious. Nell threw up into the toilet, vomiting until she felt hollow, her legs shaking, her throat sore.

'Maude? Maude, are you awake?'

She didn't think she'd heard her at first, then the shape in the bed stretched and a single hand pushed away the light summer duvet.

Maude sat up.

'How are you feeling?'

'OK. Tired.'

'Hungry?'

'Yeah. A bit.'

260

'And maybe a shower later?'

'My foot—'

'We'll work something out. We'll wrap it in a carrier bag or something.'

'I'll think about it.'

'Maude.'

'What?' Her hair was tangled and knotted, her face still smeared with sleep; she looked ridiculously young. There was a book on the floor, half-read, face down, *Tales From the North Riding*. Wincing, Nell bent and picked it up.

'Nothing. Come on then, breakfast. And we can try your dad again.'

It took far too long to get Maude out of the attic and down the stairs. She was unwilling to trust her full weight to her injured foot and was reduced to half hopping, half hobbling, clutching resentfully at Nell's arm for support; Nell flinching at every unsteady step. Maude wanted nothing more than cereal, which was a blessing, and Nell made herself a coffee before calling Chris.

When he answered, Nell tried to keep her voice even, calm, as she went through the details of the previous night, the power cut, the fall, Maude's accident.

'Will she have a scar?'

'I don't know. The doctor didn't seem worried.'

'And how did it happen?'

'I told you, we thought we heard something upstairs, it was dark, she stepped on some broken glass. Everything was very – confusing.' Nell looked across the table at Maude, who was following the conversation intently.

'Weren't you keeping an eye on her?'

'Of course I was.'

'There was blood everywhere,' said Maude, loudly.

'You should have rung.'

'I did, it kept going to voicemail and I thought a message would be . . . It was late. I didn't want to worry you.'

'You should get your phone fixed.'

'We've been through that. And anyway, what difference would it make?'

'You should have left a message.'

'Yes, all right. I'm sorry.' There was a long silence. 'We miss you,' said Nell.

'I'm – yeah, me too.' He sounded faint, far away, tired, and Nell wanted to turn the volume up, but she wasn't sure she could do it without cutting him off entirely. She wanted to tell him about the noises, about the footsteps, she wanted to be sure he would believe her. 'I know,' she said. 'When will you be back?'

'We've got to look again at the plans, the objections are all to do with altering the character of the building—'

'We?'

'Me and Sam.'

'It's a bloody barn.' Nell couldn't help it; this was all so – petty. Besides, didn't she get a say? Didn't he need her help too?

'I know. But this chap – Simeon Lee – he seems to have a lot of friends in various local history groups. And Sam reckons he's got form for stuff like this. Plus there's been a problem with some of our payments not going through to suppliers. I spoke to the bank, but I still need to make a few in-person apologies.'

It occurred to Nell that Chris was somewhere noisy, somewhere busy, she could hear the rumble of voices, the faint pulse of music.

One voice closer than all the others, muted, barely audible.

'Is Sam there? Is she with you now?'

'Yes.'

'Where are you?'

'We're in Roberto's.' The Italian cafe opposite the gallery, very cool, very hip, very popular.

'Right. Since when do we do breakfast meetings?'

'Oh, come on, Nell.'

There was a pause, and Maude stopped scooping milky cereal into her mouth.

'Anyway,' Chris went on, 'we're hoping to meet with Simeon Lee tomorrow, show him the plans, answer all his objections, see if I can't talk him round before he takes it to the council.'

And he had always been good at that, at what Nell's dad used to call 'turning on the charm'.

'What goes around, comes around,' Jess, Maude's mother, had said once, back in the early days, when they were all still trying to manage the separation, the new arrangements with Maude, back when she could barely stand to be in the same room as her ex-husband and his new girlfriend. 'He did it to me, and one day he'll do it to you.'

Nell had ignored her, of course. It had been different with her and Chris; it hadn't been infidelity, it had been love.

'The signal in here is rubbish,' said Nell, standing and heading for the kitchen door. 'I won't be a minute.'

It was chilly out in the shade of the house; the day had yet to warm up and goosebumps rose on her skin. 'Are you even going to try to get back up here?'

'Nell—'

'Are you?'

'Yes.'

'Soon?' She edged away from the house, glancing down towards Spinnaker Cottage.

'Yes. Like I said, we've got this meeting tomorrow then . . .'

But it seemed to her he had hesitated. 'If it's not too much trouble,' she said, 'because I think your daughter would quite like to see you.'

'You just said she was fine.'

'She's hobbling around the house, barely speaking to me. And I'm still – still . . .' The ache in her back, the cut on her lip, the pain in her side every time she moved; she wanted to cry. 'I don't feel very – I got my period.' She lowered her voice – wishing she could be sure Sam wasn't listening to Chris's half of the conversation. 'I'm not pregnant.'

'Oh.' She could feel him weighing his response. 'Are you – was it a – miscalculation?'

'No. I had my dates right. It didn't – I *was* pregnant.' She was sure of that, at least. 'But I'm not pregnant anymore.'

There was a long pause. 'You're sure? I mean – you were sure last time too. It wasn't—' The background noise surged, people talking, plates, cutlery clattering.

'Of course I'm sure.'

Nell closed her eyes, trying to remember what it was like to be held in his arms, the smell of him, the warmth.

'Was it the fall?'

'No – I'm a bit bashed up but . . . It doesn't work like that. I'd been feeling a bit – off – for a few days.'

'You should have said, why didn't you say, if you weren't feeling right?'

'Because that's all it was, just – a feeling, and there was other stuff going on, and – I didn't really connect it, you know?' Until it was too late.

'What other stuff?'

'I don't know – the house,' Nell said. 'I really think we should pack up and come back home.'

'It's not worth it,' said Chris. 'Give me a couple of days and I'll be back with you.'

'Only I'm a bit worried about Maude.' Pins and heaps of salt, the marks carved into the beam over Maude's bed, the footsteps she was now sure weren't just her imagination. It was too much, Nell thought, too much to make sense of, too much to explain. Dr Bishop. The poor little boy, choked, dead.

Wandering the house at night.

'You said she'd be fine.'

'Me, then. I'm worried about me. I'm not sleeping well. I'm . . .' Hearing things, seeing things.

'Well, maybe if you looked after yourself properly for a change . . .' The signal picked up, and his voice was suddenly loud, too loud, too close.

'What? This is my fault now, is it?'

'I'm sorry, I—'

'Maybe I should work on my timing too. Because let's not forget this lets you off the hook, doesn't it? It's one less thing for you and Sam to worry about.' She was crying. It wasn't fair; none of this was fair.

'No. No, no, no, let's not do this now, love.'

'Nell . . .' Behind her, the kitchen door opened, and Maude was peering out anxiously.

'Maude's here,' Nell said, rubbing at her face. 'If you want to say goodbye to her. Hang on.' Then she handed over the phone.

Nell let Maude finish the conversation with her father in private. She went back inside, drank her coffee, scraped the uneaten toast on her plate into the bin, washing it and leaving it to drain by the sink. She was wiping down the counter when Maude limped back in. 'Dad says he'll ring again later.'

'OK.' Nell tried to smile. 'Thanks, Maude. Come on, eat up, finish your breakfast.'

'I'm all done,' said Maude. 'Will you help me back upstairs now? I'm tired.'

Nell took a deep breath and tried to find a smile for her step-daughter. 'Sure, sweetheart.'

21

Last year, at her old school during GCSEs, a girl had fainted in an exam. There had been quite a fuss, although the worst bit was the way some students had kept on writing furiously – uncertain if they'd lose time, and precious marks, if they stopped to help a friend. The invigilators had dealt with it, and to be fair, she'd recovered pretty quickly.

Stress, someone had said, anxiety.

What Evie remembered most was how embarrassed the girl had looked once they'd hauled her to her feet and taken her and her papers off to the quiet room so she could attempt to carry on. She would die, absolutely die, if that ever happened to her – so it was very important that she did not faint.

The overhead light bounced off the question paper in front of her, and the printed words seemed to stretch and blur in front of her eyes.

Drowning, she thought.

Then, absurdly, she was back outside the drying ground, the silence pressing in. Waiting.

Deep breath.

The stupid thing was she liked French, she actually enjoyed the lessons, she had – and her mother always loved hearing this at parents' evening – a good ear. She knew this stuff. Or rather, she had known it at home, up in her room.

She closed her eyes; the damp grass, Flossie tugging at her

lead. She had felt it too. And now there had been an accident, Maude had been *hurt*. Should she say something? Do something?

This wasn't helping.

She opened her eyes, gripped her pen. Start at the top of the page. Read the question again and start writing.

An hour to go, then it would all be over.

Nell was sitting on the kitchen step, an old leather bound book to one side, staring blankly at the drying ground as Kym rounded the corner.

'Hello?' She was holding a bunch of flowers. 'I've been sent to check up on you, well, Maude, really. Gran says do you want to go round? And if you do, I can stay with Maude for a bit. She'd come round herself, only – she says she doesn't want to intrude.' She looked down at the flowers she was holding, peonies, roses and some sprigs of lavender. 'These are from her.'

'Oh, she shouldn't have.' Nell picked up her book and stood. It took some effort. 'Come in and we'll find a vase for them.'

'I didn't mean to disturb you.'

'You're not, I was just – reading.' Nell led the way. 'How did she know what happened?' she asked as she went through the cupboards, moving slowly, carefully.

'Evie told me.' Kym put a finger into the bowl of sea glass by the sink, swirling the water, watching the glass shimmer as it caught the light. 'Then I told my gran, you know how it goes.' She looked at Nell. 'Are you OK?' she said. 'Only Evie said – it all sounded a bit confused.'

'There was a problem with the lights,' said Nell, 'and I think . . .' She hesitated. 'It was just a silly accident. I should have been more careful.' She found a glass vase and rinsed it

268

out. 'Are you really sure?' She went on. 'About Maude? You don't have anything else to do? And you – don't mind?'

Kym wiped her fingers on her T-shirt and smiled at Nell. 'No,' she said, 'I don't mind at all.'

It sounded worse when she told Gina what had happened, mad, even.

'If I thought there was someone hanging around here,' Gina said as she poured out a cup of chamomile tea, 'I would call the police. I would definitely not go sneaking around upstairs looking for them.'

'There was no one there.'

'What does your Chris reckon to it?'

'He doesn't know, about the footsteps, I mean. Maude was there, when I last spoke to him. She's always there – I didn't want to worry her any more than she already is.'

'But you definitely heard something.'

'Yes. I think so.' Nell tried to smile. 'At the time I thought – yes.'

'Then you fell.'

'I – yes . . . This is very good of you, listening to me going on.'

'Think nothing of it,' said Gina. 'Who else would listen? Carolyn?'

'Well actually, she was incredibly kind,' said Nell. 'With Maude and everything.'

'Couldn't bear to miss out, more like,' said Gina.

'Still, I appreciate it.' It was very comforting in Gina's kitchen, and Nell felt oddly homesick. If she'd handled the phone call with Chris better, they might be on their way back now, or he would be on his way back to them. 'It's like . . .' she said, 'it's like we – I – can't get anything right. Ever since I pulled that

269

shoe out of the wall everything has – gone wrong. The business, Maude, me.'

'We all feel that way sometimes – you've had a bit of bad luck, that's all.'

'I suppose so.' Nell leant forward, reaching for a biscuit, wincing.

'And what's wrong with you?'

'Nothing. Bruises.'

'Let me see.'

Feeling slightly foolish, Nell stood, raising her T-shirt and pulling at the waistband of her jeans.

Gina's expression changed, something in it softened. 'Good Lord,' she said, probing the bruising gently. 'You'll need to put something on this – hang on.'

She opened a cupboard, and after a brief search, produced a small green jar. She unscrewed the lid, sniffing at it as if checking the contents.

'What's that?'

'Arnica, for the bruising.' Gina began to dab the ointment on her skin, raising goosebumps.

'Ow.'

'Sorry. You're lucky you didn't crack a rib. Actually, I'm not so sure you haven't.'

'Yes, I've been feeling incredibly lucky all morning.' Nell gasped again as Gina dabbed at a particularly tender spot.

'Have you slept at all? Maybe you should get yourself checked out.'

'I did. They looked me over once they'd done with Maude, no broken bones and a leaflet about concussion.' She gave Gina a watery smile 'It's not me I'm worried about.'

Kym sat on the bunk opposite Maude's, looking up at the ceiling. If she concentrated she could just make out the daisy

270

wheel etched into the beam above them. It was a nice design, she thought – simple, pleasing.

She had placed the vase of flowers on the floor in front of the trunk, their sweet old-fashioned scent masking the musty air. The kid looked better than Kym had been expecting. A bit pale, perhaps, with blotchy red patches on her arms, and she wondered if there was something going on there, allergies, eczema. The shoe lay on top of the trunk in pride of place. It was soft and stained and Kym was reminded of that time she lost her house key and as a last resort she'd had to go through the kitchen bin, through all the overripe vegetable cuttings and peelings, pulpy matter on the verge of decay.

She glanced up at Maude, then reached across and gave the dark leather a poke.

There. Not frightened of you.

'Tell me again,' said Kym. 'Tell me what happened. Slowly.'

'We were in the kitchen,' said Maude, 'and then – there was a noise, like someone was walking around up here.'

'Not like the other night?'

'No. This was definitely inside.'

'Where? Which room?'

'Nell's room, I think. Nell and Dad's room.'

'Not up here?'

'No. I'm not sure.'

'And have you told her about the other night?'

Maude snorted. 'No.'

Kym picked up one of Maude's books, and began to leaf through it. 'And on the stairs?'

Maude's expression changed, she looked furtive, guilty. 'Nell slipped.'

'Does she normally get wound up about stuff like that?'

'Stuff like what?'

271

'You know' – Kym waved the book at her – 'spooky stuff.'

'Dunno. It's never happened before. She's a bit weird about the shoe, though. She doesn't like it, I can tell.'

'And you do?'

'Yeah. It's cool.' She glanced at it again.

'What do you think it was? The noise?'

Maude sat up, leant forward, and her expression was serious. 'I don't know,' she said. 'But once it started, it sort of felt like I'd heard it before, you know? But I'd always thought it was Nell, or Dad. Only now, I think maybe it wasn't them after all.'

Kym, settled back on the bunk, closing her eyes. 'Are you sure?'

'I'm not sure,' said Maude. 'I mean, you just hear someone walking through the house and you think it's like, someone you live with because you get used to the sounds they make, so you hear it and you don't hear it at the same time.'

With her eyes closed it was surprisingly difficult to tell where the kid was, her voice, soft and light, didn't seem to be fixed in any one position. Maybe it was the sloping roof, messing with the acoustics, and maybe she had a point.

Kym opened her eyes. Maude was standing above her, hands on hips, frowning. It was warm up here, despite the open windows. Kym could feel sweat prickling in her scalp and under her shoulder blades. The kid really didn't look right, she looked – tired, anxious. 'It was like that,' she said, 'it was familiar.'

Evie waited until the exam hall was almost empty, packing and repacking her pencil case, before making her way out into the real world again.

She caught a glimpse of Marnie at the lockers, but she was talking enthusiastically to a boy Evie didn't recognise. Evie

272

grabbed her school bag, switched on her phone and was considering going over and saying hello, making a big deal of asking how the exam had gone, just to see what Marnie might do, when her phone buzzed, and she saw the messages from Kym.

One old message, and one sent just five minutes ago.

You done yet? I'm at EH with Maude. x

Seriously. Things are getting very weird. Come and say hi. xx

'Is he going to be away for long, then? Chris?' Gina asked.

'I hope not. He says not.'

Nell cradled her mug and looked at Gina. 'It doesn't feel right, you know, Elder House.' She shook her head. 'Does that make sense? I don't like it.' It felt good to say it out loud. She thought for a moment. 'You don't like it either.'

'You don't have to stay, you know,' said Gina.

'Only apparently, we do.' Nell put the mug on the table. 'We could just pack up and go back, I suppose, surprise Chris – but I think he'd think I was being . . . I think he'd think that meant I didn't trust him.'

'And do you?'

'Of course I do.' Her tone was flat. 'Anyway, the problem isn't us – it's . . .' She hesitated. 'I was reading about – the yard and Dr Bishop. I saw a clip of the ghost walk.'

'Ah. Darren something or other, I think he was called. He was a nice lad, but I wouldn't place too much faith in his stories.'

'I know, I do know that, but . . .' said Nell. 'But – I know it sounds weird, but before I fell, it felt like something grabbed hold of me and pulled.' There was a long silence. 'You don't believe me. That's OK, I wouldn't believe me either.'

'I've never much liked the place,' said Gina, 'but if you felt someone pull you – well, I'm sorry, pet, but maybe the solution is closer to home.'

Nell shook her head. 'She couldn't have, there wasn't time – she wouldn't . . .'

'Maybe it was just a joke that got out of hand.'

And it did make sense, in a way. Things going missing, then being replaced, her phone, the testing kit; the silly, spiteful random nature of it. 'There were some things in the bathroom this morning,' Nell said slowly.

'Things?'

'Salt. Pins.'

Gina raised her eyebrows. 'Salt and iron to protect a house. Have you asked her about them?'

Nell sighed. 'If I do, there'll be another scene. But if I don't . . .' She should check the time, she ought to be getting back. She looked around the room. 'Have you got a bit of paper?'

Gina opened a drawer, pulling out a pencil and a spiral-bound notebook. Nell took them and sketched the design out as well as she could remember. 'And there are these,' she said, 'up on the beams in her room.'

'Goodness,' said Gina.

'Do you know what they are?'

'Witch marks,' said Gina, then she smiled. 'Don't look so worried, pet. They're for protection, luck; they've been inside the house for a long time without doing anybody any harm. There's nothing – nothing to worry about there.'

Nell looked at the paper, thinking. 'But even so,' she said, 'it's like she's drifting away from me. No. Pushing me away.'

'It's the only power you have at that age, isn't it?'

'Power?'

'Privacy. Finding out you can say no to the grown-ups. She's testing her boundaries, that's all.'

'Oh she's doing that, all right.' Nell's throat ached, she wouldn't cry, not again. 'And she won't part with the shoe,' she said, suddenly resentful. 'There were lots of promises about taking good care, and it's only for a few days, but if it's giving her ideas . . . If she . . .' She could feel them again, small hands tugging and pinching, and her back ached, her stomach cramped.

'Maybe you should put it back in the wall, where it belongs,' Gina said.

'Isn't that – encouraging her?'

'It might – resolve things. If it's done with care.'

'Mindfully?' Nell attempted a smile.

'Think of it as setting an intention. Putting your house in order. If you get her to help, do it together, then maybe Maude will feel – I don't know – included? If she's feeling the need to protect herself, then maybe she needs to talk about – well, whatever it is that's bothering her. Putting the shoe back might give you both a place to start.'

The trouble was, Nell thought, that once they made a start, who knew where that might lead.

'Maybe,' she said. 'When she's feeling better.'

'I can't stop.' Evie hovered around the kitchen door, barely able to step over the threshold; she couldn't help glancing behind, towards the path and Spinnaker Cottage.

'I don't think she's actually going to follow you up here and drag you away,' said Kym, who seemed to think it was all a joke.

'You have no idea,' said Evie.

'Are you going to come in?'

275

'I can't – I . . . Where's Maude? Is she OK?'

'She's fine.' Kym reached out, squeezed her arm. 'She's upstairs, sleeping, and you need to stop giving yourself such a hard time.'

Evie allowed herself to be pulled into the kitchen.

'How did it go, then?' Kym said, leaning against the sink, ''cause you look like shit.'

'Shut up.'

'Honestly, you do. You should think about leaving the books alone for a bit.'

'Like that's going to happen any time soon.'

'Did she tell you? Nell?'

'About?'

'About last night. *Before* Maude cut her foot. It happened again, weird noises; only this time they were inside.'

'Right.' Evie dropped her school bag on the floor, looking around the empty kitchen. 'Where inside?' she asked.

'Her parents' room, then along the landing,' said Kym. 'But the interesting thing is, she reckons she's heard it before.'

'When you were babysitting.'

'No. Just like, in everyday life. She thinks she might have been hearing it, but thinking it was Nell or her dad.'

'Oh.'

'What if they've been hearing it all along, only they didn't realise? And now it's getting worse.'

'Why?'

'I don't know, because the house is occupied again? And it's waking up?' said Kym, and it occurred to Evie that she too seemed energised by this latest development.

'God, that's creepy.'

'Yeah.' Kym turned and stared out at the drying ground. 'So I was wondering, say it is – waking up. Then maybe it's happened

276

before? So now and a couple of years back when they decided to do it up and—'

'And before that, when your dad was working here?'

'Yeah. As if it needs people to – recharge.'

Evie moved beside her and they stood in silence for a moment, looking out of the window, at the drying ground. 'Well, it's a theory,' she said. 'The trouble is, that's all you've got.'

'Excuse me.' Kym nudged her gently. 'It's all *we've* got.'

Evie smiled, despite herself. The drying ground was in shadow, the gate still hanging open where she had left it. She had the oddest urge to go out and close it.

Kym raised her hand, tucking her hair, thick and dark, behind her ear. She wore a single earring, a long thin scarlet bead and there was a small gold hoop hooked through the cartilage inside her ear.

'Has Tyler been in touch?' Evie asked. 'Since – you know.'

Kym put her hands on the edge of the sink, leaning forward. 'Nope.'

'You've known him a long time, haven't you?'

'Small town,' said Kym.

'Yeah.' Evie put her hands on the sink too, her fingers brushing lightly against Kym's. 'Do you think you might – get back together?'

'Why, do you fancy your chances with him?'

'No.' Evie concentrated on the fine cracks in the surface of the porcelain. 'I don't – no.'

'Not your type.'

Evie shrugged, she could feel Kym looking at her.

'And now there's the witch marks, you know? And the shoe,' said Kym. 'All in this one house, and I have this feeling that if we looked at it the right way, if we could get everything in order, it would all – make sense.'

Evie turned to look at her, holding Kym's gaze; she was

almost unbearably lovely, Evie thought, delicate underneath the bold make-up, untouched. Fragile.

She looked at her for the longest time, not daring to move. 'I have to go,' she said, eventually.

'Well, if you're not interested . . .' said Kym, looking away.

'It's not that. It's – exams.'

'Well, yeah.' Kym shrugged. 'But it's only AS levels, isn't it?'

'The thing is – last year, at my old school, my GCSEs. My grades – they were OK, but they weren't brilliant, you know? They were – disappointing.' Her mother's word.

Kym looked puzzled. 'Did you have to do re-sits?'

'No. They weren't that bad, just – not good enough, for her. My mum. My dad didn't mind, not that much – I think he's happy he doesn't have to manage the fees anymore. Business sort of – quietened down for a while, so we moved. But Mum has all these ideas, expectations of me; she doesn't really get me. So, you know – I try not to get – all confrontational.'

Kym rolled her eyes.

'There's stuff I can't tell her,' Evie went on, 'about . . .' But she couldn't do it; she couldn't get the words out. She couldn't tell Kym the truth about herself. No one knew, not for sure. Not at her last school, not at this one, even if the rumours had finally reached Grace and Marnie and the others. She stood a little straighter, pulled her hand away from Kym's.

Kym was studying her. 'What stuff?'

Just looking at Kym made Evie's heart ache. She couldn't risk it. Not again. 'Nothing,' she said, 'I have to go. I have to be seen to be making an effort, you know?'

'Hang on.' Kym went to the table, rummaged around in her bag, then she pulled out a blue plastic folder, A4, bulging with notes and photocopies. 'I thought you could maybe have a look at this?'

'What is it?'

'Research. Stuff on Elder House. Old stuff, mostly. Have a look, see what you think.'

'I told you—'

'Exams. Yes.' She held the folder out. 'Come on Evie, you know you want to.'

'Fine.' Evie took the folder.

'And I was thinking we could try the museum tomorrow morning, and don't say exams again, because I already checked your timetable.'

Carolyn was up in the attic, getting organised. They had thought, a couple of years ago, once they were settled in, that they might make more of the roof space; as so many houses in the yard had. When you looked online, some of the conversions were very appealing – and of course Maude's little attic had been very nicely done. But it wasn't, Ollie had pointed out more than once, as if they needed another bedroom. They were better off using the space for storage, and they had only got as far as laying hardboard in sections over the beams, to make it easier to stack boxes, and to gain access to the water tank.

She couldn't recall the last time either Ollie or Evie had been up here, and in a way she was glad, she always enjoyed this bit, she found it soothing, reassuring; creating order out of chaos. She'd get one of them to give her a hand dropping off the bags of unwanted clothes at the charity shop at the weekend.

When she was done, she climbed down the attic ladder and went back into the kitchen, thinking yet again what a pity it was that they had no permanent neighbours, apart from Gina Verrill. She tried to remember what it had been like when they'd first moved into the yard, how it had felt to be making a fresh start, and how they had once upon a time actually got on perfectly well with Gina before all that – fuss. She was washing her hands at the sink, and considering lunch when Evie appeared at the top of the steps.

Carolyn checked the kitchen clock, then wondered what Evie had been doing up at Elder House, visiting Maude, perhaps, which was a kind thought, although there was a time and a place.

'Hi, Mum.' She closed the kitchen door carefully.

'Hello, darling.' Head down, Evie slid past her, barely looking Carolyn in the eye. 'Is everything all right?'

'Fine.'

She ran up the stairs.

The bedroom door slammed shut behind her.

Carolyn listened for a few minutes, loud music would certainly not be tolerated, but all was still. Exam nerves, she supposed. She debated tapping on the door, trying to find out what might be the matter, but maybe it would be best to let her get it out of her system, whatever it was.

Maybe things weren't going so well with Kym Swales, it wasn't as if they had anything in common, after all. Good. The sooner that particular friendship withered and died, the better.

22

'You do look like your grandmother.' Carolyn put the photograph down and took a sip of her coffee.

'Really?'

The familiar tapping at the door, not long after a late breakfast, had been a welcome distraction. A whole day and night of Maude convalescing and Nell doing her best to take care of her had left them both tired and irritable. Maude had confined herself to the attic, with Nell struggling up and down the ladder to fetch and carry for her, never quite finding the right moment to bring up the shoe, and to discuss what they should do with it. Wary still of Maude's mood and temper.

They seemed to get along better when someone else was around, even if that someone was Carolyn. She had baked biscuits and a banana loaf, which was enough to tempt Maude down into the kitchen. After inquiring into Maude's health, the conversation had turned to Nell's family and the snapshots Gina had found.

'Definitely.'

'I don't think I've ever seen a picture of Aunt Ida looking so young.'

'We could scan it,' said Maude, 'send you a copy.'

'That's very kind of you,' said Carolyn.

Maude helped herself to another biscuit. 'Was she really a

witch?' she asked. "'Cause there's no such thing, is there? Not anymore.'

'Well, not now, maybe,' said Carolyn slowly, glancing at Nell, 'but when I was little she seemed very old, very – powerful.'

Maude's expression was something between horror and awe. 'How did you know she was a witch?' she asked 'Like, for certain?'

And it was nice, Nell thought, to see a glimpse of the real Maude again.

Kym and Evie paused by one of the cabinets. Arranged carefully in rows of thick strips of yellowing linen were a selection of pins, one- or two-inches long; some blunted, some bent, all of them blackened with age.

Anglo-Saxon pins found in great numbers and in many locations. They are likely to have been worn in clothes, the hair or headband. Most are copper alloy, except where noted, cast in a mould, then hand finished.

They reminded Kym of the pin in the shoe.

'Are you sure this is OK?' asked Evie.

'Hello, Kym.' The woman behind the admissions desk was smiling at them.

'Mrs Agar. Hi. This is my friend, Evie.'

'Are you particularly interested in the pins? There are a lot more in the collection.' Mrs Agar gestured towards the double doors that led to the storage room, strictly off-limits to the general public.

'Are there?'

'More than we can display. It was such a common way to fasten your clothes.'

'Right.' Kym looked at the case again, it wasn't much, she thought, to leave behind; just a few bits of metal. 'Actually,' she said, 'I was hoping we might be able to do some work here.' She glanced towards the reference room with its cabinets of rare books. She hadn't been that keen on the Lit and Phil at the start of her work experience, she'd agreed to do it out of affection for her grandmother more than anything else, but gradually she'd found there was something about the Society that appealed to her, something about the backstage air of the reference room, and the way she could just walk past the front desk, straight into the part of the building the general public were forbidden to enter.

It had taken a bit of effort on her part, to win them over, but once they'd got past her look, the jet black hair and the heavy make-up and the skinny jeans, and realised she wasn't about to vandalise the whole collection, she'd got there in the end. Like most of the other volunteers these days, Mrs Agar was happy to turn a blind eye to Kym studying in the Lit and Phil. Sometimes she'd even help her look stuff up.

'Revision, is it?' said Mrs Agar.

'Yes,' said Evie.

'Not exactly,' said Kym. 'Research.'

Mrs Agar regarded them thoughtfully. 'Well, go on then,' she said, 'since we're so quiet.'

Kym's trainers squeaked as she led the way across the parquet floor to her favourite desk; a small oval table set by one of the windows, offering a view of the rose beds that flanked the museum entrance. The glass-fronted bookcases were locked, but the keys were easily accessible, one set in the desk by the door that also held the computer, the printer and the boxes of catalogue cards, and a spare set in the cubby – the

283

tiny cloakroom in the corner that contained a kettle, a little fridge and a range of chipped and stained mugs. If you made yourself a hot drink, then you had to stay in the cubby until you were done with it.

The first rule of the Lit and Phil, according to Kym's gran.

Then: no mobile phones; pencils, not pens; and ask permission if you wanted to photocopy anything.

'Right,' said Evie, instinctively lowering her voice as she pulled out her chair. 'What now?'

'Did you look through my notes?'

'Yeah.' Evie pulled the blue folder out of her bag and slid it across the table. Kym opened it and began to spread its contents over the table. She retrieved a spiral-bound notebook from her own bag and opened it, flicking through the pages filled with her handwriting, jagged and dense.

'What do you think?'

'I think . . .' Evie hesitated, glancing over towards Mrs Agar, who had stationed herself at the card catalogue and who gave no impression of going anywhere soon. 'It's all a bit – disconnected?'

'Yeah.' Kym dropped the book on the table. The trouble was there was no pattern, no shape to it. All her information seemed to be second or third hand, and with too many gaps – there was nothing about the witch marks in the attic, for example, in anything she'd ever read, and nothing about a hidden shoe.

She tried not to think about Ty and the expression on his face when he'd told her about Beth.

As if he felt sorry for her.

It hadn't been their imagination, the knocking, the pounding at the door, had been real. It had been – it was easier to admit this to herself now – purposeful, threatening.

'Let's start again,' she said. 'Get everything in chronological order, and then – at least we can see what we've got. You can tell me what I've missed.'

Evie was looking at her very intently, then she smiled, and shook her head. 'Fine,' she said. 'Whatever you say.'

Kym had tried asking her mum about the house, ages ago. But Kate – never one to pass on the chance to have a go at Gina – had completely missed the point. She had said something about incomers and money, and how anyone could stand to live in a pokey little yard was beyond her anyway. Then she'd more or less clammed up. Kate never set foot in Bishops Yard, not if she could help it, and certainly not since Kym had grown old enough to visit her grandmother unaccompanied.

There was something about the shoe that was nagging at her, something, she thought, to do with a pin. She fussed with the sheets of paper they had set out on the table, rearranging them.

'Can I help?' Mrs Agar joined them, looking over their work. 'Is it Elder House or Bishops Yard you're particularly interested in?'

Evie glanced at Kym. 'Both,' she said, 'I think.'

'And I keep thinking there's something I've missed,' Kym said. 'He did a sort of a dig, didn't he? In the yard. Frederick Bishop.'

'That's right, we have his finds in the collection.'

'Did they ever find pins, like the ones in the cabinet, in Bishops Yard?'

'I expect so, as I said, they were very common, and I think the finds there go back to the first abbey, which would be the correct period.'

'Can you think of a reason you'd stick one in a shoe, though?'

Mrs Agar frowned. 'I've no idea,' she said. The Lit and Phil hated not having an answer, Kym had noticed. The volunteers seemed to take a dead end in any kind of research as some sort of personal affront. 'Is this about the shoe your gran was looking at?'

'Yes. There's an old pin stuck in the seam, properly wedged in, you know? On purpose.'

Mrs Agar nodded thoughtfully. 'Well, he's not the only former occupant of the yard, is he? Dr Bishop. We could get the newspaper archives out, if you like,' she went on. 'See who else used to live in Elder House.' She glanced at Kym shrewdly. 'I assume that's the main focus of this – homework?'

'That would be great,' said Kym, 'thanks.'

'There's the transcript of the parish records too. And a couple of local histories. I'll let you get on while I go and have a rummage around in the collection. Come and get me if anyone comes in.'

'Great.' Kym looked down at the table again. 'Thanks.'

'Right. Well. When I was a little girl, I had a wart on my hand, here.' Carolyn held her hand out, palm up and pointed to the base of her thumb.

'Ew.'

'I know. Pretty hideous. So, my mum got some desperate-smelling ointment from Boots and she dabbed it on twice a day.'

'And?' said Maude.

'And nothing. I still had a wart, and my hand smelt funny. So after a while, my mum decided that the ointment wasn't working, or it wasn't working fast enough, so she – she took me to Auntie Ida and she charmed my wart away. That is – she said she did.'

'What did she do?'

286

'Oh, I don't remember, I was very young. She lived in a council house on St Mary's Crescent and I all I can really remember is that it was very warm – she had a coal fire blazing away – and it was dark, because she had the curtains closed in the middle of the day. She held my hand and she – she said a spell, I suppose. She just recited this rhyme, and I can't remember it, so don't ask – but she said it three times. I remember that.'

'And it worked?'

'Something did.' She smiled at Maude. 'Maybe it was both, belt and braces.'

Maude picked up the snapshot, peering at it. 'Wow,' she said.

They worked for a couple of hours, using the census as a starting point, then the parish records, and finally the old bound copies of the *Gazette*.

'Right,' said Kym, 'what have we got?'

Evie pointed to the first photocopy. 'In 1703 a servant – Sarah Percy – is left in charge of a little girl, Sophia Ann Mortimer, who falls ill, then dies, and there seems to be some sort of suspicion that it might be Sarah's fault.'

She pointed to the other sheets in turn. 'In 1903, a fire on the first floor killed three children living in the house, all of them under the age of five,' she went on. 'In 1927 Albert Headlam was arrested for the murder of his wife, Edith, and the attempted murder of his son, William. In 1965, there was a gas leak, a Mrs Mary Winspear survived, her infant son did not. There's a hint that it might have been a suicide attempt . . .' She paused. 'The thing is, these stories were retold or reported in the local press precisely *because* they were dramatic, yeah?'

'Yeah,' Kym said. 'You could put together a timeline of

births just as easily, with lots of happy events that no one ever bothered to report. It's an old house, and over – what – five hundred years you might even say that this is pretty good going.'

'But still – it's a lot of children, isn't it?' said Evie, anxiously. 'Apart from poor Mrs Headlam.'

'Maybe she got in the way, maybe she was trying to protect her son. A mother would do that, wouldn't she?'

'A halfway decent one, perhaps,' said Kym.

'And there's Dr Bishop's son too,' said Evie. 'Everyone knows that story.'

'So what are we saying? That there's something going on inside the house?' Kym picked up one of the reference books. 'I'm sure I've read something about weird noises there.' She flicked through the book, trying to find the right page. 'Before they lived there, the Bishops, I mean. A long time before.'

'What, like the knocking you heard?'

'No, these were footsteps, I think. Some sort of disturbance, anyway.'

'I'm sorry,' said Mrs Agar as she approached their table, 'but we'll be closing shortly. Have you got what you needed?'

'I'm not sure.' Kym began to tidy the books. 'But thank you. We'll put everything back where it belongs.'

'Will you do me a favour?' Mrs Agar said.

Kym paused. 'Sure.'

'Maybe don't mention any of this to your gran. I wouldn't like to upset her, not with – well, you know.'

Kym glanced nervously at Evie, who was sorting through her notes. 'That's OK. I wouldn't want to upset her either.'

'Right.' The older woman regarded her seriously, then gave a sad smile. 'Right, let's get all this sorted out, shall we?'

*

'Well,' said Evie as they walked down the hill and back towards the river, 'that was – unusual' – she looked at Kym – 'I had no idea you could be so well behaved.'

'Oh, shut up.'

'It's sweet – it's like you have a secret identity, as a librarian.' The swift and competent manner in which Kym had re-shelved the books, tidied the desks and helped Mrs Agar shut down the computer and lock up had been a revelation, endearing

'Curator, actually.'

Evie swung her bag onto her shoulder, it was a pale grey sort of a day, the sky was low, and she wasn't that sure how much further along they were, but it didn't matter, because she felt just a little happier, a little more in control. 'Is that what you think you'll do, then? History, or—'

'Shit.' Kym stopped suddenly.

'What?' Evie's first thought was that they had been found out, that it was her mother standing at the park gates and looking up at them; but then the jolt of guilt was replaced by a terrible sinking feeling.

It wasn't Carolyn.

It was Tyler.

Nell was sitting at the kitchen table. She had turned down Carolyn's offer of lunch and helped Maude back up to her room. She had taken possession of the phone and had intended to ring Chris. But she found all she was good for was staring idly at Gina's photographs, wondering what her gran would make of Maude, the house, everything.

She picked up the smaller picture, it was odd to see her grandmother so young, perhaps younger than Nell was now. She was walking arm in arm with Ida, along the pier. They both wore floral-print blouses and long summer skirts. Her gran carried a handbag and Ida a small basket. Ida's hair was either cropped short or pinned up, it was hard to tell, and Nell's gran wore her hair loose, dark curls caught by the breeze.

She charmed my wart away.

That was ridiculous. But Carolyn hadn't looked like she was joking.

No shoes on the table, Nell. Bad luck.

Her grandmother's voice, ringing in her head.

The flowers spiralling into the shadows.

She thought of the hands grabbing at her T-shirt. Pulling.

The shoe, hiding in the dark.

Her back ached and her belly cramped, her eyes were gritty from lack of sleep.

Nell dropped the photos on the table. Maybe Gina had a point. Maybe it would do them both, Maude and Nell, good to put it back where it belonged; to say goodbye, move on.

'I've been messaging you,' Tyler said. 'I had to ring your mum in the end. She told me you're still pissing about with the museum.'

'I should go,' said Evie, looking helplessly from one to the other. 'I should let you—'

'You don't have to go anywhere,' said Kym.

'I've come,' said Tyler, 'to do you a favour. I thought we could – you know, talk.'

They had retreated back into the park, to the kids' play area, the climbing frame and the swings.

'What about, Ty? Maths homework? Beth Harland?'

'Don't be like that.'

Kym sat down on one of the swings, and pushed back, her feet braced on the gravel. 'What's this favour, then?'

'Just you and me, you know?'

'I don't think so.'

Tyler looked at Evie, tilting his head to one side, appraising her. 'What's going on here, then?'

'Nothing.' Evie's mouth was dry.

'Oh,' said Tyler as he looked at Kym and then back at Evie, as if a new idea was occurring to him. 'Oh, this explains a lot.'

Evie couldn't bear it, the knowing smile, the patronising tone, her heart began to race.

'Piss off, Tyler.' Kym raised herself up onto her toes as if about to take flight.

'Does your mum know? Does your gran—'

'Ty? Have you got something to say, or what?' Bouncing gently now, testing her weight.

Tyler hesitated. 'I saw him again, Pete Chappell.'

'Oh. Right.' Kym lowered the swing and looked up at him thoughtfully. 'When?'

'Yeah,' Tyler went on, 'I thought you'd like that.' He turned his attention to Evie. 'Has she told you about him? This bloke who was working on your old house? I mean, he's full of shit and loves the sound of his own voice, but she—'

'When, Ty?'

'The other day – when you—'

'He was there? He was actually bloody there, and you didn't tell me?'

Ty spread his hands. 'I'm telling you now,' he said.

'And?'

Tyler's expression softened; he almost looked sorry for her. 'I asked him about it,' said Tyler, 'he saw us on the quay, he saw you and – I asked him about Elder House.'

'And?'

'It's not my old house,' said Evie.

'It was like I told you. There was stuff going missing all the time – pens and pencils, tools, his phone.' His smile was thin, unconvincing. 'Everyone reckoned it was sealed up underneath a floorboard somewhere, so they tried ringing it, but that didn't work. They could hear it, but when they took the boards up there was nothing there. And he swore he heard someone moving around, did this bloke, upstairs. Only he wanted to know about you too and—'

'It's not my house,' said Evie, louder this time, and they stopped and looked at her, the both of them. 'It's never been my house.'

'You're joking . . .' Tyler looked half-disbelieving, half amused. 'How can you not know?' He turned to Kym. 'Is she taking the piss?'

'You never said – you never told me—' Evie stumbled back. 'It's not – you let me make all those notes. You just had me lay out the whole history of that house – and for what—' She looked at Tyler. 'So he could come along and – so you could both – *laugh* at me?'

'Wait,' said Kym, standing. 'No. Wait.' She made a move as if she might take Evie's arm, might pull her close.

'Don't you . . .' And she looked at them again, both of them so alike, now she thought about it, skinny and dark, and – starved, somehow. Both of them pitying her. 'Get away from me, both of you – just—'

'Evie, it's all right—'

But whatever it was Kym wanted to say, Evie didn't want to hear it. She turned on her heel and ran.

23

'Maude.'

'What?'

Nell clearly didn't want to say it, whatever it was. She was moving round the room, making sure the windows were opened as wide as possible; fussing. 'I need to take the shoe back, sweetheart.'

'What are you going to do with it?' Maude was sitting up in bed, the duvet jumbled around her feet, a plate with the remains of a slice of Carolyn's banana bread on her lap.

'Nothing. Put it somewhere safe; just in case.'

'In case of what?'

'Do you have it?'

'Safe where?'

'Please, Maude.' Nell looked dreadful, grey, ill. 'I thought – I think the best thing to do is put it back where it belongs.'

'In the wall?'

'You could help. We could do it together.'

Strike a bargain. Maude wondered what it was that Nell was after.

'It's under the bed.' Let her get down on her knees and look for it herself. 'And I'd like my phone back.'

'In a bit. OK?' Nell found the box. 'I meant it,' she said, 'about helping.'

Maude shrugged. 'Not bothered,' she said.

'Are you all right, sweetheart? Only – if you were worried about the other night—'

'It was an accident.' Maude interrupted her. 'You said it was an accident.'

'No. I meant – before. The noises.'

Another shrug.

'If you were worried about them, you could tell me.'

'I'm not worried. They're—' Maude stopped. She looked guilty.

'They're what?'

'Nothing.' She glanced up at the witch marks on the beam. 'I'm not bothered, Nell, not by . . . You don't have to keep me entertained.' Maude chose her words with care. 'I'm not a baby.'

There was a pause.

'Fine,' said Nell as she got to her feet. 'I'll deal with this and then we'll think about lunch?'

'I'm not hungry,' said Maude, picking up her cake. 'I'll tell you when I am.'

Nell climbed carefully down the attic ladder, one-handed, her back aching. She couldn't wait any longer; she certainly couldn't wait for Maude to change her mind. She'd put the shoe back, and let the agency know when they dropped off the keys, let them worry about it.

She paused on the landing, listening for signs of life. A sign, one way or the other that she was making the right decision.

Nothing.

She dropped the box on the bed, then pulled the frame away from the wall. Without the bed head to hold it in place, the panel gaped slightly, and – she traced a finger along the crack – the wood looked fresh where it had split. She pulled gently at the panel, opening it as far as she dared, then picked up the box. It was too big, of course, but Nell found she was strangely reluctant to open it and handle the shoe directly. She tugged at the panel again, widening the gap and tried to force the box in.

She nearly had it, thought she had it, the cardboard buckling, but she couldn't quite find the shelf. There was a rattle and a scrape, she held onto the box, squeezing it, but the lid sprang open. When she pulled it out again, the shoebox – grubby, with one corner crushed entirely – was empty.

Nell picked up Maude's phone, found the torch app and shone it inside.

The angle was wrong, she couldn't see anything. She tried raising the torch, but that only revealed the cross-hatched dressing of the stone shelf, and she wasn't sure where the shoe had fallen. She could leave it where it was, close the panel and forget about it; but that didn't feel right. It felt – disrespectful.

She'd have to trust to touch alone.

She dropped the phone back onto the duvet and – sitting right at the top of the bed – she slid her hand into the void.

It was just as bad as last time, even though she knew what to expect, the thick layer of grime, the cold, the damp. Her nails digging into the dirt, her knuckles scraping against the wall, her fingers meeting nothing but stone.

'Shit.'

She tried again, methodically, tracing out the far corner of the shelf, measuring the depth of it, working her way towards the gap then sweeping her fingers against the stone, but there was nothing there.

She took a breath and tried again, slower this time, standing and reaching as far as she could, fighting the instinct to slam the panel shut and push the bed back against it. In the far corner her fingers caught against something unexpected, something different, something small, dusty and soft. There was the rattle of plastic as something scraped across the top of the shelf and fell.

But that was all.

The shelf was empty and the shoe was out of reach.

Nell pulled the bed to one side. She peeled the wood away from the wall with the tips of her fingers, and peered in. She made a neat enough job of it, first loosening, then pulling the panel free from its grooved setting, placing it carefully to one side, exposing the hidden stone wall entirely. It was coated with dust, but, like the shelf, seemed to be decorated with a simple cross-hatched pattern.

Nell picked up Maude's phone, and let the torch shine into the gap behind the panelling. The shoe had tumbled down the wall and was wedged behind the skirting board. She leant forward, changing the angle of the beam, shifting its focus. It was a small red trainer, its long lace trailing in the dust.

It was Maude's. She had put her own shoe in the box.

Irritated, Nell reached into the wall to pick it up, then her fingers brushed across something else, something different; whatever it was she had knocked from the shelf. She shone the torch into the corner of the void again, then she sat back abruptly, letting the phone fall to one side. 'Jesus,' she said softly.

She took everything down to the kitchen. She'd found a used carrier bag and scooped the contents of the void into it, knotting it firmly. She dropped the bag on the floor and went to the sink. She turned the hot tap on and, picking up a bar of soap, began to scrub, the soap foaming through her fingers.

You could date it, she supposed, the plastic cylinder, the pregnancy tester – used, as far as she could tell. Although for one extraordinary moment she had thought it was the one she had bought – you could date it from the design, the brand or logo, if there was one.

Used.

She had the urge to run upstairs and check the bin in the bathroom, to make sure no one had . . . But it wasn't a joke; it couldn't be a joke. A thick layer of dust had coated the small plastic cylinder she'd found lying in the gap between the old stone wall and the panel. The corresponding imprint left in the dust on the shelf; it had been there for a long time.

That's what she'd felt briefly, knocked, and heard falling off the shelf and next to it . . .

Something soft, dusty, yielding. Her fingers brushing over it in the dark.

A used tampon.

Blackened with age.

She lathered up her hands again. Dust seemed to have ingrained itself in every crease, beneath each nail.

Dust and . . .

Gina's words came back to her. *Why do people tie shoes to newlyweds' cars? Why do we go on about the patter of tiny feet?*

She was drying her hands, trying to reason it out, when she heard someone coming slowly downstairs.

Maude had brushed her hair and tied it back, she had washed her face and found a clean T-shirt and a pair of shorts. She limped across the kitchen. 'Can I have some juice?'

'Sure.'

Nell watched as Maude poured a drink, leaning back against the kitchen counter and draining her glass in one long gulp. 'You'll have to get some more,' she said, before belching appreciatively, and refilling her glass with water. Her sneaker lay by the bag on the floor; she didn't comment on it. 'Can Kym come and visit again?'

'If you like. She might be a bit busy, though.'

'Oh.' Maude scratched at her wrist, the little daisy on the bracelet gleaming in the sunlight, the fine ribbon blue like the veins under her skin. 'Nell?'

'Yes?'

'When's Dad coming back?'

'I don't know. Soon.'

'But he is coming back, isn't he?'

'Of course he is,' Nell said. 'He just has a lot of work stuff to sort out first.'

'I mean – you're not going to – separate, or anything?'

'Good Lord, no. Absolutely not, Maudie. Wherever did you get that idea?'

'I dunno.' She took a sip of her water, turning to look out at the drying ground.

'Do you like her? Kym?' asked Nell.

'She knows a lot about the house.'

'Does she?'

'She was telling me. Lots of people have lived here.'

'I expect they have.'

'And now there's us.'

'We don't live here.'

'Kym says that there was a family with twenty-two children that lived in this yard.'

'Goodness.'

'And not here, either. In one of the little cottages. All those babies,' said Maude, her eyes widening. 'Imagine.'

'Yes,' said Nell, 'imagine.'

'Can we go out this afternoon?'

'Maybe.'

'That means no.'

'It means we'll see how you feel.'

298

'I feel fine.'

She did look better, more alert, anyway. Her colour was still a little high, but at least she was up and about.

She drank the last of her water, then turned on the tap, filling her glass again.

'Maude?'

'Hmm?' She was still leaning against the sink, staring out of the window at the bankside.

'We need to have a chat.'

Maude sighed and turned to face Nell, clutching the glass to her chest, beads of water soaking into her T-shirt.

'You do understand we can't keep the shoe, don't you?'

Maude rolled her eyes. 'Yes,' she said, 'I do get it, Nell, not our house, not our shoe, blah, blah, blah.'

'And really, if you think about it, it belongs in the bedroom, in the wall. And I went to put it back,' said Nell, nodding towards the sneaker on the floor. 'Only it wasn't there, it was the wrong shoe.'

She started off all sympathetic and calm, like that day in Mrs Allingham's office, but she was getting pissed off, Maude could tell.

'I'm not cross.'

Maude rolled her eyes. 'I don't have it,' she said. 'You said I had to give it back and I did.' She placed her glass carefully on the draining board. For a moment the room tilted a bit, and her ears felt funny, a bit blocked, as if she'd been swimming. She wondered briefly when it was that she went swimming last, when they'd last done something normal. She wished her dad would come back.

Nell sighed and picked up the red trainer. 'Except you obviously didn't. If you wanted to play a trick on me, then well done you. It worked. Only we have to put it back, Maudie, we really do. I need it back now. Come on. Swap.'

Maude could feel that she might cry, and the hot dizzy feeling grew worse. Her hand itched, her foot was sore. 'I told you,' she said, snatching at her shoe. 'I don't have it.'

'Fine,' said Nell, as she walked towards the hall 'Fine. We'll go and check, shall we?'

'No,' said Maude as she pushed past Nell on the staircase, and turned to face her, blocking the way, still clutching the trainer. 'I told you; I don't have it.'

'This isn't funny anymore,' said Nell, stepping to one side. 'It's stealing, Maude; theft.'

'It's my room,' said Maude, mirroring her, 'it's private.'

'You can help, if you want,' Nell said. 'We'll tidy everything up, and the sooner we're done, the sooner we can do something nice together. We can go for a walk, go down to the pier again.'

'Jesus, Nell—'

'Don't,' said Nell, 'don't you take that tone with me.'

'What tone?'

'I have been more than patient, Maude. But you need to up your game. I need to see less of the spoilt brat, and a bit more personal responsibility. You need to get yourself in some sort of order, and you need to hand over the shoe.'

'Or what?' Maude's expression hardened. 'I don't have to listen to you, Nell. You're not my mum.'

'Don't you dare pull that on me, you little—' Nell bit back the rest of the sentence, but it was too late. She took a breath, and the pain in her ribs, sharp, sudden, left her dizzy. She felt sick. 'I just want us to get on,' she said, 'like we used to.'

'As if.'

'What is it?' Nell asked, her tone harsher than she'd intended.

300

'You have been a pain in the arse for – weeks, months, now. What exactly is your problem?'

Maude looked at her for the longest time. 'I know,' she said, eventually, 'I know what you did.' She backed away slowly, favouring her good foot and flinching, up one stair, then another, looking down at Nell. 'You wanted my dad, and you got him.'

'What?'

Maude's face was flushed, she looked as if she might cry. 'We were happy until you came along; me and Dad and Mum.'

'That's not what happened,' Nell said. 'Oh, God, Maude, what have you been thinking? What has Jess been saying to you?'

'She didn't say anything; I heard her on the phone, ages ago.' Now Maude just looked plain miserable. 'We were all happy, then you met Dad and that's why they split up. He left her for you. It's all your fault.' She stopped, and Nell understood that this was the bit where she should explain, fix everything, make it all go away.

Only she couldn't.

'It wasn't exactly like that,' she said.

Lying.

'You are – disgusting.' Maude turned away and began to walk upstairs, leaning heavily against the banister. 'Leave me alone, please. My foot hurts and I want to lie down.'

Nell couldn't even ring Chris to warn him. She pulled Maude's phone out of her pocket. There was barely a signal, besides, what would she say? *She knows, Chris, she's found out what we did; what I did.*

Because there had been a choice, all those years ago.

She'd rationalised it as a harmless flirtation at first, when she was dropping off her pieces at his gallery, and then after

301

the first couple of evenings in quiet bars, out of the way places, as a bit of fun.

Lies. It had been love at first sight; on her part, at least.

She'd known all about Jess and Maude when she and Chris had started seeing each other; worse, she hadn't cared.

And look where they were now.

24

Kym let herself in. She found her grandmother upstairs, sitting on her bed, slowly turning the pages of a photograph album.

She stood in the doorway for a moment. It never changed, this room, the bed neatly made and covered with a handmade quilt, the old rag rug to one side and the wall opposite dominated by the large bookcase that was crammed with novels, poetry, biographies, histories. One shelf was devoted to all the books Gina had used to read to Kym; the pair of them snuggled under the quilt. She had always felt safe here. Sunlight glanced off the large glass bauble Gina had suspended by the window, sending rainbow tinted slivers shimmering across the ceiling, and Kym felt a pang, saddened by the familiarity of it all. One day she would stand in this room with her grandmother for the last time. One day she'd have to help pack all the books away.

She had tried ringing Evie, but there had been no reply. Her texts had gone unanswered too.

'What's all this?' she said, sitting down next to Gina. 'Are you having a tidy out?'

'I was just looking,' said Gina, moving to close the album.

'Can I have a look?'

Gina surrendered the book. 'If you must.'

When she was little, Kym would beg to be allowed to look in her gran's photo albums, with no idea that it was unusual

303

for the smiling young man in the vivid snapshots to feel as absent, as far removed as the stiff figures in their uniforms, as the great great grandparents in their Victorian finery. Then, they had all been part of the same story.

Now, of course, she knew to tread carefully.

She started with the school photos, nursery, primary, then secondary school – the same boy growing up with the turn of a page. She didn't look much like him, although sometimes she thought they had the same eyes, pale blue, the iris ringed with grey. His hair was dark, like his own father, hers was darker, and had come out of a bottle. 'Handsome lad,' she said as she usually did at this point.

'And he knew it,' said Gina. The photos on the next page were more informal and seemed to have been taken by a variety of people over the period of maybe a couple of years. Kym had never asked, but she assumed this had all been put together by her gran afterwards. Maybe she had asked family and friends to contribute; and in some he was almost edged out of the frame, or looking away from the lens. In one or two he was blurred as if startled by the instruction to smile.

The photos on the final page featured her dad and her mother, Kate; tight jeans and baggy T-shirts, all long hair and eyeliner. When she was younger, Kym had thought it romantic, the way they leant into each other in the pictures, holding hands, her sitting in his lap. Now she's almost embarrassed – they couldn't keep their hands off each other.

She's glad of the last picture, though – taken when Kate was hugely pregnant with Kym herself. Because you can see it in the dopey expression on their faces – it hadn't mattered that they weren't married. It hadn't mattered that they weren't much more than kids themselves – they had been in love, they had been happy.

304

'What's brought all this on, then?' Kym asked, still gazing at the picture of her mother, self-consciously resting one hand on her baby bump, and so terribly, terrifyingly young.

'Nothing much.' Gina retrieved the album and closed it gently. 'I was just – thinking, that's all.'

'Am I like him?' Kym had asked this question before too.

'I don't know,' said Gina. 'There are times when I think I barely got to know him.'

Kym stood and went to the window, they couldn't see the Wilson's house from here, but they had a view of Elder House, side on to them, forcing itself up against the cliff, trapped in the shade.

She couldn't bear it, and she couldn't think how to put it right; she had messed everything up with Evie when they had barely begun to be friends. 'Don't you mind?' she asked. 'Being so close?'

'It's just a house,' Gina said. 'And anyway, it wouldn't matter where I went, there are some things you can't get away from.'

'Would you want to? Get away – from him. I mean?'

Gina turned and looked at her. 'Probably not,' she said. 'What is it, pet? Is something bothering you?'

'I – no,' said Kym.

Evie wouldn't answer and she couldn't think of a way to tell her. Give Kym my number, Pete Chappell had said to Tyler, tell her to give me a call. She wasn't even sure she should tell her.

Nell sat on the staircase for a long time, her head in her hands, bone weary, too tired even to cry, and waiting for some sort of solution to present itself. After a while she raised her head and listened for signs of life in the attic, but all was still. She pulled the phone out of her pocket and thought about ringing Chris,

305

but she had no idea where she might begin. She stood and slowly, carefully she made her way back upstairs.

The bed was a mess, the covers and pillows pulled back and tumbling to the floor. The oak panel was propped up against the wall and the carpet was covered with dust and grime.

Resisting the urge to crawl back into bed, to pull the covers over her head and shut out the world, she did her best to tidy up, tugging the duvet back into place on the bed and smoothing the pillows.

She picked up the discarded panel. She was turning it round, trying to work out the best way to slot it back into place, when she noticed some faint marks, running counter to the grain of the wood, and covered with a thick film of dust.

She took the panel to the window, tilting it to one side.

It was writing.

Checking the door to make sure she was quite alone, Nell swept the rest of the grime away with her hand, exposing the words and their crude but simple sentiment.

Oh Dear God

Nell ran her fingertips over the letters. They were a faded rust red, unevenly formed, but determined.

Oh Dear God God Almighty Help Me

Her heart thudding. One-*two*, one-*two*.

Help Me

It was a prayer, a blessing. A bit blunt, perhaps, but that was no reason to . . . It didn't sound like a prayer. It didn't sound like the person who had carved it thought anyone was listening.

But it was familiar too.

And there was something else, something to do with the shelf; she couldn't remember.

God Almighty Help Me

She flipped the panel and slid it back into place, then pushed the bed back against the wall before sitting heavily on it, trying to make sense of it all.

The phrase remained just out of reach. But Nell had seen it, read it somewhere else, she knew she had.

Maude's foot felt sore; hot and sore and itchy. She thought she could feel the stitches pulling through the skin as she placed her weight on it and her hip ached from walking awkwardly. She wasn't sure she'd ever felt this tired before. Nell was really cross with her about the shoe, and she'd tell her dad, and then Maude would be in trouble again. Tears stung at her eyes.

Nell had used to be all right, really.

But things were horrible now, and it seemed to Maude she was always on the verge of being in trouble. She wasn't supposed to know about Nell and her dad, of course. They all thought they'd fooled her. She'd been at her mum's, in the living room by the big window, her head stuck in a book, and when Jess had come in, Maude hadn't said anything. She probably hadn't realised she was there.

She hadn't meant to eavesdrop.

Her mum going on about the divorce and the business, and Nell.

'Both of them screwing behind my back, for bloody months, and I'm supposed to smile nicely every time I pick Maude up.'

There was other stuff too, she talked a bit about the custody arrangements, and Maude had thought for a while that meant she'd go and live with her mum full-time. But not long after there was the big announcement about the new baby, and her mother never mentioned it again.

It took a long time to cross the room and longer still to get down her ladder. She sat on the bottom rung, half hoping Nell would find her, help her, but she didn't come.

Maude leant her head against the wall and concentrated for a bit, sometimes she thought she could hear someone walking around the house. If she happened to be downstairs, then the noise came from above. If she was in her room, then the footsteps seemed to come from the first floor. She'd thought someone had been calling her name, but the house was quiet.

She was glad of the marks on the beam and the pins in the windows. She raised her wrist, so she could look at her bracelet again.

Her hand looked weird. Ever so pale, but stained with angry red patches. Both hands. She ran a finger over her arm, her skin was sore, tender. She sat up and the room began to spin, the shadows in the corner seemed to expand, leaking across the floorboards. She was thirsty again.

There was water in the bathroom. She wouldn't have to go all the way downstairs.

Rowan Cottage was empty. Before she could second guess herself, Nell ran down the steps and knocked at the door of Spinnaker Cottage. After a moment or two, it opened. 'Hi.'

Carolyn looked puzzled, then she pulled the door further back. 'Oh. Hello. Sorry, I was . . . How are you? How's Maude?'

'She's fine. She's – resting up.'

'Come in, come in—'

'No. I – I realise this is a huge cheek on my part. But I was wondering if you wouldn't mind just keeping an eye on her, for an hour or so. You wouldn't have to actually do anything. Just – be in the house with her. If you have the time?'

'Oh. Of course, yes, absolutely.'

'I'm so sorry to bother you, you've already been so kind.'

'It's no bother.'

Nell felt a flicker of guilt. She should make a point of being nicer about Carolyn in the future.

'I'll just get my bag and I'll be right with you.' Carolyn disappeared back into the house.

'That's brilliant, thank you so much.' Nell pulled Maude's phone out of her pocket, and scrolled through the contacts, looking for Gina's number.

Once her head stopped swimming, Maude risked standing and walked to the ladder. She gripped the sides so tightly as she climbed down it made her hands ache.

She should have brought the glass with her, but she managed to drink from the tap. She gulped the water down as best she could, splashing it all down her front and making herself breathless in the process. Standing up, she felt dizzy, and she couldn't tell if the footsteps had come back or if it was the thudding of the pulse in her throat that sounded so loud, so close.

One-*two*.

One-*two*.

The girl in the mirror looked ill, she thought, too pale and the rash on her arms was spreading over her face and neck. Poor thing.

'Hello?'

She thought it was Nell calling out, she was cross with Nell, and she thought she might not bother answering – give her what her mum liked to call the silent treatment – but she was hungry.

'Maude?'

Maude went out onto the landing and it was like everything suddenly came into focus, and she realised that the woman standing at the bottom of the stairs wasn't Nell at all.

'Hi,' said Carolyn, 'Nell had to go out. She asked me to keep an eye on you.'

I'm not a baby. That was what she meant to say. And she was cross with Nell, for what she'd done with her dad, for leaving her now. 'I don't feel well,' said Maude, and she began to cry.

Carolyn was nice, kind; like when she'd driven them to the hospital.

She insisted Maude bathe her face properly, and found her a clean towel to use, it was warm and soft and smelt of lavender. She kept up a gentle flow of chat as she helped her back upstairs and sat her back on the bed. And when she asked how Maude was feeling, she seemed to properly listen to the answer. The mess in the attic didn't seem to bother her, and she didn't seem to notice the shadow flickering in the corner either, so Maude did her best not to look.

She sat on the edge of the bed. 'What's happened there?' she asked, and looking at her wrist, Maude noticed that her bracelet had come loose. Carolyn helped undo it.

'This ribbon's looking a bit worse for wear.' She held it up to the light and the silver flower turned lazily. The ribbon was grubby, and beginning to fray at the ends. 'Shall I ask Evie to replace it?'

'Yes, please.' It felt odd, not wearing it; surprising how quickly Maude had got used to the warm weight of it against her skin. It was far nicer than any of the things Nell and her dad had ever given her. 'She said I should wear it all the time.'

'Well, no wonder it's in such a state.' Carolyn looped the ribbon carefully over her fingers, then shoved the bracelet into her pocket.

'So, this is a bit rubbish, isn't it?' she said.

310

'Yeah.'

'Not much of a holiday for you.'

It was a bit gloomy in the attic, despite the bright weather, and Maude switched on her lamp. Her foot ached and she kept seeing, in her mind's eye, the flesh stretching and tearing as she placed her foot flat against the floor, against the edge of broken glass – and there was a bit of her that was puzzled, that didn't really understand where it had come from, because neither she nor Nell had been carrying a glass – as her skin was sliced apart. She was supposed to take painkillers if it hurt too much, but she had left those down in the bathroom.

Carolyn was going round the room, checking the windows, scooping up Maude's collection of pebbles, tidying up.

Leave them, she wanted to say, at least leave the pins, and if it had been Nell she might have, but it was Carolyn, and Maude had the idea that she didn't want to be rude.

'And speaking of holidays,' said Carolyn, 'I was wondering. I don't mean to pry, but your mum mentioned something about school?'

'We're on holiday.'

Carolyn opened one of the drawers and dropped everything inside. 'Can you keep a secret?'

'Yes.'

'Evie used to go to a private school, until – well, until we decided she needed a change. So, I know when the holidays begin, more or less, and I know it's a bit early still . . .' She let her voice trail away, her expression a combination of sorrow and sympathy.

Maude wondered why Evie had switched schools. She reached under the duvet – she was lucky Nell hadn't got as far as searching her room again – and shoved her hand between the mattress and the wall, pulling out the shoe. She wasn't sure

311

why she'd done that thing with her trainer, only that she liked having the shoe around; she felt better when she looked at it. She held it tightly in her hand as Carolyn sat up a little straighter and looked at her expectantly.

It was a relief to talk about it all, really. A group of girls, feeling their power for the first time, perhaps, turning on the one odd kid in the class – the bookish daydreamer. Not bullying, exactly, everyone had been very careful to avoid that word, but not kind either.

Her parents had been called in, of course – her dad, and Nell, and her real mum too, dandling the new baby on her lap, pretending she still cared.

'The most important thing,' the head teacher had said, 'is that you feel you can speak to someone – to your parents, or to your form tutor, when things might appear to be – overwhelming. Do you understand Maude?'

'Yes, Mrs Allingham.'

That bit hadn't been so bad. Maude had begun to feel that everyone might be on her side after all. Then her dad had pitched in. 'We are so very, deeply sorry about this. Aren't we, Maude?'

'Yes.' Made to say sorry over and over again, as if she was a baby too. She couldn't look at any of them, she couldn't meet their eyes, she wished – more than anything – that her mum would put Leo down and give her a hug. A proper, long, breathing-in-hard hug. Instead, Nell reached over and tried to hold her hand; Maude pulled away. 'I'm very sorry and it won't happen again,' she said. She did her best to sound as if she meant it.

Her dad had tried, she was pretty certain, to put the blame elsewhere, that would be just like him, to say it was one of the others – Imogen or Tamsin – who was the ringleader, and to say that she – Maude – was just tagging along. As if that would make what she'd done any more acceptable.

'I thought I might get expelled,' she said to Carolyn, not quite daring to look up. 'But they settled for keeping me off school for a bit.' She waited for her to say something, to tell her off too.

'Poor you,' Carolyn said.

'Really?'

'It's been my experience, that people who are – well, angry I suppose – are sometimes unkind. They can't help themselves, and usually they don't mean to be cruel.'

'I did,' said Maude without thinking, 'I didn't like her and I wanted to make her – miserable.'

She could barely remember where or how it began, it must have been something small at first, the odd word, an unkind joke. But it had escalated, unflattering photos taken unawares, cruel captions added, images shared among their little group at first, then posted online, then sent to her – to Millie, Millie Butler – with messages that started out as fake queries for her health and rapidly turned into threats, instructions on how to lose weight, links to websites that encouraged eating disorders, self-harm, worse.

It had felt good, to be so certain that no one would be looking at her, chubby little Maude Clarke with her rubbish mum and dad, to know that she could make people look elsewhere. To make someone else miserable for a change. It wasn't her fault Millie had taken it all so seriously; hiding a knife in her bedroom, trying it out for real – the cutting thing. Little scrapes and scratches leading to scars that might never fade. It wasn't her fault some of the cuts had been so deep; that they thought Millie had meant to . . .

To her surprise, Carolyn burst into laughter. 'Well, at least you're honest about it,' she said, and then, 'Be careful, you don't want to damage that, do you?'

She was squeezing the shoe far too hard; the soft leather was crumpling, and the sole was beginning to buckle. 'Sorry.' Maude opened her hand and let it fall softly onto the bed. 'I'm not really supposed to have it,' she said. 'Nell says we have to put it back.'

'Well, she always was bossy,' said Carolyn, picking the shoe up. 'Has she been giving you a hard time? About school?'

'A bit,' said Maude, 'she says she's disappointed. No one else got – sent home early. Just me.' They had dropped her in it, one by one. It was all Maude's idea, they'd said. She had started it; she had found the worst of the sites online and said they should send them to Millie. She was the one who wouldn't stop – she didn't know why she bothered to stay friends with them.

'Really?' Carolyn held the shoe up to the light, inspecting the stitching that ran around the heel. 'Well, if it's any comfort, she was no angel herself.'

'But I bet she never . . .' Maude couldn't bring herself to finish the sentence, because it wasn't bullying, not exactly, because that would mean she was a bad person. But if it wasn't bullying, she wasn't sure what it was.

'Oh, you'd be surprised,' said Carolyn, and she looked different, Maude thought, sadder.

'Weren't you friends, then? I thought you were friends? When you went on that school trip?'

'There were lots of us. And Nell – everyone wanted to be friends with her, you know? She was the kind of person who never seemed to have to work for any of it – exams, friends, boyfriends. She never really took any notice of me, apart from . . .' She stared at the shoe. 'It was my idea to bunk off that day,' she

314

said. 'I didn't care about the shop – well, I did, but I wanted . . .
to be the leader as well, for a change, you know?'

'Yes.'

'The funny thing is, I got into trouble along with everyone
else, but your mum and Laura and Mark got most of the blame.
Everyone thought it was their idea. I even think they did, in
the end; it was as if no one else was cool enough to think of
it.' She looked sad. 'Shall we pop this back in its box?' said
Carolyn. 'Keep it safe?'

'I don't have it any more. I gave it back to Nell – only I put
the wrong shoe in.'

'Really?' She looked impressed.

'You won't tell, will you?'

Carolyn seemed to think about this. 'Not if you don't want
me to.'

'Gina says you could use it to – make a wish. Sort of.'

'A wish?'

'Yeah, like make a deal with it.'

'Really?' Carolyn looked at the shoe critically. 'This little thing?'

'It would be cool, wouldn't it? If you could. If you could –
make things happen.'

'And what would you make happen, if you could?'

It was as if Carolyn was playing along, humouring her, and
Maude could feel that she might cry again. 'I don't know,' she
said. 'I tried to find out more about it, but there's nothing in
the books and I'm not allowed . . . Last night,' she went on,
'when the lights went out, and I was thinking that it would
serve Nell right if . . . and – then she fell downstairs.'

'I see.' Carolyn weighed the shoe in her hand, assessing it.

'But then I got hurt too. And I don't really know – Nell
wasn't carrying a glass, but there was glass on the floor. And
Nell got – like – really hurt.'

'Did she?'

'Yeah. I heard her tell Dad.'

'Well.' Carolyn looked at her thoughtfully. 'That is odd.'

'What was she like? At school?'

Carolyn didn't answer at first; she kept staring at the shoe, and Maude had the feeling that she might like to make a wish too. 'It was a long time ago,' she said. She looked up at her. 'Shall I do your hair for you? Brush it? Braid it? I used to do that for Evie, but now she's far too grown up. And just between you and me, I miss that a bit.'

'OK.' Maude sat up and swung her legs over the side of the bed, and Carolyn put the shoe on the mattress next to her.

'Good girl,' said Carolyn, 'and when we're done, we'll think about some lunch.'

The cafe was quiet and reassuringly normal, a scattering of wooden tables, a gleaming Gaggia machine, seventies music playing softly, and Gina was sitting by the window, a pot of tea and two cups set on the table in front of her. She looked up as Nell came in. 'Hello, pet. Is everything all right? Is it Maude?'

Nell took the seat opposite Gina, trying to catch her breath. The walk across the bridge had left her chilled; another sea fret was rolling into town. It was an odd summer, she thought – it was as if the weather couldn't quite hold on to the land, as if the sea was going to claim it all.

'Thanks,' she said, 'for coming. I just needed to . . . Sorry. This is going to sound – odd. Again.'

'I don't have long,' Gina said, 'I'll need to get back to the shop. Sorry.'

'OK,' Nell said, 'OK. I was cleaning up the bedroom.' She fumbled in her bag. 'I wanted to put the shoe back, so I pulled out the panel and – there's this, written on the inside of it. It's – freaked me out a bit, I'm not sure why.' She held out a scrap of paper, the words from the panel copied onto it. 'But I'm pretty certain I've seen it somewhere before, in the museum, I think. And I wondered if you knew anything about it.' It felt good, in a way, to have something to show Gina, something tangible that might help make sense of things.

Gina unfolded the paper 'Oh,' she said. 'Goodness.'

'What? Do you recognise it?'

'Yes.' She picked up her phone. 'Let me just . . .' She hit an icon and scrolled down the screen. 'It's this.' She put the phone on the table so Nell could see the screen.

It was the display in the museum. The finds from the yard, the little brass owl and the jet beads, the scraps of glass and all the metal pins, blackened and bent; the bone comb with its broken teeth.

Not ivory, but animal bone.

Gross, Nell.

'The scratches on the comb are runes,' said Gina as Nell leant closer, zooming in on the image, examining the fine vertical scratches on the surface. They looked mathematical, purposeful, 'but there is a translation.' She enlarged the image on the screen.

The text was broken, where the original was indistinct, Nell supposed, or too obscure to read.

Oh Dear God . . . God Almighty Help Me . . . Help . . .

And underneath, another label, typed and held in place by yellowing Sellotape.

A Saxon midden recorded underneath the East Cliff. Animal bones and shells, combs and spoons dating back to the seventh

317

century were unearthed, suggesting this was the midden of
the monastery of St Hilda founded in AD 657.

'So it's a prayer, then?' said Nell.

'We think so.' The screen went blank, the image, the words vanishing. 'But I had no idea those words were inside the house too.'

'Would there be any way to date it?'

'I'm not sure. By looking at the writing? The paint used? The comb was removed from the house in the 1800s, so around then?'

'So why,' Nell said slowly, 'would you hide a prayer where you, where someone, has hidden a shoe?'

'And if Dr Bishop knew about the shoe, then why didn't he donate it to the museum along with everything else?'

'Because it was too – valuable?' Nell sounded uncertain. 'Too unusual? Maybe he just didn't want to part with it.' It had that effect on some people, she noticed, on Maude, at least.

'Not only does he not donate it; he leaves it where it belongs,' said Gina.

'And he adds a prayer too,' said Nell.

'There are a lot of protections in that building, aren't there?' said Gina. 'It's – remarkable, really.'

'I thought you said the shoe was connected to fertility,' said Nell.

'That's one theory,' said Gina, 'but this kind of magic – it's personal, private. A silent tradition. No one ever really knows for sure what the original intention was.'

'It's gone missing, the shoe.'

'Maude?'

'She says not,' said Nell, 'but yes, I think so. Anyway, I looked in the void and – there's other stuff there. Modern stuff. A pregnancy test, a tampon. Both used.'

318

Gina was quiet for a very long time. 'Goodness,' she said again.

'So maybe it's not just in the past – people have been adding to it, to the house as time goes on. More – protections. Do you think?'

Gina nodded thoughtfully. 'What did you do with them?' she asked. 'The tampon and the test?'

'I got rid of them,' said Nell. 'They were – I didn't like them.' She picked up the piece of paper. 'Was he a religious man? Dr Bishop?' she asked. 'Or, you know – superstitious?'

'Quite the opposite, was my understanding, a man of science – self-made, ambitious. When he retired from public life, someone wrote a biography. There's not much in it – because by all accounts he wouldn't cooperate with it. Too modest, apparently.' Gina sniffed disapprovingly.

'You don't look convinced,' said Nell.

'Frederick Edward Bishop was made mayor twice and his name's on half a dozen buildings around the town. I expect he was many things, but I doubt modest was one of them.'

Gina sat back in her seat, frowning. 'And what about you? Are you OK? You look a bit – flustered, flushed.'

'I'm fine,' Nell raised a hand, pressed it to her cheek. 'A bit out of breath, maybe.'

'What will you do with the panel?'

'It's back in place,' said Nell, 'until I find the shoe, at least. But I'd feel happier if that was back where it belongs before we go. Sorry, I know that sounds – daft.'

'No, no, it's not daft,' Gina said. 'That sounds sensible.' She stood. 'I'm sorry, pet, I do have to get on. And I'm out this evening.' She looked down at the piece of paper. 'Call round tomorrow morning, if you like, and we can talk properly then.'

'I might do that, thanks.'

319

'Give my love to Maude,' said Gina, picking up her jacket, 'and try not to be too hard on her, about the shoe. Everything can seem so overwhelming at that age.'

Nell was still looking at the paper, 'Yes,' she said, absently, 'I suppose it can.'

Carolyn was in the living room. She stood, closing the book she'd been browsing, gathered up her bag and sweater. 'There you are,' she said, 'everything all right?'

'Yes. Fine, thank you, I just got a bit – distracted.' Nell said, forcing a smile. 'Maude?'

'Reading, I think. I made her some lunch and then left her to it. She seems to be on the mend. A bit quiet, though, if you don't mind my saying.'

'No. We've had a – disagreement.'

'I'm sorry to hear that.'

'Oh, it's nothing, she's decided to cling on to the shoe we found, she's being a bit – stubborn.'

'Did you get – well, whatever it was you needed to do. You're all sorted now?'

'Yes. Thank you, Carolyn. I – I really appreciate – everything.' She seemed to spend all her time thanking people these days; she seemed to have lost control of her life.

'Ah, you're welcome.'

Nell thought about checking up on Maude, but if she had been fed and watered, then maybe it would be better to leave her be. There was still a difficult conversation to be had, but that could be done later, once she'd had the chance to talk to Chris. She went into the kitchen, where she'd left the laptop.

There was still no email, and after a couple of attempts she settled for the briefest of messages.

Please ring, Chris. We need to talk. Xxx

She thought for a moment or two, about Gina, and what little she knew about Dr Bishop and about the words on the panel. Then she opened up a search engine. This at least she could control. She clicked on what seemed to be a useful link, and began to read.

25

'Evie? Evie?'

It was too much to hope that she might be left alone. Evie managed to be upright and reading a book at her desk when her mother opened the bedroom door. She rubbed at her face surreptitiously. She felt so ashamed, she felt so *stupid*.

'Hello?'

'Hi.'

'How's the revision going?'

'Fine, Mum, really.'

'And what is it next? English?' Carolyn slid into the room, closing the door behind her.

'Mum. I need to . . .' It was absurd, to feel so caught out, so vulnerable. 'I'm fine.' She could ask, of course, about the house, but she wasn't sure she wanted to have that conversation all alone with her mother. It might be better to ask her dad, better still to find an answer without asking either of them. She tried to smile.

'She's not causing trouble, is she? Gina's granddaughter.'

'She has a name, Mum.'

'I thought we'd agreed you'd drop her, spend more time with Marnie and the others.'

'No. You agreed.' Evie couldn't help herself; even if it had all gone wrong, she'd rather die than let her mother find out.

The blue folder was in plain view on the desk. Carolyn picked it up. 'And what's all this?'

'Notes. French.' It wasn't even a convincing lie, surely her mother would remember she'd completed all the French papers already. 'I really should get on, Mum.'

Carolyn opened the file, began to read through it, scanning through the pages quickly then dropping them on the bed.

'That's private,' said Evie, burning to snatch it away.

Her mother looked up. 'Don't you take that tone with me,' she said, 'not on top of . . . this.'

'I—' God, she was so tired of this. 'We're friends, Mum. She's got exams too, it's not like we're bunking off school or anything.'

'Friends.'

'Yes.' At least she'd thought so.

'And what about Marnie and Grace, nice girls who—'

'I can have more than one friend, you know. I'm not five years old.' This last response was too sharp, too much, and Evie knew it.

Carolyn gave a little nod of the head. 'Fine,' she said, closing the folder and dropping it on the bed. She turned towards the chest of drawers. 'Fine. I was going to leave this. I was going to overlook your – behaviour. But obviously your father and I have been far too lenient with you.'

'Mum – please.' Evie was on her feet. 'Don't.'

Carolyn pulled out the top drawer, then upended it over the bed. 'Let's have a little look at what's been going on here, shall we?'

'Did you honestly think,' said Carolyn quietly, 'that I didn't know?' She was sitting on the bed, the contents of the chocolate box in the drawer, all the scraps of jewellery, the bright keepsakes scattered over the duvet.

Evie couldn't bear to look at her. 'Have you told Dad?'

'Don't be ridiculous.'

That was something at least. She was used to being a disappointment to her mother, but for her father to find out – she felt sick just thinking about it.

'I'd blame Kym Swales,' Carolyn continued, 'but we both know this has been going on for some time. Unless, of course, there's something else there you're not telling me?'

'No,' said Evie.

'I thought not.'

'Please don't tell.'

'And why shouldn't I? After the way you've been behaving?'

'I'll stop. I'll stay away from Kym—'

'Well, you say that now, don't you?' said Carolyn. 'But how do I know you'll keep your word?'

'Please, Mum.' Barely audible now. 'We're not even – we had an argument.'

Carolyn didn't seem to hear her. 'I don't know what it is with girls these days,' she went on. 'Nell can barely control Maude, and she's what – not yet thirteen?'

'I thought you liked her, Nell. I thought you liked them both.'

'She lost it. The shoe,' said Carolyn, 'can you imagine? No sense of responsibility.' She shook her head. 'Well, I think the best thing now is for you to tidy up this mess, then do some actual revision. I'll call you when I start dinner, you can come and help; we can talk some more then.' She stood and looked around the room, the blue folder and Kym's notes seemingly forgotten. 'OK?'

'OK.'

Once her mother had gone, Evie counted to a hundred. Then she began to sort through the papers, putting all of Kym's notes in order.

The pins, she thought, ranged in cases in the museum. *Your old house.*

She stopped and looked down at the papers. There'd be a way of checking, surely. Her parents had never owned Elder House during her lifetime, she was certain of that. But if they had before – say twenty years ago, before she was born; wouldn't there be some sort of paper trail?

She could wait until her dad got home; she could ask him then.

All those children.

She closed the folder.

She couldn't wait that long.

The living room was growing dim and Nell closed down the local history forum she had been browsing. She was scrolling through more search results when an email notification pinged onscreen. It read as though he hadn't seen her message at all.

Hi love,

Just a quick note to say we've put in a response, filed it with the planning people and sent a copy to Simeon Lee and the upshot is everything is on hold until the middle of next month. So, I'll be back – tomorrow evening, I suppose – depends on traffic, and I'll ring later. Sorry, got to go, love to Maude. X

At last.

She should go check on Maude, she might be hungry, or thirsty, she might need to see a friendly face by now, and she'd certainly be glad to know her father was coming back, but Nell was still reluctant to climb up to the attic, to disturb her. She knew in her bones that even this piece of good news would be warped somehow, that the fact he had stayed away so long would be found to be her fault, that somehow she would have failed again.

She leant back against the sofa, her head aching. All she had ever really wanted was to be a good mum to Maude. Jess was, according to Chris, far too volatile, and so Nell had made an effort to be calm. Jess was inconsistent, so Nell tried to be reliable. Jess was given to grand gestures, and to emotional outbursts, she treated Maude like a younger sister half the time, and of course now she was thoroughly taken up with her darling baby boy. And so Nell – Nell tried to be a grown-up.

Bloody Jess.

After the initial fall-out, and that had been nasty, difficult for them all, Jess had moved on with irritating ease. There had been a couple of relationships before the whirlwind courtship with Callum, the wedding, the baby.

Nell closed her eyes. Tried not to cry.

Jess announcing her pregnancy at some stupid family lunch, confiding to everyone that it had been a total accident, but actually, wasn't it wonderful.

It had never occurred to her that they wouldn't have kids of their own. It seemed so easy for everyone else, but she couldn't do it. She couldn't get it right, and she was so tired of trying, of failing.

She closed down the email without responding, and went back to her research results; she'd check with Maude in a little while.

Searching her parents' room was risky, Evie knew that, but with her dad still at work and her mum occupied downstairs, this was probably her only chance. She knew her mother kept important stuff, birth certificates, marriage certificates and the

327

like in an old leather document folder. She just wasn't sure where the folder was.

The chest of drawers first, then – if she had time – the wardrobe. It was hard to concentrate, mostly because she kept stopping and going to the door to double check that she was completely alone, but also because it seemed to be getting harder to remember where everything went – her mother would undoubtedly notice if any of her belongings were out of place – and she found she was arranging and rearranging the contents of the drawers, desperate that they should look right, undisturbed, the next time her mother went to them.

The wardrobe was easier, racks of clothes hanging neatly, sweaters folded on the top shelf, shoes in their boxes on the bottom.

Nothing.

The bookcase in the corner was undisturbed, and there was no hiding place there, anyway.

Evie walked quietly to the door and stuck her head out, listening.

The spare room next. She slipped inside, not quite closing the door so she could keep an ear out for her mother. The bed was made up, just in case they had company, not that they ever did anymore, not since her dad's business had got so quiet. There were no grandparents, no uncles or aunts, and certainly no sleepovers with friends from school, and Evie looked quickly through the chest of drawers by the window. Her mother had fallen into the habit of using it for extra storage, not for her clothes, but for the various crafting activities she took up periodically. The leather folder lay in the bottom drawer, tucked away next to a bundle of knitting patterns and a few hanks of leftover yarn. Evie picked it up, opened it – but leafing through its contents, it quickly became obvious there was nothing to do with Elder House, or any of their former houses. She put the file back, then closed the drawer quietly.

She tried to think. She was looking for old paperwork, old documents – possibly what she needed had been put away with her dad's work stuff. He rarely worked from home, but he did keep records of past projects boxed up in the attic. She looked around the room, checking that she'd left no sign of her search. It was as neat and tidy as it ever was, ready for use, a paint-spattered ladder leaning against the wall.

It was tempting to turn back, give in. If Tyler had been telling the truth, then Kym had only ever been using her to find out about the house, and her mother had been right all along. But she was committed now; she thought of Maude, standing at the top of the steps, clutching the shoe, blood trickling down her arm. She picked the ladder up and carried it onto the landing.

Evie couldn't remember the last time she'd been up here. But it certainly wouldn't have been without one of her parents. It had been last January, probably, when she'd helped her dad put away the Christmas decorations.

She took a breath. There were no lights, it was cramped and dusty, and there was an awful moment between the last step and the attic floor when she thought she wasn't going to make it. The ladder wobbled as she pushed up and against it, both hands clamped to the dusty floorboards, into the dark.

Trying not to think about spiders, she pulled her phone out of her pocket, and flicked on the flashlight app. The boxes, old books, decorations and their Christmas lights were stacked in the far corner, exactly where they should be. But there was something else, something wrong. She let the torch play over the walls, which were – different.

She moved closer. Offcuts of wood, that had been her first thought. Then, panels perhaps, or discarded cupboard doors, and smaller odd shapes, splintered and stacked against the far wall. The wall – she stopped and tried to orient herself – the wall that faced the cliff. But one of the doors appeared to have a chain suspended across it, and the larger shapes were familiar. They were free of the dust that coated everything else up here Evie noticed as she reached out and tilted one of the pieces of wood back – it was a mirror.

Close to a dozen of them; the glass shattered and in some cases broken clumsily into large, dangerous-looking shards and placed quite deliberately along the far wall, mirrored sides facing out, towards the cliff, towards Elder House.

And there in the corner, her mother's Moses basket, a smear of blood on the handle.

She edged closer.

There was something in it.

26

Nell opened her eyes, the broken nights had finally caught up with her, and she had fallen asleep. She'd had the sense to put the laptop to one side, though. She picked it up and the blank screen sprang to life.

A Tragic Loss.

A headline above a formal family portrait. The story she'd seen on the ghost walk video had been true, more or less.

The poor man, his poor wife.

She closed the computer and put it on the coffee table before standing slowly, her bruised back and ribs complaining. She tried the light switch in the hall, flicking it up and down, but the stairs remained dark. They must have tripped a fuse, again.

She went to the kitchen, opened the cupboard over the sink and found the right fuse; the hall light came on.

A loose connection perhaps. Nell tried the switch by the door again, and it seemed to be fine. A power cut, then, or a surge, or – something.

'Maude? Maudie?' She walked upstairs, pausing halfway. 'Are you awake?'

Slow, muted footsteps, and then a muffled response. 'What?' She had the impression Maude had got as far as the hatch and was kneeling down, shouting through it.

'I'm going to make dinner.'

'And?'

'I'll call you when it's ready, shall I?'

'Whatever.'

Nell turned and went back down into the kitchen. The news about Chris could wait, she decided. If Maude couldn't be bothered to come down, to have a face-to-face conversation, that was her problem. She was done with arguments and confrontation; maybe the shoe would just turn up, like her phone had.

She was chopping onions when she heard it: one-*two*, one-*two*.

Maude, she told herself, Maude coming down at last to complain that she was thirsty and that she had run out of things to read.

Maude, favouring her uninjured foot as she planted it care-fully on each tread, gripping the banister tightly, one-*two*, one-*two*, like a toddler learning to manage the stairs.

Like a heartbeat.

The poor little boy, named Frederick for his father.

The knife slipped and she nicked herself. Swearing softly, she turned on the cold tap and let it run over the wound until her finger was numb. She wouldn't think about the doctor and his wife, what had happened to their family. Chris was coming back tomorrow, she would concentrate on that. She switched the radio on, turned the volume up, and went back to the chopping board.

There was a glass of water on the trunk. Maude couldn't think where it had come from. She must have fetched it herself, but she couldn't remember. It felt heavy and the water was warm, but she drank it anyway. Exhausted, she lay down. Her mind wandered as she gazed up at the ceiling, at the marks Kym had said would keep her safe. Marian marks had something to do with the Virgin Mary, so that was probably a good thing.

They never went to church, only for Christmas and weddings.

The pins were a good thing too, the nearest she could get to iron – witches didn't like iron, apparently; and it wasn't that she believed in all this stuff, it was more that it was *fun* to believe in it, to strike a bargain, to make things happen. She wished Carolyn hadn't cleared everything away.

Kym was working at her gran's kitchen table, she had spread out the photocopies she'd made at the Lit and Phil. Evie had dated them and made the odd note, and looking at the neat handwriting as she shifted them around into chronological order, Kym felt horribly ashamed of herself all over again.

'What's all this, then?' Gina said. She was wearing a dress, a bright floral print that had seen better days, and her favourite necklace. She was fussing with her hair, which she'd pinned up into an untidy bun.

'Revision. You look nice,' said Kym.

'Thank you, pet. Are you sure you'll be all right on your own?' It was the Lit and Phil's annual get-together, a pub meal and drinks afterwards. Gina turned one of the photocopies around to get a better look at it.

'History, is it?'

'Yeah.' Kym began to stack the papers.

Gina looked at her thoughtfully. 'I don't have to go out, you know.'

'Don't be daft.'

The power went out just as they were setting the table. It was just the two of them; Oliver was over in Pickering, dining with a client, and Evie had spent an awkward hour helping her mother cook, both of them trying to pretend the scene in her bedroom had never happened. Everything seemed to fade very slowly, the music, the hum of the fridge, the soft whirring of the extractor fan over the oven, and last of all the lights.

'Damn,' said Carolyn. 'Is it us, do you think, or the whole yard?' She went to the kitchen windows.

'Dunno.' Evie rubbed her hands down the side of her jeans. She'd managed to get out of the attic undetected, to put the ladder back where it belonged, and to wash her hands and face before her mother called her down to the kitchen, but she still felt grubby, unclean.

Carolyn opened the door and looked out into the yard. 'Do we have any candles?' she said, but then the lights came on again, and the radio started up. 'There,' Carolyn said, closing the door, 'nothing to worry about.' As if she had solved the problem herself.

'I wasn't worried,' said Evie, looking up at Elder House.

'You know what?' Carolyn opened a drawer by the sink, and picked up a box of matches. 'I think I'll go and check on Nell.'

'Oh.' Evie tried not to sound too eager. 'OK.'

'Just to make sure,' said Carolyn.

'I mean it,' said Gina. 'Maybe I should stay home with you.'

The lights were on, but it seemed to Kym they were not burning quite as brightly as they had been.

'I'm not a kid,' she said, 'I'll be fine.'

The knocking made them both jump.

The radio switched itself on and Nell glanced up towards the fuse box. The lights had come back as quickly as they had faded, and she tried to tell herself it was a power cut, a glitch, nothing more.

Something was moving around upstairs; she turned the radio off and listened.

One-*two*, one-*two*.

He was closer now, making his way down the stairs.

A Tragic Loss

'Maude? Is that you?'

Closer.

A sudden rapping at the front door.

She could run away, she could run to Gina's cottage – or to Carolyn's. One of them would have a phone and Nell could call – who, exactly? The police? Chris?

She couldn't run, she couldn't leave Maude.

Nell looked down and realised she was still gripping the knife. She walked quietly through the dining room and opened the door.

The hall was dim, only partly illuminated by the lights behind her. Switch on the light, go upstairs and get Maude. That was all she had to do. Get them both out. Easy.

More knocking, louder, insistent.

She walked quickly across the hall, undid the latch.

It was Carolyn, standing on the doorstep, smiling politely. 'Hi,' she said, she was holding a box of matches and a bundle of plain white candles. 'Sorry,' she said, 'but our power went off briefly, and it occurred to me . . .' Her voice drifted away, her gaze dropping to the knife in Nell's hand. 'Is everything all right?' she asked.

'Actually,' Nell said, near breathless with relief, 'I'm not sure it is.'

Evie looked around the kitchen, smiling nervously at Gina, her glance skittering off Kym and onto the papers scattered over the table. She was clutching a crumpled linen tote bag and

335

was out of breath. 'I needed to – talk to you. I think.' She gave every impression that she might turn tail and run.

'OK.' Kym's expression was wary, she looked at her grand-mother. 'It's sort of – private,' she said.

Gina looked from one girl to the other. 'You know what?' she said, 'I'm just going to – go upstairs and finish getting ready, and I'll leave you two to have a chat.' She went to the door. 'I will be wanting some answers before I leave, though, so you might want to sort this homework out.' She looked at Kym. 'Whatever it might be.' She smiled sadly at Evie. 'It's nice to see you, pet.'

They stood facing each other, the table between them, neither sure where to start.

'I'm sorry,' said Kym, 'about Tyler. About what he said. About the house.'

'Is it true?' Evie asked.

Kym glanced at the doorway as if she was worried that Gina might hear. 'Yeah. I – thought you knew.'

'No, you didn't.'

'No. No, I didn't. Sorry.' Kym didn't seem to know what to do with her hands, she settled for folding her arms.

'And you weren't going to tell me?'

'Of course I was – I think I was—'

There was a pause.

'Sorry,' said Kym again.

'When? I mean – I looked but I couldn't – when did they own the house?'

'It was back when my grandad was working for them, my dad too' – she took a breath, looked Evie in the eye – 'he was working for them when he died.'

Evie nodded as if the answer were a confirmation, more than anything else. 'Right,' she said, 'of course. Of course he was.'

'But that's not – I wasn't, like, using you.'

The silence stretched between them, filling the room.

'Tell me again about the witch marks,' said Evie eventually, 'about why they put them in houses.'

Kym shook her head, surprised by this sudden change of subject. 'No one really knows, do they? For luck.'

'Protection,' said Evie, 'yeah?'

'Yeah.'

'And why did they build a wall around the abbey, do you think?'

'Invaders,' said Kym, 'the Vikings and all that.'

'They came later,' said Evie, 'and sometimes a wall is, like, significant?'

'A boundary.'

'Yeah.'

'Evie. Are you – OK?'

'What else did Tyler say?' The words came out in a rush. 'About me?'

'Nothing,' said Kym. 'Honestly. Nothing that matters, anyway.'

Evie hesitated, looking down at the documents scattered between them. 'There are maps,' she said, 'in your notes.' She pulled the blue folder from the bag.

The Anglian abbey had taken up most of the headland, and originally extended almost a mile out to sea. The boundary was clearly marked, running along the edge of the cliff above them.

'Here.' Evie placed another A4 photocopy next to the first. The page was slightly blurred, which Kym took to be a defect in the copying process, until she realised that the original images must have been hand drawn and then photographed. It showed the whole street, with smaller images attached, close-up plans of the yards, and there was a date in the corner: *1903*.

Peering closely, Kym could make out Gina's house, and Carolyn's too, and between them Elder Black House, in Elder Black Yard.

'They changed the name,' said Evie.

The next sheet was a plan of the headland, showing the scale and placement of the Anglian monastery. Evie blinked and tried to focus. 'So, we're here,' she said, tracing a finger up the yard, 'and the monastery . . .' She stopped and checked against the previous map. 'It was very close, wasn't it?'

'Yes,' said Kym. 'I mean, there's been a bit of erosion over the years, but yeah, very close. More or less above the yard.'

It was, in her opinion, an odd place to build, there must have been so much space to choose from – and even allowing for the variation in scale, it looked as though the house had been placed underneath the boundary wall of the abbey above. Not underneath, she thought, but below it and just outside. As close as possible but still with a gap; a void.

There were other photocopies too and she picked them up, flicking through them. One was a reproduction of an eighteenth-century engraving of the street view that clearly showed a wrought iron gate barring entrance to the yard.

Keeping everyone out.

Keeping something in.

She pushed the thought away.

'So they build a wall around the abbey,' said Evie, 'and inside, people are – safe.'

'More protection.'

'And outside . . .' She ran a finger along the boundary. 'Outside . . .'

338

'What is it?' Kym looked up, still wary.

'It's my mum. It's like she's been going on about the house, the house and the drying ground, for ever.' Evie frowned. 'And if you look at where it is, and . . . I didn't know they used to own it. I couldn't see why it meant so much to her.' She looked at the papers Kym had been working on, picking one up. 'But it occurred to me, that maybe it's not Elder House, or the drying ground – or maybe not just that.' She pointed to the little patch of land marked on the map. A blurred square that had never been properly occupied. 'Maybe it's not what it is, but *where* it is.'

It seemed to Nell that the kitchen lights weren't burning quite brightly enough. It seemed to her that she could hear someone walking across the landing upstairs.

'I'll take that, shall I?' Carolyn said softly, putting the candles on the kitchen counter, and extending her hand. Nell looked down, then surrendered the knife. 'Good,' Carolyn seemed to visibly relax. 'Why don't we sit down and you can tell me what's wrong. Is it Maude?'

'Oh, God. Maude. I didn't . . .'

'No. You listen to me, you' – Carolyn led Nell to the dining table, and sat her down – 'are going to wait here.'

'But—'

'I will nip up and check on Maude. And then we can have a chat, OK?'

'OK.'

'I won't be long.'

Evie reached into her pocket and pulled out a small grey pebble. She looked down at it, then slid it along the table, barely able to look Kym in the eye. It was Kym's hagstone.

Kym looked at it for a long time, before picking it up. 'I thought I'd left it at school, dropped it somewhere,' she said.

'I – yes. I'm sorry.' Evie rubbed at her face. 'It's difficult, sometimes, to stop myself. Taking things. I mean, I know I shouldn't – I'm sorry.'

'Bloody hell, Evie.' Kym held it to her eye, squinting through the hole. 'You are full of surprises, aren't you?'

'I think . . .' Evie had to clear her throat and try again. She picked up the linen tote bag she'd brought with her. 'I think you should look in here too.'

It seemed to Maude that it was far too dark in the little attic, but no matter how she tried she couldn't get the bedside lamp to switch on, and then when she leant over to try again, she couldn't reach, it was too far anyway.

The little boy in the corner had stopped playing with his toys and was looking at her, clutching a painted toy soldier.

She blinked. No one there.

She pushed the bedclothes down – she was far too hot – and thought about getting up to drink some water, or maybe even have a shower. She'd like that, cold water rushing down on her, filling up her eyes and nose, like diving, like swimming. She closed her eyes and imagined it, swimming through seaweed, dark ribbons of it wrapped around her arms and legs, pulling her further in, further down. Vaguely, far above her, beyond the waves she could hear someone calling her name.

Nell sat quietly at the dining table waiting for Carolyn to come back. She was gone for the longest time and it seemed to Nell that the kitchen lights dipped and flickered more than once, and the smell that seemed to pervade the room – the damp, the smouldering was growing worse. Her back ached, her mouth was dry.

When she spoke to Chris, she'd tell him they needed to have a long talk, that they needed to go home, that she needed – and the word came as a shock, blunt, vicious – she needed to grieve. She allowed herself to start planning; cleaning, packing, returning the keys. She would see him soon; he would hold her, and they would try to make everything right.

The tapping at the door was so gentle Nell thought that it might be her imagination. When she opened it, they were standing there on the step, the two of them, one dark, one fair, and both of them looking anxious.

'Sorry,' said Evie. 'Only, we were wondering – is my mum here?'

'Yes,' said Nell. 'Come in.'

Evie closed the door behind them but didn't seem very willing to move any further into the house. There was a faded cotton tote bag dangling on her shoulder. 'She said she wouldn't be long.'

'She's just checking on Maude. I'm not feeling too good and she – she's been very kind. Come in, come and sit down. She won't be long.' But before anyone could move, the lights flickered and died once again.

'No,' said Evie.

'It's OK,' said Nell. 'There are some candles by the sink.'

'Hello?' Carolyn said, softly. She was sitting on the floor by Maude's bed, and to be honest she wasn't quite sure how long she'd been there, watching over her. It reminded her of when Evie was little. Back when everything was simpler.

Then the lights had flickered out and she heard them quite

341

distinctly, perfectly familiar even after all these years. Halting footsteps that brought to mind a child learning to walk, managing the stairs as best he could.

Some people were frightened of the dark, but not her.

'Hello?' she said again. 'Are you there?'

But there was no answer, only Maude's laboured breathing, slow and painful. Reaching for the knife, Carolyn stood.

She had done her best.

All she had to do was wait until her eyes adjusted, it wasn't even fully dark outside, not quite. It was an effort, though, Kym thought, to stand still, and to not think about what might be hiding in the shadows.

One-*two*.

Inside the house.

Getting closer.

Gradually the room resolved; the solid forms of the furniture, observable, recognisable, familiar.

One-*two*.

She caught her hip against the sink, but she lay her hands on the box of matches easily enough.

'The door,' Evie said, 'open it.' Kym did as she was told and stood there, breathing in the cool evening air. Matches, Kym thought, light. It took a lot of effort to open the box.

She struck the first match, lit a single candle, then a second. 'There,' she said.

'Is it the same at your house, then?' Nell asked, picking up a third candle. 'The power?'

'Yeah. The whole yard, I think. We . . .' She looked at Evie. 'We've been talking and – my gran thinks – we think you and Maude should stay the night with us. She says you should come back right now.'

She was expecting an argument, but to her surprise Nell simply nodded, 'Yeah, that sounds like a good idea,' she said.

'Right.' Kym said. She glanced at Evie. She wasn't looking too good either in her opinion. 'But before – before you go, there's something we need to do.'

The shoe lay on the table, glowing in the candlelight, the leather a rich dark brown, as if it had been cleaned, polished.

'I've been having a few – like, problems and – sometimes I – take stuff – sometimes.' Evie's voice was barely audible. 'I don't really know why. It makes me feel – better.'

'Jesus.' The poor kid. All Nell really wanted to do was hug her.

'And no one really notices, because people trust me, and anyway – I thought no one knew, but it turns out Mum did.' She shifted in her seat. 'She's not – pleased, obviously.'

Kym reached out and gave Evie's hand a tentative squeeze.

'And we were talking about – that – and she said about the shoe. She said it had gone missing. And I thought, I thought she'd blame me. Only she didn't – not even a . . .' Evie cleared her throat and sat up straighter. 'Which was weird, you know? She didn't even ask. Like she already knew it wasn't me. And she said something about you not knowing what it was for. And she sounded like she, sort of – does.'

'Carolyn?' Nell knew she had to put the shoe back, but she was faintly repelled by the idea of picking it up, touching it, the warm leather yielding underneath her fingers.

'When you came round, and she said about her Aunt Ida? She used to have a real thing for her – a couple of years ago, she got really into homeopathic and folk remedies and there were stories, more stories, I mean, like she was proud of Ida. Like she could really – do things. And she has some books,

343

upstairs in her room. Dad used to tease her, but he thought it was just a phase, like quilting or knitting or . . .' Evie looked like she might cry. 'Only she's had those books forever and we've been talking and it's important, I think – we think – to put it back.' She leant forward her expression urgent. 'And you should do it quickly, and not let her see, because – I was looking for . . .' She glanced at Kym. 'I was looking for something else and . . . When I found the shoe, she'd put it in the Moses basket. She hid it in our attic and there are – mirrors. It's hard to describe, they're all facing the wall.'

'We should get Maude,' said Kym, 'take her up to Gran's and then – we can put it back, yeah?'

Nell thought for a moment, then she stood, picking up a candle and led the way into the hall.

'Carolyn?' Nell held up her candle, shadows danced and wavered around the hall.

She was sitting at the bottom of the stairs, her head resting against the banister, her eyes closed.

'Carolyn, are you OK?' Nell asked.

'Fine. I'm fine.' She pulled herself wearily to her feet. 'You shouldn't have come,' she said to Evie. 'Everything is – under control.'

'I was worried.'

'So I heard.' Her gazed travelled over Kym and she smiled. 'And you brought your friend too.'

'Mum—'

Carolyn shook her head. 'No,' she said.

'I just need to speak to Maude,' said Nell, but as she moved towards the staircase, Carolyn stood, blocking her way. She was still holding the vegetable knife, the blade gleaming, the edge still a little bloodied.

'No,' she said again, 'there's no need. She's fine.'

'Mum, please,' said Evie.

'Don't fuss,' said Carolyn. She gestured towards the kitchen, and after a moment's thought, Nell nodded and led the way back.

'Why don't you tell us about the mirrors,' she said, putting her candle back on the table.

'They reflect negative energy away from the house. Sympathetic magic. Protection. It's a simple principle, really,' Carolyn said. She stayed back by the door, in the shadows, blocking the way. High up in the house there was a distant thud.

Nell glanced at the ceiling. 'Maude,' she said.

'She's fine,' Carolyn said. 'She's sleeping.'

And then they heard it, travelling along the ceiling above them, the halting rhythm, one-*two*, one-*two*, one-*two*.

'Please,' said Nell, but Carolyn didn't seem to be listening, her gaze fell on the shoe on the table, and she moved closer.

'That belongs here,' Kym said. 'You can't have it. We're going to put it back.'

'And what would you know about it?' said Carolyn.

'It keeps everything – I don't know – in check. Safe.'

'Is that what you think?' said Carolyn. 'Once upon a time, perhaps, but now I'm not so sure; what if that little shoe means different things to different people? What if it means something different to me? What if I need it more than you do?'

'Mum,' said Evie, 'you can't keep it. Please.'

'Do you know,' Carolyn went on, 'the hidden shoe represents a human sacrifice? Because they are worn and moulded over time, because they're the imprint of a person.' She looked at Nell. 'That's why they used a child's shoe, because that's the best kind of sacrifice. Children make the best offering, even if they try to protect themselves with bent pins and piles of salt.' She smiled. 'I tidied up, in the attic,' she said.

345

'It's not yours,' said Nell. 'It belongs to the house.'

'You're not listening,' Carolyn said, waving the knife idly. 'It's not just the shoe, it's your intention; it's what you are willing to do.'

'Like Dr Bishop,' said Nell. 'You must know all about him, surely? He dug up the drying ground, and he donated his finds to the museum.'

Help me, God Almighty

'And I think he found the shoe, but that – that he put back in place. But . . .' Nell glanced at Kym who seemed to be edging towards Carolyn. 'At around the same time there was an accident. His little boy went missing. He went missing, and they found him in the attic, and he'd died. And all this time I've been hearing . . . I thought it was . . .' She ran a hand across her belly, the ache there was too much. 'I felt sorry for him. It must have been unbearable,' she said.

'Or not,' said Carolyn, 'because the really interesting thing about Frederick Bishop is that after the tragic death of his only son, his luck changed. He became a successful man. He became mayor, he built a hospital, devoted his life to good works and there were more sons eventually; more babies, all boys. He lived a long and happy life, with everything he could wish for, a happy ending.' She paused, smiling. 'He struck his bargain, he got what he wanted.'

'He made a sacrifice,' said Evie, and her mother looked at her closely.

'My clever girl,' she said. 'I didn't think you had it in you.'

'You don't know that,' said Kym, 'not for sure—'

'Of course I do,' said Carolyn. 'My Aunt Ida knew, she told me. She knew lots of things.'

'Maybe he felt ashamed, or maybe,' Kym said, 'maybe he

346

realised in moving the shoe he – he – allowed something into the house. Moving it makes everything go wrong.'

'Too late, by then, of course,' said Carolyn.

'No,' said Nell. 'He put it back, with a prayer. He had seen the words on the comb and he thought they would protect him.'

'From what, though?' asked Evie.

Carolyn turned on her daughter, her expression mild. 'She's very invested in all of this, isn't she – your new friend?' She smiled. 'Has it never occurred to you to wonder why?'

'We haven't the time for this,' said Kym. 'You should put that knife down and let Nell go see to Maude.'

'I know,' said Evie, glancing at Kym. 'I know about her dad. She told me all about it.'

'Well, good for her.' Carolyn tilted her head to one side. 'We didn't go to the inquest, your father and I, but a statement was read.'

'Inquest?' said Nell. 'Why—'

Carolyn ignored her. 'We had no idea why he was here, trespassing, although we could guess. Things had been going missing on site all the time, tools, wallets, people's phones. We were just as upset as everyone else when it happened, and the *Gazette* kept bothering us for a comment.'

Nell grabbed the back of the chair, as if she might fall. 'Here,' she said. 'He died here?'

'And we couldn't move in, of course. We owned the house, but once we'd finished the renovations, well – Oliver felt that we couldn't – that it might seem – insensitive. So we sold it. We had to give it up.' Carolyn shook her head. 'That just – broke my heart. There were other houses after that, quite a few, but none of them were right. None of them were – home. We've never been able to settle, not really. There was talk of

347

legal action, at the time. Compensation.' She kept a firm grip on the knife. 'Of course, that came to nothing because that boy shouldn't have been in the house in the first place. Although she wouldn't have a word said against him at the time, Gina. Goodness knows what nonsense she's told Kym, though. I wouldn't be surprised if they were still after money.'

'Fuck you, Carolyn.' Kym took another step closer.

'No,' said Evie, uncertainly. She shook her head. 'I don't care. Please, Mum. Please. We should put it back.' In the soft glow of candlelight the shoe looked as good as new, as if a child had kicked it loose and run away, as if they might come back to reclaim it at any moment.

'You,' Carolyn said, taking a step nearer, 'have no idea what you owe to that – to me. No idea at all.'

'It's – not good for people,' said Evie. 'We weren't meant to find it, to move it.'

'Not you,' said Carolyn. 'Not Nell, maybe, but if you know what to do—'

'You knew,' said Nell, and it was almost a relief to make sense of it. 'You knew the shoe was here all along.'

The mark in the dust where the little plastic cylinder had lain undisturbed on the top of the stone shelf, and the corresponding mark for the shoe. Dr Bishop had left the prayer on the panel; a woman had left a used tampon and a pregnancy test. 'You found the shoe once before, and maybe you took it away, but you made sure to put it back in place.'

'Oh, I did more than that.' Carolyn looked at her, her expression soft, almost pitying. 'I saw you, you know, in the supermarket that day. I saw what you bought. Picking through supper that night for the things you can eat, discarding the things you can't – when you daren't take a risk, because *it's not good for baby*. It wears you down, doesn't it?' she said. 'The times when you're late, five days, a week, two – but it never comes right and it's the hope, every month, that destroys you in the end. Because no matter how careful you are, it always comes to nothing. And it's so easy for everyone else, isn't it? The ex-wives and the silly little schoolgirls, falling pregnant like it's an accident, an inconvenience. We were desperate. *I* was desperate. So I struck a bargain too.' She looked steadily at Nell. 'You understand that, don't you?'

'But you don't need it now, do you?' said Evie. 'I mean, we're all right without it, aren't we?'

'I want another chance,' said Carolyn. 'I want another baby. I've been trying for . . . It worked before, and it will work again.'

'Seriously?' Kym couldn't help herself. 'That's why you stole it? You wanted – a lucky charm? Because whatever that is, you do realise that's not how it works, right?'

'I know exactly how it works,' said Carolyn. 'Which is why we're all going to stay here for a little while longer.'

'I want to see Maude,' said Nell.

'No,' said Carolyn.

'Mum,' Evie said, and she began to cry.

It seemed to Nell that the poor kid might crumple, collapse entirely. She let go of the chair, edged towards Carolyn, trying to make it look as if she was just straightening up, shifting her weight; maybe if she rushed her, knocked her off balance, made a grab for the knife . . . the electric lights above them buzzed and flickered and faded away.

'That's why you kept going on about the drying ground,' said Kym. 'You wanted to get access to the house, to the shoe.'

'Well, yes. Between you and me, I was never quite cool enough to be friends with Nell Galilee and it would be a bit of a push, to go from using the drying ground to just nipping

349

inside to get upstairs – but, yes, I thought I could try it. And it's not as if I'd have to search for it. And anyway' – she turned her attention to Nell – 'there's something out there, something about that little patch of land, don't you think – it's – connected somehow, I think – almost like it's—'

'Alive,' said Evie.

Carolyn nodded approvingly at her daughter. 'That's it.'

'Everyone thinks it's the shoe,' said Evie, wiping her tears away. 'Or the house, but really it's the place – it's the ground in between. There's something – wrong there.'

'A reason,' Carolyn said, 'for all these protections.'

The kitchen lights brightened once more, then flickered out again. Nell leant forward. 'And it was you all along, who opened the panel, that day you brought round the cake.'

'I wasn't quick enough,' said Carolyn. 'Maude came in just a little too soon. Which was – irritating. But then she hurt her foot and you were only too eager to palm her off onto me; and it was me she confided in, when she stole the shoe.'

It might have been Nell's imagination, but Kym seemed a little closer to Carolyn too, and was keeping a wary eye on the hand that held the knife.

'She didn't really have a plan – she was acting on instinct, I think, when she hid it from you. But it was easy enough to persuade her to give to me – for safekeeping. I told her I would give it back to her when you left, that she would get to keep it and you would never know. She does have a problem with you, Nell, doesn't she? And it will only get worse, just you wait and see. Evie is verging on the uncontrollable. Lying. Stealing.' She shook her head. 'Gay, for God's sake, as if that means she's going to have any normal sort of life.' She looked at Nell, confiding, almost friendly. 'I couldn't believe it, when I saw it was you. Fate again, you see, stepping in because I needed it

– the shoe – another chance. I need another chance to be a mother. To get it right this time.'

'Then you understand,' said Nell. 'It's Maude, you see – we have to make sure she's all right.'

Carolyn shook her head. 'I don't think so,' she said. 'Books are all very well, but when it comes down to it, you have to go on instinct. Good intentions are one thing, but when it comes down to it – you have to be willing . . .'

'Are you actually out of your mind?' Kym was definitely closer to her, angry too. The lights flickered again, flaring briefly, and Nell could feel it, the house tensing, then expanding; when the footsteps started again, they would be closer. 'Look at her, at your child, look what you've done to her—'

'As if you care.'

Kym could smell something, something smouldering, something burning. 'Of course I do, she's . . .' She looked at Evie, smiled sadly. 'She's smart and kind and – beautiful – and she deserves better friends than me and she certainly deserves a much better mother than you—'

'It worked before,' said Carolyn. 'You have to hold your nerve, that's all. A flick of the switch is all it takes. Nell knows what I mean, she knows what she'd do.'

'No.'

'It's all right for Chris, isn't it? He's already fathered a child. He doesn't know what it's like to want something so very terribly, and to be denied. He's not the one who is – damaged.'

'You're talking nonsense,' said Nell.

'I don't think so,' said Carolyn. 'It speaks to me, this house, it always has; it speaks to you too. It knows what we want.'

There was a silence; Nell couldn't find an answer.

'What do you mean?' said Kym. 'Hold your nerve? What did you do?'

'I didn't do anything,' said Carolyn. 'I waited; and that's what we're going to do now. We'll sit quietly and wait, and hope that next time round, the child won't be quite so – defective.'

With a half swallowed sob, Evie grabbed hold of the shoe, before turning to face Carolyn. 'You don't mean that,' she said, 'I'm not – not—'

As the air crackled with static and the lights burst back into life, Kym moved – launching herself at Carolyn, missing the point of the knife more by luck than judgement. Carolyn fell back, hitting the wall, sliding to the floor and dropping the knife. Nell snatched it up as the kitchen lights flickered then settled again; bathing the room in a sickly yellow glow. 'Maude,' she said.

'Yes,' said Evie.

'Maybe,' Kym said to Nell, nodding at the shoe, which Evie was still clutching, 'you should deal with that too.'

27

'Maude? Maudie, sweetheart?' Nell shook her gently, then again, more firmly. She dropped to her knees beside the bed and lay the back of her hand against Maude's forehead. She was running a temperature; there was a rash, vivid patches of red splashed over her pale clammy skin, and scratches too, long raised welts on her wrists, arms, neck.

This was wrong, it couldn't be – she was supposed to be getting better.

On the mend. That's what Carolyn had said.

She tried to recall the last time she'd seen Maude and had a proper conversation with her, lunchtime? Earlier that morning? She had assumed Maude was sulking. She had relied on Carolyn, trusted her. She'd been grateful to have Maude taken off her hands. She hadn't even bothered to pass on Chris's message.

Love to Maude.

She was covered in a thin film of sweat, her eyes fluttering behind their lids, and there was a peculiar rasping quality to her breathing.

'Maude?'

The girl's eyes fluttered open, her gaze fixing upon Nell, looking right through her. 'Serve . . . serve you right . . .'

Meningitis might have been Nell's first guess, but now – some

353

sort of infection, perhaps, connected to the cut on her foot. She knelt up, leaning forward, the better to see the expression on Maude's face, and to check on her breathing.

Nell was holding the shoe. It was an odd thing, supple, alive, almost. And she had brought it up with her for a reason, hadn't she? She had to think for a moment.

Carolyn believed it would give her what she wanted if she kept it close by.

But she was supposed to put it back.

It speaks to me, this house, it always has; it speaks to you too.

Nell held up her hand, balancing the shoe in her palm. A child's shoe, a child – no more than three or four years old, perhaps.

What we're really talking about is sacrifice.

Poor Carolyn, she must have been – desperate. And the shoe seemed to offer some sort of comfort. Nell understood that much at least.

It knows what we want.

She closed her eyes, and she could hear it once again – footsteps passing slowly along the landing below.

She'd read all about him earlier. Dr Bishop, so eager, so ambitious. He'd probably been delighted with his find – a little prestige at last, even if his practice was struggling with so many mouths to feed.

A bargain struck.

A sacrifice.

There was something about it that let you think about these things, she noticed – consider them. Something about the house.

Nell looked around the attic.

A little boy playing in the corner, his father watching over him, moving closer, reaching out.

And worth it in the end; he'd filled his life with good works. Did all those good deeds make up for that one bad thing?

Oh God God Almighty

The words of the prayer floated into Nell's head. They were very old, buried for centuries in the drying ground, the midden. Another idea, less seductive, began to form.

Why did he bring the prayer into the house? Why place it so close to the shoe?

The shoe was a sacrifice made over and over again, time out of mind, for the greater good, to keep something at bay; but then you can't tell where one ends and the other begins. And in the end, the shoe isn't enough.

A little boy, choking on a pin.

Wire burning.

God Almighty Help Me

Carolyn thinking she could strike a bargain with it, not once, but twice.

A bargain with . . .

One-*two*, one-*two*. Closer now.

Who's there?

She couldn't think about that and she was almost grateful as the question slid away.

Maude's room was a mess, a red trainer – the left one – lay abandoned on the floor, its laces trailing along the rug, its twin poking out from under a bunk.

Carolyn was right about one thing; it did wear her out, the hope – and the secret fear that she was at fault. Defective.

She turned her attention to Maude. Her eyes were closed, her hair damp with sweat.

It wouldn't hurt, surely, to stay here, holding the shoe, for a little while longer, listening for – for . . .

355

Chris would understand. It had worked for Carolyn; it would work for them. All she had to do was turn off the lamp, flick the switch, sit in the dark for a while. Just – wait.

Too late, she would say, I got there too late.

'Nell?' Kym was standing at the foot of the ladder, calling up. 'Are you OK? Nell?'

All that sacrifice, all those hopes and desires, all that fear and need congealing around that single shoe, tainting it.

'Nell?'

The long scratches that ran the length of Maude's arms had begun to clot – the cuts were not too deep. Maybe she had lost her nerve – or maybe she needed to take her time. Nell didn't know where this new idea came from, that a slow death was a welcome thing. She tilted Maude's head to one side, there were more marks, purplish bruising under the jaw, a scratch running from below Maude's ear and down her neck; the blue pulse of the vein, so fragile. She had brought the knife with her, although she didn't remember snatching it up. It lay on the floor beside the bed.

She picked it up.

Maude's breath was growing more laboured.

The little boy had choked to death, on a pin.

It's what you're prepared to do.

She looked at Maude, so small, so still.

A bargain struck.

A sacrifice.

'We need—' Nell stood up and the room swayed. 'We need an ambulance. Go and call for an ambulance – I can't wake her up.' She went to the ladder. 'Do you understand?'

'Yes. Yes, of course.'

356

'And there are marks, cuts on her arm – I think it was Carolyn. And a cut on her neck.'

She turned back to the bed, the knife in her hand.

Evie was hovering over her mother, who was still slumped on the floor. She was conscious and – thank God – she had finally stopped talking when Kym ran back into the kitchen.

'Do you have your phone?'

'Yes.'

'Right. You need to ring for an ambulance, Maude's really ill.' Kym couldn't help looking down at Carolyn. 'Nell can't wake her up.'

Evie fumbled in her pocket. 'No signal,' she said after swiping at the screen. 'Hang on.' She picked up her bag, opened the kitchen door and vanished into the gloom.

'It hurts,' said Carolyn, looking up at Kym, then rotating her wrist experimentally. 'I think something might be broken. Give me a hand up, will you?'

'I don't think so,' said Kym, 'not yet.'

Carolyn sighed, and shuffled back until she was resting against the wall, her legs stretched out in front, one shoe loose, adrift. Kym sat down next to her, almost as if they were friends, and regarded her seriously. 'I was chatting with Pete Chappell earlier. I think I'd like you to tell me what you did to my dad.'

It took a surprisingly long time to persuade the person on the other end of the line to send an ambulance. She kept asking peculiar questions about the patient, and her symptoms, and she didn't seem to understand that Evie wasn't actually there, right next to her.

It was Maude's age that tipped it, in the end, and the fact that Evie was beginning to sound frantic.

'Go to the end of the yard,' the woman on the phone said, 'and wait for the ambulance there.'

'Right.' Evie shoved her phone in her pocket, then hesitated, looking up at the drying ground.

It wasn't yet fully dark, but it was still difficult to find her way. The security lights weren't working, and the light from the kitchen didn't help much; it only seemed to cast deeper shadows the higher she climbed up the bank. Evie followed the fence until she found the open gate; she looked up at Elder House, then taking a deep breath, stepped inside.

It was cold. Still.

But it seemed to her that very faintly, beneath her feet, there was – something, a tremor, a vibration.

And it was getting stronger.

Nell pulled the panel out of the wall. She picked up the shoe – one last time, just this one last time – and tried to clear her mind, to focus; to set her intention. Outside, on the landing, the lights wavered; there was someone, something there, just out of sight.

'We were doing up the house, when we found it – or rather, when I did,' said Carolyn. 'That bedroom used to have the most hideous wallpaper, can you imagine? God-awful chipboard covered with these enormous violent pink roses. It looked ridiculous, and I was dealing with that, when I found the panel, and then the void, and the shoe. And I knew what it was, straight away. My Aunt Ida had told me, you see about – traditions, superstitions, little things you could say and do to smooth your way through life, to overcome difficulties.' She seemed to lose her thread for a moment, smiling slightly, caught in the memories of the past, a happier time. 'I'd done everything you were supposed to do, I looked after myself, I even planted parsley in some little pots, and it had worked and I was pregnant,' she said. 'I was certain of it, although we hadn't told anyone, and the shoe seemed like it was an omen. So, I took it out of the wall, took it home – to our flat over on the West Cliff. For luck.' The smile faded. 'Then everything went wrong.'

'The testing kit,' said Kym, 'the tampon. Gran told me about – that was you?'

'Oliver said he didn't mind, but he did. Almost as much as I did. And I knew, you see, I knew what the shoe was – what needed doing.' She paused, gathering her thoughts. 'Just putting it back didn't seem like enough, though. And it was – difficult too, I remember that, because I very much wanted to keep it close by. And I began to think about Dr Bishop and what he'd done. She'd been in service, my Aunt Ida, did you know that? And people talk, stories get handed down—'

'Did your husband know?'

'Good Lord, of course not. The house was just wood and stone to him, an investment.'

'And then?'

'Afterwards, your grandmother tried to sue us,' said Carolyn, sharply. 'All she wanted in the end, was money.'

'She wanted you to take some responsibility for what you had done,' said Kym. 'When you offered to settle out of court, she told you to shove it.'

'It was an accident, and we didn't have to offer her anything,' said Carolyn. 'We were trying to be kind.' She looked towards the back door and frowned. 'Where's Evie?'

'Getting help,' said Kym. 'Tell me what you did.'

*

359

The land fell away steeply, the long grass cold against her legs. She should leave, go and wait at the end of the yard like she'd been told to, make sure the gate was open. But she might not get another chance. Taking the shoe from her mother hadn't been enough, and she wasn't sure that putting it back would help either, it all seemed too much, too close now.

Slowly, Evie turned her back on the yard and looked up at the cliff, craning her neck, trying to work out where the yard and the drying ground stood in relation to the church and the abbey. Fixing it in place on the map.

There was no real way of telling, but that was OK, if she—

She didn't hear the noise, exactly, it was more like she *felt* it. At first, she thought it might be Flossie, the stupid animal, snuffling through the long grass, scrabbling at the earth. But when she turned around, there was nothing there. The kitchen windows were a dull yellow, and the house was still. She turned her attention to the roof, the attic where Maude slept, and wondered if Maude could see the whole yard from her room; the Wilson's cottage and the gate they'd put up. Sealing them all in.

This time the noise came from behind her, a trickle of pebbles falling, and Evie turned quickly. Rock falls were rare, but they did happen, and she was close to the cliff after all.

Too close.

It was getting colder, and she stood for a moment listening to the pounding of her heart as the skin on her arms prickled. Goosebumps.

She clutched the linen bag, took a deep breath.

'He was nice enough,' said Carolyn, 'friendly. And I wasn't that much older than him.' She looked at Kym. 'What did Pete say? He worked for us for a bit, did you know that?'

'Not until he told me. When he was eighteen he had a year out between school and university, and he spent it labouring. He knew my dad, and they both worked for you,' said Kym.

'Always a smile and a hello whenever I was on site. He couldn't do enough for me.' Carolyn shifted position, trying to get comfortable. 'He and Pete, they made a big deal of explaining the system to me. How we should always check the fuse box, and to mind out for exposed wires. Like I was thick, or something. The little woman.'

Kym hoped Carolyn was in pain, that she had broken a bone; she was in the mood to break something else.

'What else did he tell you?'

'He said my dad told him he'd arranged to meet you at the house. And he never told anyone, not even at the inquest – because he thought you two were . . .' Kym hesitated. 'You know – he thought it would make the both of you look bad.'

'Yes, that's Pete all right. It would never occur to him that there would be any other reason I needed Robin to come to the house.' Carolyn shifted her weight, winced again. 'I told him there was a bit of extra work on offer,' she said. 'Cash in hand, helping me strip the walls, sand down the paintwork. I told him not to tell anyone else, because I wanted to keep it a secret from Ollie. I put everything back in the wall where it belonged. I told him to come to the house that evening, once everyone had gone home. And I waited. I had it all worked out. I'd get here first, get everything ready, and if he came – it was up to him, you see. I'd say I'd left my phone here, and what a shock it was finding him like that; what an awful accident. There was no light switch in the hall, you see. Just the exposed wires, and people get into habits, don't they? You'd just expect a switch to be there, to be safe.' She looked Kym straight in the eye. 'I turned the power on, and I waited. *We* waited.'

'We?'

'This house isn't empty, you know that as well as I do.' Carolyn lifted her chin, defiant. 'I didn't touch Robin Verrill. It was his choice to come. And when he did, it took him.'

'It?'

'It's here now – it doesn't matter what you do to me – it's here and all we have to do is wait.'

'For what?'

'You'll see,' said Carolyn. 'It'll all come out. Poor Maude – disruptive at school, excluded, unhappy. Neglected. Left all alone in that condition, she's a remarkably impressionable girl. No wonder she took a knife and – what is it called? Self-harm? Not my fault, anyway, and she's very ill.' She smiled. 'All we have to do is wait,' she said.

Kym could smell it again, the strongest it had ever been, burning wire, melting plastic, smoke, and – and . . . 'Jesus,' she said. 'You're – mad. You're actually mad.'

'I found out I was pregnant late the following month, with Evie.' She shook her head. 'She has no idea, what I did for her. I wasn't sure, you know, if it would be enough. A young child is better, you see. But it worked.' She looked at Kym, her eyes glittering. 'Will you tell her, do you think? What I did for her? Where she came from? Do you have the nerve to do that?'

Kym scrambled to her feet, backed away.

'Gina's child for mine. That's what it came down to.' Carolyn's face crumpled, and for a moment she looked old, weary, afraid. 'You can't imagine,' she said, 'that I'm happy about any of this.'

The quartz pebbles rattled at the bottom of the bag as she pulled out the salt, a packet snatched from the kitchen cupboard, and turned towards the fence, lurching in the dark, scattering salt along the edge of the boundary, pausing to drop a couple

362

of the pebbles in the corner, one hand holding the bag, the other her scrap of paper, her prayer, a charm hastily torn from one of her mother's books. She stumbled in the dark, tried to focus, to still her mounting panic. She'd meant to wait, to find a quiet time when no one was around, but now – there was no time left.

It was as if, as if – there was someone behind her, breathing onto the back of her neck; her skin puckered into goosebumps. She should go, get to the street. Evie turned, then stumbled; she fell to her hands and knees, her fingers clawing into the earth as the ground shuddered.

The paper fluttered into the dark.

She shook her head, there was a pain, like a single long scratch at the back of her throat. She coughed, once, twice, tasting blood, but the pain grew worse, and she couldn't catch her breath, and the ground seemed to be shifting below her. Her mother's words came back to her.

A reason for all those protections.

She looked up towards the house, it wasn't enough, any of it, the salt and the pebbles and the prayer; it was just childish nonsense.

Then it seemed to her that the land beneath her began to twist and shudder, that the shadows had come to life and one of them was moving closer.

The light in the master bedroom cast a sickly glow, and the smell was back too; damp, decaying.

One-*two*, one-*two* – closer now.

Kneeling by the bed, Nell paused, she could almost see the child framed in the doorway, but then the shadows stretched and she realised she'd made a mistake. It was a man, but the air around him seemed to shift and fold and he vanished and

363

there was something else, something *old* forcing its way into the house.

It took an effort to turn away, to drag her attention back to the gap in the wall.

One-*two*, one-*two*.

She couldn't look, wouldn't look; certain now that whatever was limping towards her was no child.

One-*two*, one-*two*.

Two shoes, lying on the bed.

One-*two*.

Time to choose. Time to go on instinct. Nell worked as quickly as she could, fumbling in her haste, then pressed the panel back into place.

One-*two*.

Not a shadow, Evie realised, but Gina, all dressed up in a cotton print frock, shivering in the cool night air; reaching down and helping her to her feet, a silver charm dangling from a chain around her neck, the faint scent of violets warming the night air. 'Come on, pet, that's enough, don't you think?'

She knelt and pushed the bed back against the wall.

Oh God

She bowed her head, wondering if she'd left it too late.

God Almighty

She should have taken better care.

One-*two*.

It was inside the room, it was with her.

She made her choice.

She closed her eyes.

364

28

'I should have been quicker,' said Gina. 'I left it far too long before I decided to come and see what was keeping you.'

'There's no point thinking like that,' said Nell. 'It doesn't do anyone any good.'

They were sitting in the garden, Nell and Gina. Chris was in the hospital, thirty miles up the coast, with Maude. They had been assured there was no need for him to be there. Maude was responding well to treatment and there was nothing he could do – but he couldn't, wouldn't, be parted from her.

Nell drank her tea, regular builder's tea today, and looked at the view. Late spring was tumbling into summer, the garden was flourishing, and purple and white columbine nodded their heads in the breeze. After gentle inquiries about Maude's health, the conversation had circled back inevitably to Carolyn. 'And you are not to blame,' she said, 'for her . . . fixation.'

'Well. I should have realised there was something up.'

'How? You couldn't have known. Nobody else did, apart from poor Evie. She knew something was wrong long before the rest of us. Really, Gina, it's OK.'

'Only just.'

Sepsis. Hard to diagnose, and no one's fault, they'd said at the hospital, a complication from the cut on her foot seemed to be the general consensus. There had been a difficult twenty-four hours, but Maude had stabilised, and the prognosis was good.

Once she had started to improve, Chris and Nell had begun commuting to the hospital. But that morning, when Nell had said she was feeling tired, Chris hadn't tried to persuade her to drive up with him. There was still so much to say, and neither of them seemed to have a clue as to where to start. Nell had spent the morning pottering around the house, unable to settle to anything before deciding to call on Gina.

'So, have I got this right? Maude had the shoe all along?'

'She couldn't bear to give it up, and Carolyn – well, she persuaded her she was on her side, that she'd look after it for her. She had her believing that I'd picked on her at school, that I deserved to be – upset.'

That was as much as she'd been able to piece together. And while Chris had apologised, for leaving them, for not being there, Nell was far from sure that she herself had been forgiven for the mistakes she had made, the poor decisions. 'The other stuff, the things she'd put in the attic, the pebbles, the salt – I think Maude was trying to protect herself.'

'Against?'

'I don't know. I'm not sure she knows.' She thought again of Maude's diary, the swirling patterns and half-formed thoughts. She'd been lost; and Nell had no idea.

But she had made the right choice in the end, and surely that counted for something. Sam was working at the gallery, holding the fort until they could get back, but she'd handed in her notice; the email was formal, impersonal, not really like Sam at all.

'I'm so sorry,' Nell said, 'about Robin. I had no idea that it had all happened – so close by. I can't imagine—'

Gina cut her off, shaking her head. 'You weren't to know,' she said firmly. 'And I – we – are used to it.'

Nell might have said more, but she could hear footsteps, two sets moving rapidly up the path.

'Hiya.' Kym and Evie appeared around the corner, Kym swinging her bag extravagantly before she dropped it onto the grass.

'All done?' Gina asked.

'All done. Roll on the summer holidays,' said Kym, flopping down next to her bag.

'I thought you'd be visiting Maude,' Evie said. 'It's nice to see you.'

'I wanted to let you all know how she's doing,' said Nell, 'and to thank you, again, for helping.'

'I didn't do very much.' Evie looked embarrassed. 'I mean, none of it's provable, is it? It's all theory.'

'A matter of interpretation,' said Kym. 'Like the shoe.'

'Well, thank you anyway.'

'Cup of tea?' said Gina.

'I'd rather have a coffee,' said Kym.

'It'll have to be instant.'

'Go on then.'

'Evie?'

'Coffee, please.' She had some colour back in her cheeks at least, even if she was still a bit on the thin side. 'I'll do it though,' she said, and went into the kitchen, vanishing into the cool green light.

'Is she OK?' Nell asked softly.

'OK might be pushing it,' said Kym. 'But she reckons her dad has stepped up a bit.'

'And Carolyn?'

'In hospital, for the moment, and Evie reckons she's cooperating with the therapy; it might even help. She's still insisting that Maude pinched the knife, though, that she was the one who – you know . . . That she found her self-harming and took it away from her for her own good.'

367

Nell looked at her closely. 'You've not really said what happened with her that night,' she said. 'You were on your own with her for a bit, weren't you? What did she say?'

'Not much, not really,' said Kym. 'I mean, she'd totally lost the plot by then, hadn't she? She was talking about sacrifice and Ida Green and – there wasn't a great deal a person could take to the police, even if she wanted to.'

'That doesn't seem fair on you, or your dad.'

'But fairer on Evie, I think,' said Kym. She smiled at her grandmother. 'I got enough, in the end, and what good would it do everyone else to drag it up all over again? With no proof?'

'I wasn't an easy woman, Ida,' said Gina, 'for all her advice and remedies. There was something about her that seemed to enjoy other people's misfortunes a bit too much. It was as if once she'd helped someone out, then she was – entitled, I suppose, part of the family. I can imagine her clinging on to someone young and insecure, trying to mould them.' She swirled her tea around in her mug, frowning. 'Giving them ideas. She had her fallings out with people, too, you know – as she got older she seemed to push folk away.'

'Except for Carolyn?'

'I suppose so.' Gina put her mug on the grass. 'She's been gone a long time, but she casts a shadow still, doesn't she?'

'And you?' Nell asked Kym in the silence that followed. 'Are you OK?'

Kym's expression was calm, her make-up impeccable. 'I like to think of myself as a work in progress,' she said. The beginnings of a smile flitted across her face. 'What about Maude? How's she doing?'

'Fine. She doesn't seem to remember anything, which is a blessing, I think.' They hadn't spoken much, and on the few occasions they had been alone together Nell had barely known where to start. She didn't know what Maude had felt and seen in the house, she wasn't sure she ever would. She stood. 'I'll go give Evie a hand.'

She was standing by the kitchen sink, staring blankly out at the garden as the kettle boiled furiously. Then a switch flicked and it fell silent.

'Are you OK?' Nell asked.

'Sorry. I was – thinking.' Evie turned to her. 'I'm glad Maude is getting better and you're . . .' She smiled anxiously. 'You'll go soon, though? You won't stay in the house any longer than you need to, will you?'

'As soon as we can, yes.'

'Good.' Evie brightened. 'That's good.'

'Is there something bothering you? Something I should know?'

'Nothing. Only I tried – the other night . . .'

'Gina told me where she found you.'

Evie nodded. 'I was trying to fix it. Stupid, really.' She fiddled with a bracelet on her wrist. Today it was a tiny silver anchor on a bright blue ribbon. 'She's always had this collection of books, you know, my mum – old paperbacks – about . . . I've been reading them. There's a story about a man called John Shorne – and I know all the stuff we were saying about boundaries and protection and superstition only . . .' She hesitated. 'This was a long time ago, the thirteenth century, when people believed in demons.'

'Evie. It's all over and done with now.'

The girl looked up at her. 'People thought he'd trapped the devil in a boot,' she said. 'Imagine if you could do that.' She was pale, verging on tears.

'No. No more.' Nell wrapped her arms about the girl, and pulled her close. 'No more of this.'

'Sorry. It's OK— Sorry.' Evie's voice was muffled. 'I just think – you shouldn't stay.'

'We'll be fine, sweetheart, I promise,' said Nell.

Evie seemed more like her old self as they talked in the garden, and after an hour or so Nell stood. 'I should probably be going.'

'You'll come back, won't you?' said Gina. 'Say goodbye properly, you and Chris and Maude. No – sneaking off.'

'Of course.'

'And give Maude my love, when you see her next.'

'I will.'

'I'll come too,' said Kym, picking up her bag. 'Mum's expecting me.'

'Make sure you close that gate,' said Gina.

'You don't like that gate.'

'Even so. Please.'

Kym led the way, down the narrow garden path, along the side of the cottage, towards Elder House.

They came to the drying ground, and they stopped; Kym looking thoughtfully at the overgrown walls and the long grass. 'Someone should do something about that,' she said.

The air here was still chilly, almost damp. 'I think we've done the best we can,' Nell said, 'for now.'

'You put it back then? The shoe? Only, you did seem to take a long time.'

'I put it back.'

'I still can't get my head around it – does the shoe keep everything in place or is it, I dunno, part of the problem? Either way, Carolyn must have realised it belongs in the house. She must have known she couldn't keep it.'

'I'm not sure,' Nell said, thinking of Evie in the kitchen, so pale and serious, and unwilling to cast her mind back to that night, to the shape she thought she might have seen, hidden in the shadows, struggling to get through. 'Maybe it's a bit of both? But yes, I think it's best off where it is.'

Nell unlocked the kitchen door. 'Thank you,' she said, 'for – well, you know . . .'

'I quite enjoyed knocking Carolyn Wilson on her arse, to be perfectly honest. So, you're welcome.'

'Did Evie tell you where she found the shoe?'

'She showed me, once her dad was off the premises, visiting Carolyn. We took it all apart – I wanted to bin the bloody Moses basket, but Evie wouldn't let me. Carolyn had smashed up some old mirrors – I mean, how do you do that? You've got to be organised, right? You've got to be – planning ahead.'

'I suppose so.'

Kym looked up at her. 'And she'd put the shoe inside the Moses basket, wrapped up in a baby's blanket. Only she must have cut herself somehow as she did it; there were – stains.'

'Carolyn is not well.'

'No. She is not.'

'And Evie will need someone to stick by her for a bit,' said Nell.

'I know,' said Kym, 'I'm on it.'

'Right.' Nell pushed the door open. 'I'll see you later.'

Kym hovered for a moment. 'You did your best for Maude, you know,' she said, 'under the circumstances.'

'I think my husband would disagree, but thanks.'

They were none of them out of the woods yet. But they could fix that, if they tried, and she wanted to. She would do anything to make it right.

'Give her my love when you see her.'

'I will.'

The house was empty. It smelt of beeswax polish and lavender. Nell dropped her bag and her keys on the kitchen counter, the bowl of sea glass still sat on the window ledge. She should go through it soon, she thought, decide which pieces to keep. It occurred to her that she might make something for Evie, a pendant perhaps; something for Kym too.

She climbed up the little ladder into the attic. They weren't sure when they'd be able to leave, but Chris had already made a start on Maude's packing, and the room was tidier now, orderly; lonely. A suitcase lay open on the bed and Nell spent a few minutes putting away the last of Maude's clothes. The books she was done with, her collection of cheap tinny jewellery, and a handful of postcards, plus a few of the quartz pebbles she was so fond of. She closed the case and picked up a single discarded shoe, a red trainer.

She went around the room closing all the windows, before going back downstairs into the bedroom.

The panel lay flush against the wall, and Nell tried very hard not to think about what lay behind it; what she had put there. Looking down, she was almost surprised to see she was still holding the trainer, the right one, still missing its twin. The left one was on the stone shelf, behind the panel alongside the little leather shoe – both smeared with blood, Maude's blood, that had been unavoidable, although Nell had done her best to be calm, to set her intention before sealing them up.

Striking her bargain.

There was time to change her mind, to take it back, but she didn't move.

372

She would do anything to make it right; to give them the life they deserved.

She thought for a moment, then opened a drawer, burying the remaining shoe among her T-shirts and sweaters.

She would hang on to it, for a little while.

For luck.

Acknowledgements

This book is a work of fiction, but some elements have been borrowed from real life. Shoes and other objects, including mummified cats, have indeed been hidden in old houses as a form of magical protection for centuries. If you're interested in finding out more, or if you make a discovery of your own, The Concealed Revealed Project, which can be found online, and Brian Hoggard's website Apotropaios are both excellent places to start.

The museum Nell and the others visit is based on Whitby Museum, which houses a fascinating collection of local and seafaring artefacts. Sadly, since I started work on *The Hiding Place*, real life has overtaken fiction, and while many of the objects I describe are on display, the comb, complete with runic inscription, is currently on loan to English Heritage and can be seen at Whitby Abbey, where it was originally found. Maybe it's safer there.

I'd like to thank Katrina Naomi and The Brisons Veor Trust for awarding me a Writer's Residency way back in 2017, where I began working on the first draft of this novel. It was offered at a particularly difficult period in my life and provided much-needed time and space to regroup and focus. I greatly enjoyed my visit, and I hope to return some day.

I'd also like to thank The Society of Authors and The Authors' Foundation who in 2019 awarded me one of their generous grants to support a work in progress, essentially buying me time to write. The support they have offered over the past couple of years – both financially and creatively – has been invaluable.

And as for everyone else – well, it's been quite a year. My agent, Julia Silk, who has the unenviable job of reading the first and worst draft, has been as brilliant as ever; she helped shape this book, letting me see what I wanted to do with it, and she sends excellent care packages when the going gets tough.

Everyone at Zaffre has been similarly wonderful, working with passion and commitment in the most difficult of circumstances, particularly Sophie Orme, who is a voice in my head in the nicest possible way, and Katie Lumsden, who edits with such care and precision.

I need to thank my family and friends for their love and support; my sister, Deborah, and my brother, Andrew. Tracy Kuhn, for her advice on schools and teenagers in general, and Laura and Poppy, for their willingness to offer clarification as to what girls do and don't say these days. Ian Havelock, who told me a tall tale about a witch, and Lauren Gigg, who told me a true story about magic with mirrors.

And lastly, to the usual suspects – I hope you know who you are – to Bidi, who continues to live in inspiring places, and to Wendy, who continues to insist that I am a writer, my thanks and all my love.

Hello,

Thank you for picking up *The Hiding Place*, I hope you enjoyed it.

The practice of placing objects in a building to protect it is a very old one and I'm fascinated by this sort of superstition; the idea that a certain action, or habit, or even the right words in the right order can protect a person from harm. These concealed objects can be bits of clothing, sometimes they are mummified cats, but most often they are shoes. It's such a personal kind of magic, the rules are rarely written down, and what's left behind are incredibly ambiguous objects which accumulate an odd sort of power in and of themselves. They can remain undisturbed for centuries; once they are found, we can only guess at the intentions of the person who hid them away. And that is really where *The Hiding Place* began.

I wanted to write about this rough, informal magic that seems once to have been a part of everyday life. Why would someone hide a shoe, a child's shoe in particular? What might they have hoped to gain? What were they afraid of? If you found one in your house, what other secrets might you unearth? What does a child's shoe mean to a mother, or to someone struggling with motherhood?

I knew I wanted to write a book about mothers and daughters, and I knew that the central character would be someone who very much wanted to have her own baby. For a while Nell was alone in Elder House, but the story came to life for me when I thought about how there is more than one way of being a mother, and that being a step-parent might have its own conflict and stresses. Motherhood, in any form, is hardly a simple thing. I knew that Nell was going to meet someone from her old life, and I became interested in the battles that this character, Carolyn, has with her teenage daughter, Evie.

What might she have sacrificed to become a mother? Had it been worth it? And all the time, I was thinking about a little shoe, hidden in a bedroom wall. What did the shoe mean in the past, and what does it mean now?

I like to think I'm not superstitious, yet deep down I know I am, all the little rituals of my childhood — don't open an umbrella indoors, don't put shoes on the table, don't walk under a ladder — are now habit. And if I notice these habits at all, I find them comforting, they remind me of my mum, my grandad, my great-aunt. Superstitions are stories; they tell us how we fit into the world, as well as ways to keep ourselves safe. There is power in them, too, because they deal with our greatest fears and our greatest desires, and they give the illusion, at least, of control. As I worked on the book, I began to wonder about just how powerful a hidden object such as my little shoe might become, if it was the focus of so much emotion and intent over such a long time. I began to wonder if people might begin to overlook its original purpose . . .

If you enjoyed *The Hiding Place*, then you might like my first novel, *The Wayward Girls*. It tells the story of two sisters in the 1970s who find themselves at the centre of an investigation into a poltergeist. The present-day section follows the younger sister, Lucy, when she returns to the family home with a new team of paranormal investigators to uncover exactly what did happen all those years ago. It's a novel about sisters, loss and the strange melancholy of a long hot summer when there is nothing to do, where it seems you will never be allowed to grow up.

If you would like to hear more about my books, you can visit **www.bit.ly/AmandaMason** where you can become part of my Readers' Club. It only takes a few moments to sign up, there are no catches or costs. Bonnier Books UK will keep your data private and confidential, and it will never be passed on to a third party. I won't spam you with loads of emails, I'll just get in touch now and again with news about my writing. And of course, you can unsubscribe whenever you want.

If you would like to get involved in a wider conversation about my books, please do review *The Hiding Place* on Amazon, on Goodreads, on any other e-store, on your own blog and social media accounts. I can be found on Twitter as **@amandajanemason** and on Instagram as **@amandajmason**. Comments and feedback from readers make such a difference to authors and for my books to be read and shared and discussed is just the most fantastic feeling, and it's always great to hear from people.

Best wishes,
Amanda Mason

Reading Group Questions

1. *The Hiding Place* begins when Nell brings her family to the seaside town where she grew up. How do you think the setting influences the story in this novel?

2. What did you think of Nell? Did your perception of her change?

3. Nell and Maude's relationship intensifies throughout the novel. How else does *The Hiding Place* explore the theme of motherhood?

4. Events begin to ramp up when the characters discover an object hidden in Elder House. How is the idea of concealment explored – and in what way is this related to power?

5. Kym and Evie find new friendship in the novel, but how is this friendship tested?

6. Kym, Evie and Maude all face individual challenges as children/teenagers; how is coming of age explored in the book?

7. What did you think of Carolyn? Did your view of her change as the novel progressed? To what extent does she drive the events of the novel?

8. How does the history of the Elder House and the drying ground contribute to the events in the novel? Does the real danger come from the house, or the people inside and around it?

9. Were you frightened by events in the novel? Which section did you find the most unnerving?

10. What did you make of the book's closing paragraph? Do you think Nell made the right choice?

If you loved *The Hiding Place*,
why not try *The Wayward Girls* . . .

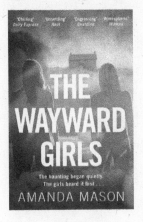

THEN

1976. Loo and her sister Bee live in a run-down cottage
in the middle of nowhere, with their artistic parents and
wild siblings. Their mother, Cathy, had hoped to escape to a
simpler life; instead the family find themselves isolated and
shunned by their neighbours. At the height of the stifling
summer, unexplained noises and occurences in the house
begin to disturb the family, until they intrude on
every waking moment . . .

NOW

Loo, now Lucy, is called back to her childhood home.
A group of strangers are looking to discover the truth about
the house and the people who lived there. But is Lucy ready
to confront what really happened all those years ago?

Available now, read on for a sneak peek

1976

'Stand still.' Bee tugged at Loo's petticoat, trying to straighten it.

'I don't like it,' said Loo. The cotton was soft and cool but it smelt funny, as if it had been left out in the rain. It made her skin crawl.

'Oh, shut up.' Bee stood back, concentrating. Her own petticoat had a frill around the skirt and the top she wore – the camisole – had lace edging at the neck; she looked different, not pretty exactly, but more grown-up. She stood with her hands on her hips, her head tilted to one side, scowling, her long dark hair flopping into her eyes.

'It's too long.' Loo kicked at the skirt. 'I can't walk in it.'

'Well, we'll pin it up, then,' Bee said, as if her sister was either very small or very stupid. 'God, Loo, it's not – stay here, and don't let Cathy see you.' She opened the door, then turned back, her expression stern. 'Don't move a muscle,' she said, before ducking out of the room and running lightly across the landing, disappearing into their parents' bedroom.

They had found the box in the pantry, shoved out of sight under the shelves, and had brought it up to their room while their mother, Cathy, was busy in the garden with everyone else. The cardboard was speckled with damp and there was bold blue print running along one side: GOLDEN WONDER. It was old, but not as old as the clothes they'd found inside.

Cathy wouldn't be pleased. She might even take it away; it wasn't really theirs, after all. She might want the clothes – for that was all the box held, petticoats and nightgowns and camisoles, a lot of them, too much for one person, surely – she might insist they hand them over to their rightful owner, whoever that might be.

Bee was taking ages. Loo ran her hands across the fabric, trying to smooth out the deep creases that criss-crossed the skirt, some of them a faint brown. The fabric was paper-thin and she wondered if it might tear if she pulled it hard enough. What Bee would say if she did.

It was stuffy in their bedroom. She went to the window and, pushing it as far open as she could, she leant out.

They were still there, all the grown-ups and Flor and the baby, sitting on the grass under the apple tree at the far end of the garden, not doing much, any of them; it was too hot.

Simon was sitting next to Issy, and they were talking to each other. Loo wondered what they might be saying. Issy raised her hand to her face to shade her eyes whenever she spoke and Simon leant in close, as if he was whispering secrets in her ear.

Odd words drifted up to the open window, but nothing that made much sense. Issy laughed once or twice and Loo suddenly wished they would look up, one of them, see her, smile. She leant further out, bracing her hands on the window ledge, on the warm, blistered paint, letting the sun bake her arms.

There was a shift in the air as the door swung open. She felt Bee cross the room and stand behind her, looking at the same view, at Simon. She leant in closer. Her breath was stale, her hip nudged Loo, one arm draping around her shoulders and her weight settling on her, skin on skin, edging Loo off balance. It was too much, too hot; besides, they never hugged. Loo tried to pull away and felt an answering pressure across her shoulders as her sister refused to budge, her fingers digging into the soft skin at the top of Loo's arm.

'I told you not to move.' Loo jumped back from the window, startled. Bee was standing by the door, well out of reach, her mother's pin cushion in one hand, needle, thread and scissors in the other. Loo felt dizzy, the room seemed to shimmer briefly, then everything came back into focus, sharp, solid. Bee was giving her a funny look.

'You're bloody useless, you are.' Bee dragged her in front of the mirror again. She grabbed the waistband of the skirt and pinched it, pulling it tight, pinning it into place before she knelt and began to work on the hem. 'You can sew it yourself, though,' she said. 'You needn't think I'm going to do it.' She worked quickly, so quickly Loo was sure the hem would turn out lopsided.

'Bee?'

'What?'

'Will Joe come back soon?'

Joe, not Dad. Cathy, not Mum. Loo wasn't sure when they'd started using their parents' proper names, or even whose idea it had been in the first place, but they all did it now, except for Anto, who was too little to say anything.

Bee stopped what she was doing and looked up. She didn't look angry, exactly, but still Loo wished she hadn't said anything. 'Suppose so,' she said, turning her attention back to the hem. She sounded as if she didn't care at all, but it was hard to tell. Bee was such a bloody liar, that's what Joe used to say whenever he caught her out. He thought it was funny, most of the time, and Loo had often wondered if she did it for that exact reason, to make him laugh.

'Bee—'

'Shut up, Loo.'

There was no point in asking anything else.

'There,' Bee said as she got to her feet. 'That's better.'

Bee's outfit didn't need altering. Her skirt didn't sag down onto the floor, and the camisole she wore was a little bit too tight, if anything. As if the girl they once belonged to fitted between the two of them, between Bee and Loo.

She should say something, about the window, about the . . .

'It looks stupid with this.' Loo plucked at her T-shirt, which had once been bright blue, and she could see that Bee was torn. 'I don't mind,' she said, 'you can have it all.'

And she didn't mind – the clothes in the box, she didn't like them. She tugged at the skirt again. It felt – wrong.

'Well, that won't work, will it?' said Bee. 'We have to match.' She rifled through the clothes on her bed, pulling out a little vest, greyish white and studded with tiny bone buttons. 'Here. Try this.'

Loo didn't move.

'Bloody hell, Loo. You're not shy, are you?' Bee chucked the vest at her. 'I won't look,' she said, turning back to her bed and making a show of sorting through the remaining clothes.

Loo turned her back on her sister and the mirror too, peeling off the T-shirt and letting it fall to the floor, shaking out the camisole and pulling it over her head as quickly as she could, her skin puckering despite the heat as the musty cloth settled into place.

It was too big. She didn't need to look in the mirror to see that, but she looked anyway. It was almost comical, the way the top sort of slithered off her shoulder, as if she had begun to shrink, leaving the clothes behind. She might have laughed, if it hadn't felt so . . .

Bee grabbed her and swung her round. 'We'll have to fix this too,' she said, pulling the camisole back into place and digging the pins through the double layers of cotton.

'Ow.' Loo flinched as Bee scraped a pin across her collar bone.

'Oh, give over. I didn't hurt you.' Bee swung her around again and began to gather the fabric at Loo's back. 'Now, stay still.'

Loo did as she was told. It was always easier to do as she'd been told, in the end. Anyway, the sooner Bee finished, the sooner she could have her own clothes back.

'Right.' Bee stood back. 'That should do.'

Loo looked in the mirror, straightening the camisole, trying to get used to herself. Bee stood next to her, admiring the effect, how alike they looked now. She posed with one hand on her hip. 'Say thank you, Lucia,' she said. She'd been in a funny mood ever since they'd found the box: loud, giddy, frantic.

Loo didn't say anything; she went back to the window.

The scene in the garden had changed. Michael was helping Cathy to her feet, and Flor was jigging around next to her, Simon and Issy were drifting towards the house. No one seemed to be missing them, the girls, at all. They were saying their goodbyes, getting ready to go. One day, soon, Michael and Simon would be gone for good. And then perhaps Joe would come back.

Loo placed her hands on the window ledge again and leant as far forward as she dared. As she watched everyone, it seemed to her that she could feel something underneath the paint, inside the wood, a sort of humming, and the more she concentrated on that, the clearer it became. Just like it had before. There was something scratching, something trying – she thought – to get in. Then she felt it, a sharp pinch, sharp enough to make her catch her breath.

She stretched out her arm, but all she could see was a little brown smudge. She licked her thumb, and rubbed at it, then watched as more marks appeared, not much more than shadows at first. They darkened, blooming under her skin, resolving gradually into a series of purplish bruises, each one the size of a thumb print.